MELISSA ANNE

Worthy of Her Trust

A Pride and Prejudice Variation

Melissa Anne
AUTHOR

Cover art by GetCovers

This book was professionally typeset on Reedsy.
Find out more at reedsy.com

Dedicated to my husband, who is probably my biggest cheerleader as I have embarked upon this process of writing. Thank you, sweetheart, for all your encouragement as I write, and for understanding the times when the muse strikes and everything else falls to the wayside.

Contents

Acknowledgement

So many people have helped me as I have written this story or have offered feedback after it was completed. One of the biggest reasons I love to post on fan fiction sites is the encouragement I receive as I move through the process of turning an idea into a story. Many of you have read this as it was written and offered suggestions and feedback, caught errors I missed, or just cheered me on. I appreciate all of you!

Specifically, I'd like to thank all of those who assisted with the editing and revising process and the ARC team, who provided feedback before it was published. Thank you all so much! Your help was invaluable, and I cannot thank you enough.

Prologue

March 1791

Elizabeth Bennet Tomlinson, frequently called Beth by her friends and family, grew up at Longbourn, her father's estate in Hertfordshire. She was the youngest of three children and was closest to her eldest brother, Edward, who doted on her. Thomas, her other brother, was away at school during her formative years, and she did not know him well.

When she was 18, while in London, she met Frederick Tomlinson, the only son of a large landholder to the north of the country. They married after courting for six months, and Beth moved to Briarwood, Frederick's family's estate, located on the border of Staffordshire and Derbyshire. Frederick was the sole heir to the estate, which garnered approximately seven thousand pounds per annum.

Beth had never been more pleased than the morning she felt the quickening of their first child. She was anxious for her husband to return from riding out on his family's estate with his father so she could share the news with him. The couple had been married for nearly a year before they noticed the cessation of her courses in December and began to suspect her condition — the quickening she felt that morning provided conclusive proof of the coming child.

When Frederick returned with his father from the fields, Beth accompanied him to his rooms and told him her news while he bathed and changed. They celebrated as young couples in love were wont to do, leading to their being late arriving for supper that night. This was quickly forgiven when the news was shared with Frederick's parents, Alexander and Susannah Tomlinson, who were ecstatic about the prospect of a grandchild.

As Beth's condition was now confirmed, Frederick rewrote his will to include the coming child. It was not that he was concerned about his mortality — he was a reasonably young man in good health — but his father had taught him to be prudent, which meant making arrangements for a child as soon as possible.

Twenty thousand pounds was set aside for a daughter's inheritance, placed in a trust to prevent her future husband from acquiring or accessing her funds upon their marriage. The couple hoped for a son who would inherit Briarwood. However, since the estate was not entailed, if the only child born of the marriage were female, she would inherit the estate in its entirety, in addition to the 20,000 pounds. His father owned Briarwood, and its disposition would be addressed in Mr. Tomlinson's will.

Among other stipulations included in the will, Frederick named his father the child's guardian and trustee, with a neighbour and friend, George Darcy, appointed a secondary trustee of the child's inheritance.

Only a month later, something spooked Frederick's horse while he surveyed the fields, causing it to respond poorly. He held on through the first tumultuous moments, desperately trying to regain control, but the situation quickly escalated beyond his control. With a sudden jolt, he was thrown from the saddle, landing heavily on the ground, breaking his back. The world around him blurred, the impact stealing the breath from his lungs and pain engulfing him. The skittish horse bolted toward home, but when the horse was found, it was too late for its master. By the time they found him, he was dead.

Beth was heartbroken by the loss of her husband. She carried her child to term and gave birth at her husband's estate in August of that same year. The child was a girl and was a little small for a babe, but she was determined to be heard from almost the moment she entered this world. Her mother struggled to recover and never truly regained her strength. In truth, her heart was broken, and despite the child, the product of the love between her and her husband, she simply gave up on life. A few days short of the anniversary of her husband's death, she, too, passed from this world, leaving Elizabeth Rose Tomlinson an orphan.

Despite this, the child's grandparents loved her dearly, and she did not lack for anything. Since Frederick was an only child, there were no aunts and uncles for the infant Elizabeth on the Tomlinson side of the family, though there were two uncles on the Bennet side. The elder, Edward, was the master of a small estate in Hertfordshire and regularly sent letters and small gifts to his niece. Her grandparents often corresponded with him about her progress since he had loved her mother dearly. Edward even visited Briarwood several times to see his niece as she grew.

Elizabeth's other maternal uncle, Thomas, two years younger than Edward and a professor at Oxford College, was a lackadaisical correspondent at best. He was aware of his sister's death, though he had not attended the funeral despite his brother's offer to convey him there. He married Frances Gardiner, most often called Fanny, who mistakenly believed Thomas to be the reclusive master of Longbourn. When that proved incorrect, she turned bitter, and this bitterness was made worse when she first birthed a girl child and then, nearly two years later, gave birth to a stillborn boy. Over the next several years, she gave birth to three more daughters. This further upset the lady, since she hoped to have a child who might eventually inherit her husband's family's estate. Edward Bennet was over thirty and showed little inclination toward marriage.

* * *

Under her grandparent's care, Elizabeth, called Ellie, grew into a lively and intelligent child. She was fascinated by books at an early age, and her adoring grandparents sat with her to teach her letters and numbers and answer her many questions.

The Tomlinsons were close friends with George and Lady Anne Darcy and the Earl and Countess of Matlock, Hugh and Grace Fitzwilliam. These families gathered together each summer at one of their respective estates, alternating between Briarwood, Matlock, and Pemberley, as the estates were within 50 miles of each other. The summer of Elizabeth's fourth birthday was the Tomlinsons' turn to host the gathering.

The Darcy and Fitzwilliam cousins, all boys and considerably older than the almost four-year-old Ellie, proved to be delightful playmates that summer despite the difference in their ages. Immediately, she joined in the adventures of ten-year-old Fitzwilliam Darcy and twelve-year-old Jonathan Fitzwilliam, demanding to participate in their escapades. She rarely played the role of the 'damsel in distress' since she often insisted on being the valiant hero alongside the older boys. At seventeen, the older Fitzwilliam child ignored the others and rarely participated in their adventures.

One morning found all in the park that surrounded the estate. "Will! Jon!" she called out, using her newly acquired nicknames for Fitzwilliam and Jonathan. "What are we playing today?"

With a mischievous grin, Fitzwilliam looked at Jonathan, who merely sighed and asked, "Another daring adventure, I suppose."

Ellie clapped her hands, her eyes sparkling. "Yes! And this time, I get to be the fearless hero who saves the day!"

Fitzwilliam chuckled, "You're always the hero, Ellie. We have not had a single adventure this summer without you rescuing us from imaginary perils."

Rolling his eyes, Jonathan added, "And I can never escape being the villain, can I?"

"But you make the best villain!" Ellie exclaimed, her enthusiasm infectious.

Despite the age difference, Ellie's boundless energy and creativity always included an interesting element to the boys' games, and even Jon reluctantly agreed that she added much to their play.

Later that evening, after their adventures had concluded, the trio gathered in the nursery with the nurse overseeing their interactions. Ellie, perched on a small chair, looked up at Will and Jon eagerly.

"Tell me a story, please! A really exciting one!" she pleaded.

Fitzwilliam glanced at Jonathan before smirking, "Alright, Ellie, but you have to promise not to get scared tonight and keep your nurse awake."

Ellie nodded vigorously, wiping away imaginary tears. "I promise! But do try not to make it too scary."

Fitzwilliam began weaving a tale of knights, dragons, and daring rescues, his eyes twinkling enthusiastically. Despite his initial reluctance, Jonathan joined in, adding twists and turns to the narrative. Ellie listened wide-eyed, occasionally interjecting her ideas. They only left when the nursemaid insisted and retired to their own rooms for supper.

Days after Elizabeth celebrated her fourth birthday and Fitzwilliam marked his eleventh, the families concluded their month-long visit and returned to their respective homes. Tomlinson orchestrated a spectacular fireworks display on the last night of their party to commemorate the end of summer and the children's birthdays. Fitzwilliam tenderly held Elizabeth in his arms as they marvelled at the vibrant bursts illuminating the night sky. Initially startled by the noise, Elizabeth quickly found joy in the spectacle, particularly when her "Dearest Will" — a nickname inspired by his parents' endearments — embraced her. Laughter ensued when she planted an appreciative kiss on his reddening cheek, creating a heart-warming moment for them all.

This interaction gave Fitzwilliam's father and Elizabeth's grandfather much fodder to tease each other, and they playfully entertained the idea of the two children one day marrying. Although both were too young to take such thoughts seriously, the men playfully speculated about the potential brilliance of such a match since it would unite two great estates. However, they both desired for their offspring to find happiness in marriage and seeing how the two responded to each other, they believed they likely would.

Likewise, they did express some hope of witnessing how young Ellie would lead her "Dearest Will" on a merry chase when the time came for them to consider a match as, despite her age, it was already apparent Elizabeth would be a beauty and given her present impertinence, they doubted that would alter much as she aged. Both gentlemen prayed they would be around to see and experience it.

Sadly, such things would not come to be.

* * *

The following spring, Lady Anne welcomed a new addition to the family —
a baby girl named Georgiana Elizabeth Darcy. Fitzwilliam, who returned
home from school in June, finally met his new sister and discovered his
mother was still weakened and recovering from the birth slowly. That
summer, the Tomlinsons and little Ellie visited Pemberley briefly and
celebrated the children's birthdays once again, though in a more sedate
fashion.

When Fitzwilliam departed for school at the end of that summer, Lady
Anne still had not fully recovered. Sadly, she passed away later that year,
leaving his father consumed by grief and struggling to face his son and
daughter since their presence constantly reminded him of her absence.
Fitzwilliam's attempts to comfort him were thwarted when Mr. Darcy
began to prefer the company of the steward's son, George Wickham, his
godson. Wickham appeared determined to win favour with his godfather
and did all he could to "best" Fitzwilliam, who resented his father's apparent
partiality.

Eventually, Wickham began attempting to harm Fitzwilliam, and he
succeeded in breaking his arm and giving him many cuts and bruises.
When asked by his father and godfather, the young Wickham explained
Fitzwilliam's injuries as accidents. Still, his constant taunting of the young
Darcy made it clear to Fitzwilliam and Jonathan that he acted intentionally.
Jonathan Fitzwilliam did what he could to protect his cousin, teaching him
how to defend himself and encouraging him to be cautious.

When they attended school together, Wickham ignored his studies and led
a life of dissipation, frequently posing as Fitzwilliam to obtain credit with
merchants who demanded payment from Fitzwilliam instead of Wickham.

Despite his son's efforts to tell him of Wickham's true nature, Mr. Darcy
remained oblivious and allowed himself to be charmed by his godson. Mr.

Darcy never overcame his heartbreak, and he joined his beloved wife in eternal rest not long after his son reached his majority and could assume responsibility for his sister.

After devoting so much of his time entertaining his godfather, Wickham was livid at the paltry thousand-pound bequest left him by George Darcy and the Kympton living if he took orders. He had expected substantially more and demanded the value of the living from Fitzwilliam since he had no intention of becoming a member of the clergy. Still dissatisfied, he vowed to avenge this slight against him.

* * *

While Lady Anne Darcy's health waned, Elizabeth found herself enduring her own significant loss not long after her fifth birthday — the passing of both her grandparents. Shortly after her grandmother's death that autumn, her grandfather also fell seriously ill. Alexander Tomlinson asked Terrance Elliott, a close friend and neighbour, to be the trustee of Elizabeth's inheritance, along with George Darcy, who would also be her guardian.

As the Tomlinsons' sole heir, Elizabeth would inherit Briarwood and their funds and investments. Added to what her father left her, Elizabeth would be a significant heiress, and Mr. Tomlinson was concerned about protecting her in the future. He put the deed of Briarwood in her name and established a second trust on her behalf, into which he placed all of the Tomlinsons' assets. Based on legal advice, both trusts were worded to prevent her future husband from claiming her assets as would typically be the case when a woman married; Briarwood would not transfer to her husband upon her marriage and was to remain under her sole ownership and direction. George Darcy was to manage the estate until Elizabeth came of age.

Mr. Elliott spent hours discussing matters with his friend, ensuring all necessary arrangements were in place for Elizabeth's care and to protect her fortune should the worst come to pass. He composed letters on his friend's behalf, including one addressed to George Darcy, updating him on

Elizabeth's inheritance and providing details regarding Briarwood so he could manage the estate after her grandfather's death.

George Darcy could not journey to Briarwood during this period; instead, he stayed near the side of his ailing wife. However, he and Mr. Tomlinson frequently exchanged letters to clarify Mr. Tomlinson's expectations for his granddaughter. She was to be given the finest of everything, and the money used for her care was to provide her with all that was required for a girl of her station — fine clothing, a governess, masters in music, art, and languages, and a season in town when she reached the proper age. When she married, Elizabeth would have amassed a significant dowry in addition to her inheritance. Mr. Tomlinson's will required that both George Darcy and Terrance Elliott, and Elizabeth herself agree to the match before any funds were released.

Mr. Darcy reached Briarwood in time for the funeral, where he extended his stay by a few days to fulfil the requisite formalities. This included signing essential documents appointing him Elizabeth's guardian and one of her trustees, a responsibility he shared with Mr. Elliott.

Due to Lady Anne's fragile health, Mr. Darcy could not immediately take charge of Elizabeth. Consequently, Mr. Elliott acted as his agent to arrange for Elizabeth to live temporarily with her uncle in Hertfordshire. To ensure proper care without imposing undue burden, he established that the trust would provide for Elizabeth until she reached her majority.

The payments would automatically increase upon Elizabeth's fifteenth birthday when she was to receive 200 pounds annually for her allowance. The extra funds were intended to cover the increased cost of clothing she would need when she approached her debut in society. All of this was conveyed to Mr. Edward Bennet through letters, and he agreed to the stipulations for the funds in the same manner. Mr. Bennet was allowed to retain one-third of the annual payments for hosting Elizabeth and was required to furnish the trustees with a yearly account of these funds.

When she arrived at Longbourn, Edward Bennet ensured there were people in place to care for his niece — as a bachelor and something of a recluse, he had little idea of what the child would need. Soon, little Elizabeth

Tomlinson was ensconced in the nursery at Longbourn. While she missed her grandparents, she liked living with her uncle, whom she knew from his visits to Briarwood over the years. The two muddled on well enough, but in December of 1796, only a few months after arriving, Elizabeth suffered the loss of yet another relative. Edward Bennet died from a terrible cold just before the new year.

Her other uncle, Thomas Bennet, was now the master of Longbourn. At Mr. Darcy's request, Mr. Elliott quickly wrote to him to apprise him of the agreement between his elder brother and George Darcy regarding the child's care. He offered the same arrangement to the new master, and it was readily accepted — for the first time, Thomas Bennet answered a letter on the same day it arrived.

When Thomas Bennet and his wife and four daughters arrived at Longbourn, Fanny quickly diverted the nursemaids and governess hired to care for and educate Elizabeth Tomlinson into helping care for eight-year-old Jane, four-year-old Mary, an almost two-year-old Kitty, and the baby, four-month-old Lydia. Elizabeth's clothing was distributed amongst her cousins, taken without her permission, and soon she was considered just one more of the Bennet daughters.

At five, Elizabeth had known her name was Elizabeth Tomlinson. The maids who originally accompanied her to Longbourn also knew her name and background, but they left soon after Thomas Bennet's family arrived. The first few times Elizabeth was introduced as Elizabeth Bennet, she attempted to correct her aunt and received a slap for her impudence. Elizabeth knew that she was Ellie, but soon, her new family began to call her Lizzy. She did not care for this name and tried to insist on the other. Any attempts to correct it were met with harsh words, and she soon learned it did not matter what she said. She forced herself to respond to "Lizzy Bennet" and attempted to forget, thinking her prior life had merely been a lovely dream.

Mrs. Bennet was determined to have the neighbours think well of her, so at their first visit to the dressmaker in Meryton, she informed everyone that Elizabeth was an orphan the couple had taken in out of the goodness of their hearts. She implied that Elizabeth was a poor relation to the Bennet family and hinted that she was Edward Bennet's natural daughter. She also did not want an orphan dressed better than her own children, so she outfitted Elizabeth in the poorest of materials while dressing her daughters in the best.

Thomas Bennet was unconcerned with these matters. His wife did not know of Elizabeth's dowry or her eventual inheritance and never asked questions about where the stipend came from. She eagerly spent the stipend for Elizabeth's care to outfit the girls in a style more appropriate to their new situation. Elizabeth's clothing was shared amongst his daughters, and her uncle never noticed when Elizabeth was dressed in somewhat poorer materials than the others.

* * *

Not long after arriving at Longbourn, Mr. Bennet engaged a governess to teach the older girls. Unlike Elizabeth, Jane was uninterested in learning, and Mrs. Bennet complained that her daughters did not need such "nonsense." Mr. Bennet silenced her with the reminder that their girls were now the daughters of a gentleman and, indeed, some education was essential.

Despite her lack of interest, Mr. Bennet insisted his oldest daughter attend daily lessons. However, Mrs. Hatcher, the governess, focused more on Elizabeth, who desired to learn all she could and was already far more advanced than her cousin despite being two years younger.

As the other girls grew, they also attended lessons. However, that ended shortly after Elizabeth's twelfth birthday and Lydia's sixth.

From nearly the moment of her birth, Lydia had been spoiled. Whatever she wanted, she received, and it did not matter what it was, whose it was, or whether she needed it. Lydia resented having to attend lessons, and, in retribution for being punished for some infraction in the schoolroom, she stole some ribbons, a few coins, and a piece of jewellery from the governess. Mrs. Bennet was outraged at what she believed were false accusations against Lydia by Mrs. Hatcher, and the matron summarily dismissed her.

Instead of fighting his wife, Mr. Bennet paid Mrs. Hatcher her wages for the quarter, gave her a character, and paid her way back to London. He informed Mr. Elliott that the governess left voluntarily and promised to hire a new one to continue Elizabeth's education per their agreement. In the same letter, he indicated his intention to send her to London for instruction from masters in music and languages.

Although Mr. Bennet may have intended to follow through on his commitment to Mr. Elliott, he was an indolent man. It proved too difficult to provide the education and other things required by the terms of Elizabeth's trust without disrupting his household and upsetting his wife. He soon concluded that he should not have been expected to raise Elizabeth according to a higher standard of living than his daughters.

And so, soon after Mrs. Hatcher departed, he stopped his efforts to do so. No governess ever stepped foot inside Longbourn after that, though Mr. Bennet did send to London for some books he wanted. He also expanded his library — there was a small room next to his study that was only rarely used, and he was able to hire carpenters to add a doorway and then bookshelves in the room next door. Mr. Bennet justified using funds meant to pay for Lizzy's education by claiming she would have access to his library and the books purchased to fill it.

With no governess, the girls were left to fend for themselves. They were allowed to spend their time in idle pursuits and not encouraged to learn anything more than the most basic skills required. Elizabeth would, when allowed, sequester herself in the library with her uncle and learn all she could from books and from him. When she could not, she escaped to the outdoors. She offered to teach each of her cousins the piano, although only Mary was interested in the instrument, and she preferred to muddle through on her own.

Eventually, he grudgingly complied with Elizabeth's request for new music and sent her to his brother-in-law's in London for a month to take piano lessons from a neighbour. She repeated this trip twice annually for instruction in music, among other things, over the next several years, but that dropped to just once when she turned seventeen. Mrs. Bennet resented that Lizzy always returned from London wearing new clothes, much finer than what she could obtain for her daughters. She attempted to send Jane instead, and Mrs. Bennet commanded her sister-in-law, Mrs. Gardiner, to purchase Jane elegant dresses and introduce her to wealthy men.

Neither occurred; Mrs. Bennet did not seem to understand that Elizabeth's gowns were purchased with the funds provided for her care. Mr. Bennet had never told his wife about the additional four hundred pounds a year for Elizabeth's care that began when she turned fifteen. Each year, he sent a portion of this to London secretly to provide some finer clothing for Elizabeth in case she encountered one of her trustees while in town.

Mrs. Bennet despaired of ever making Elizabeth into her ideal of what a gentlewoman should be and frequently disparaged her appearance and abilities. All four Bennet daughters resembled Mrs. Bennet, though Mary and Kitty had a little more of the Bennet side in their appearance. Elizabeth looked more like the Tomlinson family and bore little resemblance to her cousins. Jane and Lydia looked the most like their mother and were their mother's undisputed favourites. They received the nicest clothing, the most praise, the most indulgences. As they grew older, Mrs. Bennet spent most of her clothing allowance on those two girls and had their cast-offs remade to outfit the other girls.

Most of Elizabeth's best clothing remained in London. The one time she had brought home all that was purchased for her there, it was taken from her room by Mrs. Bennet and distributed between Jane and Lydia. However, as Elizabeth grew, though she was of a similar height to Jane, she became curvier, and her dresses could not be easily remade to fit her elder cousin. Lydia was stout and a bit taller, making it difficult for Elizabeth's dresses to be stolen to fit her youngest cousin either, so the few items she brought home with her were not touched. That was partly due to Mr. Bennet's putting his foot down on the issue. Mrs. Bennet had not cared for the restriction, though she grudgingly complied because the only time she had attempted to fight him on this, he had restricted her pin money for a month.

Chapter 1

September 1811

Elizabeth Bennet dressed carefully for the upcoming quarterly assembly. Netherfield Park, largely vacant for the past five years, had recently been leased to a wealthy young man with an annual income of four or five thousand. The local gossip fuelled speculation about the size of his party, ranging from as few as two to as many as twenty residents. Elizabeth found this amusing, particularly given the neighbourhood's lively rumours surrounding the matter.

Mrs. Bennet had already claimed the tenant, a Mr. Charles Bingley, as the property of her eldest and most beautiful daughter, Jane. She commanded all her girls to make themselves as presentable as possible for the event in case other wealthy gentlemen accompanied him. Her most beautiful daughter needed to marry well because of the entail of their property, and Mrs. Bennet decided their new neighbour was just the man to save them from the hedgerows. To Elizabeth, she merely instructed her to stay out of the way and not to make a nuisance of herself.

When the party from Netherfield entered the hall sometime in the middle of the second dance, all eyes turned towards the newcomers. While the residents of Hertfordshire watched them, the newcomers turned a critical eye toward those in attendance. It was clear that they all, except the younger red-headed gentleman, were displeased with what they saw.

While a popular dance partner, Elizabeth was not a marriage prospect for the few gentlemen in the village since it was widely believed that she had nothing, not even the twelve hundred pounds that her cousins would inherit upon their mother's death.

Due to this, Elizabeth occasionally directed the available gentleman to ask other girls to dance and would choose to sit out several dances at each assembly. During one of these times, Elizabeth heard a conversation between two of the gentlemen from Netherfield.

"Come, Darcy, you must dance," Charles Bingley said to his friend, who was standing by the wall. "I hate to see you standing about in this stupid manner."

"Charles, you are fully aware the sole reason I am present tonight is to avoid being left alone with your sister," Fitzwilliam Darcy responded with a brusqueness not uncommon to him. "Had you informed me of tonight's assembly, I would have delayed my journey a day to avoid attending. Now, return to your partner and enjoy her smiles. I have an excruciating headache and no desire to dance tonight, particularly not with a lady I am unacquainted with."

Unnoticed by both men, Elizabeth smiled slightly at their conversation. She had seen the predatory lady in their party grabbing at the taller gentleman's arm when they walked in and watched with amusement as the gentleman repeatedly attempted to extricate himself from her grasp — much to the lady's displeasure. She could certainly understand why he had a headache if he was constantly subjected to that.

Silently, she walked into the kitchen attached to the assembly room, prepared a glass of willow bark tea, and carefully returned to her spot by the gentleman she understood to be Mr. Darcy.

Careful to keep herself hidden from the rest of the room, she quietly spoke to the gentleman. "Sir, I hope you will forgive my impertinence, but I overheard you speaking to Mr. Bingley. My family often uses tea with willow bark to help with pain, and I have prepared a cup for you. It tastes bitter, but it should help your head if you are willing to try it."

He startled and then turned slightly to look at her. She appeared vaguely familiar, but the pain in his head had kept him from paying much attention to the introductions. "I must apologise as I do not remember your name. While I appreciate your effort, I am not accustomed to accepting drinks from women I do not know. In my position, it is unwise."

"I had not considered that, sir, but having watched Miss Bingley's pursuit of you, that seems wise. My name is Miss Elizabeth Bennet. We were introduced earlier, but if your head hurts as much as you say, I dare say it is difficult to remember so many introductions in such a short time," she replied, keeping her voice low and attempting to avoid notice. "I will leave the tea here if you change your mind, and then I will leave so my aunt does not observe me talking to you. I must confess she *is* one to watch out for."

He barked a laugh and quickly covered it with a cough. "I appreciate your help, Miss Bennet, and I will take a chance and try the tea. It was a pleasure to meet you, though I also feel you are familiar in some way. Have we met before tonight?"

"We might have seen each other in London at some event," she offered before dipping a shallow curtsy. She made one final comment before slipping away. "I must correct you in one respect, sir. My elder cousin is Miss Bennet; I am called Miss Elizabeth. Do take care, Mr. Darcy, and I hope you feel better soon."

Darcy watched her as she left and laughed inwardly at her pertness in introducing herself to him and correcting his address. She was unlike most women he knew. It was refreshing to meet an attractive woman who exhibited genuine kindness, bringing him tea to relieve his headache while not attempting to curry his favour. Even more astonishing, she warned him about her aunt's matchmaking schemes.

He desired to get to know her better; however, he idly wondered if there was any point. In this small market town, it was unlikely she had a fortune or any worthwhile connexions. Since infancy, his duty to marry for fortune and connexions had been drilled into him, first by his parents and, since their deaths, by his uncle, the earl. Could he genuinely throw those expectations aside for a country maiden? Shaking his head, he wondered what had come over him and how a short conversation that she had been careful to ensure no one had observed could have caused him to begin pondering marriage to a woman he had just met. Perhaps it was simply that she had not attempted to attract attention to their conversation and the genuine kindness in her actions.

* * *

From across the assembly hall, Caroline Bingley kept a watchful eye on Mr. Darcy. She observed him conversing with an indistinct figure, the identity of whom eluded her, as the person remained in the shadows. Her keen eyes detected him sipping from a cup of tea, leading her to believe he had been speaking with one of the attendants.

Miss Bingley had been especially pleased to learn of Darcy's visit to her brother's leased estate, as this presented her with the perfect opportunity to show that she would be his ideal wife. If, for some reason, he failed to succumb to her charms, she had contingencies in place to ensnare him. The necessary arrangements had been discreetly set in motion long before his arrival. Although her brother did not overtly endorse her designs, he was well-informed of her plans. Despite Darcy's insistence that he would never marry Caroline, they both had faith in Darcy's honour to choose the path of righteousness in the event he was compromised.

Indeed, at this juncture, Bingley felt an almost desperate urgency to marry off his sister to anyone — willing or unwilling. Her extravagant spending habits were syphoning his resources at an alarming rate, and frankly, her sour disposition made her a challenging companion. While Darcy genuinely liked Bingley, he harboured a strong aversion towards his unmarried sister, and his agreement to visit Bingley at his leased estate was contingent upon Caroline's absence while he was there. Darcy was livid when he arrived and discovered Caroline in residence and acting as Bingley's hostess. This, coupled with the upcoming assembly that evening, had nearly led to Darcy's immediate return directly to London. Despite his initial reluctance, he ultimately agreed to remain, yielding to his friend's pleas to assist in his endeavour.

* * *

Bingley's other sister, Louisa Hurst, and her husband were also present for Darcy's visit. Louisa was privy to Caroline's plan for a compromise, having been briefed on all its particulars by her sister. She shared the details with her husband.

Gilbert Hurst intended to be on guard and would apprise Mr. Darcy when the plot was ready to be acted upon. The Hursts genuinely appreciated Darcy's company and did not want to risk injuring their relationship with him. Therefore, they intended to thwart Caroline's efforts and were ready to act if required. To avoid unnecessarily alarming Darcy about plans that might never come to fruition, they did not disclose Caroline's plans to the man himself. Instead, Hurst's valet notified Darcy's valet and kept him apprised of any developments. When this was first discussed, Hurst was amused to learn that the man always slept in Darcy's dressing room and took extra measures to protect his master whenever he was in the same house as Caroline — at the gentleman's request. The valet, as well as the rest of Darcy's staff, was very familiar with his master's insistence that he would never marry Miss Bingley, regardless of the circumstances she created.

With all this in mind, both Hursts kept an eye on their sister and guest at the assembly, and Hurst, from his location sitting near Darcy, observed the exchange with the young lady. He had likewise noted Darcy's pleasure in it and observed to himself, *"This should be interesting to watch."* When they returned to Netherfield that night, the couple would discuss what they had seen in great detail.

The rest of the dance proceeded as one would expect. Bingley danced every dance, two with the eldest Miss Bennet, which was observed with mixed emotions by those in attendance. Darcy, whose headache had largely abated by the end of the evening, did not dance at all but did speak briefly to Miss Elizabeth to thank her for her assistance, and he found that, once again, he thoroughly enjoyed her conversation. It had ranged beyond a simple thank you into their shared love of books and nature; in fact, they had spoken for the entirety of one dance, giving them a full half hour in each other's company. The longer they talked, the more a nagging sense of familiarity struck him, although he could not recall ever meeting an Elizabeth Bennet. He wondered who her family was and if they had, as she suggested, crossed paths in town at some point.

When the Netherfield party departed, Caroline spent the ride complaining bitterly about the assembly and the lack of breeding displayed by the entire company. Only Miss Bennet was spared from the general disdain and was given scant praise as being "passably pretty." So determined was Miss Bingley to disparage the town and its society that she failed to notice no one else spoke the entire way to express either agreement or disagreement with her words.

* * *

In the Bennet carriage, the conversation centred on the charming Mr. Bingley and his equally charming sisters, although the other gentlemen of the party did not receive such praise. Mrs. Bennet had observed Mr. Darcy speaking to Elizabeth towards the end of the evening and was unhappy about *that* development. Mrs. Bennet believed the possibility of Elizabeth marrying well, or at all, could harm the rest of her family. As a result, Mrs. Bennet glared at her niece and disparaged that "unpleasant Mr. Darcy" at every opportunity.

Once all the girls were in bed, Mrs. Bennet spoke to her husband about the gentleman from the north and his apparent interest in Elizabeth. Since this summer had marked Elizabeth's twentieth birthday, Mr. Bennet had finally confessed the facts about the stipend to his wife. Mrs. Bennet worried that if Elizabeth married before she came of age, the stipend would stop sooner. Regardless, Mrs. Bennet was ready to cast Elizabeth from her home on the day she turned twenty-one because without those funds coming in, she felt they had no obligation to house the child.

Although she knew Elizabeth would inherit an estate in the north, it did not occur to Mrs. Bennet that treating the girl well was a way to guarantee her own welfare. As she saw it, an Elizabeth with a substantial inheritance would make her more likely to attract a suitor than Jane. Mrs. Bennet did not want to imagine anyone else's daughter being more attractive to a gentleman than Jane.

Mr. Bennet was far more worried about the end of the stipend because, without it, Longbourn would not be enough to support the habits of his family. He had been indolent in its management since taking over its management and had not done anything to increase the profits; instead, they had decreased under his management. Without the stipend, he faced the daunting prospect of making substantial cutbacks in his family's expenditures, and he still had four daughters to settle. The stipend they received for Elizabeth's care enabled him to spend much more freely on books and port and allowed his wife to spend as much as she liked on dresses and other fripperies. Their own daughters' allowances were also paid out of the stipend, and his daughters, particularly Lydia, would not appreciate those funds being cut.

Chapter 2

The morning after the assembly, Elizabeth rose early to walk to Oakham Mount, as was her habit on most fine mornings. The encounter with Mr. Darcy the night before had left Elizabeth flummoxed — she could swear she had met him before. They were unclear recollections, and she wanted to laugh at the dreams his voice had evoked. She knew they could not be real memories; they were far too fanciful — vague impressions of fighting dragons with him as a child or playing the "damsel in distress" to his Sir Galahad and lying beside him in the grass, watching the stars as he made up stories. The memory that caused her cheeks to redden was him carrying her in his arms while calling him "Dearest" and kissing his cheek as explosions of light burst around them. Shaking her head as she attempted to cool her cheeks, she laughed at herself, determining she would never dance at an assembly again if it caused her to have such wild imaginings.

Still, there was something so familiar about him. It was more than his looks, although he was quite the most handsome man she had ever met, and just thinking about his person made her cheeks heat again. He was tall and well-formed, and while they had not danced, she felt confident there was no padding under his jacket. He had been kind when he spoke to her, and while he had not spoken to anyone else at the assembly, she had known it was because of his headache. He was a little proud, to be sure, but he had confessed to feeling awkward when he heard his wealth and status bandied about the room nearly as soon as he entered it.

His voice, too, was familiar, though quite a bit deeper and more resonant now than in her dreams. He was much younger in her dreams — then, she would guess him to have been a boy of perhaps twelve or thirteen. It seemed odd to dream of him as a boy when she had only met the man the night before, but as she walked, she recalled she had dreamt of him before that night as well. Somehow, he was connected to the Will and Jon of her imaginings, although it made no sense. Other vague memories — a long journey by carriage, a large estate, mountain peaks, and the grandparents she was told she had never met — felt more real to Elizabeth than her family would admit.

In the middle of these musings, Mr. Darcy arrived, riding a rather tall stallion, tall, at least, from Elizabeth's perspective, since she had always been a little fearful around horses.

"Good morning, Miss Bennet, oh, pardon me; good morning, Miss Elizabeth," Darcy greeted the lady he had dreamed about as he dismounted his horse. It was strange, he thought, to encounter her so soon after such an odd dream. When he finally found sleep the night before, he dreamed of laying beside a much younger version of Elizabeth in the grass, telling her stories about the stars. In his dreams, he called her Ellie, and she called him Will. It had been years — before his mother died — that anyone had called him by that name.

Darcy harboured faint recollections of a young girl, merely three or four years old, who had once affectionately addressed him as "dearest" during a summer visit to Briarwood, an estate approximately fifty miles from Pemberley. Even now, he occasionally visited the estate, having assumed the role of trustee upon his father's demise. Another trustee, a friend of his father, maintained contact with the girl and her family. However, Darcy, having not heard the girl's name in years, struggled to recall it. As his father's will outlined, his responsibilities were confined to the estate's property and investments. It was understood that Mr. Terrance Elliott oversaw the girl's well-being.

Darcy exchanged a few words that morning with Miss Elizabeth before

21

separating; however, they continued to meet this way for several mornings, and their conversations grew longer each day.

One morning, Darcy noticed how Miss Elizabeth seemed to shy away from his horse. "Might I introduce you to Bucephalus, Miss Elizabeth?" he asked.

Despite her fear, her eyes twinkled when she retorted: "Should I suppose your Christian name to be Alexander, sir, to have a horse with such a name? Or do you simply prefer to have your friends add "the Great" to your name when referencing you in company?"

Surprised by his low chuckle at her comment, she was further astounded when he bowed gallantly and stated in an affected voice, "Fitzwilliam Alexander Darcy, at your service, madam. Perhaps you might be Roxana?"

For a moment, she was startled by his words, but then she suddenly laughed. "Having never been to Asia, sir, I could scarcely be considered the most beautiful woman on that continent. My cousin Jane is widely considered to be the most beautiful woman in Hertfordshire, and I know I can scarcely compare. You, Mr. Darcy, are a flatterer."

She noted him shaking his head and answered his previous question a little more timidly. "I would be delighted to be introduced to your horse, sir, but I admit that horses and I do not always seem to get along. My uncle attempted to teach me once to ride when I was perhaps seven or eight, but he was unwilling to help me overcome my fear of the animals. Having a smaller horse or a pony might have helped, or a little more concerted effort on his part, but I was too afraid, and he never attempted it again. I have a faint memory of riding a horse as a young child with someone named 'Jon', and in that instance, I fell from the horse and injured my leg. My aunt and uncle claim it must have been a dream since we do not know anyone named Jon or Jonathan, but still, the memory made it difficult for me to overcome those feelings, and, as I said, my uncle would not try anything further to encourage me."

"How old were you in this dream?" Darcy asked, intrigued as her 'memory' made him recall a similar event that had happened one summer at Pemberley. "Do you remember anything else?"

"The horse seemed enormous, but as I was only four or five in my dream, I believe most horses would have appeared that way to me. Jon was not a boy, perhaps a young man nine or ten years older than I, and I recall a discussion of slaying a dragon with him and another boy. Jon dismounted first, but something distracted him for a moment, and before he could help me down, I fell off the other side. The other boy rescued me, carrying me to the house and taking me to my nursemaid. I think it was only a slight injury, but the memory of it stuck with me."

Darcy started, remembering a similar event at Pemberley the summer his sister was born. "Do you remember the name of the other boy?" he asked, his voice betraying his interest in the matter.

Elizabeth trilled a laugh. "I believe I called him 'dearest'. I feel fairly certain it is a dream; my relations have told me often enough that I have a fanciful imagination," she finished when he appeared shocked at her revelations.

Darcy's conviction that these were not merely dreams intensified, and his suspicion that Elizabeth Bennet was something more than she seemed deepened. The previous day, he had penned a letter to Mr. Elliott, seeking insights into the Tomlinson family, specifically the girl who was the heir to the estate. Since his father's passing, the two men had corresponded sporadically regarding the trust, though most were about business matters. He possessed limited knowledge about the heir, and encountering Elizabeth stirred his recollections of the young Ellie Tomlinson.

At other times during these meetings, Mr. Darcy spoke passionately about his estate, relishing the opportunity to share his knowledge with Elizabeth. His descriptions of the area around his home piqued her interest. She was always curious about travel and genuinely interested in Darcy's estate, so she could not resist the urge to inquire about the sights he mentioned. "Mr. Darcy," she began one morning, her eyes fixed on the distant horizons, "would you describe those Peaks you have seen? I am intrigued by your descriptions as something about them niggles at my memory."

Mr. Darcy's eyes softened as he recounted the majestic scenery. "The Peaks are remarkable, Miss Elizabeth," he replied. "The rugged beauty of the landscape, the rolling hills, and the commanding peaks that seem to touch the sky are a sight that takes one's breath away. My home, Pemberley, is in the middle of this area, and I delight that I can visit there frequently."

Elizabeth nodded, her mind racing to connect these descriptions with her vague memories. "You know, Mr. Darcy," she confessed with a playful smile, "I have had some rather peculiar impressions of seeing similar sights in my past. However, I have always dismissed them as the imaginings of an avid reader. You see, I have frequently devoured many books with vivid descriptions of places I long to visit someday."

He regarded her with a thoughtful expression. "Could it be that you have a deeper connexion to such landscapes than you realise, Miss Elizabeth? Perhaps your heart has journeyed through these terrains long before we met."

She laughed her charming laugh as he had intended her to do. "Yes, perhaps I have visited them in a past life."

A few days later, the two families were in company again at Lucas Lodge. Since he had begun meeting with Miss Elizabeth in the mornings, he observed the family dynamic more closely. At the assembly, it appeared something was not quite right with them, and, given his conversations with the enchanting lady, he had often wondered about her family.

Darcy noted that Elizabeth looked very different from her relations. Granted, they were cousins, and she was not related by blood to her aunt, but something about Elizabeth struck him as familiar. However, he could not recall any Bennets amongst his acquaintances. An off-handed comment by Charlotte Lucas also revealed the date of Elizabeth's birth — August 14, 1791 — only a few days before his own birthday. Hearing that date stirred another memory and Darcy was determined to ask her about it the first chance he had.

After they exchanged greetings the next morning, Elizabeth fed Bucephalus an apple she had brought just for him. She had become familiar with his horse throughout the last fortnight and had begun bringing him a treat, along with something for herself and Darcy to eat as they spoke. It was evidence of the trust she was forming in them both. "Miss Lucas mentioned that your birth date is only a few days before mine. It brought to mind a memory that I wanted to share with you. On my eleventh birthday, my family and I celebrated at the estate of a friend of my father's, Mr. Alexander Tomlinson. The estate is called Briarwood.

"That particular date stands out in my memories because it coincided with the birthday of the estate owner's granddaughter, who was also turning four. Mr. Tomlinson purchased fireworks for our last night to celebrate his granddaughter's birthday and, coincidentally, mine. Despite the differences in our ages, Ellie and I had become friendly over the summer, and she was initially frightened by the fireworks. She wanted comfort, so she came to me and insisted I hold her during the rest of the display. When it was over, she patted my cheek, called me her dearest, and then kissed my cheek. My cousin, now an army colonel and a couple of years older than me, teased me mercilessly the next day.

"The following summer, I saw Ellie again on our birthdays, but this time, we were at my family's estate because my mother had just given birth to my sister. She was still rather weak. I learned later that before that year was out, Ellie was sent to live with a relative as both of her grandparents died. My father was appointed her guardian, though my mother was too ill for her to live with us at the time. I still am the trustee of her estate, although I have not seen her since."

Elizabeth sighed. "It is a lovely memory. It is odd — I have always had a vague memory of a knight protecting me from bright lights in the sky one night when I was small. Like your Ellie, he allowed me to kiss his cheek when they were done, but as I have been told I have never seen fireworks, I determined it was merely a dream," she whispered.

"How do you know it was a dream, not a memory?" Darcy asked.

"Other than trips to London, I have lived all my life at Longbourn, or so I have been told," Elizabeth stated. "My aunt and uncle have told me on more than one occasion that I am too fanciful as I often have dreams of things they say could not have happened. I was told I had a rather active imagination when I was young and was constantly making up stories about dragon-slaying knights. When I tried to tell others about these memories, they teased me or accused me of lying, as there are no boys in our family of the proper age to have been my playmates. When I was small, these imaginary playmates seemed much older than I, but they would have been boys, perhaps ten to thirteen. None of my cousins have similar memories, so I am quite convinced I made them up. Perhaps they are memories of things I read or came from stories someone made up and told me."

Darcy started at her recollections. "Miss Bennet, are you certain you have always lived at Longbourn?"

Elizabeth laughed. "My aunt and uncle say it is so. The present Mr. Bennet inherited when I was five, and I was at the estate before they arrived, so they claim I must have memories from that time. When I was young, I insisted I had another family than those at Longbourn and spoke of a grand house surrounded by peaks, though when I made those claims, I was told I was being very hateful to imagine a life without my family. There is a John in our neighbourhood, but it is not the same boy from my dreams. "

"How do you know they are not the same?" Darcy asked.

"He is only a couple of years older than me — the boys in my dreams were quite a bit older, perhaps ten or more years. John also does not have the same memories or dreams as I and does not have an older brother," Elizabeth replied. "Do not trouble yourself, Mr. Darcy. I am convinced it is a matter that will never be solved. Why would my relations not be honest with me? I believe I would feel equally annoyed with a child if she insisted she had a different family somewhere. It would be rather hurtful — once I realised that, I quit saying those things. I may have these memories from when my other uncle lived before Aunt Fanny and Uncle Thomas came to Longbourn, but it seems better not to speak of them."

As Darcy considered this, he realised everything about Miss Elizabeth captured his attention. Each morning he met with her, he liked her more and began contemplating how to call on her or request a courtship. However, something about her family made him hold back and wait before he asked. He felt something was not right at Longbourn and wanted to discover more, especially as Elizabeth's "imaginings" coincided with his own memories. To that end, he had begun to ask Elizabeth more questions about her family when they met, and those questions were returned until the two knew quite a bit about each other and were in a fair way towards falling in love.

Chapter 3

While Darcy was riding the fields and coming to know Elizabeth better, Caroline Bingley was plotting. The night before, they had attended a card party at the Lucases, and Miss Bingley did not care for the attention the gentlemen of her party paid to the Bennet family. She was frustrated with Charles's flirting with Jane Bennet, although she knew it would not go anywhere. Still, *her* Mr. Darcy's eyes were drawn entirely too often toward the second Miss Bennet, the penniless, orphaned cousin, who might be the natural child of the previous master of Longbourn.

Miss Bingley surreptitiously watched the interactions between the two. It was apparent they knew each other better than their brief acquaintance should have allowed, which made her wonder how *that* came to be. She knew Mr. Darcy went out for a daily ride, but other than that, he was in the house, often ensconced in the study — or on the estate with her brother. This bothered the lady nearly as much as the attention he paid to Eliza Bennet. She could not engage herself to the gentleman if she were never in company with him.

Despite her best efforts, she continued to be unsuccessful. The footmen seemed to be taking orders from someone else since she demanded one leave her alone in the breakfast room on at least two occasions as she waited for Mr. Darcy to appear. However, he never appeared when a servant was out of the room. Not only that, the door to his bedroom and sitting room, even the servant entrances, were locked at all hours, and Caroline could not obtain a key. It seemed the housekeeper had been instructed, although she could not discover by whom, that no family member was to have a key to his rooms or the servant entrances. Aside from the housekeeper, only Mr. Darcy's valet, Mr. Roberts, had a key to that gentleman's room, and he was always present when the maids went in to clean, preventing Caroline or her maid from being able to slip in.

"Charles, I cannot compromise Mr. Darcy if I cannot get into his rooms. He departs early each morning for his ride, and his valet keeps the doors locked — all of them — as though he does not trust the residents of the house. His man opens the doors for the maids to clean, though he remains within the rooms and locks them immediately when they depart. The footmen will not leave the breakfast parlour while Mr. Darcy is there, and despite all of my efforts, it appears he will not ask me to marry him without some provocation. What are you going to do to force your friend to propose to me?" Miss Bingley screeched at her brother the morning after the gathering at Lucas Lodge.

"I never promised to help, Caro, only to encourage him to act as a gentleman if you succeeded in compromising him. It seems he does not intend to be compromised," Bingley replied, laughing inwardly at his sister. "I know you are determined, and while I would welcome him as a brother, I am not willing to lose his friendship. If I were to do anything to aid you in your efforts, he would sniff it out, and, should you succeed, he would cast my friendship away without a second thought. I might be his brother-in-law in that instance, but he would no longer allow me in his company. I am still unsure whether your compromise would get you what you desire. While Darcy is honourable to a fault, he can also be harsh when crossed. No amount of persuasion has ever convinced him to do what he does not want to do."

Caroline changed tactics as she continued to screech her displeasure. "Another thing, Charles, you are far too enamoured of that mousy Miss Bennet. That Bennet family is positively awful—the second daughter is the worst of the lot—but you are being taken in by the eldest. You cannot marry

29

so far beneath yourself; you should stop pursuing the chit, or you will give her expectations."

"She's beautiful and a fun diversion. Should she offer me more than her smiles, I would not turn her down, but you are correct: I will not marry her. However, nothing will come of a harmless flirtation."

"Mr. Darcy is enamoured of that hoyden Eliza Bennet," Caroline nearly yelled, showing the true reason for her upset. "If I cannot persuade Mr. Darcy to propose to me soon, we must depart Netherfield for London. I will not stand for remaining here much longer. If nothing else, I must get Darcy away from her. I will not allow that … that woman to take my place."

Bingley attempted to placate his sister. "Darcy would never offer for an impoverished woman, as I understand the Bennet daughters have next to nothing as a dowry. He may be, as I am, engaging in a harmless flirtation with the girl. Continue to work your arts upon him and just see if you cannot persuade him to offer for you without affecting a compromise. It will go much better for you that way."

"What if that Eliza Bennet succeeds in compromising him first?"

"I think you are being ridiculous if you think that will occur. He rides in the morning and then spends his days here, usually with Hurst and me when we go out shooting. He spends the evenings in company with you and Louisa when you flirt with him. He has never even called at Longbourn and has been in company with the Bennets twice. And surely you observed how he looks at the parents? He cannot stand them."

Mollified, Caroline decided to do as her brother suggested. She began dressing even more provocatively and noticed Mr. Darcy eyeing her costumes with interest. Each time she came near him, she immediately latched onto his arm and flattered and simpered up at him as she had seen done in all the best ballrooms. She had no idea that each time she did those things, she pushed any future as Mrs. Darcy further and further away.

* * *

"Miss Bingley is in a right snit that I will not give her a master key. She has specifically questioned your master's habits of locking all the doors and your practice of being on hand while the maids clean the room. If she gets her way, she'll compromise the man, and I wouldn't put it past her to try something soon. She's frustrated, that one is, since he does not pay her the attention she thinks she deserves," the housekeeper, Mrs. Nicholls, warned Mr. Darcy's valet when she encountered him one afternoon.

She was not finished and continued, her tone indicating not a little curiosity: "Not only that, but she thinks he's paying too much attention to Miss Elizabeth Bennet. Everyone in Hertfordshire admires Miss Lizzy, and it seems she and your master have been meeting atop Oakham Mount each morning since the assembly, did you know?"

Roberts, Darcy's valet, was like his master, tending to be a quiet and solemn man. He considered the matter before he spoke. "My orders are to prevent Miss Bingley from compromising my master, and I have spoken to several other servants willing to aid in this. Many of the local servants do not seem to like the Bingley family very well and do not want to see my master tied to the mistress," he finally said.

"And has he said anything to you about Miss Lizzy?"

"He has not."

Her face fell. "Oh."

"But he seems to be rather pleased after his rides each morning, more so than a mere ride would normally bring, and was aggravated the morning he was prevented from riding out due to the weather," the valet revealed slowly, his lips twitching slightly at the corners.

That returned the smile to the housekeeper's face. "He could not find a better woman, should he decide in her favour."

"I will tell him you said so," Roberts replied with a slight grin.

* * *

Nearly a week after the evening at Lucas Lodge, Darcy received a response to the letter he had written to his father's friend. It had been sent to Pemberley first and had to be forwarded to him at Netherfield, causing the delay. At first, his steward had been uncertain about whether he should send it on, but after recalling that it was likely a personal matter, he decided to include it with that week's mail. He would have sent it sooner if he knew Darcy awaited this letter.

As soon as Darcy saw the package of letters from Pemberley that arrived by that morning's post, he shuffled through the letters and was surprised to find the one he had been waiting for, along with a note of explanation for its delay.

Setting the rest of the post aside, he quickly opened the letter from Mr. Elliott.

> *Darcy,*
>
> *I was taken aback upon receiving your letter inquiring about the Tomlinson estate and its heiress. As you are aware, following your father's demise, you assumed the role of trustee for Miss Elizabeth Tomlinson, entrusted primarily with financial matters and estate management. Given the circumstances surrounding the passing of the Tomlinsons and your mother's illness at the time, the young girl could not join your family then, and I arranged for her to be placed in her uncle's care. That uncle passed away not long after she arrived, and she was placed with another uncle, the next heir to the estate after his brother, who was married with two or three daughters at the time. I do commend your dedication to overseeing her investments and estate, which have flourished under your care.*
>
> *Miss Tomlinson has recently celebrated her twentieth birthday, and with her approaching majority, it seems fitting to initiate her introduction to her inheritance. Oddly, her uncle has chosen not to reveal her true status as an heiress and treats her in a similar fashion to her cousins, perhaps to shield her from potential fortune seekers. Regardless, she is set to assume control of her inheritance next summer and deserves to be informed. Despite the lack of a societal debut and a proper season, she appears well-prepared, as indicated by her uncle's letters describing her involvement in estate management and assistance*

with his affairs.

Given your current presence in Hertfordshire, you may have already encountered Miss Tomlinson. It would be beneficial for you to assess her aptitude for managing her estate. If her uncle has not provided the claimed education, we must prepare to acquaint her with the necessary knowledge once she assumes control. I entrust you to collaborate on a plan to impart the required information, should that be the case.

Darcy nearly dropped the letter when Mr. Elliott confirmed that Miss Tomlinson was in Hertfordshire. It must be her, as the only Elizabeth he had met was Elizabeth Bennet, and he recalled that she was 20 and her birthday was in August.

My involvement in her upbringing has been minimal due to assurances from her uncle regarding the agreed-upon allowance and training. However, recent doubts about her uncle's honesty and concerns raised by Edwin Gardiner have prompted me to reconsider what I believed I knew about matters. I request your discreet investigation into Miss Tomlinson's upbringing, verifying her intelligence and accomplishments.

As her co-trustee, you possess complete authority to divulge any pertinent information using suitable means if you believe it to be necessary. Her uncle was never designated her legal guardian; your father was given that role in the will. However, in the wake of his passing, uncertainty clouds the current legal custodian. This issue, coupled with Miss Tomlinson's impending attainment of majority, necessitates our thorough investigation, particularly in light of her grandfather's desire for her to partake in a social season and the possibility of attracting a fitting suitor.

The terms of her grandfather's will ensure that her property and wealth remain under her control after she comes of age, with specific conditions in the event of an elopement. Both trustees' approval is mandated for her marriage, even after she turns twenty-one, securing her inheritance as her property, not her husband's.

*Please keep me updated on any findings regarding Miss Tomlinson,
and let me know if you deem my involvement necessary. My knowledge
of the family she resides with is limited, and I regret my negligence
in fulfilling my duties as her trustee. I placed too much reliance on
her uncle's assurances without verifying their accuracy. I hope my
shortcomings have not adversely affected Miss Tomlinson.*

Sincerely,

T. Elliott

The letter confirmed what Darcy believed—Miss Elizabeth Bennet was not, in fact, a Bennet but was Miss Elizabeth Tomlinson, an heiress in her own right. He knew beyond a doubt why he had always felt that Miss Elizabeth was so familiar to him—she was the picture of her grandmother as a young woman and retained much of the liveliness of her younger self. He had often viewed the portrait of the elder Mrs. Tomlinson at the estate when he visited, as her likeness was prominently displayed above the fireplace in the study. She also bore a remarkable similarity to several other portraits in the gallery, which was likely why she did not resemble many of those in the family with whom she resided.

Memories of those two summers with little Ellie ran through his mind. He thought of how she had lived up to the promise of that first summer—she was as impertinent and lively now as she had been then. Since their first meeting at the assembly, Darcy had felt a powerful attraction to Elizabeth. Her family was beyond understanding, and the information he was acquiring made the situation far more challenging to comprehend. He wondered if Mr. Bennet were to be trusted as he had often noticed Elizabeth's clothes were obviously less expensive and of a lower quality than Miss Bennet's gowns.

While Elizabeth appeared well educated, he knew from speaking to her that she had not had a governess past her twelfth year and that her education after that had been conducted rather informally. She seemed to have risen above that due to her own desire for knowledge, but it was apparent the other girls had not taken the same advantage. Admittedly, he had not observed the other girls as frequently, though he had noted the disparity between what the two eldest wore and Jane's apparent lack of accomplishments, that is, if Miss Bingley was to be believed. It was one of the points she liked to harp on when she spoke of the "rustics" she was being forced to tolerate in the country. If the family received a stipend for Miss Elizabeth's care, as Elliott stated they were, it was not utilised on Elizabeth's behalf. Idly, he wondered how it was being used, especially given what Mr. Elliott said about doubting Mr. Bennet's honesty regarding how the funds were spent.

After contemplating everything he knew, he wrote a reply informing Mr. Elliott of what he had already observed about their charge. He expressed his concerns about what he had seen, confirming the trustee's fears about Bennet's trustworthiness. Since he had already met the lady before learning her identity through this letter, he had learned a great deal about both her and her family, and he agreed with the other trustee's opinion — the Bennet family's treatment of Elizabeth was hardly what it should have been.

Chapter 4

Once again, Darcy deliberately sought Elizabeth's company at Oakham Mount the next morning. When she arrived, he was waiting for her, having dismounted and tied his horse at the base of the path.

"Miss Elizabeth," Darcy called as Elizabeth approached the spot where he stood waiting for her. "I received a letter yesterday and wanted to speak to you about what it contained."

"Of course, sir, I would be happy to help," she replied cheerfully. "What might I do for you?"

"This is perhaps an improper request, but I am wondering if there is a place we could go and speak where we would not be observed?" he asked.

"Mr. Darcy," she exclaimed, alarmed by his apparent disregard for propriety in making such a request. "Are you absolutely certain of what you are asking?"

"I am," he affirmed. "I have a rather weighty matter to discuss, and it might require some time to address it properly. I would prefer our conversation remain private, away from prying eyes. I assure you, I mean you no harm."

Elizabeth gazed at him for a moment, but the sincerity in his eyes convinced her of his good intentions. She slowly nodded her consent and guided him down the path towards a secluded grove of trees, shielding them from unwanted attention. Over the weeks of their acquaintance, they had met numerous times during her walks, and he had yet to demonstrate any threat. She felt secure in her choice to place her trust in him, even finding herself admiring him, though fully aware of the vast difference in their social status and the unlikelihood of him ever desiring anything more than friendship with her.

They were both quiet as they walked, and once they settled in the grove, he remained silent for several long moments. "Mr. Darcy, I cannot stay here all morning and must return before too much longer. Please say what you need to say," she scolded lightly.

"I apologise, Miss Elizabeth; I am trying to determine the best way to approach this topic," he replied. "Please forgive me in advance; I do not intend to offend you with my questions, and sometimes, I express myself in a way that might be misunderstood. I also hope you will trust me enough to believe what I tell you is the truth."

Elizabeth once again eyed him warily. "I will try not to be insulted and will ask for clarification if you word something in such a way that it does," she agreed.

Darcy began his tale: "Since my father passed away five years ago, in addition to the care of my estate, I have managed an estate as a trustee for a young lady who has not yet reached her majority. My responsibility, and my father's before me, was to ensure the estate operated as it should and to manage investments on her behalf," he began. "I have had no actual responsibility for the young lady in question, although apparently, my father was appointed her guardian." Darcy proceeded to explain the circumstances that led to George Darcy not being able to take charge of the girl at that time.

"Instead, her other trustee, Mr. Terrance Elliott, conveyed her to her uncle's estate, where she has lived since. Mr. Elliott was responsible for overseeing her care, although her uncle was responsible for ensuring she had the expected upbringing. His oversight has largely occurred through annual letters from her uncle that told of her health and care and updated Mr. Elliott about her education and accomplishments. Mr. Elliott's wife could have sponsored her for a season, but not long after she came to live with her uncle, Mrs. Elliott became ill, and while she lingered for several years, she never recovered. Like my father, Mr. Elliott struggled with depression for several years upon losing his wife and did not, perhaps, superintend her care as he should." He watched Elizabeth carefully to see how she reacted to this information.

Elizabeth merely nodded. "This is an interesting story, Mr. Darcy, but how can I help you?"

"Mr. Elliott has tasked me to learn what I can about this young woman because he believes her uncle is no longer being truthful with him about the young lady and her care. The young lady is unaware of her situation, believing she is the family's impoverished relation. The family receives a quarterly stipend for her care, although when she comes of age next year, that stipend will stop, and she will come into control of her inheritance. This includes an estate near my own and a rather large sum of money invested on her behalf for her dowry," he stopped there for a second before speaking again, somewhat self-consciously. "In the last five years, I have been rather successful with my investments, and I have done well with hers, increasing the amount significantly. According to the terms of her grandfather's will, it will all remain with her, even after her marriage, as it is clearly outlined that her marriage settlements must state all she brings into the marriage will remain hers."

He stopped and drew a deep breath before he continued. "What I want to ask you is, when I acquaint her with this information, what is the best way to go about it? If my co-trustee is correct, her uncle has been misleading him about how the money has been spent on her behalf. " Darcy explained some of the facts he knew from Mr. Elliott and then finished by asking: "How can I confirm these claims without offending her or the family? I want to know if she is treated as a valued family member who is paying for her own care or as someone who is barely tolerated due to her penniless state?"

Elizabeth gasped lightly at the implication, recognising that many of these things he said described her treatment within her home. "Mr. Darcy," she said quietly, her sense of unease growing the longer the two spoke, "might I ask why you are telling me all this? It begins to feel that your stated purpose is not your true intention."

"I knew you were clever, Miss Elizabeth, so your uncle was not mistaken in his description of you," he said softly. "Given what Mr. Elliott has said, I believe you are the girl we have been discussing. He did not mention the gentleman's surname, though he did name the uncle in London whom he had recently met. Knowing what I do about his occasional absent-mindedness, he assumed I was aware of the name or simply forgot to include it. I have already written to him again, asking for the information he neglected to include. Assuming I am correct and you are the lady in question, I gave your name and my observations of the family so far.

"It was in that meeting with the gentleman in London that Mr. Elliott began to wonder if this girl's uncle has been completely honest with him over the years, and if you are indeed who we are discussing, it appears as though he has good reason to question the veracity of the letters. According to the letters her uncle writes annually, the child was provided with a governess to assist with her education and has been regularly exposed to London society, visiting the theatre and the opera, along with the museums and other cultural attractions. She has also been provided with masters to teach her languages and music. While she was not brought out in London, she is fully prepared to take her place in society when the time comes, according to her uncle.

"However, if you are, in fact, Miss Tomlinson and not Miss Elizabeth Bennet, I would guess that much of what has been written is untrue based on our conversations. Am I right to suppose that your cousins, particularly Miss Bennet, receive higher quality gowns and other items than you do? I have yet to meet your uncle, but is it safe to assume that your relations spend more on their own children, particularly the eldest, than on you? The family of the girl I am speaking of presently receive three hundred pounds each quarter to provide for their ward, most of which is supposed to be spent directly on her, with fifty pounds of that amount intended to be given to her directly each quarter as her pin money."

Elizabeth gasped at this number as she often had noted an entry for that amount each quarter day in the account books. Her uncle never told her where it came from when she asked, but she knew that the estate would not be nearly as profitable as it was without those funds. The estate itself had at one point brought in more than two thousand pounds per annum, but due to her uncle's indolence, it was now bringing in less than fifteen hundred. In the last few years, Elizabeth had begun taking steps to recover that lost amount. However, her uncle's reluctance to entertain many of her proposed ideas hindered her success.

She had managed to achieve some success with changing the rotation of the crops, but that had required little effort from Mr. Bennet to accomplish. The additional twelve hundred a year from that unexplained source paid for her uncle's books, much of Mrs. Bennet's finery, and what Jane and Lydia received from their mother. Elizabeth received the same allowance as all her other cousins — fifty pounds per annum — but Mrs. Bennet's generosity did not supplement what Elizabeth received. Mary and Kitty were similarly overlooked, though Elizabeth was given the least by her aunt and always with complaints about having to spend their money on a penniless relation. She had wondered about this and, knowing Mrs. Bennet's shallow nature, assumed it was because she did not take after the Bennet family in appearance. Mrs. Bennet often complained about this, going so far as to disparage Elizabeth's looks, especially in comparison to Jane or Lydia.

Mr. Darcy was not finished with the story. He watched the emotions play across Elizabeth's face for a moment, and he saw the moment she realised the truth. Sadness, anger, and resignation all warred within her. Finally, he saw her nod as though she had come to some kind of resolution, and then she looked up at him again, and he continued. "Since meeting you, I have observed a marked difference between your clothing and that of your elder cousin, except for that night at the assembly. You are everything lovely, Miss Elizabeth, but Miss Bingley has commented on your clothing several times in my hearing. There is also the matter of how Mrs. Bennet speaks of you in public. I have scarcely heard her say anything positive of you, and she frequently disparages you in company. Considering how she treats you in public, I suspect it is much worse in the privacy of your home. As Mr. Bennet has not attended any of the events where I have met with you,

I cannot be certain how he treats you within your family, but his lack of attendance indicates a lack of concern about the well-being of the family as a whole. I am sorry if this offends you, but it is what I have observed."

Elizabeth hung her head. "You are not wrong, Mr. Darcy," she whispered. "I have often noted the difference in how I have been treated and assumed it was because I was, as you have said, merely a penniless relation relying on the kindness of my relations. Jane receives new dresses frequently, as does Lydia, but I typically am given Jane's dresses to make over. When I receive new dresses, I am always directed to the cheaper fabrics and embellishments unless I am in London, where my Aunt and Uncle Gardiner pay for much higher-quality clothing. Mrs. Bennet does not hide her displeasure when she sees what has been purchased for me there." She paused and took a deep breath. "What other information makes you believe I am the woman in the letter?"

"Her name is Elizabeth, she is twenty, her birthday is in August, and she lives on an estate in Hertfordshire. There is also your uncanny resemblance to your grandmother — her portrait is in the study in Briarwood, and I have often sat there and admired it. Finally," Darcy said, "I cannot disregard your memories of 'Will' and 'Jon' and my own memories that were triggered when I met you. Since encountering you, I have often dreamed of little Ellie, the girl I knew at Briarwood and Pemberley all those years ago. I believe meeting you brought back memories I had almost forgotten, and the dreams you recounted are similar to real experiences from those times."

"And the name of the uncle in London?" she pushed again, not reacting outwardly to his words, but she was glad she was sitting, as she felt herself grow weak as he had listed each item.

"Ahh, yes, he said he met a man named Edwin Gardiner, the brother of the lady's aunt," Darcy replied softly.

Elizabeth gasped and felt tears prick her eyes. "I cannot believe it! You must be telling me the truth. Other than the portrait, which I cannot confirm because I have never seen it, all you have said has been true of me. And your face, though older, is so similar to the image I have of the 'Dearest Will' from my dreams.

"Ultimately, what does this all mean, Mr. Darcy? Apparently, I will inherit an estate when I come of age in August, but until then, what difference does this make in my life? Perhaps I can insist that I am no longer made to feel as though I am a penniless relation, and I will know that I have contributed greatly to my care over the years. Must I stay at Longbourn?"

He shrugged out of his great coat and laid it down so she could sit on a fallen long. Once he had her settled, he sat beside her. "I am uncertain, Miss Elizabeth," he replied. "You will be of age in August, though that is still ten months away, and you will eventually need to learn about your estate. However, neither I nor Mr. Elliott can take you there without the presence of another woman for the sake of propriety. Of more immediate concern is the fact that your uncle has lied to the trustee and diverted your funds for his own use. That will need to be remedied, though I believe it best to wait to speak to Mr. Elliott before we pursue that.

"You, of course, should be presented at court and be given a season in town. With your fortune, you will garner significant attention amongst the *ton*. Both trustees must approve any match, but as I stated before, your estate remains in your control even after marriage."

He stopped at her laugh. "Mr. Darcy, I hardly think marriage is worth considering at this moment. The boys I have grown up with are now men, but I cannot imagine marrying any of them, and I doubt the men in the *ton* will overlook my lack of beauty, especially if they would not receive the estate and fortune themselves."

Darcy shook his head in wonder that such a lovely and enticing woman could think so little of her own beauty. "Miss Elizabeth, whoever said you lack beauty was dissembling. You are incredibly alluring."

She noticed his voice had grown a little husky and saw something in his eyes that made her heart flutter. The mix of admiration, fondness, and a hint of vulnerability intrigued her, and her hand flew to cover her mouth in surprise.

"Even without your fortune, you would be a great temptation for many men," he began earnestly, looking her directly in the eye. "Since we began meeting at Oakham Mount, you have drawn me in with your intelligence, your wit, *and* your beauty. You had already impressed me with your kindness that night at the assembly. I am dismayed you have not noticed that I have been informally courting you for some time now, though perhaps you just believed we were becoming friends. I pray you will trust me when I say I have only been reluctant to formally ask you because I was concerned that not all was as it should be with the Bennets."

Elizabeth felt her cheeks heat at his compliments.

Darcy took her hand and continued. "As it turns out, now that I have discovered I am a trustee of your estate, I am uncertain I can even ask to court you as I wish. If you are willing to agree to a courtship, I must address matters with Mr. Elliott to see what must be done."

"Mr. Darcy," Elizabeth asked haltingly, "I must ask my question before I can answer yours. Although, it occurs to me that you have not actually asked a question, and I may be thinking too much ..." she trailed off, realising that while he had mentioned courting her, he had not actually made the request.

He laughed. "Do not doubt it, Miss Elizabeth; nothing will prevent me from pursuing you. My delay is due solely to my not knowing how to ask for a courtship under the circumstances. I must first speak to Mr. Elliott and perhaps consult with my uncle, but please, ask your question. I would prefer to discuss this with you openly. There is the matter of my trusteeship that must be dealt with as well."

"It is just that, well, you only said you wanted to court me after you discovered my identity. I wonder if you would have courted me as the penniless orphan Elizabeth Bennet or whether I have only become acceptable to you now because I am this Miss Tomlinson. Regardless of my status or fortune, I will still be the same girl I am now," she said in a rush.

Again, he chuckled, a low, rich sound she suddenly found she adored. "Miss Elizabeth, trust me when I say I have wanted to court you for nearly the entirety of our acquaintance. Since that first night when you exhibited kindness toward me, you have intrigued me, and I have enjoyed our meetings and discussions at Oakham Mount very much. I feel that we have been getting to know each other already during these encounters. I assure you I would have made the request regardless of your fortune or lack thereof.

If you are worried about my interest, you only have to ask my sister or cousin; I wrote to them frequently about my admiration for you since that first meeting. This letter from Mr. Elliott was merely an impetus to speak more purposefully, especially because I fear losing you to another gentleman once you are introduced to the *ton*. And while I feel nearly certain that you are the woman described, I am still waiting for him to confirm the matter absolutely."

She sighed and took a deep breath in an attempt to calm herself. Then, drawing herself up, she spoke. "I ask again, sir, where do we go from here?"

Darcy smiled at her bravery in the face of what was undoubtedly a considerable shock. "First, Miss Elizabeth, I would like you to know that I admire you, and as I said earlier in this conversation, the more I know of you, the more I want to know. I am amazed at how well you are handling this information, and that speaks highly of you. Based on what I know of you now, I also think we would do well together, and I would like to see if you could feel the same way about me. Regardless, we will be tied together in some way for the next year as you learn about your inheritance for when you eventually are given its control. As I previously said, I have run Briarwood along with my own estate these last five years, and I can start to teach you whatever you need to know about running it as soon as you would like. And then, of course, I will be a near neighbour if you begin running your estate independently after your majority.

"However, I do not know how to go about informing Mr. and Mrs. Bennet that I am one of the trustees of your estate and that I have told you about it," he exhaled deeply. "It appears to me that there is something deeper at work, and it seems best they do not know that you are aware."

"I agree with you," she sighed. "I believe it is best if we consult with Mr. Elliott about our next steps since there appear to be several matters that require attention before we delve further into them. You have revealed much today; perhaps we should both consider matters and speak again in the morning."

Chapter 5

Elizabeth returned to Longbourn deep in thought, pondering all she had learned that morning. Mr. Darcy intended to follow up with the other trustee, but she felt confident, as he did, that the lady he described was definitely her. She knew his father was dead, but she wondered if this other trustee had personally known her parents or grandparents. Her feelings were in turmoil — partly elation, given Mr. Darcy's statement that he desired to enter into a courtship with her, but a more significant part of her was angry and upset with the Bennets and the secrets they had kept from her.

"What do I do now?" she thought. *"Knowing what I now know, how do I face Uncle Thomas and Aunt Fanny and continue to treat them as I always have? Who can I trust to do what is best for me?"* These thoughts and several others pushed her possible courtship with Mr. Darcy to the back of her mind as she turned them round and round in her head.

She entered the breakfast room where most of the family, at least the female contingent, was gathered. Her slipping in was largely unheeded in the noise of the room, and she sat down after serving herself from the sideboard. However, she struggled to eat much, and Lydia eventually noticed her silence.

"What is wrong with you this morning, Lizzy?" she cried loudly, gathering the attention of all at the table. "You are barely eating, and you look like you have been crying."

Elizabeth looked up at Lydia's words. "I am well, Lydia, just a little tired from my walk."

"Do not waste our good food," Mrs. Bennet said sharply, eyeing the girl carefully.

"Yes, madam," Elizabeth responded, looking back down to her plate and forcing herself to finish the rest of the food she had taken.

The conversation returned to the discussion of the coming militia — and all the officers that would come with it — and Mr. Bingley at Netherfield. Mrs. Bennet encouraged Jane to do whatever she could to ensure Mr. Bingley continued to pay her attention and suggested she flirt and act in a way that would entice him to propose. Jane flushed scarlet at such talk and bashfully listened to all her mother's suggestions. After breakfast was over, everyone was finally dismissed to their individual pursuits. Mary went into the music room to practise the piano, Lydia and Kitty went to their room to fetch bonnets to redo, and Jane and Elizabeth went into the sitting room to work on their sewing.

Elizabeth remained contemplative throughout the morning. Jane occasionally attempted to engage her in conversation, but Elizabeth had little to say in reply. After lunch, she retreated into her room, claiming a need to rest, but really, her mind was engaged with the news from the morning.

After a few minutes of contemplation, she decided she simply could not deal with the question of her not being who she thought she was and instead chose to focus on Mr. Darcy. Her first impression of him had been that of a haughty man, but then she had overheard his conversation with his friend and began to feel compassion for his frustration and pain. Since that night, they had met nearly every day at Oakham Mount, first by accident but obviously now by design. Elizabeth considered briefly that if anyone became aware of these meetings, they could be forced to marry, and she wondered what Fanny Bennet would do in that instance. She also wondered what the Bennets knew about her inheritance. While Mr. Bennet was intelligent enough, he was lazy and likely would not have bothered reading her grandfather's will in its entirety. Mrs. Bennet would not have understood it, even if she had bothered to read it. What would they know about the terms of the will?

She realised her thoughts had drifted back to her circumstances and focused them back on Mr. Darcy — the very handsome man who had told her that morning he wanted to court her, had wanted to court her for some time, but was concerned about how her aunt and uncle might receive the request.

Later that afternoon, she broached the idea of visiting London with Mr. Bennet. She still called him Uncle Thomas, and it was not wrong to do so, but it felt strange now, knowing that things were not as they seemed. "Uncle," she began, hesitating over the familiar name that now felt so ... wrong, "I was wondering if I might be permitted to go to London to visit the Gardiners soon. Aunt Maddie wrote that she is expecting again, and I would like to be of aid if I can. I know she writes that she is well, but her last confinement was difficult. If you allow me to go for a time, I could help with the children while she rests. It has been some time since I have visited London, and with the guests at Netherfield presently, my aunt is distracted and would not miss me."

Mr. Bennet agreed readily since Mrs. Bennet had been complaining just the day before about how unfair it was they had to care for their niece. That lady was becoming more fractious the closer it came to Elizabeth reaching her majority. While it was still months away, Mrs. Bennet was angry that the funds they received for her care would soon stop. "You may go; ask Edwin to send the coach halfway if he can. Although, keep your ear out for anyone else who might be travelling to London soon — perhaps someone else can fund your travel for once."

After that casual dismissal, Elizabeth determined never to return to Longbourn from this visit if it could be helped. She did not know why suddenly, after so many years of it, this simple dismissal hurt so much more than before, but she would speak to Mr. Darcy about helping her find a way to London that did not cost her uncle a farthing. He might receive that stipend until August, but after that, the Bennet family would be entirely on their own. What to do about her cousins was a different matter, but Mr. and Mrs. Bennet would receive no further assistance from her or her estate if she could help it.

* * *

At Netherfield, Mr. Darcy was also thinking of his meeting with Elizabeth that morning while he bathed. "She seemed interested in the idea of courting me," he murmured to himself. "She has so much to consider; how will I get her to London and away from the Bennets?"

"What was that, sir?" his valet asked.

"Oh, I did not realise I had spoken out loud, Roberts. I am nearly certain Elizabeth Bennet is actually Miss Elizabeth Tomlinson, the daughter of my father's old friend. We spoke this morning, and while I cannot yet ask her for a courtship, I intend to marry her once we have figured out how that can be arranged. I need to speak to Mr. Elliott to see what can be done about several matters related to her guardianship."

"Congratulations, sir, on finding a lady you want to marry. Might I suggest you not mention it outside this room for now? And it may be best to depart sooner than you originally intended, particularly if you can convince your lady to visit London to court her there. Miss Bingley has continued to ask questions about your rooms being locked and is frustrated that she has been unable to 'persuade' you to marry her."

His valet's emphasis on the word 'persuade' made Darcy look at him with interest. "What do you know, Roberts?"

"Mrs. Nicholls has told me Miss Bingley has on several occasions attempted to obtain a key to your rooms and is annoyed that one has not been given to her. She claims that as mistress of the house, she is entitled to every key, but Mrs. Nicholls has reminded her she is only *acting* as mistress since the house is leased. As I am certain you have seen, she regularly attempts to dismiss the servants so she can be found alone with you, but they have been well compensated to ignore such commands."

"Why has this not been mentioned before?" Darcy asked in a sharp voice.

"Mr. and Mrs. Hurst took care of some of these arrangements, and some have been handled locally. Apparently, the neighbourhood greatly admires

Miss Elizabeth, and your interest in the lady has been noted. They also despise Miss Bingley and find her harsh and rude. The neighbourhood does appreciate your more welcoming attitude."

Darcy grimaced. "Well, I appreciate the efforts made on my behalf, but next time, I would prefer to know about them sooner. Let me know if you need additional funds to compensate anyone on my behalf."

"Mr. Hurst has assumed responsibility for managing the affairs, and Mrs. Hurst has been discreetly keeping Mrs. Nicholls informed of any pertinent matters," the valet explained, pausing briefly. Upon a glare from Darcy, he continued, "Mr. Bingley is well aware of Miss Bingley's endeavours to compromise you. Though he offers no support to her cause, he has refrained from interfering. He even finds amusement in her aspirations toward you, though, as I said, he has not attempted to stop her. However, if she is successful, he would undoubtedly attempt to insist on your marriage to her."

Darcy started upon hearing that. "He has said nothing to me, and I have told him many times I would not marry his sister under any circumstances. It is galling that Mr. and Mrs. Hurst are proving better friends than Bingley."

"He wants her married but is unwilling to completely sacrifice his connexion to you by overtly aiding her efforts. Neither was he willing to claim any prior knowledge of the attempt, but still ..." The valet trailed off as the feeling of betrayal sunk more deeply into Darcy's mind.

"I would not have expected it of Bingley, but I am uncertain why I am surprised to learn that my *amiable* friend proves so unsteady regarding his sister. He has forever given in to her," Darcy replied. Sighing, he asked his valet a question in his frustration. "I need to depart as soon as can be arranged, but I will need to see what can be done about Ellie ... Miss Elizabeth — now that I have found her, I do not want to lose her so soon. And I must wait until I receive Elliott's next letter before I can leave this area. Have you any suggestions as to how these matters can be accomplished, Roberts?"

Chapter 6

It rained the next morning — and the following day as well. During this time, most residents near Meryton were practically housebound as the rain made most outdoor activities impractical, and carriages could not travel without getting stuck in the mud. At Netherfield, this news was met with mixed emotions. Caroline Bingley was thrilled since it meant Mr. Darcy could not escape the house for his daily rides or go shooting with the other gentlemen. He, however, was quite literally trapped inside the house with her, with few places to go to where he could avoid her.

And trapped, he certainly felt. During the two days of continual rain, Darcy had never been as irritated as he was at that moment. He had begun to make the arrangements for his departure but knew that with this weather, it would take an additional day or two of sun to dry the roads sufficiently to make the journey advisable, at least in a carriage. A part of him was ready to ride straight to London, rain be damned, but his rational and sane side knew that was inadvisable, regardless of the provocation. Therefore, he hid in his rooms each day as long as he could without being rude and spent more and more time in the company of Mr. Hurst. On one or two occasions, he noticed Bingley slip from a room he was in upon Caroline's entry, but usually, Mr. or Mrs. Hurst were not far behind the harpy. She would huff her annoyance when they entered since she had asked her sister to help capture the gentleman from Derbyshire, but Louisa was unwilling to do so and seemed to be actively disrupting her sister's plans.

"If you attempt to compromise Mr. Darcy, you risk ruining not just yourself but our entire family with you," Louisa had tried to reason with her sister. "I do not believe Mr. Darcy can be forced to marry you as his family has much more wealth and power than ours. He will make you a laughing stock in the *ton* if you follow through with this plan, and his family will ensure we will never be able to enter society again. Keep in mind that a man can get away with such things, but women cannot recover if it becomes known they have been ruined, or if it is even hinted at."

"I *will* be Mistress of Pemberley, and if you do not assist me, I will ensure you are never invited there or to our London home. *You* will be the laughingstock of society, not me," Caroline cried before stomping down the hall and back to her bedroom.

As she had done several nights of late, she dressed in a thin silk nightgown that clung to her scant curves and made her way to Mr. Darcy's room. There was still a little light under the door, so she knocked on the door and posed in what she believed to be a seductive pose.

"Is there anything I can do for you, madam?" Roberts asked when he answered the door.

"Yes, Mr. Darcy invited me to join him tonight. I did not want to keep him waiting," she stated brazenly as she attempted to push past the valet and into Mr. Darcy's rooms.

"Mr. Darcy informed me of no such invitation," the servant replied. "I am under strict orders not to allow anyone into his rooms without his express permission, and certainly not a harlot. I doubt he would make an exception for you, as my master has never been one to consort with 'ladies of the night'."

She spluttered in rage. "How dare you accuse me of such?" she raged.

"Madam, you are at a single gentleman's door late at night, wearing that" — he waved toward her nightgown that did little to hide her negligible charms — "and expect to be treated with respect. A *lady* would never behave as you have, madam, and my master would not care to be importuned by the likes of you."

"I will ensure you lose your place for your rudeness. You are merely a *valet*, and you have no cause to speak to me in such a way," she screeched.

Darcy appeared at the door to see what caused the disturbance and immediately looked anywhere but at Miss Bingley. "Please shut the door, Roberts. There is little reason to continue this conversation. I will have a letter for you to post to Lady Matlock in the morning to inform her of this incident. I would not want anyone to form the wrong impression of what has happened here. I will need it sent by express at first light."

"You cannot mean that, Mr. Darcy?" Caroline cried. "Lady Matlock will ruin me in polite society if she makes this known. No, you must marry me; you have compromised me."

"I have done no such thing. *You* came — uninvited, I might add — and knocked on my door in the middle of the night dressed as a common trollop. I do not know what you expected this outcome to be, but it will not garner a marriage proposal from me. Roberts, would you care for a wife?"

"I would not, sir. If I take a wife, it would not be one with as little to offer as this one. No, I enjoy being in your service and look forward to the day you take a *respectable* wife," Roberts replied, emphasising the word respectable as he glared once more at Miss Bingley before shutting the door in her face. She heard the sound of the lock click and fell to the floor in tears.

Charles Bingley found her this way a few minutes later, having been alerted by several servants of a disturbance in the hallway near Darcy's room. He found Caroline still on the floor, barely dressed and crying miserably. He was shocked at her attire and more so by what she said.

"He … will … not …. marry … called … trollop … door in face," she sobbed, and her brother struggled to understand her mutterings. He garnered enough to realise she had attempted a direct approach, which had failed.

"Did he take advantage?"

Caroline sat up, realising this might be her opportunity. "Yes," she sobbed. "He took what he wanted and then threw me out. You must … you must make him marry me."

"I told you I would have no part in this, Caro. I warned you that it would be on your own head if you failed. Had I found you with him, not on the floor outside his room, I could have tried to convince him to act honourably, but as matters stand, I cannot. He is far above us in consequence, and despite our friendship, I do not think he will be persuaded in this case," Bingley replied sadly.

"He ... intends ... to write ... countess," she gasped as she began crying again. "Must ... stop."

"He intends to write to his aunt, the countess, about what happened tonight?" Bingley cried, this time, genuinely shocked. "That will ruin all of us. Caroline, you stupid chit; how could you? The Hursts might survive the scandal, but this will ruin anyone named Bingley if it becomes known. You worried *I* would ruin the Bingley name by offering for Miss Bennet, but you have done far more damage than I ever could. If this gets out, I would be fortunate if Miss Bennet *did* accept me, as no one in polite society will speak to me again."

This only caused Caroline to sob even more loudly. Louisa and a maid carrying Caroline's robe had arrived by this time.

"I warned her against this course," Louisa told her brother as she laid the robe over her sister's form. "She has made a colossal mess of things — we will need to see if we can send her away and convince people she is ill." After motioning a footman over to assist Caroline to bed, she told her brother. "See if you can convince Mr. Darcy to delay his letter. I have no doubt he is writing it now, but see what can be done to mitigate Caroline's disgrace. Perhaps Lady Matlock would not make this known if we agree to send Caroline away from London?"

Bingley reluctantly agreed and knocked on his friend's door to make the attempt. Darcy answered and looked at his friend in disgust. "Bingley, I have heard everything that was said outside my door. Your sister lied — I did not touch her and did my best to avoid even looking at her. Obviously, she showed up uninvited."

"I know that, Darcy, but she has clearly lost her mind. She believed you accepted my invitation to spend time with her and would offer for her on this trip, and nothing I said to her could convince her otherwise."

"Yet you told your sister a moment ago that you would have attempted to make me 'act honourably', but only if she were caught in my room. Had you been called earlier and found me still speaking with her, despite my valet's presence, would you still have attempted to *convince* me then? You have been lying to me even before I arrived at Netherfield, and I have learned that the Hursts prevented your sister from successfully compromising me when you took steps to leave us alone. Were we ever truly friends, Charles, or did you attach yourself to my coattails just to use me for my connexions to society?" Darcy demanded

"We were friends, Darcy," he cried. "We still are unless you throw years of friendship away because my sister has gone slightly mad."

"You knew what she was attempting, and while I know you did not assist her, you did nothing to stop her or to warn me. I heard you tell her so just now. You knew that I would have never touched her, not under any circumstances, and I have told you time and time again that I would never marry her," Darcy retorted. "No, we are no longer friends, and I will never willingly be in your company again. I will recognise the Hursts if I encounter them in town, but no Bingleys."

"Why them?" Bingley demanded.

Darcy glared at him. "They at least warned Miss Bingley about the foolishness of her efforts and attempted to dissuade her from the attempt. They warned my servant, who in turn warned me. To my knowledge, neither of the Hursts has ever lied to me. They followed Miss Bingley into several rooms following your hasty departure, as obviously, you were attempting to leave me alone with her. I will remain here until it is safe to depart for London, but our friendship is done."

"Will you cut me?" Bingley asked anxiously.

The hard stare returned. "I will make no effort to recognise you, but neither will I deliberately cut you. I *will* cut your sister should she approach me or mine. If you attempt to pretend a closeness that no longer exists, I will ensure it is known throughout the *ton* what your sister has attempted. I will write to my aunt to inform her of what happened, but as long as nothing is said against my honour, she will not need to repeat any of it. I want her informed of the particulars to counter any gossip should *anyone* here attempt to start any."

Bingley scowled but could say no more. He angrily departed from the room of his former friend, muttering as he went. "Jane Bennet may be the best I can do now, so I will remain here. I will send Caroline away, but then I will pay my addresses to Miss Bennet. At least if I purchase Netherfield and marry a gentlewoman, I will remain a gentleman, even if I no longer have Darcy's patronage. That should garner me some notice in the *ton*, and they will recall that we *were* friends, even if we no longer appear together."

Several footmen heard this and wondered what they should do about it, as they liked most of the Bennet girls and distrusted the Bingleys. They informed Mrs. Nicholls of all that transpired that night, and she sent them to bed with an order that no gossip should leave the house. While they owed no loyalty to the tenants, they did like the Hursts and Mr. Darcy and were aware of the budding friendship between Darcy and Miss Elizabeth. It was for *her* sake, as much as anyone else, that no gossip would leave the house.

* * *

Elizabeth found herself equally despondent, confined within the walls of Longbourn. Although she had dispatched a letter to her aunt and uncle in London, their invitation and her departure were thwarted by the relentless rain. Moreover, her inability to see Mr. Darcy during this period weighed heavily on her, almost as heavily as her seclusion within the estate. Her aunt — Mrs. Bennet, she corrected herself again — had grown increasingly irksome over the last days. Elizabeth had become the primary target for her grievances, constantly tasked with attending to her cousins' needs as some sort of retribution for whatever great ill she had wrought upon the family.

Since learning of the lies her aunt and uncle had told her over the years, making her feel the dependent and, frankly, unwanted orphan for so long, she had been uncomfortable with referring to them so familiarly. She did not want to maintain the connexion after she left and struggled not to feel overwhelmed with anger or sorrow over the revelations.

During these trying moments, she felt more than ever like an orphan. She was — she had always understood that both her parents were gone — but she felt even more alone now. Honestly, little had changed; Uncle Thomas was still her uncle, but rather than being the natural child of Edward Bennet as many assumed her to be, she was the child of her uncle's sister, who had been legally married to her father. Instead of being penniless and accepting the generosity of her relations, she was contributing to the household for her care. It was unjust for her extended family to have made her feel like she was beholden to them for their notice for most of her life, and she almost hated them for it.

It was distressing enough that her parents were deceased, and she had never had the chance to know them. Everyone who had loved her was gone, and instead of telling her any of this, her relations had kept it a secret and made her feel ashamed of her heritage, not even letting her keep her name. This revelation once more ignited her curiosity about the hidden motives behind the family's deception, inciting her need to escape the sitting room where the rest of the family, except Mr. Bennet, of course, were gathered.

She momentarily thought of hiding in her bedroom but diverted herself into the still room. At least the various flowers and herbs reminded her of the outdoors, and she took some small solace in that. While there, she contemplated her status as an orphan — and that of an heiress, as she had finally learned.

Elizabeth had helped Mr. Bennet with the administration of Longbourn for the last several years, and she wondered about the estate Mr. Darcy mentioned — Briarwood, he had called it. It would be hers on her twenty-first birthday, though that was still months away. She wished she could have asked him more questions about it, but that would have to wait until they were again in company. Elizabeth hoped he would be willing to cut his trip to Netherfield short and return to London with her. Perhaps he would even be willing to find a way for them to make the journey together.

They could discuss these matters openly if they travelled with a trusted maid or companion — perhaps Mrs. Hill could be spared. She could ask him all the questions she had about the estate, and maybe he even knew something of her parents. She wished she could raise these questions with her ... with the Bennets, but she was not supposed to know about these matters. She scowled at this thought as she wondered how long they would have waited to tell her the truth, if ever.

Chapter 7

After enduring several days of confinement indoors, Elizabeth yearned for a refreshing walk. Upon waking that morning to find the rain had ceased, she donned attire suitable for traversing the fields.

Typically indifferent to dampness and mud, Elizabeth found herself making more of an effort that day to sidestep puddles. Although she anticipated her hems might end up muddy, she resolved to present herself with some degree of composure in case she encountered Mr. Darcy once more. Amid these thoughts, she chuckled at her own concern. "What difference can it make?" she mused aloud, only to be taken aback when a voice unexpectedly responded.

"I would imagine that it depends on what it is," a low, resonant voice replied.

"Mr. Darcy," she turned, her hand going to her heart in surprise. "I did not see you there."

He grinned at her. "Might I persuade you to join me atop my horse as you used to do, little Ellie? It would undoubtedly keep your skirts and boots from getting so filthy as you walk."

"Scandalous, sir," she quipped with a grin but raised her hands toward him as he approached.

He grinned as he leaned down, assisting her in scrambling up to sit on the horse sidesaddle. Once settled in front of him, she wrapped her arm around his waist. "This is the most improper thing I have ever done," she admitted, briefly hiding her face in his chest.

"Me as well," he replied huskily in her ear. "This was perhaps not my best idea, but it is too late to reconsider now."

She looked at him in surprise. "I am not certain I take your meaning, sir, but perhaps that is for the best. I am glad you came today; I worried you would not. I have missed speaking to you and found I have much to say."

"I apologise; I know that I told you I want to court you, but until matters are a little more settled, I cannot yet ask. I should not have asked you to ride with me, yet I relish the closeness this allows us. I have also missed speaking with you, Miss Elizabeth. Netherfield felt like a gaol these last few days, but I must speak to you about some things that happened there. I will depart for London on the morrow; had I not wanted to speak with you, I would have departed on horseback as soon as the rain stopped," he told her.

"Are you well? Did something happen requiring you to leave?" she asked, concern evident in her voice.

"Yes, to both questions. Unfortunately, there was an incident at Netherfield that necessitated me to depart sooner than planned. I am afraid these incidents have led to Bingley and I parting ways," Darcy replied coolly.

"That sounds rather ominous," she replied. "I believe I can guess what has occurred. How terrible for you. However, I also have news. I am also departing for London to visit with my Aunt Madeline…" She stopped speaking abruptly and put her hands to her mouth. "Oh!" she cried and buried her face in his chest.

"What is it, dearest?" he asked, slowing the horse and wrapping her more firmly in his embrace.

"I did not mean to startle you. It just occurred to me that my Aunt and Uncle Gardiner are not truly my aunt and uncle. Mr. Gardiner is my … is Mrs. Bennet's brother. I am not related to them at all. They are … were my favourite relatives. Though, I suppose, I have never been truly related to them." He felt her shoulders slump.

"As you say, they are still related to you through your aunt, and while they may not be related by blood, they will likely not change their treatment of you because of these new revelations. If they held you in affection before, the fact that you are related to your uncle's sister rather than his brother should not change matters. I do not understand why Mr. and Mrs. Bennet were not more open about the relationship from the beginning and why no one ever explained matters to you. Mr. Elliott wrote further of what he knows, and none of it makes sense," Darcy crooned as he held her.

For a few moments, she relaxed into him as she sobbed; she had never felt so cherished nor protected. However, after the tears abated, she felt suddenly bashful and a little foolish for giving in to her emotions.

"I am sorry," she said as she pulled away and used her handkerchief to dry her eyes. He offered her his own, and she dabbed at his waistcoat. "Have I ruined it?"

He looked down at the damp spot on his chest. "Not at all, and even if you had, I would not be upset at the opportunity to demonstrate that I care for you. I do care, you know, and I am pleased you feel at ease in my presence and are able to express your emotions. You have had many changes suddenly come upon you, and I think you must wonder who, if anyone, in your life you can trust."

"I do. I cannot speak of this with Jane; she would be troubled by this knowledge and unable to hide it from her parents. I am not ready to face the Bennets — they should have been honest from the beginning and not made me feel as though I was a penniless orphan who imposed on the family. They obviously had to know I would learn it someday. Why could I have not always been a niece born of his sister and her husband and not made to feel worthless? What purpose was there in claiming me as a Bennet? After we spoke, I remembered attempting to correct the Bennets as to my name when they first arrived at Longbourn, but my aunt slapped me each time I claimed I was not a Bennet and I was told I was wrong to claim another name. I was told I was Lizzy Bennet and that I was to forget any other life I thought I may have lived before.

"I have so many questions, Mr. Darcy, but I am concerned about how they might react if I were to ask them. Mrs. Bennet has become so much more hateful of late — I think she despises me and only tolerates my being in their family because of the stipend they receive for my care. I think she fears it not continuing, but she despises me for it nonetheless."

"Do you fear for your safety at Longbourn, Ellie?" he asked, his worry causing him to address her again as informally as they had done as children.

"I do not think so," she replied. "Besides, Mr. Bennet has permitted me to visit London, and I may stay there for some time. Is Mr. Elliott in London? Might we be able to speak with him there? I would like to visit Briarwood and begin to learn more about it. I do not ever want to return to Longbourn."

"Some of the estate's books are actually at my townhouse," Darcy responded. "I make a point to visit a few times each year, and a competent steward is in charge. The house itself is in excellent condition, though it is currently rented out. An Admiral of the White leased it for the summer, and they decided to extend their stay into the autumn. Luckily, they have no children, which I found to be an ideal situation when my solicitor presented the offer. The estate generates an annual income of approximately seven thousand pounds and operates on a four-crop rotation system. I have noticed that the stewards of Longbourn and Netherfield follow a similar approach."

"Yes," Elizabeth confirmed. "I managed to persuade Mr. Bennet to adopt this system several years ago, and the tenants at Netherfield followed suit once they saw its success at Longbourn. Convincing Longbourn's tenants was quite an effort initially, but after a few of them agreed to give it a chance and found it successful, it became easier to sway the others. It has helped to bring the annual income of the estate up slightly, though not to bring it back to what it was before my uncle took charge."

"I am not surprised to learn you led that charge," he teased. "What else have you done to improve Longbourn?"

As they made their way to Oakham Mount, they continued to speak of the estates. She was a fast learner and asked good questions. This impressed Darcy. Except for his Aunt Catherine, he was unfamiliar with women taking such an avid interest in what were typically considered male pursuits. When he said as much to Elizabeth, he unintentionally offended her.

"I meant it as a compliment, Miss Elizabeth," he quickly replied. "I am impressed with the breadth of your understanding in these matters. Many of the women of the *ton* would never dream of speaking or thinking of such matters, and I am pleased that you are unlike them. I always hoped for a wife who would be concerned about more than fashion and the weather."

"Oh," she replied, realising she had misunderstood him and flushing at his implication. They had reached the base of the mount, and he helped her dismount. After offering her his arm, they approached the top to watch the sunrise. "Forgive me for assuming you meant it differently," she said after several moments. "I suppose I am not used to being paid compliments. Mrs. Bennet was more likely to scold me for my interest in such things even though I have incrementally increased the estate's income. Of course, she does not realise that."

She paused briefly. "I have been assisting Mr. Bennet with the estate's accounts for years and frequently noted the quarterly stipend payments. I am well aware of where it goes — books for Mr. Bennet and dresses and other fripperies for Mrs. Bennet and the girls. My allowance is on par with my ... my cousins', and I do not hold any ill feelings towards them for it. However, I do wonder, are there any stipulations on how that money should be allocated? Is there any recourse to recover the misspent funds? I would not want to injure my cousins, especially Jane, by bringing any legal action against them, but I do wonder what can be done to hold Mr. and Mrs. Bennet accountable."

"I have pondered the question over the last few days. It is quite apparent that the money has not been spent for your benefit as it should have been. Did you receive any of the instruction he claimed you did? I have heard you play a little, and it is delightful, but what about the other things he claimed, the languages and other accomplishments," Darcy inquired.

"We had a governess until the time I turned twelve. Lydia objected to being instructed in anything, and Mrs. Bennet insisted she be dismissed. After that, I would receive piano instruction from a neighbour of the Gardiners whenever I would visit. I insisted on being taught French and Italian — Mrs. Gardiner spoke both languages tolerably well and would teach me when I visited, and I would hone those skills further with Mr. Bennet. He would not teach me, but he would speak to me in the languages. He did help me learn a smattering of Greek and Latin, mainly because I think he enjoyed practising those skills himself. I was terrible at sewing, so I never bothered learning any more than the most basic of skills, and of course, Mrs. Bennet insisted that we all learn dancing from a dancing master. Once I turned fifteen, I was considered 'out' in society and, according to my aunt, no longer needed such instruction and was forced to spend more time on my sewing and other pursuits she felt were important for a lady. My time in the library, and even at the Gardiners, was shortened, although, after some time, she loosened those restrictions. I believe she preferred me to be away from her drawing room," Elizabeth explained, with a hint of bitterness in her tone, Darcy thought.

"We know a portion of the funds should have been spent on you — your allowance should have been four times what it was — but it is obvious to me that other things were ignored, and Mr. Bennet claimed to do far more than he did. Longbourn will suffer significantly when you gain your majority, as they will lose those additional payments. Surely, Mr. and Mrs. Bennet cannot expect you to choose to remain with them at that time, given all they have kept hidden from you," Darcy replied.

"I begin to think they hoped to keep me ignorant of the facts and that my trustees would continue to be uninvolved or unconcerned. They will be unhappy when they discover I know the truth. I would like to go to London before they find out — does Mr. Bennet have a right to force me to return to Longbourn before I reach my majority?" Elizabeth asked, suddenly worried about the next year.

"That is another question we will need to ask Mr. Elliott. I confess I have done what I was tasked with regarding Briarwood and the investments because it was one of the responsibilities passed down by my father, but I have not paid careful attention to the particulars that did not come under my direct oversight," Darcy said. "Now, I have a vested interest in learning all I can. I will also have to speak to Mr. Elliott about us and what will need to be decided so we might court. I trust you know I intend to marry you one day, Ellie. That is, if you are willing."

Elizabeth coloured brightly at both his words and the address, but neither spoke for several minutes as they considered all that had been discussed. Suddenly, Darcy turned to Elizabeth with a question. "How do you intend to get to London, dearest?" he asked.

She felt her cheeks heat again at the endearment. He had used it several times that morning, and she admitted to herself that she enjoyed hearing it from his lips. "Normally, Mr. Bennet sends me in his coach halfway, and Mr. Gardiner sends his to convey me the rest of the way. I intended to ask if you had an alternative plan and vaguely wondered if I could somehow travel with you, that is, if you would not mind taking me."

He grinned broadly. "My carriage is at your service, madam," he said with a courtly bow, causing her to laugh. "I would enjoy travelling with you, and if we can find a companion, someone who can be trusted, we can continue to speak of matters as we ride."

"I had the same thought. I wondered if Mrs. Hill, the housekeeper at Longbourn, might be spared, but I am uncertain Mrs. Bennet would allow her to go," Elizabeth offered.

"What about Mrs. Nicholls?" Darcy suggested. "She apparently likes you and seems trustworthy."

Elizabeth laughed. "She and Mrs. Hill are sisters and are both wonderful women," she replied with a wry curve to her lips. "Do you think the Bingleys would mind sparing her for a day or two to accompany us to London?"

"I need to tell you about the Bingleys," he said, and he proceeded to disclose what had happened at Netherfield during the two days of rain. "The Hursts thwarted Miss Bingley's efforts to compromise me and acted in my interest during my brief stay. I believe Mrs. Hurst will agree to anything I request at this moment as she does not want to risk my displeasure after her siblings have incurred my wrath. I do like the Hursts, and I appreciate what they have done for me. I will ask Mrs. Hurst and Mrs. Nicholls what can be arranged for today or tomorrow. Could you be ready to leave as soon as this afternoon?"

"I can, but how can we explain how things were arranged for you to convey me to London?" she asked, then looked at him again. "Mrs. Hill," she stated, answering her own question.

"Mrs. Hill?" he asked, confused.

"I believe Mrs. Hill will write to her sister regarding an urgent errand Mrs. Nicholls must suddenly complete in London. Her note will include information and my trip and suggest that she accompany me. Mrs. Nicholls will respond that you have offered to convey her to town since you were already planning to go, and she is certain you will not object if I travel with you. This would save both my ... Mr. Bennet and Mr. Gardiner the expense of using their own carriages. Uncle Gardiner cares not about the expense, but Mr. Bennet would be pleased not to have to use his funds or his carriage. You can come to Longbourn later this morning with the offer, stating that it was Mrs. Nicholls' suggestion, and Mr. Bennet will surely not turn it down."

"Ellie, you are brilliant!" He kissed her forehead, catching them both by surprise. Each felt their cheeks flame with his impromptu gesture. After a moment, he regained his composure. "That is an excellent idea, dearest, and I will see what I can arrange as soon as I return to Netherfield." He offered to escort her back to Longbourn atop his horse. She shyly agreed and once again rode sidesaddle in front of him with her arms wrapped tightly about his waist.

Darcy dismounted just before they reached Longbourn. As he helped her down, he held her slightly longer than he had earlier. Slowly and deliberately, he bent toward her, pressing a light kiss to her lips, retreating almost before Elizabeth realised what he had done. "I will see you soon, sweetheart," he whispered before he mounted the horse again and took off quickly.

Elizabeth was a little dazed as she walked the rest of the way to Longbourn's garden. She spoke briefly to Mrs. Hill about what had been planned before retreating to her room to pack for her stay in London.

Chapter 8

It took some manoeuvring, but Darcy and Elizabeth were able to make the arrangements for them to travel to London the following morning without too many lies having to be told. While Darcy initially hoped to depart that very day, all the necessary arrangements made that impractical. At Elizabeth's request, Mrs. Hill sent a note informing Mrs. Nicholls of Elizabeth's intention to travel to London. With Mrs. Hurst's help, Mrs. Nicholls invented an errand in London that required her to travel to London with Darcy.

Once the arrangements were settled with the housekeeper, Darcy arrived at Longbourn in the early afternoon to confer with Mr. Bennet. He offered to escort Elizabeth to her uncle's house in London based on a conversation with the housekeeper who had mentioned Elizabeth's need to travel. Mr. Bennet, without any hesitation, concurred, and soon, he consented to Elizabeth's journey in a manner that caused him the least inconvenience.

Darcy spoke to Mrs. Nicholls about Elizabeth's situation when he requested her accompaniment to London. "Mr. Darcy," she warned as they left Netherfield that morning, "do take care not to injure Miss Elizabeth's reputation. She will be facing many changes in her life with this news, and while it appears you have come to care about her in this short time, your attention to her must be different in London." Her voice, cautious yet reminiscent of the scolding tone he had encountered from Pemberley's housekeeper before, prompted a slight smile. He recognized her careful choice of words considering their different statuses, yet he was impressed that she had not let that hinder her.

"I admit that we have met many mornings atop Oakham Mount in the last weeks. Initially, it was by happenstance, but it became a habit, and through these meetings, we have come to know each other well, and, I hope, I have gained her trust. We have discovered and spoken of Miss Elizabeth's true parentage as I vaguely remembered her from the time our families spent together as children. If I were not a trustee of her estate, I would have asked her for a courtship already, and while I realise that our meetings have not been strictly proper, there was no other way for us to speak in Hertfordshire. I needed to be wary of the Bingleys, and Miss Elizabeth is uncertain how the Bennets will react to our courtship, given their deception. We intend to seek the advice of the other trustee while we are in London, and since he and Miss Elizabeth believe the Gardiners to be trustworthy, we will ask for their assistance as well. However, I do appreciate your willingness to speak up in this matter," he replied gently.

"My sister has told me countless stories about Miss Lizzy's kindness and generosity over the years. I have always had a soft spot for the girl. She deserves the best, and neither my sister nor I could fathom why the Bennets treated her so poorly. When they were younger, there was little less of a difference in their treatment, but I began to notice a change when Miss Lizzy was around twelve, I think it was. Then, when Miss Jane was introduced to society at the tender age of fifteen, Mrs. Bennet couldn't stop raving about her beauty and how she deserved only the finest things. She started adorning both her daughter and herself in elaborate attire.

"Miss Lizzy never received even half of what the others did except from the family in London. It was evident to everyone in town that Miss Lizzy received the other girls' hand-me-downs, although she had a talent for transforming them into something beautiful, despite how much she hated it." Mrs. Nicholls grew increasingly indignant on behalf of her favoured Miss Lizzy as she continued her narrative.

Darcy extended his hand, gently covering the housekeeper's, which was moving erratically in her agitation. "I am committed to rectifying this situation for Miss Tomlinson and ensuring she receives what she is entitled to. She is an heiress in her own right, and when she reaches her majority, it will all be under her control. She will have her own estate to oversee, which is quite prosperous, and a substantial inheritance, so her practice at Longbourn will be of great use to her. Her grandfather's will specifies that it is meant for her, not her husband, and that no one else may lay claim to it. I do hold the hope that I may one day be her husband, and in that case, I will make certain she is well provided for. However, should she ultimately decide against me, I am still committed to ensuring her well-being as a trustee of her inheritance."

Mrs. Nicholls beamed at the gentleman. "You are a truly honourable man, Mr. Darcy," she declared. "I've heard of your attempts to aid your friend; though he does possess a gift for eloquence, he seems to fall short of actually doing anything. I can assure you that none of the local staff will ever breathe a word about the other night. They wouldn't want someone as decent as you tethered to such a difficult person, and they'd be even less likely to speak out if your courtship with Miss Lizzy were made public. I've observed how you treat the servants, and while a few may find you a tad reserved, you've always been kind to everyone."

"Thank you, Mrs. Nicholls. I admit, you remind me of my housekeeper at Pemberley. You even sound like her — well, not your accent, but your tone," he teased. She responded with a grin, but they fell silent as the carriage had just pulled up at Longbourn.

Netherfield's housekeeper was pleased that the girl she watched grow up would have a far better life than she might have at Longbourn. Both Mrs. Hill and Mrs. Nicholls thought well of Elizabeth and frequently commiserated over the girl's treatment, which they never understood. They had been in their respective homes in some capacity long enough to remember Elizabeth's true parentage, and, in the case of Mrs. Hill, she recalled the girl's mother as a child, though both women were afraid to speak of her situation to anyone since it was obvious the Bennets did not want it known.

They arrived at Longbourn that morning precisely at eight o'clock. Just as Darcy disembarked, the front door opened, and several servants exited with a trunk. The coachmen had already jumped down, and together, they began to attach it to the back of the carriage. Rushing out, tying her bonnet strings, Elizabeth smiled when she faced Mr. Darcy. "Right on time, sir, as always," she jested.

No member of the Bennet family was present to bid her farewell; at this early hour, only the servants and Elizabeth were typically awake, and the ladies of the house were never seen at such times. Meanwhile, Mr. Bennet, firmly ensconced in his study reading, remained unaware that Elizabeth had packed some of the estate's books to take with her. If questioned, she would claim to be working on a project, but as the sole user of those books, she doubted Mr. Bennet would notice their absence.

"I do what I can," he replied dryly. "Mrs. Nicholls and I are ready to escort you to London, and I do hope you will be able to remain with the Gardiners for some time."

She frowned a little. "At least until Christmas, as the Gardiners usually travel here for the holidays. I do not know if I would be permitted to return to London after that," she said, a trifle sorrowfully.

He squeezed the hand he held as he helped her into the carriage. "We will find a way," he whispered.

Elizabeth smiled sadly at him as she stepped into the carriage and patiently waited for him to follow. With Darcy's assistance, she took her place on the forward-facing seat alongside Mrs. Nicholls before speaking. "I certainly hope so. Mrs. Bennet was insufferable last night, but I believe she took some satisfaction in my absenting myself. It is strange; she sometimes appears to be half afraid of me, yet her disdain is evident. I can understand the fear to some extent, as her life will change considerably when they cease to receive the funds for my upkeep. What I do not comprehend is her animosity toward me or her failure to at least pretend to like me in order to remain in my good graces. The only explanation I can find is that she despises me because I will inherit my estate while Longbourn is entailed away from the female line. Yet, would it not serve her better to treat me kindly? Then, when Mr. Bennet passes away, and she needs a place to reside, she could come live with me. You would think she would realise that her ill-treatment of me makes that prospect rather unlikely"

"Angry people are not always wise, dearest," Darcy responded, once again causing Elizabeth to blush at his endearment. "She is undoubtedly feeling angry, frustrated, and perhaps even jealous. When the true extent of your inheritance is more widely known, you will be far more sought after than your cousin. Given that 'dear Jane' is supposed to be the most beautiful of all her daughters, or even in the country, she likely cannot bear the thought of someone else catching the eye of the eligible gentlemen in the area. Since you are at least as beautiful as Jane — if not more so — she is determined to diminish your standing in the eyes of others."

He reached out to touch her hand, and she gazed up at him. "I was present at the assembly, as you will remember, and that night, she had much to say about her dearest daughter while undermining you. She also belittled her other daughters, emphasising Jane and offering a few flattering words for her 'lively Lydia.' However, she clearly promoted Miss Bennet to all within hearing. Yet, you were the one who attracted more attention, and I did observe that you declined several dances, directing those gentlemen toward other young ladies on more than one occasion."

Elizabeth extended her hand to touch his but abruptly withdrew it when she noticed their chaperone glancing towards her. Mrs. Nicholls was ostensibly gazing out the window, but Elizabeth noted her watchful eyes on the pair through the reflection of the glass. Darcy observed both of these actions and responded with a tender smile, experiencing the thrill that she wanted to touch him while appreciating her cautious and innocent nature.

"Thank you, Mr. Darcy," she said in a hushed tone. "I had not considered the possibility of her being jealous. Indeed, Jane is the most beautiful of my cousins, and I know I can never compare. I am far too plain and too much of a hoyden ever to capture a suitor, or at least that is what Mrs. Bennet has told me and anyone else who would listen." He started to object, but she raised her hand to halt him. "I have eyes, sir, and I am aware Jane is far more beautiful than I could ever aspire to be, but I am not envious. It is not just about the clothing — Jane possesses all the qualities a gentleman would

70

desire in a wife. If I happen to garner more attention now, it will be because of my fortune. I know you said you wanted to court me even before you realised who I was, but few men think as you appear to."

Darcy inhaled deeply, carefully contemplating how to provide reassurance without upsetting her. "Some men do seek a wife based solely on her beauty, although few can afford to marry without at least some consideration to fortune. Not to sound arrogant, but trust me when I say that I am among those who can marry as they please. It would not harm me to marry a woman with no dowry — as I contemplated when I first considered pursuing a courtship with you. I was not concerned about your lack of wealth, and I am in earnest when I say the only reason I had not broached the topic with you sooner was my uncertainty about your family dynamics. I could not fathom why you were treated so differently and was unsure if your relations would welcome my interest. I apologise for not discussing this with you before I did; perhaps we could have found a solution together."

Elizabeth grimaced. "I am sorry, too. You have been very kind and have explained your reason for delaying already. I ... I admit that I have a hard time trusting that a man could be interested in me given how often I have heard that I was undesirable."

"Allow me to convince you, dearest," he whispered. "I find you incredibly desirable."

She extended her hand to lightly graze his cheek, though she promptly pulled it away, her cheeks flushing with embarrassment over her bold gesture. He took her hand to press a kiss to the back of it, and for a moment, they were lost in each other's gazes. They heard Mrs. Nicholls clear her throat, prompting them to shift the conversation to more general and less emotionally charged topics.

* * *

The remainder of the journey unfolded in amiable conversation. Mrs. Nicholls offered a few suggestions on how the couple might proceed in their courtship, circumventing the Bennets, and shared with Darcy additional information about the Bennet family, including the Gardiners, whom they would soon encounter. The Gardiners had a favourable reputation in Meryton, even though their visits were infrequent. The entire town was well aware of Mr. Gardiner's prosperity as an importer. Having spent his early years in Meryton, many locals still remembered him and liked him.

Mr. Gardiner stood in stark contrast to his sisters. Perhaps it was due to his early schooling or a difference in how his parents treated him because of his sex, but he displayed amiability and intelligence where his sisters were frivolous, flighty, and, in Mrs. Bennet's case, mean-spirited. He and his brother Bennet shared several common interests, particularly their passion for books. However, while Mr. Bennet was indolent and preferred to avoid family interaction in favour of his books, Mr. Gardiner took an active role in his family's life. He had not only turned his business into a resounding success, amassing considerable wealth for himself but chose to reside near Cheapside to ensure he could spend ample time with his family when not occupied with work.

His wife shared a similar disposition, working diligently to be a gracious hostess for her husband and devoting herself to preparing their children for their futures. The couple married when Elizabeth was six and waited almost four years before welcoming their first child. During that period of waiting, they took a keen interest in all their nieces, including Elizabeth, and though they extended invitations to all the Bennet children, it was typically Elizabeth who was sent to London. Jane occasionally accompanied her, but she was often kept at home as Mrs. Bennet preferred not to be separated from her.

Elizabeth had relished those opportunities to leave Longbourn, as it would give her a respite from Mrs. Bennet. It was during these visits that she would spending learning from others and would hear words of praise instead of censure. These visits seldom exceeded a month in duration, but during these times, the Gardiners imparted a wealth of knowledge to Elizabeth and provided role models she had not had at Longbourn.

As Darcy listened to this narrative, he gained a deeper understanding of Elizabeth's upbringing and why she stood out from her cousins despite being raised under the same roof. It became evident that this aunt and uncle, though unrelated by blood, held a special place in her heart and were the family she cherished most as she looked to the future. While he typically would not associate with tradesmen — Bingley was in the process of entering the landed gentry, even though his fortune had its origins in trade — Darcy decided to hold this tradesman and his wife in high regard because of the influence they had on the woman he hoped to someday call his wife.

Likewise, he was interested to learn that Mrs. Gardiner was the daughter of a vicar and had spent most of her formative years in Derbyshire. After the passing of her father, the late Samuel Hobbes, she and her mother relocated to London, where she met Mr. Gardiner. This connexion to Derbyshire was of interest to Darcy as he vaguely recalled a Mr. Hobbes having served in Lambton when he was a child.

Chapter 9

Darcy's carriage delivered Elizabeth to the Gardiner's house a little before noon. Knowing his niece was expected, and uncertain of the reason for her trip to town, Mr. Gardiner came home early for his afternoon meal. Therefore, he was waiting with his wife when the carriage arrived. All three travellers were escorted into the house, and refreshments were ordered. Mrs. Nicholls was uncomfortable with the invitation to join the family and instead asked to be introduced to the Gardiners' housekeeper and join her for tea. She would stay at the Gardiner's house until she returned to Netherfield on the morrow in a hired coach.

Once settled in the Gardiners' parlour, Elizabeth introduced her aunt and uncle to the gentleman. They were all then seated, and Elizabeth spoke first. "I met Mr. Darcy at an assembly just after Michaelmas a little more than three weeks ago. A few days ago, he received a letter that seemed to concern me, and we wondered what you might know of these matters and if you might be able to provide aid."

Mr. Darcy picked up the story and began to tell about the estate and investments he maintained as the inheritance for a friend of his father's and the letter he received that led to the confirmation of his belief that Elizabeth was not who she thought she was, as well as their subsequent discussions.

"Miss Elizabeth, I did not say anything in the carriage, but I received a reply from Mr. Elliott yesterday afternoon. He confirmed that you are, in fact, Miss Tomlinson," Darcy told the group when the recitation ended.

Though they had heard the rumours of Elizabeth's origins when visiting Longbourn, Mr. and Mrs. Gardiner had never received a satisfactory answer to her origins. Therefore, they had long suspected there was more to her arrival at Longbourn but were nonetheless shocked at what Darcy revealed, especially regarding the stipend for her care.

Mr. Gardiner was particularly annoyed with his brother and sister at this. "He always asked me to have my wife purchase appropriate clothing for Elizabeth and would forward a trifling amount to provide for her. Knowing my sister as I do, I knew she would never purchase Lizzy what she truly needed, so we supplemented those funds to provide her with the best we could. I thought Bennet was doing his niece a good turn, though he was truly taking advantage. I believed it was out of kindness that he sent his niece to London for masters, and again, we supplemented the small amount he would send. But to know that he was manipulating all of us angers me." He was seething, but a touch from his wife helped him calm.

"Lizzy, do not think we begrudged you anything we spent. We would have done the same for you regardless of the amount Thomas sent. However, I am angered that he did what he did in a manipulative way. He could have sent enough to cover several wardrobes for you, but sent a small amount and always did so in such a way that made it seem that we were doing you both a favour."

Elizabeth nodded at the Gardiners, acknowledging their words. She understood how they felt, as she felt similarly. The Gardiners were just learning of the Bennets' duplicity while she had had some time to process the news.

After a few moments, Darcy broke the silence: "Mr. Gardiner, Mr. Elliott will be in town early next week and asked to meet with both of us as soon as can be arranged. I would like to request your presence as well, as Miss Tomlinson is not yet of age. My father was appointed her guardian, though we are uncertain who presently has that responsibility, legally."

"He only confirmed I was the girl in question, nothing else?" Elizabeth inquired, furrowing her brow as she looked at him.

"No, there was more, but, Miss Elizabeth, I prefer to speak of it privately to your uncle first," Darcy admitted, wincing slightly. "It is not that I do not think you are capable of hearing it, but that the information is delicate, and I prefer to speak it over with Mr. Gardiner first if you do not mind."

Elizabeth was unsure whether to be annoyed or worried as this was the first time he had been reluctant to speak to her about anything concerning herself. She reluctantly agreed. "I insist you two get it over with quickly then because if it concerns me, I would like to hear it as soon as possible."

Darcy hid a grin at her impatient tone but requested to speak to Mr. Gardiner privately. That gentleman agreed, and the two removed to Mr. Gardiner's study.

As soon as the gentlemen left, Mrs. Gardiner moved closer to Elizabeth, squeezing her hand as she attempted to understand what she had heard. "Lizzy, this is much to take in in such a short time. How are you doing with everything?"

Elizabeth breathed deeply to compose herself. "It has been difficult, Aunt, to realise everything I believed was true is not. I have always known that technically I was incorrect in calling you Aunt, since we are not related whatsoever. However, I feel more comfortable continuing to refer to you in that way than in continuing to refer to Mr. and Mrs. Bennet familiarly." Again, she sighed deeply. "I feel betrayed by them, and the more I have discussed things with Mr. Darcy, the greater the betrayal seems. I am an heiress, Aunt; on my next birthday, I will come into a significant fortune and will own my own estate. I will answer to no one and never have to marry if I do not choose to do so. I have a freedom I never knew, but my entire life has been built upon a lie."

She covered her face with her hands for a moment to think. "I think the most shocking realisation has been to learn that I am not the penniless natural child of my Uncle Edward, as many have assumed, but the daughter of Mr. Bennet's sister and her husband. At the moment, I cannot fathom having anything to do with Mr. and Mrs. Bennet ever again."

"I do understand your feelings, Lizzy, and a part of me feels the same way. However, I apologise for changing the topic but tell me of Mr. Darcy and how he came to assist you in this way," Mrs. Gardiner asked softly. "How is he a part of all of this?"

Her smile was radiant as she replied. "He wishes to court me, Aunt. He did not mention it until he told me of the letter from Mr. Elliott, and the pieces began to fall into place. He has assured me he desired a courtship even before he became aware of my true background, though he was uncertain how to navigate matters at Longbourn. He sensed something was amiss but could not pinpoint it, believing it prudent to wait until he had more information. I do not want to doubt him, but it is difficult for me, especially after learning how Mr. and Mrs. Bennet have lied to me for so long," Elizabeth confessed, her eyes on her tightly held hands in her lap.

"However, he has not yet broached the subject with Mr. Bennet — he wanted to seek Mr. Elliott's counsel before proceeding. I suspect that even if we did decide to marry, it may not be possible before I come of age. I am unsure he would be willing to endure such a long wait."

"Lizzy, I have little doubt he has already begun to consider all these things if he has spoken to you of courting. He is seeking advice on approaching your uncle, and it seems he has taken good care of you. Even if you do have to wait the better part of a year to wed, I doubt he will be unwilling to do so," Mrs. Gardiner soothed. "You pay too much attention to what my sister has said all of these years and do not realise your own value. She belittled you because she felt better about her own circumstances. It was a mean thing to do to a child, but my sister has always been cruel to you."

Mrs. Gardiner patted Elizabeth's arm and tugged her chin up so she was looking directly at her. "Mr. Darcy is extraordinarily wealthy and does not need your wealth, my dear," she told her. "He is the furthest thing imaginable from a fortune hunter."

Elizabeth laughed. "I never envisioned Mr. Darcy as such," she replied. "No, I was more worried that my inheritance was all a man like that might be interested in. Even if he does not need my fortune, is it not possible that my possessing one makes it that much more pleasing of an idea to him? He could have resisted me as the natural child of a gentleman, but now that I have a dowry ...? I wonder how anyone could love someone like me?" she sobbed.

Mrs. Gardiner wrapped her arms around her niece. "Hush, child," she whispered into her hair. "You are well-loved by many, and any man, particularly one like Mr. Darcy, would be inordinately lucky to have you as a wife." The two remained that way for several minutes as Elizabeth regained her equanimity in the comfort of an embrace from a beloved aunt. "Tell me, Lizzy, you said he has spoken of a courtship, but has he said more?"

Elizabeth shook her head. "Not explicitly, or well, he has not asked me outright, though he has hinted at it several times. He has, on several occasions, addressed me as 'dearest' and has made other remarks that suggest deeper feelings. He... he did kiss me yesterday after our conversation at Oakham Mount when we were discussing our plans for travelling to London today. It was brief, our lips scarcely touched, but, oh, Aunt." Elizabeth paused momentarily, her hands covering her face as she blushed. "It was absolutely wonderful."

"Do you love him?" she asked.

She dropped her hands and looked at her aunt. "I ... I think I might, but how do I know? We have not even known each other for a full month. We ... we have met at Oakham Mount nearly every morning for a little over a fortnight. Of course, I nearly always walked that way even before he came, though I think he sought me out after the first few meetings. Except for yesterday, we have always maintained a distance from each other, but we have spoken of so many things during this time. At first, our meetings were accidental, but after that, I think it was on purpose. He was the only person I could talk to about my situation, and I wanted to see him." Glancing at the concern on her aunt's face, she quickly tried to reassure her. "No one saw us, and, as I said, we never stood close to each other, although, the day he received the letter, we did speak much longer than usual."

"Calm yourself, Elizabeth," Mrs. Gardiner said, again taking her niece's arm to calm her. "I do not doubt you and am hardly worried about gossip in Meryton. The tenants of Longbourn and Netherfield think too well of you to spread scurrilous tales about you, even if someone had seen something, and Mrs. Hill and Mrs. Nicholls would never allow servants to gossip about you."

"Thank you, Aunt," Elizabeth said but then gasped. "Oh, you do not mind if I continue to call you my aunt, do you?"

"Of course not, dear," she replied, patting her hand. "No matter what happens, you will always be my niece. Nothing will change that."

* * *

In the study, the conversation between the two men took a markedly different tone. "Mr. Bennet has written to Mr. Elliott, seeking his approval for a marriage contract between Elizabeth and the heir presumptive to Longbourn, a man by the name of Mr. Collins. He indicates that Mr. Collins is willing to renounce his rights to the entail, as he will gain a more valuable estate, Briarwood, upon his marriage to Elizabeth. Mr. Bennet is intent on orchestrating this match and clearly anticipates the consent of the trustees. He is disregarding the fact that Miss Tomlinson's consent is also required. It appears he has also conveniently overlooked the fact that Miss Tomlinson's future husband will have no rights to any ownership of the estate." Darcy's tone carried a hint of frustration.

"I must add that this Mr. Collins happens to be my aunt's clergyman, and, based on that alone, I can confidently assure you he is not a suitable match for Miss Tomlinson. My aunt has a penchant for hiring sycophants; her previous rector was an imbecile."

"Mr. Darcy, is there anything else you want to speak with me about? You seem far more involved in this situation than just as a trustee, and I still am unclear how Lizzy ended up coming to town in your company," Gardiner asked.

"I spoke to Miss Elizabeth about my desire to court her several days ago. At first, I waited as I was uncertain how my request would be received by Mr. Bennet, but once I heard from Mr. Elliott and learned for certain she is the young lady for whom I am a trustee, it complicated matters. Until we speak to Mr. Elliott, nothing can be done. I …. I care about her very much, sir, and if I believed she was ready, and if there was not the additional complication of the trusteeship, I would have already asked her to be my wife. I have told her I would like to court her, but have been unwilling to press too much, given what she is having to endure at the moment," Darcy confessed. "I intended to ask you and Mr. Elliott for advice on how to proceed."

"Bennet does not know of your interest?" Gardiner clarified.

"No, I have only met him once, when I offered to convey Elizabeth to London. He has never been at any of the events I attended in Meryton."

"Thank you, Mr. Darcy. I am well-acquainted with the personalities of my brother and sister and find it difficult to believe that either of them would be amenable to your proposal, particularly if they are entertaining this plan to marry Elizabeth off to this fool. I wonder which one of them concocted this scheme." Mr. Gardiner leaned back in his chair, closing his eyes for a brief moment as he contemplated the situation. "What did your Mr. Elliott say about this proposed marriage?"

"He is acquainted with my aunt and cannot fathom her employing a man as her vicar that any sensible woman would desire to marry. Naturally, he will reject it based on the erroneous notion that Mr. Collins will own Briarwood once he marries Elizabeth, and he will emphasise that no marriage contract will be sanctioned without the agreement of both trustees and, of course, that of Miss Tomlinson. She cannot be coerced into this or any marriage. My concern now is that Mr. Bennet agreed to this trip to London to remove her from Longbourn while the contracts were being negotiated, only to return her later and attempt to tell her she has no choice in the matter. Miss Tomlinson has been kept in the dark about her true identity for all these years, and her relations have treated her quite poorly. I am apprehensive about what might unfold should she return to Longbourn. If she does, I will lease a residence in Meryton to monitor the situation closely," Darcy concluded.

"Mr. Darcy, I must pose a question as the nearest male relative to my niece; well, regardless of any true connexion by blood — she is and will always be my niece. Please do not take offence, and appreciate that I need to understand this. You have expressed your wish to marry my niece, yet you display a deeper attachment than what is customary for couples in the courting stage. Would you have pursued her with the same fervour had she been Elizabeth Bennet rather than Tomlinson?" His tone was firm though he still strove to maintain a conciliatory approach with the more influential gentleman.

Darcy's countenance briefly hardened at the tradesman questioning his honour before softening. "I agree, sir, you are fully entitled to such an inquiry. I have the responsibility of caring for a much younger sister, and I would extend the same vigilance to anyone who sought to court her. Yes, I was interested when I believed her to be Elizabeth Bennet. A certain restraint held me back, though, and it was not linked to her wealth or connexions, or even the rumours of her birth. I found myself troubled by the way her aunt treated her in public, and as I delved deeper into her background, I encountered more questions that I needed answers to before I felt I could proceed. An inner voice cautioned me that my suit might not find favour with Mr. Bennet, prompting me to wait. When I disclosed the truth about her identity to Miss Elizabeth, I felt compelled to be forthright about my intentions. I believed she should have at least a glimpse of my true feelings for her. I know she is unsettled by all the changes in her life at the moment. I worry she has agreed because she sees me as a way out of her difficulties."

"I do not think Lizzy would agree for that reason," Gardiner told the younger man. "It may be a part of it, but it is not the only reason. Lizzy has always said she would only marry for the deepest love, and she will want to be certain of that before she agrees to more."

"Thank you for that reassurance, sir. I will wait before moving further unless you or Mr. Elliott think it wise."

"Mr. Darcy," Gardiner said thoughtfully, then trailed off and shook his head to clear it. "We need to discuss this further, but you need to make Lizzy aware of this latest development. It will be one more shock to her, but she is unlike many young women and will be able to handle it."

Darcy nodded. "I wanted to discuss it with you before I said anything to her. I was … I was worried I could not restrain my anger at her uncle if she was the first one I told," Darcy confessed.

"Lizzy probably could have handled your anger, but, knowing her as I do, will likely desire to walk after she is told. It is better to do it here where she can escape to the garden or the park. I will even allow you to accompany her," Gardiner teased.

"I have noticed that trait in her," Darcy laughed. The two rose and returned to where the ladies waited.

Chapter 10

When the gentlemen returned, Elizabeth was feeling much more herself. Her eyes were twinkling when the ladies greeted them, and Darcy hated to, once again, take that away from her.

"So, you have returned and are ready to discuss that 'delicate' matter with us poor females?" she quipped playfully.

He nodded and gave her a slight smile. "I apologise for not telling you directly, Miss Elizabeth. It also was not the kind of news I wanted to share with you in a carriage, so I opted to wait until we arrived," he said earnestly before leading her to a settee across the room from the Gardiners.

This action surprised her relations, and Gardiner merely shrugged at his wife as he quietly told her what had been discussed in the study. Then, they turned to watch the other couple.

"Miss Elizabeth," he began after a minute of contemplation, then shook his head and tried again. "Ellie, I hate to tell you this, but Mr. Bennet wrote a letter to Mr. Elliott asking him to approve a marriage contract for you." She gasped, and he took her hand in his, lightly caressing it as he spoke softly. "He desires to engage you to the presumptive heir of Longbourn, who is willing to give up his rights to Longbourn because he has been led to believe he will receive Briarwood as part of your dowry. Mr. Bennet either forgot or is unaware of the terms of your grandfather's will that left Briarwood in trust for you with the other assets you inherited. The will also specifically states that, if you marry, your future husband will not have any entitlement to the estate or any other portion of your assets."

"He is attempting to trade my future for his wife's comfort and security," Elizabeth said baldly.

"Yes."

Elizabeth let out a shuddering breath. "Obviously, you will not approve the contract, but will Mr. Elliott?"

Darcy squeezed the hand he held. "No, of course not, my dear. Remember, under the terms of the will, your approval is required for your marriage as well. I cannot imagine why Mr. Bennet expects you would consent to this. Moreover, even without your inheritance, Mr. Bennet cannot force you into a marriage you do not desire. The Church of England is very clear on this. There is no point in worrying about that.

"On Monday, I will consult with Mr. Elliott and my solicitor to see what must be done about appointing a guardian for you to consent to *our* courtship. Indeed, once the Chancery Court learns of the Bennets' conversion of your funds for their own use and their deception regarding your true parentage, it may be that the court will simply grant its consent without appointing anyone."

"That is good to know," she replied, sounding very tired. "What else do I need to know?"

"Mr. Collins, the heir, is most likely a sycophantic fool," Darcy told her. "He is my aunt's rector, and she likes to surround herself with people who would never dare disagree with her. I would not expect him to be anything else; he probably believes he is doing you a favour by marrying you, as I am certain the Bennets would have allowed him to believe the story in Meryton of your being the natural child of his brother. Gardiner asked a relevant question about how long this had been planned and if the Bennets ever planned to tell you the truth. They will likely be upset to learn that I have told you the truth of the matter, and, frankly, I am somewhat astonished they have not attempted something like this before now."

"I need to move," Elizabeth replied, and Darcy had to hide a smile. She asked permission from her uncle to escape to the garden. Permission was granted, and Elizabeth flew through the house toward it without even bothering with a coat or hat. Darcy could only follow behind.

She paced through the back garden for several minutes, her frustration evident. "Despite my contentment in being with my aunt and uncle, I long to be in the countryside right now, where I can roam much farther than the boundaries of this garden. I am not in the mood for a leisurely stroll in the park; I yearn for a place where I can embark on a lengthy, invigorating walk to relieve my frustration."

Darcy watched her as she paced, uncertain how to best support her. He had simply followed her and stood and waited for her to speak. "I know of some places I could take you outside of town. Of course, it would be better if you could ride there."

"And I am afraid of horses. Perhaps if Mr. Bennet had kept a horse appropriate for a young girl to ride, I could have overcome my fear. Mrs. Bennet would not have permitted her husband to spend money on things I wanted and did not think riding horses was a necessary accomplishment for any of her girls, and certainly not for me. I would guess Mr. Elliott was told I was taught to ride as one of my many accomplishments," Elizabeth replied bitterly.

"Twelve hundred a year could have afforded me many more opportunities than I was given. Mr. Bennet has stolen much from me — that was money I was entitled to. I would not have complained had they kept back part of that money for themselves, but nearly *all* of it was spent on them; none was spent on providing me with the accomplishments I should have had. Despite my fear, I wanted to learn to ride; I asked for tutors who would teach me about things I found interesting; I begged to be permitted to go to school. Although, if Miss Bingley is an example of what I would have learned at school, perhaps it is best I did not attend. Regardless, my uncle took what was not his and deprived me of what I was entitled to. He robbed me of so much, and even should he have to pay it back — which he never will be able to do — he cannot restore to me what I lost due to his selfishness. And there is also the damage to my reputation the Bennets caused by falsely making known I am illegitimate."

Elizabeth began to sob heavily, and Darcy rushed to take her in his arms before she collapsed. He caught her and sat down heavily with her in his arms. Pulling her into his lap, as he was uncertain of what else to do, he merely wrapped his arms around her and let her cry.

Gardiner found them like this sometime later and gave Darcy a stern look. Darcy merely shrugged helplessly and continued rocking Elizabeth in his arms as he muttered soothing words. Gardiner sat on a bench and watched the couple. After a few more minutes, she finally seemed to recollect herself.

"I am sorry, Mr. Darcy," Gardiner heard her whisper.

"I am happy to help, Miss Elizabeth," Darcy replied. "It is time you gave into your emotions, and I am glad I was here when you finally felt safe enough to do so."

Gardiner felt the need to interject himself into the conversation. "Lizzy, Darcy, shall we return inside to a more appropriate setting for further discussion?"

Elizabeth suddenly started and realised she was seated in Darcy's lap on the ground in the garden. Her embarrassment was clearly reflected as her cheeks turned a brilliant shade of pink, though she simply nodded in acknowledgement of the less-than-subtle command in her uncle's voice. Darcy extended his hand to assist her in standing and then lifted himself from his somewhat uncomfortable position.

"I am not even certain what happened. I was stalking through the garden, and then I was … overcome by it all. How did we end up … as we were?" she asked Darcy as they walked inside.

"I caught you just as you collapsed, but I did so awkwardly and fell with you. It was simpler to hold you than to try to do anything else. I cannot say I regret it, though I hate that you are in this position at all. I would gladly hold you any time, my dear," he whispered, causing her face to redden again.

"You are a rogue, sir," she whispered back.

"No, but I do care about you very much, Ellie. I am so sorry that we have not had a chance to get to know each other in less fraught circumstances, but I would gladly comfort you whenever you feel the least bit like crying. I only hope that I can make you equally as happy someday."

Elizabeth laughed lightly. "I have changed my opinion, sir. You are not only a rogue; you are a charming rogue."

"No one else will believe it, dearest. I will bring my cousin, Colonel Fitzwilliam, whom you called Jon as a child, and he will tell you. I have been called many things in my life, but you are the only one ever to describe me as charming … and he would laugh uproariously at me being called a rogue."

"Then I am pleased to know I have been the one to bring this out in you," she replied as they entered the parlour with the Gardiners. "Now, we need to speak to my aunt and uncle again and decide what to do next."

As different ideas were debated, Darcy was impressed with the breadth of understanding of both ladies present. Several ideas were discussed and cast aside just as quickly. Obviously, marriage to Mr. Collins was not even a consideration, and Darcy was reluctant to press his own suit right away. He wanted them to have the chance they needed to come to an understanding without rushing matters.

Of course, Mr. Elliott also needed to be a part of any conversation. They would schedule a time to meet with him as soon as he arrived in town, but for now, Darcy would continue to call on Elizabeth, glad he could now do so openly, though, at the same time, he wished for the intimacy they had managed at Oakham Mount.

Finally, Darcy became aware of the time and stood to take his leave.

"I apologise for remaining far longer than I intended; however, much needed to be discussed. I will let you know when Mr. Elliott is available to meet with us, but I do hope to still call on Miss Elizabeth each day while she is in town. I have several business matters to attend to tomorrow, but might I come in the afternoon?"

Darcy addressed this question to Mr. Gardiner, but that gentleman looked at his niece and, seeing her nod, agreed. "My wife intends to take Lizzy to do some shopping in the morning, but they will return by two in the afternoon," Gardiner said, glancing at his wife for confirmation. Darcy agreed and promised to arrive around three. He also asked for, and was granted, permission to bring his sister when he came.

"Mr. Gardiner, I apologise, but I did need to ask one more question before

I departed. Will you accompany me to the door?" Darcy requested.

Surprised, Gardiner agreed, and Darcy took his leave of Mrs. Gardiner and Elizabeth. He kissed Elizabeth's hand slowly, caressing it slightly as he did so and leaving her feeling warm.

As the two gentlemen moved toward the door, Darcy hesitated. "Ask your question, Darcy," Gardiner commanded.

"I do not mean to offend, but I am aware of what Elizabeth's estate earns. Can I ... would you allow me to advance some funds for Elizabeth to receive a new wardrobe while she is in town? She is entitled to so much more, but the Bennets have denied her what she is due. I would also like to take her to the theatre and perhaps a dinner or two; her acceptance into society would be easier if she were dressed well. She is a very wealthy landowner, and while I do not want to give any other gentlemen a chance with her, it would be best if she were accepted before our relationship, such as it is, is known publicly."

"Do not worry, son," Gardiner replied. "My wife will ensure she is properly outfitted, and it will not be difficult for us. She has several dresses she left here the last time she visited, and they are far superior to anything she would have at Longbourn. My wife and I have always ensured she was well dressed when she was with us, even without knowing of her inheritance, though Bennet would send some funds for this purpose. It was one thing he insisted on, and my sister did not fight him on it that I am aware of."

"Thank you, sir," Darcy replied. "I did not mean to offend..."

Gardiner cut him off. "You did not, and I appreciate your desire to ensure my niece is taken care of. It demonstrates your care for her. How long will you wait to propose?"

Darcy sighed. "I would propose and marry her today if I thought it could be arranged. However, you are aware several questions must be settled first. She collapsed in my arms earlier because the reality of her circumstances finally hit her. I suppose it is because she felt safe enough in your house to finally give in to all she felt. I am still working on encouraging her to trust me, given all that she has been through."

"Not in my house, Darcy, in your arms," Gardiner replied. "She finally felt safe enough because she was with you. I do not think she would have given in to her feelings in that way with me. My wife, perhaps, but she felt safe enough with *you*. I feel certain you have earned her trust."

As he departed, Darcy allowed that thought to linger and loop in his mind, ruminating on it until he returned the following day.

Chapter 11

The next afternoon, Darcy arrived on the Gardiners' doorstep accompanied by a young lady. Elizabeth supposed the young lady was his sister, Georgiana Darcy, who would soon turn sixteen. Elizabeth and Darcy had discussed the girl several times, and on one of those occasions, Darcy confided some of the troubles his sister had recently been through. He did not state it directly, but Elizabeth heard enough to know that she had been disappointed in love, having been pursued by the worst sort of scoundrel and fortune hunter.

Georgiana Darcy was lovely, appearing older than her age in looks, but her actions were those of a young girl. She was terribly shy and constantly looked toward her brother for confirmation whenever she spoke, so Elizabeth did all she could to make her feel at ease. Mrs. Gardiner did the same, and within an hour, the three were speaking together easily. Darcy watched them, smiling at how quickly Elizabeth had made his sister feel comfortable in her presence. He realised she had a similar effect on him, as she had made him feel at ease from the first time they spoke together.

Darcy was surprised when the mantel clock struck the hour. "Ladies, I apologise for the extended visit, but I hated interrupting your conversation before now. I am afraid we have overstayed, and I do have business to conduct yet this afternoon," Darcy said during a break in the conversation. The younger ladies appeared startled by his voice as they had nearly forgotten his presence in the room.

"Oh, I apologise, Mr. Darcy; we forgot you and completely excluded you from our conversation. Do forgive me," Elizabeth apologised.

"It is quite all right, Miss Elizabeth. I was pleased to see how easily you befriended my sister and contemplated other matters as you spoke. However, if you do not mind, I will call on you tomorrow morning by myself. Perhaps your aunt will also allow me to escort you to Darcy House afterwards for tea and perhaps a walk through Hyde Park."

Elizabeth turned to her aunt, who nodded, and the invitation was readily accepted. Mrs. Gardiner and Miss Darcy spoke to each other for another moment, allowing Elizabeth and Darcy to talk quietly between themselves.

"Miss Elizabeth, I introduced you to my sister today as Miss Bennet, but I wondered ... would you prefer to be introduced as Miss Tomlinson? Of course, we can wait until we consult with your other trustee to be certain, but well, I wanted to speak to my aunt and uncle about you and ask them to invite you to dinner soon. As you may remember, they were acquainted with the elder Mr. Tomlinson, although they likely knew your father at least a little."

"Perhaps that should wait until we learn more from Mr. Elliott. Today is Friday, and he will arrive in town next week: is that not what you said? Surely you can delay a little longer to tell your relatives about me?" she teased.

"I worry about what your uncle intends to do," Darcy confessed. "I have had too much time to think of scenarios where Mr. Bennet could force you to somehow return to Longbourn and into a marriage with Mr. Collins. I worry that I could lose you."

She smiled gently at him. "You told me I cannot be forced to marry; even if Mr. Bennet requires me to return, he cannot make me agree to marry that man or to speak the vows. I suppose we need to discover if he has a right to force me to return, do we not?"

"Elizabeth, he could do things that would make a marriage necessary. He could allow that man to take you somewhere and ruin you, and I do not mean only your reputation. I love you and would marry you regardless, but ..." he stopped as he realised what he had revealed.

"You love me?" she asked, her voice barely a whisper.

"I do, Ellie," he replied, his voice equally soft. "I felt the first stirrings of love the moment you handed me a cup of tea at the assembly, and the more I have learned about you, the more my love has grown. I told Mr. Gardiner I would marry you as soon as you would have me but wanted to wait until you were ready."

She smiled up at him, her eyes sparkling with unshed tears. "And how will you know when I am ready?"

He wanted to touch her, to pull her into his arms and show her his love. He mentally cursed himself for starting this conversation when they were in a room with her aunt and his sister. "I do not have the slightest idea, Ellie. I was hoping you would tell me?"

"Was that a question, sir, or a statement?"

"I think I told you I have never courted a lady before now, nor have I even wanted to do so before, and I tell you, and only you, that I do not have any idea of how to go about this, my dear. I am relying on you to assist me." He was far too aware of the others watching them as they spoke.

She sighed as she also noticed their onlookers. "Perhaps it would be best if we continue this conversation tomorrow when I come for a visit." Darcy nodded his agreement with her statement.

"Please do not worry that Mr. Bennet will somehow arrange for me to be compromised and forced to marry Mr. Collins. While he might consider taking such action should his request for consent be denied, Mr. Bennet has an inflated opinion of himself and believes few are more intelligent than he. I am sure he is confident that the trustees will agree to the match. And remember, Mr. Bennet does not know I have discovered my true identity and that I am aware of my inheritance, so he has no reason to be concerned. I do not intend to travel there. Surely, we can invent an appropriate excuse for me to stay at least until Christmas."

She smiled at him mischievously, hoping to change the serious turn of the conversation. "Now, perhaps you will share why you keep calling me Ellie."

He grinned broadly at her. "It is what Jonathan and I called you that summer at Briarwood. I had nearly forgotten little Ellie until I made your acquaintance, but now I have difficulty thinking of you as anything else."

The two Darcys took their leave and soon departed the house. Mrs. Gardiner began speaking almost immediately after the door closed behind them. "What were you and Mr. Darcy discussing so intently just before he left?" she asked.

"He is anxious that Mr. Bennet might attempt to call me home and do something to force me into marriage. I do not think he has a very good opinion of Mr. and Mrs. Bennet. While I confess he has just cause, I struggle to think of Mr. Bennet being so terrible as to be capable of what Mr. Darcy seems to believe possible," Elizabeth admitted.

Mrs. Gardiner looked at her askance. "What did he suggest?"

"That Mr. Bennet might attempt to force the matter by having me ruined … in more than just reputation."

Gasping, Mrs. Gardiner brought her hand to cover her mouth. "I would not think Mr. Bennet capable of ordering that, but we do not know what Mr. Collins might attempt if he believes he can get his hands on your estate. Mr. Darcy thinks the man is likely a fool, but is he so mean? Perhaps my husband and Mr. Darcy should have him investigated to see what they can learn about the man."

"I would not be surprised if they have not already considered it. Mr. Darcy also asked whether I should be introduced as Miss Bennet or Miss Tomlinson while in town. I deferred the question for now, saying it was best to seek the opinion of my uncle and Mr. Elliott. I believe Mr. Darcy would prefer to have me known for who I truly am, though I am not certain his reasoning is completely disinterested."

"Because you are courting, even if unofficially?" she asked. Elizabeth merely nodded, not ready to confess everything that had been discussed. She still needed to sort through her own feelings toward the man before speaking of them to anyone.

She had an opportunity to do that later that evening. As she thought over their relationship — had they truly only met a little less than a month ago — she realised that she did care a great deal for him. She had never felt as though she belonged in her home, and now she realised she had not.

Longbourn had never been her home, and her vague memories that the Bennets had waved away as fanciful were real. She desperately wanted to go home — to her real home. She longed to have somewhere she belonged and was not just a visitor.

The question of Mr. Darcy made this all a little less clear. Briarwood was her home, though she had not seen it again since spending most of her first five years there. It was hers, but she did not remember it, though perhaps when she arrived, she would feel some familiarity with the place. But would it feel like home?

She remembered the day before when she collapsed and was caught in Mr. Darcy's arms. She had felt safe in his embrace and a sense of belonging she had never experienced. *"Is this love?"* she asked herself.

Still uncertain, she wondered if she could talk it over with him the following day when he called. *Would it be improper for them to ride together in an open carriage without a chaperone?* she wondered. She needed to speak about it with someone, and he seemed the ideal choice.

* * *

Darcy was cursing himself as the worst sort of fool. Making a declaration of love at that particular moment and in that manner was not what Elizabeth required. She needed time to become more familiar with him. She was also undergoing a substantial upheaval in her life and needed the opportunity to let the complexities of her changed circumstances sink in. Adding further pressure from him was the last thing she needed, especially as he was uncertain he would be able to court her, much less marry her before her birthday in August.

More than any other time in the last five years, he missed his father. He needed to speak to someone, though he did not know who. His cousin would never understand, not really, and he was uncertain what his uncle would say. Of course, Lord Matlock would be pleased that he was finally taking a wife and that the woman in question was an heiress, though he would have preferred him to marry a titled lady. However, the earl would scarcely allow for feelings to be a consideration and would gladly make the contract regardless of the bride's feelings — or the groom's. According to the earl, marriage was about building wealth and connexions; the feelings of the parties involved were irrelevant.

No, he needed to speak to Elizabeth. He would apologise for pressuring her and reassure her that he would wait for her — however long that might be. He would also speak to her uncle to ensure she was well protected. The more he thought about it, the more he believed that Mr. Bennet had had this plan in place for longer than they realised and would do all that was required to make it a reality. He wished he knew more about both men involved in the contract.

Feeling the need to do *something*, he sat down to pen a note to his man of business asking him to hire investigators to find out anything he could about Thomas Bennet and William Collins. To be safe, he also requested they investigate Mr. Phillips, the solicitor in Meryton and brother-in-law to Mr. Bennet. Darcy did not know his Christian name but felt Meryton was a small enough community that it would not be hard to discover what they could about the man.

This done, he drafted a letter to his solicitor to prepare a marriage settlement. He knew it would be an unusual settlement since it would stipulate that all property the bride brought into the marriage would remain in trust for her. While she did not need additional funds, he would still settle an additional thirty thousand pounds on her. It could someday serve as a dowry for a daughter or provide a good start for a second or third son, should it be required. Darcy was suddenly distracted by two images appearing together in his mind — the image of *his* Elizabeth carrying their child and, the more tantalising of the two, the image of what it would require to get Elizabeth with child. It took him quite some time to return to his work after *that* thought crossed his mind.

Chapter 12

Before Darcy's intended visit to Elizabeth the next morning, he received a message from Mr. Elliott indicating a change in plans. Mr. Elliott would arrive in London later that afternoon rather than next week. In his message, Mr. Elliott requested Darcy's presence for a meeting with him and the solicitors responsible for drafting Alexander Tomlinson's will and establishing Elizabeth Tomlinson's trust. The meeting was scheduled for the first thing on Monday. Darcy responded immediately with his agreement.

Upon his arrival at the Gardiner residence, Darcy promptly shared this information with Elizabeth. He left a note for Mr. Gardiner, asking for Elizabeth and Mr. Gardiner to be ready to meet with Mr. Elliott after the initial discussion with the solicitors. The purpose would be to openly discuss matters concerning Mr. Bennet and the stipend assigned for Elizabeth's care. Acknowledging Darcy's intention to consult Mr. Elliott first regarding their potential courtship and marriage and recognising the inappropriateness of her presence at the solicitor's office, Elizabeth smiled in agreement with the proposed plan.

Darcy conversed with Elizabeth and Mrs. Gardiner for half an hour, allowing Elizabeth and Darcy to discuss their plans for her stay in London. Mrs. Gardiner interjected occasionally, sharing insights into the upcoming weeks based on the arrangements she had already made. Additionally, Darcy invited the three of them to join him for dinner at his residence the following evening. He intended to acquaint Mr. Gardiner with his earlier connexion to Elizabeth from their childhood, an omission he felt was necessary to rectify.

With the plans made the previous day for tea and a stroll in Hyde Park, Darcy made a further request. "Mrs. Gardiner, I rode here in my phaeton and hope you do not mind if I take Miss Elizabeth for a short ride on the way to Darcy House. I have my tiger accompanying me, of course, but there is no room in the carriage for a maid. It is an open carriage; we will be easily seen by anyone passing by."

Mrs. Gardiner considered this for a moment before she agreed. "I believe that will be acceptable." The two hastily gathered their accoutrements, and Darcy helped Elizabeth into the carriage, his hands lingering a trifle long on her hips as he helped her up.

"Mr. Darcy, I hoped to speak to you privately today," she said hesitantly once they were seated on the high perch.

"To continue the conversation from yesterday that was interrupted?"

She nodded. "Do you truly believe me to be unsafe?"

He sighed, his brow furrowed in deep thought. "I am uncertain. I have sent a message to my man of business instructing him to investigate Mr. Bennet, Mr. Phillips, and Mr. Collins. I am eager to uncover any underlying motivations behind their actions. After I escort you back to the Gardiners, I want to speak to your uncle about the possibility of arranging for your security. Specifically, I wonder about the possibility of hiring one or two footmen dedicated to ensuring your well-being while you stay in town." He stopped for a moment to think before continuing.

"Naturally, I will raise this matter with Mr. Elliott as well. As trustees overseeing your estate, Mr. Elliott and I feel we are obligated to inform Mr. Bennet of our intention to discuss your inheritance with you before any decisions regarding a potential marriage can be made. I propose meeting with him face-to-face to judge his response more effectively. Mr. Elliott, at this point, has yet to reply to Mr. Bennet's note regarding the marriage contract, so I anticipate he is eager for information on the matter."

Elizabeth grinned and could not resist a tease. "You also have a personal interest in the matter, sir."

He laughed. "That I do. I have also considered what might happen were I to spirit you away to Scotland and marry you there." He paused at realising what he said and sent her an apologetic look. "No matter what happens, the estate belongs to you, not your husband, so I am uncertain if eloping would change anything other than enabling us to marry before you come of age. However, I would not wish for either of us to suffer from the resulting scandal from such an action. While I would happily marry you in any circumstances, I also want to ensure you are protected should Bennet or Collins attempt anything untoward. This is another reason I want to ensure you have protection always near you."

She covered her mouth with her hands. "What sort of untoward actions?"

"I honestly do not know, dearest," he sighed, pausing momentarily as he navigated the phaeton through the crowded streets. "I am imagining the worst possible scenarios as I am terrified of losing you. Yesterday, I confessed that I love you and immediately regretted it ..."

Her gasp caused him to stop. "You regret telling me you love me?" she asked shakily.

He stammered, his expression reflecting a mix of emotions. "Yes... no," he began, then wiped his hand across his mouth as he took a breath to start over. He used his free hand to cover Elizabeth's. "I do not regret loving you, Ellie, though I had not planned to reveal my feelings until things were more settled with your family situation. I understand it may have been... unfair to you to express my emotions while you grapple with so many other concerns. I intended to wait for a better time. Moreover, it was not the ideal moment or setting for such a confession. I would have preferred to share those words with you privately when I was more certain of your sentiments toward me."

"Oh," she responded, brushing away tears that had welled up in the corners of her eyes. "I do understand. I was disappointed that our conversation was interrupted. I... I want you to know that I do care for you. I... it is too much for me to say that I love you at this moment, but I sense that it is on the horizon. You are correct — things are too much in disarray for me right now, and I scarcely know whether I am on my head or my heels. I barely know who I can trust, but I sense that you are one who will never fail me."

"I do not want to put additional pressure on you, Ellie," he whispered, hating their terrible timing once again. This was far too serious a conversation to be had while driving through the streets of London. She echoed his sentiment, and he laughed. "Our minds are in accord; I was just thinking the same. Someday, we will talk about this where we will not be interrupted and where we can give each other our full attention. First, I could not speak to you as I would like because we were standing in the entryway with my sister and your aunt, and now I cannot because I am driving a carriage through London."

She smiled at him, her eyes sparkling once again. "What is the fun of that? Nothing in our relationship has proceeded as usual; why should we change that now?"

He laughed before he replied. "That is true. You are a most unusual woman, Elizabeth Tomlinson."

Her smile changed to something else, something more ethereal. "We likely still should speak to Mr. Gardiner, but please, call me by that name in the future. I like it, and I believe I am ready to throw off the name of Bennet entirely."

"Once again, our timing is terrible. I would love to embrace you right now," he replied, smiling rakishly. Darcy then suggested, "Perhaps I can steal you away for a moment once we reach my house?"

Her laughter floated in the air behind them as they moved toward Darcy House. The sight of his home — soon to be their home — took Elizabeth by surprise. Having grown up at Longbourn, she had never entered such a grand home as it appeared from the outside. Upon entering, however, it was no surprise that it felt warm and inviting, elegant rather than opulent. Elizabeth found that the house, much like its master, was comfortable and perfectly aligned with her tastes.

* * *

On Sunday, the Gardiners and Elizabeth joined Darcy, his sister, and his cousin, Colonel Fitzwilliam, for an intimate family dinner. It was a pleasant meal, and, once again, Elizabeth and Georgiana found much to discuss. During their visit the day before, the two had begun to address each other by their Christian names and had dismissed Darcy to work in his study as they came to know each other better by practising duets on the pianoforte.

Both young ladies were accomplished performers, although Elizabeth's technical proficiency was not on par with Georgiana's. Elizabeth had a gift for infusing more emotion into her music, making her quite enjoyable to listen to. Despite the distance that separated them, Darcy found great pleasure in hearing her play. Elizabeth also had a beautiful singing voice, a talent Georgiana did not possess due to her shyness and reluctance to perform publicly. In private, Elizabeth gently encouraged Georgiana to prepare her to perform in front of others, as she believed Georgiana had a delightful voice.

The colonel was surprised by his cousins' guests since, other than Bingley, Darcy had a habit of looking down on those in trade. However, it did not take him long to discover Darcy's motivation behind this change, as it quickly became evident that his cousin was utterly besotted with his youngest guest. To that end, he did what he always did — he intentionally raised his cousin's ire by flirting with Elizabeth.

A skilled and charming flirt, the colonel soon had Elizabeth colouring at his forwardness. When dinner was announced, he quickly stood and offered her his arm before Darcy could. "Miss Tomlinson," he said as he extended his arm, "might I have the pleasure of escorting you in to dinner?"

Glancing towards Mr. Darcy, she tried not to show her disappointment. "Certainly, Colonel," she replied, taking his arm lightly while still looking toward his cousin.

Seeing this, the colonel increased his efforts, "Thank you. I confess, I was surprised to meet you here tonight; my cousin had not mentioned you at all until just before you arrived. I think he was trying to get rid of me, but I planted myself in his study and refused to take his hint. Is there a reason he does not want me to meet you?"

"Perhaps he was afraid of you stealing my attention from him? Or that I would be frightened off by your boldness?"

Darcy, his irritation growing, interjected, "Miss Elizabeth, I believe the colonel has a natural gift for flattery, but his words are as fickle as the wind. You should not be swayed by whatever he is saying to you. I hesitated to have the two of you meet because I know what a rogue he is and did not want to subject you to him so soon in our courtship."

The colonel flashed a sly grin in Darcy's direction. "Ah, but Darcy, you underestimate the power of a well-turned phrase. Miss Tomlinson deserves all the admiration we can offer her, do you not agree?"

Darcy took Elizabeth's other hand and pulled her away from the colonel to claim her as his own. "You may escort Georgiana to dinner; I will escort Miss Elizabeth. Go away, Jonathan," Darcy nearly growled.

Elizabeth arched her eyebrow at him before saying so only he could hear: "That was quite the display of possessiveness, sir."

Darcy let out a soft sigh. "I apologise, Miss Elizabeth. My cousin delights in provoking me and intentionally attempted to anger me in a method common to brothers. While we are cousins by birth, we are as close as brothers, and he seems to think it is his role to torment me."

"Yes, I recall," she said, laughing lightly as she allowed herself to be led to the dining room and seated to Darcy's right. The seating was informal, and everyone else was encouraged to sit where they liked, although Georgiana did take the hostess's seat at the end of the table. Colonel Fitzwilliam sat to her left, allowing the Gardiners to sit next to each other on the other side of the table.

Dinner progressed easily, with conversation encompassing the entire table most of the time. The colonel was intrigued by Darcy's frequent references to his guest as "Miss Elizabeth" when she had been introduced to him as "Miss Tomlinson" and the oblique reference to a courtship. He was somewhat surprised Darcy would enter into a courtship without informing at least the earl and countess, although he considered it might be recent enough that he had not yet had time. He had been amused by his cousin's show of possessiveness regarding the lady and by the lady's apparent preference for his cousin.

When the meal was finished, the ladies retreated to the music room to continue their practice from the previous day. The three gentlemen retreated into Mr. Darcy's study, where Fitzwilliam immediately asked his cousin for an explanation, which was hastily given.

"That is our little Ellie?" Fitzwilliam asked incredulously. "I never saw her again after that summer at Briarwood, and neither mother nor father knew what happened to her when her grandparents passed away. They would be delighted to meet her again."

"I intend to bring her to meet your parents soon. However, for now, I need to see what can be done to protect her from the marriage Mr. Bennet hopes to arrange. That is one of the things I will discuss with Mr. Elliott and the solicitors tomorrow. Do you know a few men who could be hired to protect Miss Elizabeth?" Darcy asked, then turned to Mr. Gardiner to explain. "It may be unnecessary, but I would feel better knowing Miss Elizabeth has a footman or two to accompany her wherever she goes for her protection. You know your brother better than I, but can he force Elizabeth to do as he wishes? I worry that he might attempt to abscond with her or force her to wed Mr. Collins against her will. I fear he has had all of this planned for some time."

Gardiner started. "I would not have considered Bennet capable of it in the past, but I also would not have believed he would have kept such information from Elizabeth and the rest of the family. I doubt this was his intent when he first accepted her care, but he has obviously grown used to the extra funds from her estate. I do not know how far he may be willing to go to ensure his plan comes to fruition."

"What will you do about that, Darcy?" Fitzwilliam asked.

He sighed. "Ellie does not want him to get away without any consequences, though she does not want her cousins to suffer. For years, he has lied to Mr. Elliott about how the funds were spent. Elliott and I seek to find out what crimes he may have committed and whether he can be prosecuted for any of them in our meeting with the solicitors tomorrow," Darcy explained.

"Can Bennet require her to return to Longbourn?" Gardiner asked.

Becoming aggravated by these questions, as these were the very ones he had himself and had so far been unable to answer, he replied tersely. "I have many more questions than I have answers to at the moment, gentlemen. Can we cease this inquisition and rejoin the ladies? I hope to discuss all of these during our meeting with Mr. Elliott and the solicitors on the morrow."

Fitzwilliam laughed at his scowl. "I think we must, or you will become even more surly," he quipped, earning another glare from his cousin. "You are just out of sorts because the lovely Miss Tomlinson prefers my company to yours."

"Not a chance, Fitzwilliam," he retorted, breaking away from the group as he entered the music room. Inside, he found Elizabeth seated beside Georgiana at the piano, and an instant smile graced his face as he gazed upon the heartwarming scene. *"This,"* he thought, *"this is what I wish to cherish for a lifetime."*

Chapter 13

Thomas Bennet was feeling rather pleased with himself. Since receiving a letter several months ago from Longbourn's heir, he had hatched a plan that would allow him to keep Longbourn in his family, thereby providing for his wife and daughters after his death. He had even negotiated with the fool to ensure he would continue to receive the stipend from his niece's estate for his lifetime.

The heir, William Collins, had readily agreed to relinquish his claim to Longbourn in favour of Briarwood, a larger estate than Longbourn. He also agreed to continue and even increase the quarterly stipend Mr. Bennet had come to rely on so he could maintain his current lifestyle without fretting over reducing their expenses or bothering with his estate. The contract had already been drafted, and the week prior, Mr. Bennet had sent it to Mr. Elliott, asking for his signature and instructing him to contact the second trustee, who would also be needed to sign the contract.

His brother, Mr. Phillips, had taken great care crafting both the marriage settlement and a private agreement regarding the entail. This second agreement would not be shared with the trustees and would be executed solely between Mr. Bennet and Mr. Collins, though he did not realise he had hinted at this part of his plan in the letter to Mr. Elliott.

Mr. Bennet did not even mind Elizabeth's absence in London for a month or two. With Mr. Collins visiting soon, it had seemed wise to remove her until all the contracts were signed. Mr. Bennet imagined she would be more compliant in marrying a stranger than she would be after meeting the man. The letters he had exchanged with Mr. Collins revealed his foolishness, and Mr. Bennet anticipated that Lizzy might not willingly accept him, at least not at first. However, he was certain he would eventually convince her to comply with his demand. And if she resisted, well, there were ways to compel her into marriage, he knew.

A fortnight after Elizabeth departed for London, Mr. Collins made his way to Longbourn. He expressed dissatisfaction with the absence of his future bride from the house. Mr. Bennet, however, sought to appease him by assuring him that everything was in order for the wedding to proceed as planned. They then set the wedding date for the twenty-seventh of January, enabling the reading of banns to commence on the Sunday after Epiphany, with the marriage scheduled for the day following the third reading.

Mr. Collins asked his cousin, "Are you absolutely certain that everything is proceeding smoothly, Mr. Bennet?"

Mr. Bennet, with a feigned air of confidence, replied, "Rest assured, Mr. Collins, there are no impediments to our plans. I have taken care of everything. You only need to show up before the wedding date, and all will occur as planned."

Mr. Collins hesitated momentarily before conceding, "Very well, Mr. Bennet. I trust your judgement in this matter, though I had hoped to meet my bride on this visit."

"Her aunt needed her in London," Bennet explained.

"I did not think she had any other family," Mr. Collins questioned.

"Mr. Gardiner is my wife's brother. Lizzy has always considered them her relations, and she greatly favours them," Bennet replied, waving away the man's concerns. "She will return to Longbourn when the family gathers for Christmastide." Mr. Collins nodded, although he remained displeased about not meeting his bride.

Bennet was confident the trustees would sign the marriage settlement soon. *They had not shown concern for Elizabeth over the last fourteen years; why should that change now,* he thought. He felt that if he presented the marriage as a *fait accompli*, they could do nothing about it, and they would simply turn the estate over to Mr. Collins without question. It never occurred to him that they would not follow his plan.

* * *

Mr. Collins' life's ambition was to emulate the rector he so admired in his home parish in Hampshire. He yearned to bring hope and happiness to his parishioners through his benevolent counsel, and surely, as a man of God, all he served would gladly seek his wisdom. Securing the position of rector in Hunsford fulfilled his deepest aspirations. Not only was he appreciated by his congregants, but his patroness, the esteemed Lady Catherine de Bourgh, was gracious enough to share her counsel in all matters, large and small. There was nothing not significant enough for Lady Catherine to have an opinion about, and she expressed these often and forcefully. Mr. Collins saw no harm in adopting her words as his own, which he frequently did, taking pride in imparting her proclamations to anyone who would listen.

He showed Lady Catherine the letter from Mr. Bennet about his unexpected inheritance, and she encouraged him to relinquish his claim on his cousin's estate in exchange for the more profitable one, even if it meant marrying his cousin, the natural-born child of Mr. Edward Bennet. She assured him it was the godly thing to do. His wisdom in following Lady Catherine's advice was celebrated, although she was greatly affronted on behalf of her rector that the lady had not been present during his visit.

Mr. Collins had no knowledge of estate management and planned to hire someone to oversee the estate so he could remain where he was.

Overjoyed by his unexpected inheritance and anticipated marriage, Mr. Collins celebrated at a nearby tavern. Normally, he abstained from drinking, but this was a special night, and he overindulged, loudly conversing with anyone who would listen, seeking advice on what he ought to do, and, above all, bragging about his beneficence in considering marriage to the natural daughter of his cousin.

Pure chance resulted in George Wickham crossing paths with Mr. Collins that day. Having fled from Ramsgate after his ill-fated attempt to elope with Georgiana, Wickham found himself in Kent at the same tavern. He had been toying with the idea of stopping at Rosings to inform Lady Catherine of how close Darcy had come to allowing Georgiana's ruin, believing he could use this information to avenge Darcy's interruption of his elopement by igniting Lady Catherine's rage and hopefully forcing the match between Darcy and his cousin, Anne de Bourgh. It was during this contemplation that he overheard Collins discussing Briarwood.

Wickham knew much about Briarwood as he had accompanied his godfather, George Darcy, to the estate several times before that man's death. When George Darcy ran it, it earned something like six or seven thousand a year. If Wickham could swindle the estate from this simpleton, he would be set for life. He also would enjoy owning an estate in the vicinity of Pemberley, something he was certain would cause Darcy great mortification.

With that in mind, Wickham struck up a conversation with Mr. Collins. He introduced himself as a solicitor and pretended to be shocked at the mention of Briarwood, as he was very familiar with that estate. He spun a tale about his father's experience as a solicitor and later as the steward for a large estate in the north that abutted Briarwood. He himself had frequently visited Briarwood with his godfather, who was charged with overseeing the property, held in trust for an absentee owner. Wickham said he was trained by his father to be a steward and then later studied the law. He humbly offered his assistance but cautioned Mr. Collins that he had been barred from his godfather's estate for falling in love with the master's daughter. His heart had been broken, and he had yet to recover.

Swayed by Wickham's account of hardship at the hand of a cruel estate master, Mr. Collins' gullibility allowed this fabricated tale to draw his sympathy. "My dear sir, your story deeply moves me, and I find your offer of assistance most generous."

Without requesting references or conducting any kind of due diligence, Collins hired Wickham as Briarwood's new steward on the spot. Shockingly, he also failed to seek his patroness' guidance.

Wickham offered to go to Briarwood to ascertain its condition, but he would need his expenses paid in advance. An enthusiastic Mr. Collins handed him five pounds, promising more once he acquired the estate.

Wickham responded with a manipulative smile, "I assure you, Mr. Collins, your trust in me will not be misplaced. I shall assist you in every way possible."

Although he was not a solicitor, Wickham had studied the law enough to know how to use it to his advantage, and he drafted a contract between them that made him the estate manager and the recipient of the majority of its profits. He assured Mr. Collins he need not worry about the legal language contained within, which would only serve to confuse him. "Do not concern yourself with the legal intricacies, Mr. Collins. This contract is simply a formality."

Mr. Collins readily accepted Wickham's representation and signed the document without reading it, offering a contented smile to the charming man who expressed his delight at their future arrangement.

Wickham could not believe his luck at having so easily manipulated the cull and could not wait until the twit's marriage so he could begin reaping the estate's profits and living the life to which he was entitled. Ultimately, Collins would be powerless to change the course of events.

For a moment, Wickham thought how fortunate he had been that Darcy had shown up when he did and blocked his elopement with his sister. This arrangement regarding Briarwood would keep him living well far longer than he would with Georgiana's dowry, and he would not even be saddled with such a passive and unwelcoming wife.

Following Collins' unsuccessful visit to Longbourn, he wrote to his "solicitor," asking him to gather more information about his cousins, particularly his bride. With another twenty pounds in his pocket and a promise to cover all expenses, Wickham began his trip to Meryton to see what he could discover there.

* * *

During this period, Mr. Elliott and Darcy met with the solicitors, delving into the details of Alexander Tomlinson's will and its stipulations. They established conclusively that Mr. Bennet had defrauded Elizabeth of a minimum of nine hundred pounds owed her for her allowance over the last six years, as she had received only fifty pounds per annum instead of 200 pounds. By examining Mr. Gardiner's financial records, which validated the sums he disbursed and received from Mr. Bennet over the last five years on behalf of Elizabeth and the account ledgers Elizabeth had taken from Longbourn, they had clear proof that very little had been spent on her during her residency at Longbourn. They could also support Elizabeth's claim that she had not had a governess after age 12, she had never had a companion or masters and that virtually nothing was spent on her clothing.

While there was little doubt that Elizabeth was owed a significantly larger sum, it was ultimately decided by Darcy, Elliott, and Gardiner, with input from Elizabeth and Mrs. Gardiner, that when they met with Mr. Bennet, they would demand repayment of three thousand pounds which represented the maximum amount they could irrefutably prove. This request was confirmed by the solicitors engaged to support their claims.

One additional revelation emerged during their examination of the will. Although George Darcy was appointed Elizabeth's guardian, no alternate was identified, and Mr. Tomlinson's solicitor was unaware of anyone being appointed after Mr. Darcy passed away. He agreed to review court records to determine if that was the case. He also proposed filing a petition with the Chancery Court immediately asking that Mr. Elliott be appointed. That appeared to be a prudent course of action, so he was authorised to proceed.

"This is a good start," Mr. Elliott told them when they met at the Gardiners later to discuss what had been discovered. They summarised what occurred in their meeting with the solicitors and then reported on the investigation of Mr. Bennet and Mr. Collins.

Darcy addressed the group. "The investigators have ascertained that Mr. and Mrs. Bennet hatched this scheme to keep the estate in the family and protect Mrs. Bennet and their unmarried daughters if they survived Mr. Bennet. They have also confirmed that Bennet engaged his brother Phillips to draft the contracts, and it appears that Phillips has been privy to

Elizabeth's true parentage for all these years. Mr. Collins's background is something of a mystery. From what we have gathered so far, he appears to be a sycophantic fool and is easily swayed. This might explain why Bennet succeeded in convincing him not only to relinquish his claim to Longbourn but also to continue the stipend throughout his lifetime."

"Does Mr. Bennet have a copy of my grandfather's will?" Elizabeth asked.

"Presumably, although we do not know for certain. Surely, at some point, he would have seen it and read it," Gardiner stated. "Bennet may be lazy, but he is not a fool."

The others agreed with that conclusion, and the conversation drifted to other topics, including a planned outing to the theatre in a few days.

"Now, after Collins departs from Longbourn, you and I" — Elliott indicated Darcy — "will pay Bennet a visit. We will not let on all we have discovered but will speak to him about the legalities that require filing trust fund expenditures and the marriage contract. Darcy, I worry a little about your involvement in this meeting, so I urge you to allow me to lead. Bennet may remember you from your offer to escort Miss Elizabeth to town. How attentive was he when you met him?"

"I think our meeting lasted less than five minutes," Darcy replied. "He knew little of me other than I was conveying Mrs. Nicholls to town and offered to take Miss Elizabeth at no cost to him. He approved it immediately."

"Would he recall your name?" Elliott asked.

"I would hope so, but I think he barely looked up from his book the entire time I was there," Darcy replied, looking apologetically at Elizabeth.

She waved off his concern. "After all we have learned, it is of little surprise to me that he cared so little about my safety. I would like to think that he has enough faith in Mrs. Hill and Mrs. Nicholls to trust their judgement, which is why he agreed so readily. However, I also know that he was pleased that things were so easily arranged with so little effort on his part," she replied, her voice equal parts sarcastic and hurt.

Chapter 14

When Darcy told his aunt and uncle, the Earl and Countess of Matlock, about Miss Tomlinson, they were delighted to realise she was the granddaughter of their close friends, the same girl who played with Jonathan and Fitzwilliam all those years ago. They had always wondered what had become of her after her grandparents passed away but had not heard anything. However, when Darcy told them of his unofficial courtship of Elizabeth, the earl was not pleased. While he was relieved that her fortune, at least, was what he hoped for Darcy, he insisted Darcy should marry a lady with a title. Darcy promptly interrupted his uncle, asserting his resolution to marry Miss Tomlinson despite her absence of noble lineage. In his view, she possessed all the qualities he sought in a bride.

The informal courtship between Darcy and Elizabeth was progressing apace. Despite all the necessary conversations about Elizabeth's inheritance, Darcy spent time with her each day discussing other matters. As she had ordered several new dresses, paid for with her funds, they were able to go to more places, including museums and other venues.

More than a fortnight after she arrived in London, the two attended the theatre accompanied by Mr. and Mrs. Gardiner. Darcy's aunt and uncle, the Earl and Countess of Matlock, were also to be in attendance that night.

Since their discussion of his courtship, the earl had been silent on the subject, though Darcy still felt his disapproval. Lady Matlock would be more welcoming, fondly remembering the elder Mr. and Mrs. Tomlinson, and her acceptance was of greater value since she could help introduce Elizabeth to the *ton*.

When Darcy arrived at the Gardiners' home to collect Elizabeth, he was once again taken aback by her extraordinary loveliness. From the first moment he had laid eyes on her in Meryton, he had considered her beautiful. Throughout their relationship, he found her becoming more exquisite to his eyes each day. It was not only her physical beauty that captivated him; her kindness, sharp wit, and warmth combined to make her even more attractive.

On this particular evening, Elizabeth seemed to radiate a special allure as she descended the steps. She was adorned in a gown far more elegant and of much higher quality than anything he had ever seen her wear before. Her gown was a vision in ivory with deep green embellishments that made her fair skin radiant. The dress accentuated her graceful figure, enhancing her natural charm.

What truly caught Darcy's attention was the small emerald pendant gracing her neck. The deep green hue of the emerald perfectly complemented the accents on her gown, creating a delightful harmony. Darcy could not help but be captivated by the enchanting sight before him, his heart stirred by the eternal elegance and grace that Elizabeth always exuded.

This exquisite necklace had been discovered among the treasures stored for her in her London bank. Mr. Elliott had decided to give her access to these a few days before, as she should have had them since her debut into society. This was her first foray into London society, so both he and the Gardiners felt she would be better received dressed as the heiress she was.

"You are stunning, Miss Elizabeth," Darcy finally said, taking Elizabeth's hand and kissing the back of it.

Lowering her eyes for only a moment to glance at the hand that held onto her own, she looked up to gaze directly into Darcy's eyes. She saw his love and devotion for her shining in them, and tears briefly stung her eyes. "Thank you, sir," she said, far more demurely than was her wont. Taking his offered arm, she moved more fully into the hallway where her aunt and uncle waited.

"Shall we depart?" Mr. Gardiner inquired as soon as the young couple appeared. They nodded in agreement and began moving toward the door to don their outerwear. With a tenderness that had become second nature to him, Darcy assisted Elizabeth by draping her cape gently over her shoulders. His hands lingered for a moment on her shoulders, causing a shiver to trail down her spine and her heart to race at the delicate touch. Darcy noticed her reaction and was secretly thrilled that she was so responsive to him.

When they arrived at the theatre, Darcy stepped out first, swiftly followed by Mr. Gardiner, who graciously assisted his wife as she descended from the carriage. Darcy then moved to assist Elizabeth and gently placed her hand on his arm, covering it with his free hand. Together, they entered the theatre in this fashion, immediately drawing the attention of the crowd.

The spectacle of Darcy, who was well-known for avoiding the company of young, eligible ladies, arriving with a stunning and unknown brunette on his arm, accompanied by an older couple, piqued the interest of many theatregoers. Elizabeth's extraordinary beauty only added to the intrigue. As they moved through the crowd, their party exchanged greetings with several acquaintances, but Darcy was selective in making formal introductions to a chosen few. By the time they had crossed the lobby and begun their ascent to his box, the chatter and gossip surrounding them reached a fever pitch.

"I apologise, dearest. I believe we will be on display tonight," Darcy whispered to Elizabeth, noting the intense interest of the crowd. "Our box will likely be inundated with visitors during the intermissions."

Elizabeth, while somewhat anxious about the attention, felt a surge of courage. "Our box, sir?" she playfully teased in a hushed tone.

He felt his cheeks heat, but still, he managed to retort, "Yes, well, it is our box in the sense that we are all sharing it tonight, are we not?"

Her light laugh echoed in the narrow space. "That is true, although I had assigned quite a different meaning to your comment. Now, tell me more about what we might expect tonight. I have attended the theatre on only a few occasions, but this is my first time viewing the performance from a box."

They continued their quiet conversation while removing their outerwear and handing them to the accompanying footman. After asking the footman to fetch refreshments, Darcy guided Elizabeth to her seat and discreetly pointed out a few noteworthy individuals in the audience. They observed others taking their seats until their conversation was interrupted by a couple from the adjacent box.

"Darcy," a voice exclaimed, "You simply must introduce me to your charming companion."

Darcy leaned in to whisper to Elizabeth, "My aunt, Lady Matlock," and then rose to perform the introductions to his party.

Lady Matlock expressed her approval of Elizabeth for all to see, and numerous eyes from the other boxes were drawn to the interaction. The earl was also introduced, and while he was less effusive in his greeting, he remained pleasant. There was little time for more than brief pleasantries before the bell signalled the start of the play.

"Do you always garner so much attention at the theatre?" Elizabeth whispered to Darcy as the lights dimmed.

He sighed. "Unfortunately. I am, by society's standards, considered quite the catch. Available first sons are rare, and those who have already inherited their estates are even rarer. Additionally, my wealth is a magnet for many women who aspire to be associated with it, not unlike Miss Bingley. Moreover, being the nephew of an earl…" He paused, reluctant to sound overly conceited. While he took immense pride in his role as the present owner of Pemberley and the other estates he oversaw, he viewed himself as their caretaker. He diligently managed his properties, overseeing the many tenants and servants employed at his properties. Unlike many of his social standing, he was keenly involved in the day-to-day affairs of his estates. Under his careful management, Pemberley and his secondary properties had all flourished. Briarwood, Elizabeth's estate, had also prospered under his direction.

Elizabeth placed her hand on his arm, remembering a similar conversation before. "I understand. You are pursued for your wealth and status, not for yourself, and you despise that."

Darcy smiled at her understanding and whispered into her ear. "You understand me so well. It is one of the many reasons I adore you."

Her smile was radiant. "I love you too," she whispered so quietly he had to lean closely to hear.

"Did you ... what did you just say?" he whispered in reply. "Did you really have to say that now?" His voice rose slightly in pitch as he once again considered their terrible timing.

She grinned at him. "Yes, sir, I said that I love you, too," she told him, struggling to restrain her laughter at his discomfiture.

"You are cruel, madam, to taunt me in this way," he replied, bringing her hand to his lips for a lingering kiss. He did not release her hand but hid their clasped hands in her skirt, where they remained until the intermission.

At intermission, Lady Matlock joined the Darcy party and spoke to Elizabeth and Mrs. Gardiner, while Lord Matlock spoke with Darcy and Mr. Gardiner. The earl was surprised to learn that Gardiner was a tradesman and asked several intelligent questions about his business. They were not able to speak long before they were interrupted by a few friends of Lady Matlock, who came at that lady's unspoken invitation.

When these women met Elizabeth and heard her surname, one of them, Lady Constance Harrington, recalled her grandparents and told Elizabeth a story about them. "Your grandparents were heartbroken when their son was killed, followed soon after by the death of their daughter-in-law. We wondered who had raised you after their deaths, but it is obvious you have become a lovely young woman. You must be something rather special to have attracted Mr. Darcy's interest. He is extremely eligible if you did not already know."

"I am lucky to have garnered Miss Tomlinson's agreement to a courtship," Darcy interjected. "I was first attracted to her kindness, and I have seen countless examples of her exemplary qualities during our acquaintance."

This public acknowledgement of their courtship caused ripples of talk to run through the theatre. At least one person who overheard this comment fully intended to share this news with young Darcy's other aunt as soon as she could, to the point that she debated leaving the theatre early to send an express that very night. However, she decided to continue to watch the couple, as she had seen him kiss her hand at the beginning of the play and wanted to know what other information she might glean.

Caroline Bingley was also at the theatre that night. When Darcy left for London nearly a month ago, Caroline also insisted she must depart. Since her sister wanted nothing to do with her after that, Caroline had written to several friends to beg an invitation. One arrived a few days later, though it was obvious the writer was not pleased to do so, having only agreed because Caroline threatened to reveal something her "friend" preferred to keep private.

She had kept a low profile for a time, worried that Darcy might have followed through on his threat to inform Lady Matlock about the attempted compromise. However, as she heard the rumours that a long-lost heiress, who was not only wealthy but reported to be beautiful, was being squired around by Darcy, Caroline was determined to put an end to his infatuation before it got out of hand. Her spies assured her he would be at the theatre that evening, so she planned on taking care of things that night. First, however, she needed to evaluate her competition.

Hiding behind her fan, she stared at the occupants of the Darcy box, hoping for a good look at the interloper. She was astounded! Standing next to the man Caroline intended to marry was none other than that chit Eliza Bennet. How had she managed to fool Mr. Darcy? Despite calling herself by a different name — Elizabeth Tomlinson, indeed! — she could not be competition for Darcy's hand. As for the rumours of her being a heiress, they clearly were false.

No, Elizabeth Tomlinson, or Bennet, or whoever she was, despite being dressed in a gown made by one of London's premier modiste and wearing an emerald necklace — they must be paste, she told herself — was no match for a man like Mr. Darcy. She was still the plain, unsophisticated, ill-mannered Eliza Bennet of Hertfordshire — the baseborn daughter of a nobody.

Incensed, Caroline was intent on revealing *Eliza* for the imposter she undoubtedly was.

Deciding that boldness was the key to obtaining her desires, she made her way toward the Darcy box, resolved to enter at the next intermission. She did so, sneaking in with another party, and addressed her rival. "Miss Eliza Bennet," she exclaimed loudly, drawing attention to herself, determined all would know the fraud for what she was. "I am astonished to see you here tonight ..."

Before she could say more, she was accosted by Mr. Darcy. "Madam, I am uncertain how you have managed to make your way into this room uninvited, but I insist you leave at once," he barked.

"Why, Mr. Darcy, this chit is ..." Again, before she could finish her sentence, she was cut off, this time by Darcy's footman physically pulling her toward the door.

"Mr. Darcy asked you to leave, miss," the footman said.

In the Darcy box, those who had witnessed the scene took a moment to recover from Miss Bingley's audacity. Colonel Fitzwilliam, who had accompanied his parents to the theatre, could not help but chuckle before saying loud enough to be overheard. "She is exceptionally dense, Darcy, to think of forcing her way into your company again. And in such a public way after what she attempted at Netherfield."

Darcy nodded in agreement but refrained from saying more. "I apologise for not preventing her entry, Miss Tomlinson. I did not realise she had returned to London and am shocked that she would attempt to speak to me or anyone around me after I cut the connexion the last time we spoke."

"I thought you and her brother were good friends, Darcy," the earl inquired, recalling what his wife had mentioned regarding Miss Bingley's attempts to force a compromise in Hertfordshire.

"Our friendship has been dissolved, sir. I will no longer recognise the Bingleys and have refused the entry of either Mr. or Miss Bingley to my house."

"As I understand it, this is not the first time she has attempted to enter a room uninvited," the earl commented. "She is shockingly obtuse." These words were immediately followed by murmurs from those listening to the conversation.

"She is determined, though she will never obtain her object," Darcy responded calmly, his restraint evident.

Elizabeth noticed his discretion and saw it as a sign of his character, appreciating that even in the face of disloyalty, Darcy was unwilling to ruin his former friend entirely. If she were honest with herself, she knew it made her fall in love with him a little more, and she looked forward to a moment alone with him later to talk more about her earlier confession. Unfortunately, Darcy and Elizabeth did not have an opportunity to speak privately after the theatre or for the next several days.

Chapter 15

After investigators confirmed that Mr. Collins had returned to Hunsford, Mr. Elliott and Darcy made their way to Hertfordshire to pay a visit to Mr. Bennet. Numerous discussions had taken place before and during their journey regarding how this meeting should proceed. Once again, Darcy had been advised to allow Mr. Elliott to lead the way since he could maintain an impassive demeanour concerning Elizabeth, something Darcy would find challenging given the nature of their relationship.

Part of him was unwilling to do so, but he recognised that his feelings for Elizabeth — which had only grown since her own confession of love — would make it difficult for him not to react to Mr. Bennet's plans for her.

When they arrived at Longbourn, Mrs. Hill escorted them to Mr. Bennet's study. Darcy surreptitiously handed a note to the housekeeper from Elizabeth explaining her circumstances and requesting that she pack several of her books and a few other small items she left behind. These could be placed in Elliott's carriage without anyone noticing.

Bennet received the two gentlemen with little ceremony. He was surprised that Mr. Elliott had bothered to visit; he assumed the second gentleman was the other trustee.

He greeted them with a sardonic tone. "Welcome, gentlemen. Mr. Elliott, I know you from our correspondence these many years, but who is Mr. Darcy? Is he the second trustee? Have the two of you come to sign the marriage contracts?"

Darcy's hackles rose upon hearing this, and Mr. Elliott cleared his throat to signal to him to calm himself before speaking. "Yes, Mr. Darcy is the second trustee, and we have come to discuss the marriage contracts, amongst other things."

Struggling to keep his voice even, Darcy spoke for the first time upon entering. "Is Miss Tomlinson home now? Her agreement is, of course, required for the marriage to proceed. We would like to meet with her and her intended before we sign any documents related to any future marriage."

Mr. Bennet demurred. "Elizabeth is in London obtaining her trousseau, and her intended has returned to his rectory. He intends to remain there with Elizabeth after they marry, until she reaches her majority, at which time he will resign and take up the management of Briarwood. As I wrote, he has agreed to resign his claim as the heir to Longbourn since he will have Elizabeth's estate in its stead."

"He will not," Mr. Elliott said. "You have obviously forgotten the stipulations of old Mr. Tomlinson's will. The estate belongs to Miss Tomlinson, not her husband, and her marriage contract must state that fact before it is turned over. The income from the estate remains under her control as well. Her husband will be entitled to nothing and has no claim upon any part of her inheritance."

Mr. Bennet spluttered. "What?" he cried.

Mr. Elliott continued as though Mr. Bennet had not spoken. "Those are the terms of the will. If she marries over the anvil, then her uncle — you — immediately stops receiving any funds from the estate, and it is up to the trustees to decide what happens next. No one person can approve her marriage; Darcy and I have to approve, and, of course, Miss Tomlinson herself must agree. No one can force another person to speak the vows, and if she marries without the approval of her trustees, the estate remains under our control until we agree to turn it over to her."

Mr. Bennet was angry at these revelations. He managed to keep his composure, though it was a near thing. "So, will you approve the marriage then?"

"Since Miss Tomlinson is in London and cannot be asked her opinion, we must seek her out in Town to inquire. Please give us the direction of where we can find her. Once we have spoken with her, we will return to Longbourn to address any outstanding issues. During the interim period, you will need to have the marriage contract redrafted to ensure it contains the necessary clauses regarding the inheritance. You can have your solicitor copy the language from Alexander Tomlinson's will if necessary.

"There is also the matter of the accounting the trust must file with the Chancery Court prior to Miss Tomlinson's marriage documenting how the funds you received from the trust were spent. There is no need to be alarmed; based on your annual letters, you should have no problem providing such documentation. Among other things, you should begin making a list of your niece's governesses, companions and masters and gathering receipts or other evidence of your payment to them. We will also require receipts for her clothing and entertainment in London."

"Of course," Mr. Bennet said, thinking quickly about how to avoid giving the requested information. He needed to devise a reason why Lizzy did not have a companion with her if they visited her in Town or how to arrange for one temporarily who would claim to have been with her for several years. However, convincing Elizabeth to lie about having a governess or a companion would be tricky. "Unfortunately, her companion has taken a brief leave to tend to a sick relative, and Lizzy is staying with my wife's brother in London. I would prefer you wait to visit her until she has returned home, which will be just before Christmas. Her wedding date is set for January, and we intend to have the banns read after Epiphany. Elizabeth would not like to delay, so you should visit again between Christmas and the New Year. I will have to search to find the direction of her governess — it has been some years since we have had a reason to contact her."

Darcy could not hold back any longer. "I do not believe we can delay our meeting until after Christmas in light of the plans you have made. In fact, as there does not appear to be a good reason for rushing the wedding, you should postpone it until we are in a position to file the accounting and approve of the match."

"And why the governess not have stayed on for your other daughters? I understood that you had four, and the youngest is, what? Just fourteen or fifteen?"

Mr. Bennet started at this, wondering what all these men knew about him and his family. *"Is it possible they know more than I have told them? Could they have had me investigated?"* he thought, suddenly worried.

"Lydia recently turned fifteen and is now considered 'out' in our local society. I realise it is not the 'done' thing in London, but here in our country town, it is not unusual," he explained.

"Surely Miss Tomlinson was not pushed out at fifteen," Mr. Elliott asked. "The will stipulated she was to receive a London Season before reaching her majority so she would be able to meet eligible gentlemen. She is a substantial heiress who deserves a chance to meet more men than she could have met here. No, you said she had not had a season, and I will insist upon it before she weds. You will need to write to her aunt to ask her to obtain appropriate clothing for her debut, along with forwarding the necessary funds. Since Miss Tomlinson is a substantial heiress, she needs clothing that reflects her status.

"Her allowance is substantial, but even her two hundred pounds a year is not enough to pay for the dresses she will need for her first Season. You will need to send her the funds from her clothing allowance that you have received."

Again, his visitors watched as Bennet blanched. "Two hundred pounds," he stammered out.

"Yes, the will stipulated that beginning at age fifteen, she would receive fifty pounds from each quarter's stipend as her allowance. Of course, that is in addition to her clothing allowance, which was also to be paid from the twelve hundred pound stipend you received annually. Mr. Darcy, you have a younger sister; what does she spend on clothing?"

"She is just fifteen and not yet out, but still, I spend at least one hundred pounds a year dressing her. Of course, she does not need finer gowns yet. For a full season, I would expect to spend at least two hundred pounds to provide appropriate clothing.

Having recovered some composure, Mr. Bennet attempted to make demands from the gentlemen. "Why does she need a season at all? She is engaged and does not need to meet additional men."

"She cannot be engaged, as she does not have the permission required to be so," Mr. Elliott stated calmly. "We will meet with her when we return to London to speak to her about these plans. Mr. Darcy's aunt is the Countess of Matlock, and she can sponsor Miss Tomlinson's debut. If, after she has had a Season, she still desires to marry this heir, then we can arrange a date in the summer for the marriage to take place."

At this point, Mr. Bennet wondered how all his plans could have gone so wrong. Lizzy still believed she was a Bennet and did not know about her inheritance or engagement. *"How will she react to this news, especially if these men tell her before I can?"* he thought as he considered what else to do. It was apparent these gentlemen would not relent in their intention to speak to Elizabeth, but he wanted to control that conversation.

Finally, he arrived at a plan. "Well, sirs, I will need to notify my brother before I send you to his home to speak to Elizabeth. I will write to you in a week to give you their direction after I have had a chance to discuss matters with him."

It was evident that Mr. Elliott was reluctant to agree, but eventually, he did so. "I expect a letter no later than a week from today, Bennet. I will not tolerate a delay in this, especially in light of your rush to marry her off."

Mr. Bennet readily concurred and hastened to guide the gentlemen out of his study. He was taken aback when they crossed paths with Jane during their exit, and it seemed as though she regarded the younger man with a hint of recognition. At that moment, a vague sense of familiarity also struck him about Mr. Darcy, but he could not quite pinpoint why.

Once the gentlemen departed, he sought out Jane to ask about him. He was surprised to learn that Mr. Darcy had been in Hertfordshire for several weeks and was the one to escort Elizabeth to London.

The realisation hit him suddenly. "They know!" he nearly yelled, leaving Jane confused and unsettled. He rushed from the room and sent a servant to the stables to order his horse saddled. He changed into appropriate clothes for riding and went directly to Netherfield.

Chapter 16

Upon arriving at Netherfield, Mr. Bennet promptly sought an audience with Mr. Bingley. Their prior interactions had been limited to Mr. Bennet's initial visit and Mr. Bingley's subsequent return call, both of which had been somewhat awkward. Skipping the customary formalities, Mr. Bennet immediately inquired about Mr. Darcy.

"Mr. Darcy?" Mr. Bingley replied, somewhat puzzled by this line of questioning. Believing this was an opportunity to introduce a hint of scandal, he recounted the version of events presented by his sister, Caroline. "Well, he did visit for a time, but I had to ask him to leave. It appears he invited my sister to his rooms one evening while he was here, and then he refused to do the honourable thing and marry her. I had never believed any of the gossip circulating in Town about him until this event."

"So, he is not a gentleman then?" Mr. Bennet was eager to gather any tidbits he could use against Mr. Darcy, believing he could achieve his goals if he could convince one of the trustees to follow his plan. If one of them agreed, he surely could persuade the other, and they would convince Lizzy to go along with it.

Mr. Bingley recounted tales of his own exploits with women, none of which were particularly nefarious. He had a propensity for quickly falling in and out of love, but with the right spin, he could portray Darcy as quite the scoundrel and rake. Since Darcy had severed ties with the Bingley family, and given the Bennets' lack of ties to London, Mr. Bingley believed his tales would do little more than tarnish Darcy's reputation in the local area. As a thank you, Mr. Bennet invited Mr. Bingley and his family to join him at Longbourn for a meal in the coming week. Mr. Bingley readily accepted the invitation, having decided he needed to secure Jane before Caroline returned from London. She had left only a day or two after Darcy, intending to see how badly her reputation had been affected and what, if anything, Darcy had done as a result of Caroline's actions. The news of the scene she created at the theatre had not yet reached Meryton.

By the time Mr. Bennet left Netherfield, he had garnered quite a bit of information that would no doubt cause a scandal in London were it widely known. When he arrived at Longbourn, he informed his family he would not join them for the evening meal and secluded himself in his study. He composed a long letter to Mr. Darcy, offering to keep silent about what he knew if he agreed to the marriage contract. As he wrote, he also contemplated how to deliver the letter, deciding that when he wrote to Mr. Elliott next, he would arrange a meeting for the three of them in London. At this meeting, he would find a way to hand Darcy his note and then arrange a private meeting. If all went well, he would gain Darcy's approval for the marriage and begin moving forward with his plans.

That Darcy already knew Elizabeth did concern Bennet somewhat, and he wondered if that gentleman realised the lady he conveyed to London was actually Elizabeth Tomlinson. If he did not, it was all the better for Bennet. He momentarily wondered if he were being played for a fool, but since he had become so used to thinking himself more intelligent than everyone else, he decided that it was unlikely these men were deceiving him.

* * *

Darcy requested Mr. Elliott to leave him in Cheapside so he could tell the Gardiners and Elizabeth about their visit to Longbourn. The Gardiners were unsurprised by Mr. Bennet's attempts to delay the matter and would let both trustees know if they received word of his plan to visit. They anticipated Bennet would require some time to get his story straight, but they could not conceive of how he expected to convince them that he had acted properly, and they fully intended to catch him in his lies.

While he was at the Gardiners, Darcy was able to ask for a few moments to speak to Elizabeth privately. After she confessed her feelings for him at the theatre, Darcy was nearly desperate to finally propose to her. Aside from Darcy's desire to marry her for personal reasons, Mr. Elliott agreed with Darcy that marrying Elizabeth quickly was the best way to protect her and prevent any further attempts from either Collins or Bennet to claim her inheritance.

He had initially eschewed the idea of an elopement, but as matters progressed, it seemed a more viable option. However, once he was alone with her, words briefly seemed to fail him. For several long moments, he merely remained staring at Elizabeth as he sat beside her. Seeing the confusion in her eyes forced him to finally act.

Standing, he paced away and blew out a deep breath to regain his composure. He approached Elizabeth and knelt beside her, gently lifting her hands from where they rested on her lap. He brought both hands to his lips, kissing each tenderly. Gazing deeply into her eyes, he began, "I declared my love for you in this same room days ago, and you have now expressed the same feelings for me. Now, I ask you, Elizabeth, will you be my wife? With each day I spend in your presence, my love for you deepens, and I can no longer envision my life without you. I want to be the one you run to when you feel afraid and the one you can always trust."

She smiled tenderly and reached her free hand to caress his cheek. "Yes, Mr. Darcy. I fall more in love with you every time I see you and long to be your wife. I will be thrilled to marry you."

"Call me William," he whispered, nuzzling her hand where it lay on his cheek. After a moment, he hesitantly asked: "May I kiss you?"

She nodded her agreement, and slowly, briefly, his lips caressed hers. He leaned back a moment and, seeing her eyes still closed and the soft smile on her lips, leaned in and kissed her again, a little more firmly and longer than the last. When Elizabeth sighed, he retreated and brought her hand to his lips once more.

"That was lovely," she whispered.

"There is one other matter, my dear," he said, his forehead pressed to hers as he attempted to slow his racing heart. "There is still the question of permission since you are underage. As I told you before, your grandfather's solicitor does not believe Mr. Bennet is your legal guardian, and he has filed a petition to appoint Mr. Elliott. Once he is appointed, Mr. Elliott can approve our marriage, and we can marry anywhere at any time by special licence. My uncle has graciously taken on the responsibility of obtaining one for us. If we are fortunate enough to do so, we may marry at Pemberley; at least, if that is acceptable to you.

"Unfortunately, we do not know when the licence will be issued nor how long it will take the court to act on Mr. Elliott's petition. Until both events occur, your situation remains precarious. Neither Mr. Elliott nor I wish you to remain in London because, despite the security we have arranged for you, you are vulnerable to Mr. Bennet's plotting. Although we know he is not your guardian, the rest of the world does not. Indeed, it is possible he does not even know. Should he find you here and attempt to force you to leave with him, it is doubtful anyone other than the men we have engaged to protect you will intercede on your behalf. And there is the possibility that Mr. Bennet would attempt to have them arrested for interfering with his rights.

"Mr. Elliott believes we should make for Scotland and marry before Mr. Bennet arrives. He feels that is the best way to protect you. Although it is likely the safest thing to do, I disagree that we must hie to Scotland to marry immediately. You should be safe if you are far away from London and Mr. Bennet does not know where you are. We can make our way north and wait at Pemberley for several days. If the stars align in our favour, we can marry at Pemberley, though if it is delayed or becomes necessary, we can still marry in Scotland. When we return to London after our marriage, we can end all of Mr. Bennet's efforts to marry you to Collins and begin suing him for the funds he stole."

"Is that necessary? Suing Mr. Bennet, I mean."

"Yes and no," Darcy answered with a sigh. "We do not need the money, but he should not be able to get away with what he did. He has stolen thousands of pounds from you, dearest. Should he not be made to pay for at least a portion of that?"

"What about my cousins? What will this do to them?"

Darcy moved from where he knelt on the floor to the seat beside her. "That remains to be seen. Perhaps we can assist them by investing whatever you recover to give them each a small dowry."

Elizabeth nodded her agreement, then gave him a teasing look. "So, when do you suggest we leave for the border?"

"Are you truly willing to elope with me? We can take my sister and my cousin along as chaperones, that is, if Fitzwilliam can obtain leave. Otherwise, I will see what else we might be able to arrange," he replied.

Elizabeth groaned. "Why must this be so complicated? Could we not abscond tonight and take a ship directly to Scotland? Then, after we are wed, we can go directly to Pemberley and pretend the rest of the world does not exist."

He laughed. "I would like nothing better than to do that, dearest. However, it is November, and I am uncertain about the weather travelling so far north."

"Come," he said, standing and bringing Elizabeth with him, "let us find your aunt and uncle and make definite plans. We can leave tomorrow afternoon after we discuss matters with the solicitor."

Mr. and Mrs. Gardiner did not favour an elopement but suggested that if the couple travelled to Pemberley along with Georgiana, they could begin having the banns read. A common licence might also be an option if Lord Matlock did not arrive in time.

Regardless of whatever else might transpire, the couple could be married before Christmas, and both the Matlocks and the Gardiners could travel to Derbyshire ahead of the wedding. Aside from the fact that reading the banns would require they be read in Longbourn parish in addition to Darcy's parish, Darcy reminded them that Elizabeth was underage and they required the consent of her guardian to marry in England, so Scotland was their only option until the court appointed Mr. Elliott to that role.

Once again, it was suggested that Lord Matlock take over for Darcy as trustee, and with that in mind, Darcy decided to go early the next day to Matlock House to speak to his uncle about transferring the trusteeship to him. While Gardiner could have assumed this role, Mr. Elliott believed that having a peer like Matlock would more effectively address the complex circumstances.

Chapter 17

Darcy had no difficulty obtaining his uncle's agreement in light of Miss Tomlinson's significant holdings. He accompanied Darcy to Mr. Tomlinson's solicitor's office, where they met with Mr. Elliott.

"Now, what is this about an elopement?" Matlock demanded, after signing the necessary papers that made him Miss Tomlinson's second trustee. "As I understand it, once Mr. Elliott and I approve the match, the lady and my nephew might wed immediately or as soon as a licence can be obtained."

The solicitor spoke up. "Miss Tomlinson is underage, my Lord, and until she reaches her majority in August, she must have her guardian's consent to marry since her parents are no longer living. According to the courts, a more trustee cannot provide such consent. However, Alexander Tomlinson's will stipulated that the trustees must approve the match for the inheritance to be turned over fully. Having said that, I must bring another matter to your attention, gentlemen." At the earl's nod, he continued. "We have confirmed that Mr. Bennet was never Miss Tomlinson's guardian. In his will, Alexander Tomlinson appointed George Darcy, but no alternate was named, so when Mr. Darcy passed away, Miss Tomlinson no longer had a legal guardian."

All of the gentlemen eyed the solicitor warily, but it was Darcy who finally spoke. "So what does that mean exactly?"

"As you know, Mr. Elliott petitioned the Chancery Court to be appointed in George Darcy's place. I am happy to report that his petition was granted yesterday afternoon. That means Mr. Elliott can consent to Miss Tomlinson's marriage, and it will not be necessary for you to marry in Scotland.

"Will Mr. Bennet need to be notified of any of this?" the earl asked.

"No, he is not mentioned in either Mr. Tomlinson's will or the trust regarding Miss Tomlinson's care. He has no legal right to any information concerning her." the solicitor answered.

"But will he have any recourse?" the earl again asked.

The solicitor thought for only a moment before replying. "No. If he learns about it and files an objection with the court, he will probably claim he has acted on her behalf since her grandfather passed away, and there are no grounds to change guardianship at this point. Please permit me to assure you that he is unlikely to succeed in this attempt. You have accumulated evidence that Mr. Bennet has misused Miss Tomlinson's funds, neglected her care, and misrepresented his actions to the trustees. With the earl's backing, I believe it will be a simple enough matter for the court to dismiss any such claims.

"Moreover, any objection Mr. Bennet might make will be too late to prevent the marriage from occurring with Mr. Elliott's consent, especially if he does not know Miss Tomlinson's location. However, I still recommend that Mr. Darcy and Miss Tomlinson marry as soon as possible to ensure Mr. Bennet cannot interfere with their plans. I also strongly advise the removal of Miss Tomlinson immediately from London, particularly from the Gardiners' home before Mr. Bennet arrives in Town."

"What about Bennet's contract with Mr. Collins?" Darcy asked. "He cannot, of course, actually exchange Longbourn for Briarwood, but since he signed a marriage contract with Mr. Collins, does that obligate Elizabeth in any way?"

"No. The contract is not valid. It violates Mr. Tomlinson's will, and, in any event, since Mr. Bennet is not Miss Tomlinson's guardian. Therefore, any contract he signed would be null and void as he had no authority to act on her behalf. Since the court has appointed Mr. Elliott, he is the only one who can consent to Miss Tomlinson marrying."

Mr. Elliott spoke then. "I think we can all agree that Miss Tomlinson's safety is a concern, and ending Mr. Bennet's involvement is of utmost importance."

"With your permission, once they are married, I will prepare a letter informing Mr. Bennet of what has occurred and notifying him of our intention to pursue him for the illegal conversion of Miss Tomlinson's funds," the solicitor offered.

Darcy thanked the man. "You have given us excellent news. We were planning to depart London within the next day or two, but both Elizabeth and I prefer to marry in England to avoid any possibility of a scandal."

Turning to Lord Matlock, Mr. Elliott asked, "What is the status of the special licence?"

"I have arranged for it to be issued and hope to have it by Monday. If it is delivered after you and Elizabeth depart for Pemberley, I will bring it to you myself so I can attend the wedding."

"Elizabeth will be very pleased. And so will my sister! I had better let her know to begin planning the wedding breakfast — discretely, of course."

After a few more questions, the gentlemen began to leave the office to head in their separate directions with plans to meet again at Darcy House that night for dinner.

"I heard from my investigator last night," Gardiner said as he and Elliott made their way to the latter's carriage, which would take them toward Cheapside. "As you know, I asked him to learn more about Mr. Collins. Apparently, Collins has spent quite a bit of time lately with a solicitor who is advising him and supposedly helping him make plans for when he acquires Briarwood. However, Collins is being duped. My man followed this individual and learned he is not a solicitor. We knew Collins to be a fool and easily led, and this has proven true since it appears this fellow is attempting to swindle Collins."

"Do you know the pretender's name?"

"Yes, his surname is Wickham, and he claims a connexion to the Darcys. He is not particularly careful with what he says, especially when he is in his cups, and he claims George Darcy was his godfather. His father was

Pemberley's steward before he passed, and the elder Darcy provided this man's son with an education."

"Wickham, you say? I vaguely recall him. Mayhap George Darcy mentioned him a time or two. You say he is not a solicitor but is merely pretending to be one?"

"Yes, and he has run up substantial debts in the area on the basis that he will come into an inheritance soon that will enable him to pay them all — not only with the merchants but debts of honour from gambling as well."

Elliott considered this for a moment. "We should keep an eye on him. Has he run up enough yet to be thrown into debtors' prison?"

"I believe so. His debt to the local merchants is already more than twenty pounds, and he has only been there a short time. I do not know about his debts of honour, but that is someone else's concern — I am less concerned if someone with a penchant for gambling is not paid. But the merchants he owes could be ruined if he never pays those bills."

"I will send a note to the magistrate in the area asking him to purchase Wickham's debt on my behalf and then, when he cannot pay, to throw him into the local gaol. Once we have this situation with Bennet handled, we can turn our attention to him to see if we can determine his intentions. We do not need one more person attempting to take advantage of the poor girl. He can remain in the gaol until after the new year. I will be in no hurry to deal with someone like him." Elliott had no time to worry about someone so inconsequential as he dealt with what he believed were more weighty matters.

"This claim that he is awaiting an inheritance is troubling. Is he intending to lay some claim to the Tomlinson estate? Surely he has some nefarious plot in mind," Elliott replied. "I prefer to have him safely locked up where we can deal with him in our own time rather than running free to wreak havoc."

"That is probably for the best. If there is a connexion to the Darcys, we should likely mention it over dinner. Perhaps Darcy will know how to best deal with the man," Gardiner said before the two went their separate ways.

In Hertfordshire, things were as Elizabeth's supporters suspected. Almost as soon as Bennet returned to his home from visiting with Mr. Bingley, he wrote a letter to Mr. Collins informing him of the potential delay in the marriage plans. He asked the gentleman to continue with his planned visit at Christmas, as he had several thoughts about ensuring that the marriage happened sooner than the trustees believed it would.

Bennet informed his wife that Bingley would be dining with them that evening, encouraging her to push their eldest, Jane, toward their guest. "I believe he is interested in our girl, and surely, once he realises Jane will inherit Longbourn, he will be even more interested in her. There may be a delay in the wedding, but I hope that by telling all and sundry of Lizzy's engagement to Collins, I will be able to force Mr. Elliott and Mr. Darcy to agree to the match far more willingly," Bennet said to his wife.

"Mr. Darcy?" she asked, suddenly concerned. "What has he to do with Lizzy?"

Bennet scowled. "I did not realise when he offered to convey Lizzy to London that he is her second trustee. I have only dealt with Elliott all these years and had forgotten the name of the second gentleman. This Darcy is the son of the original trustee, as the elder Mr. Darcy died some years ago. I suppose I was informed, but I do not remember, not that it matters. What do you know of Mr. Darcy?"

Mrs. Bennet shook her head. "He is very wealthy, far more so than Mr. Bingley, but he was haughty and proud and never spoke much to anyone outside his party. I only saw him twice, and he never danced a single dance, not even with Mr. Bingley's sisters. I found it odd, and then he departed suddenly. Mr. Bingley never mentioned his departure, and Miss Bingley left for London shortly after. Mrs. Hurst would not give a reason but seemed to imply that Miss Bingley had acted in a way that she disapproved of."

"Or their guest did," Bennet replied darkly before sharing a portion of Bingley's story about his friend's behaviour.

"And you allowed Lizzy to travel with that man? What if he compromised her? All of our plans would be for nought. If she were forced to marry Mr. Darcy, then Mr. Collins would still take control of this estate instead of Lizzy's. Perhaps we could persuade him to marry Mary instead," Mrs. Bennet said in a rush of words. A few months ago, after receiving a letter from Mr. Collins, Mr. Bennet conceived a plan to exchange Mr. Collins's interest in Longbourn for Elizabeth's estate. To appease Mrs. Bennet's incessant complaints, he shared this plan with her, and now she was pushing for the marriage to "save her from the hedgerows."

"Mr. Darcy will not marry Lizzy, and our plans are still in place. In fact, I have encouraged Collins to visit at Christmas, and we will ensure that Lizzy is forced to marry him. I do not care how he does it, but Collins will compromise Lizzy if I have to lock the two of them in a bedchamber myself," Bennet declared. "I will not let all my careful planning go to waste. I must go to London in a week or two and meet with the trustees. You are to focus on getting Jane married to our neighbour, and I will worry about Lizzy's marriage."

With a huff, Mrs. Bennet departed the study and began scheming.

Jane and Mary were just outside the open study door and had heard everything their parents said. Some of it was unclear, as there had been a mention of Lizzy having her own estate, and there had been talk of trustees. While neither girl was particularly wise in the ways of the world, they knew how poorly Lizzy had been treated by their parents. Jane recalled the stories Elizabeth had told when they met at Longbourn all those years ago, including the surname she claimed and stories of an estate somewhere in the north.

"We need to write to Lizzy," Mary said after a moment.

"Hush," Jane hissed. "Not here." She thought for a moment, pulled her sister into the music room, and shut the door behind her. "Hill packed a few of Lizzy's things and placed them in the carriage with Mr. Darcy when he visited yesterday. Do you think she might know something of the matter?"

"Perhaps," Mary replied quietly. "Do you think she would tell us what she knows?"

"I do not know, but we can ask her. When?"

"Shall we go into the kitchens to see her for a minute? Perhaps she will tell us what has happened?" Mary suggested.

When the two girls found Mrs. Hill, they convinced her of their sincerity and desire to warn Lizzy about what their parents were plotting. That news persuaded Mrs. Hill to share the letter she received yesterday explaining some of what Elizabeth had learned in the last weeks. Jane and Mary were shocked to learn that Lizzy was not the natural child of their uncle as had always been implied but rather the daughter of Mr. Bennet's sister and her husband. Together with Mrs. Hill, they pieced together a small part of what their parents had done.

"We must write to her immediately. I sincerely hope she does not remain in London for long," Jane said.

Chapter 18

Darcy was greatly alarmed when he learned of Wickham's involvement in the matter. "Wickham is a liar, a thief, and a seducer of innocents. I believe it advisable to remove Elizabeth from London at once, sir," Darcy protested when the gentlemen spoke after dinner. "I know him entirely too well to be unconcerned when his name is mentioned in connexion to *anyone* I care about."

"Gentlemen, I suggest we speak to Elizabeth regarding this matter. My niece will not be pleased to be excluded from this conversation. She is not some easily overwrought maiden," Gardiner inserted into the conversation. At this, Darcy flushed slightly and seemed to release some of his frustration. He nodded and began to lead the others from the room.

However, he was halted by his uncle's arm. "We need a plan before we speak to the ladies," he insisted.

"Elizabeth will not respond well to a plan formed without her input. She is not a lady who would allow the men in her life to command her; she is an intelligent woman who is able to consider matters rationally and without excess emotion. Perhaps you would excuse your own wife from such a conversation, but I will not," Darcy stated.

"She is not your wife yet, Darcy," the earl observed.

"But she will be, and I intend to act now as I will then. If you prefer to remain here and discuss it amongst yourselves, you may do so, but I will go and solicit her opinion," he retorted before stalking from the room, followed by his cousin.

Gardiner laughed as he watched the young man depart. "He is quite a young man," he said quietly, causing the earl to nod.

"He is a very good man. I wish my elder son had turned out half as well. He has always been a responsible child and, since inheriting the estate from his father, has only become more so. I confess, his ease with Miss Tomlinson is surprising, especially given the short duration of their acquaintance." With that comment from the earl, the rest of the gentlemen followed Darcy into the parlour, where the ladies waited.

Darcy was already seated next to his intended and the colonel next to Georgiana. The other gentlemen rushed to sit next to their wives though Mr. Elliott, a widower, sat in an armchair between Elizabeth and Gardiner. After a few moments of general conversation, Georgiana was encouraged to depart to the music room so the others might speak of weightier matters.

"Should she not be involved, William?" Elizabeth whispered to her intended.

"No, I will tell her what we discuss later, but there are things that it is best she not hear in company with others just now," Darcy whispered back. "Your uncle just informed me that Wickham is involved, having offered his services to Mr. Collins to 'help' claim your inheritance."

Elizabeth's mouth dropped for a moment into an O. "Is that the man who attempted to elope with your sister?" she whispered back. At Darcy's nod, she looked at him with concern. "What do you think he will do?"

"I would not put it past him to attempt to swindle your uncle's cousin. He is pretending to be a solicitor and knows just enough about the law to be dangerous. That is what we were discussing in my study, but before we make plans, I wish to consult with you. I would like to take you to Pemberley to remove you from any danger."

"Before we wed?" she inquired with an arched eyebrow.

"Would you rather go to Scotland first, dearest?" he teased before becoming more serious. "I am concerned about your safety. I know Wickham too well to doubt he will do something to injure me once he

139

learns I am involved. Right now, he is only hoping to fleece a foolish man out of his future fortune, but when he learns I am involved, he will become vengeful. He will not hesitate to harm you if he thinks it will ultimately harm me." Darcy quietly informed Elizabeth about what they had learned in their meeting at the solicitor's that morning. Some she already knew from her uncle, though some of what was conveyed had been unknown to her.

"Scotland is sounding better and better, William," she said when he finished.

The booming voice of his uncle brought an end to their *tête-à-tête*. "Darcy, I know that you and Wickham have had a falling out, but you were friends in your youth. Do you really believe the man would injure Miss Tomlinson to get back at you?" It was apparent the earl had eavesdropped on their conversation.

"I do," Darcy replied seriously, his tone grave. "Wickham and I have not had a mere 'falling out', Uncle. It was far more serious than that."

Darcy told the company about his experiences with Wickham — excluding the incident with Georgiana — and they gradually agreed that Darcy was correct to worry about him. They were very relieved that Gardiner had already sent a man to Kent to purchase the debts left by Wickham and to use those to imprison the man, at least temporarily, until they could deal with him.

The colonel perked up at this idea; he would enjoy a trip to Kent to "assist" George Wickham in coming to town. The debts paid by Gardiner, combined with those Darcy already held, would put Wickham in Marshaelsea for some time and would likely neutralise any threat he presented.

A half-hour later, it was determined the party would remain in London for a few more days to allow for Elizabeth to be seen by the ton. Several footmen would be hired, at Darcy's insistence, to accompany Elizabeth for her protection. Something gnawed at him that made him insist more than he typically would have done, and Elizabeth acquiesced easily enough.

"I do not like the restrictions placed on me, but my walks would be curtailed in town regardless, and I will allow it for your peace of mind. However, do know that I do not like to have my actions restricted, at least not without cause. I appreciate that you took the time to explain your reasoning to me," Elizabeth told him when they sneaked into the library to steal a few moments together. After exchanging a kiss or two, he expressed his concern for her safety and nearly demanded that she not leave the house without accompaniment.

Darcy held her closely. "Now that I have found you, I cannot stand the thought of losing you, dearest Elizabeth," he whispered before kissing her once again. They were breathless when they parted, and Elizabeth stepped away from his arms.

"I can see how easily a woman can lose her sense of what is proper," she stated breathlessly. "I fear I am in some danger from you, William."

"Danger? From me?" he stammered.

"Yes," she replied seriously. "I lose all sense of decorum when I am in your arms, and I believe you do as well. It is yet uncertain when we will be able to marry, so we will need to take care."

He was abashed by her words. "I apologise, dearest." His eyes were cast down until he heard her melodic laugh.

"It is well, William," she replied. "You have done nothing I did not wish for."

Darcy smiled down at her for a moment, but his expression quickly changed to a frown. "I hate not knowing what lies ahead. I confess I am not certain how I feel about their insistence that we remain in London."

"I know, but we will still be able to see each other while I am here," Elizabeth soothed, stepping forward to place her hand on his arm. "Come, let us join the others. My uncle will want to depart soon."

They returned to the drawing room, where they found the others preparing to leave. "Darcy, we will speak more on the morrow," the earl stated loudly. "My wife has invited your intended for tea — come early so we might talk first."

Reluctantly, Darcy saw his company out and kissed Elizabeth's hand in farewell.

"I will call on you tomorrow morning, dearest," he whispered before releasing her. "Good night."

He watched her carriage depart before returning inside. His cousin waited for him in the study and the two talked until later into the night.

Chapter 19

Darcy arrived at the Gardiner's home the following morning as soon as it was an acceptable hour for a visit. He had slept poorly, imagining all manner of scenarios that would take Elizabeth from him. The more he considered these possibilities, which had become more preposterous the later it grew, the more anxious he became. Finally, he fell into an exhausted sleep and awakened feeling far less rested than he would have wished.

"Are you well?" Elizabeth asked nearly as soon as he entered the Gardiner's drawing room.

He kissed her hand, wishing Mrs. Gardiner could be persuaded to leave the two alone at some point during his visit. "I am better now that I am in your presence. However, Fitzwilliam and I spoke after everyone left last night, and he shares my concern about Wickham being involved in this now, especially since our connexion has become common knowledge. I do not like the idea that others might attempt to take you from me."

She arched her eyebrow at him in question. Darcy continued, "Several people have a vested interest in trying to obtain your estate and inheritance. I worry about what Mr. Bennet may do, especially once he realises all his planning is for nought, and I confess, the fact that Bingley is still at Netherfield adds to that sensation a little. I have spoken to my aunt and uncle about what occurred at Netherfield, but what if Bennet remembers the connexion and speaks to Bingley? Is Bingley sufficiently angry at me to attempt retribution for severing ties between us? And then there is the matter of Wickham and Collins. I worry less about Collins if left to himself, but what if he is manipulated by either Wickham or Bennet to do something to harm you?"

Elizabeth sighed and pressed her hand to his briefly, looking over at her aunt, who was focused on her sewing as she allowed the couple to speak. "I worry, too. I do not wish to be at the Gardiners, where Mr. Bennet expects me to be. I spoke to my uncle in the carriage last night, and he and my aunt have a similar worry but are uncertain where else I could go. I wish we could simply marry, which would alleviate most of our concerns, am I right?"

It was his turn to nod. "It would," he replied simply.

Taking a deep breath, Elizabeth came to a resolution. "I know I have not yet reached my majority, but I believe it is time to take control of my life. Mr. Elliott has signed the marriage settlement, has he not?" At Darcy's nod, she continued. "I will remove to Darcy House today, and instead of waiting a sennight or more, we should depart for Pemberley on Monday. That gives us three days, including the Sabbath, to prepare, and then we have the whole week to travel if necessary. I do not want to wait to marry and would like to be married as soon upon our arrival as possible."

Darcy continued the train of thought. "It may take a few days to obtain a common licence. We can marry as soon as someone arrives from London with the special licence in hand. My uncle was going to do what he could to expedite obtaining it."

"I am not even completely aware of the full amount of my dowry, though I know it is substantial. It seems unnecessary for you to settle more on me."

"It was what my father did for my mother. The funds can be used for any children — our first-born son will inherit Pemberley, and another child, son or daughter, will have Briarwood. The Darcys own two or three additional smaller estates that can be left to any subsequent children. If we have only daughters, they will have substantial dowries of their own, along with an estate, though Pemberley would be inherited by the first son of our eldest daughter, provided he takes the Darcy name."

Talk of children caused Elizabeth to blush profusely, and she did not reply for several minutes. Finally, she managed, "Then I will allow you to do as you see fit, sir."

He glanced over at Mrs. Gardiner before lifting his hand to caress her cheek. "Any children we have will be well provided for, my love, and know that I will include you in all decisions. In fact, once we arrive at Darcy House, I would like to review your settlement with you if you like. You should know what funds you have available, and I promised to speak to you about Briarwood when we left Hertfordshire. We have been so busy with other matters we have not had a chance to do so."

Elizabeth silently agreed with his suggestion. "I would appreciate that, William. I have felt like I have not had much say in how things have gone lately, and Mr. Bennet's attempts to steal my inheritance, not to mention what he has already stolen, have been upsetting." She sighed heavily. "I look forward to having matters permanently settled and that there no longer be this threat hovering over me."

"When will your uncle return home? We ought to inform him of our plans. We can speak to my aunt, uncle, and Mr. Elliott when we meet at Matlock House for tea. My uncle asked me to come early, but I will escort you there if you do not mind."

Mrs. Gardiner interjected into their conversation. "I believe you two have the right of it. This waiting around for Mr. Bennet to arrive troubles me, and I told Edwin so last night. He has received several messages from Kent regarding Mr. Wickham, and he believes that gentleman could be thrown into the gaol within the week. Mr. Elliott has purchased several of the markers Mr. Darcy holds for the man — enough to ensure a long stay in debtors' prison — so they can keep Mr. Darcy's name out of the matter as long as they can. Unfortunately, Mr. Wickham left Kent a sennight ago, and he has not yet returned, so these plans are on hold until he reappears."

She looked at Mr. Darcy meaningfully as she spoke, and he knew this had been done to prevent Wickham from speaking out against either Darcy sibling. With Darcy's permission, Elizabeth had confessed to her aunt the extent of Wickham's actions against the Darcy family the previous night, knowing she would say nothing to injure his sister. He also trusted Mrs. Gardiner to tell her husband what he needed to know about the matter, believing it would also help the Gardiners protect Elizabeth.

"I do wonder if it would not be better to have Elizabeth stay at Matlock House instead." She held up her hand to stop the protest from the couple. "Mr. Darcy, I know that you would like to have Elizabeth housed under your roof for her protection, to be the one to ensure her safety, but you also want her with you, in your home. However, Mr. Bennet knows of your involvement and might attempt to visit your house. He is unaware of Lord Matlock's involvement, and his status as an Earl would do much more to ensure her safety, as my brother would never think to invade the house of a peer."

Darcy frowned even as he nodded. "As much as I do want you in my house, under my protection, Elizabeth, Mrs. Gardiner may be correct. I think my aunt would be willing to house you for a few days, and perhaps we can persuade her to wait to conduct you around town until you might do so as Mrs. Darcy. If we can convince her of the need to remove to Derbyshire quickly, then she will be more likely to convince my uncle of the same."

Mrs. Gardiner excused herself for a few minutes to ask a maid to begin packing Elizabeth's things. This brief time alone gave Darcy the chance he had wanted since he entered the house. "Dearest," he whispered before kissing her, keeping things mostly chaste after their fiery kisses of the previous night.

* * *

Before too much time had passed, Elizabeth's trunk was loaded behind Darcy's carriage, and the three made their way toward Matlock House. Mrs. Gardiner was somewhat self-conscious about intruding on the visit, which had not officially included her. Still, she felt she needed to help convince Lady Matlock to do as she had suggested. Mr. Gardiner had returned home briefly, and he reluctantly agreed with the plans that had been made, as he had received a report from Kent that Wickham had still not returned and had most likely travelled to Hertfordshire to 'investigate' the Bennet family. This report heightened Darcy's reservations about waiting, although he understood that the Sabbath would necessitate them to stay in an inn for an additional day if they departed before Monday. Resigned, he knew that Elizabeth's plan was for the best, though he continued to feel anxious.

Lady Matlock's parlour was empty when their party was announced. "Welcome," she greeted her guests. "Mrs. Gardiner, I realised after you left last night that I had forgotten to extend my invitation to include you. If you had not arrived with your niece, I would have asked Darcy to send his carriage to collect you. I want to speak to you about what our men have planned. Darcy, your uncle is waiting for you in his study."

"Aunt, with Wickham lurking about, we have decided it is best to remove Elizabeth from London as soon as possible. Since it does not make sense to leave before the Sabbath, we will depart for Derbyshire at first light on Monday. However, Elizabeth cannot remain in the Gardiner's home since her uncle would know to find her there. We considered Darcy House, but ..." Here he trailed off to allow Lady Matlock to draw her own conclusion. She did not disappoint.

"Oh, no, she cannot stay there. Even if you were to remove to your club, her reputation would still be questioned if she stayed at your home. No, Miss Tomlinson, you must stay at Matlock House, and if you, Mrs. Gardiner, cannot accompany them to Derbyshire, I will. I know that Georgiana and Mrs. Annesley will also travel with you, Darcy, but my going along will lend further respectability."

Elizabeth agreed with Lady Matlock and graciously accepted the invitation. While Mr. Darcy went to his uncle, Lady Matlock showed Elizabeth and Mrs. Gardiner the room that would house Elizabeth until Monday and assigned a maid to unpack her trunks.

* * *

The conversation in the study was less easy than the one in the drawing room.

"What do you mean you are removing to Pemberley on Monday?" Lord Matlock scowled his displeasure. "You can marry from London once the licence has been obtained. The archbishop implied it would be ready soon, so there is no need to depart."

"I would like to take Elizabeth where I can protect her while Wickham still presents a threat. I do not trust him at all, and Gardiner has been unable to locate him. The investigator believes he may be in Hertfordshire learning what he can about the Bennets to aid Collins in claiming Elizabeth's estate."

Lady Matlock entered the study then. "Malcolm, I will be travelling to Derbyshire along with Darcy. Mrs. Gardiner cannot accompany them, and my presence will lend the group respectability. If they have the licence in hand, so much the better, but I still believe they should marry at Pemberley. If the licence is not ready when we depart, you can follow in a day or two, bringing Mr. Elliott with you."

"You agree with our nephew?" he asked incredulously.

"If you wish her to remain in town to confront her uncle, I am against it. He neglected her for all these years while allowing her aunt to abuse her. Instead of telling the truth about her heritage, they damaged her reputation and allowed their neighbours to believe she was the natural child of her other uncle, knowing all the while that was untrue. They hid the truth of her parentage, and her aunt regularly spoke ill of her in her presence while her uncle hid in his library and ignored the estate. He stole from her and not once gave her what she was entitled to. Now, he is attempting to barter her inheritance for his own security, or that of his wife and daughters, instead of taking steps to provide for them himself. He is indolent, yes, but also manipulative, mean, and not worthy of our notice. I suggest merely having the solicitors serve him with a writ demanding repayment of the funds and letting him scramble. If we are all from London, he will waste his time looking for them, allowing us to get our nephew married. Once that is done, he can do nothing."

Grudgingly, Lord Matlock admitted her plan had merit. He sent a note to the archbishop regarding the licence and, after receiving assurance it should be available Monday afternoon, sent a note to Elliott requesting his attendance as they finalised the plans for travel.

Chapter 20

Charles Bingley was unhappy that Caroline had returned to Netherfield. Louisa and Gilbert Hurst were likewise disgusted with her attitude and behaviour within an hour of her returning, and half of that time had been spent with her refreshing herself from her travel.

His sister was terribly upset that Darcy had her expelled from his box at the theatre and was ranting about the natural-born daughter of a country squire being seen on Darcy's arm. Her brother had tuned her out, knowing that Caroline had done something foolish in Town, making herself *persona non grata*, not just to Darcy, but likely to most of the *ton* as well. Due to her arrival, he had travelled into the village to escape hearing her voice and to spend time with more congenial company.

However, upon his arrival at the tavern, he noticed someone he knew, even if only slightly. Bingley vaguely recalled meeting George Wickham while at Cambridge with Darcy. He knew the two men had fallen out and wondered if Wickham also had a sister who had set her cap for Darcy, though he doubted it.

Vaguely, he recalled that Darcy had seemed to look down on Wickham for indulging in vices that he did not — gambling, drinking, and women, all the pastimes of the wealthy, though Wickham had not been wealthy. Wickham was ... he was the son of Pemberley's steward and old Darcy's godson. Bingley wondered what Wickham might be doing in Hertfordshire and sat beside him.

"George Wickham, is it not? I recall you from our time at Cambridge, I think," Bingley said as he approached the man.

Wickham looked up at him with bleary eyes. "You look familiar, but Cambridge was many years ago. What's your name again?" he slurred in reply.

"Charles Bingley. I believe I met you when I was with Fitzwilliam Darcy."

"Darcy, the ol' prig. Did me wrong ... so nearly 'ad his sister's dowry." He hiccoughed as he seemed to recall himself and shut his mouth rapidly. His near slip seemed to sober him up just a bit. "What d'ya want with me? Friend of Darcy's is no friend of mine."

"Well, Darcy and I ... well, we have had a falling out. My sister wanted to marry him and attempted to compromise him, but Darcy refused to act the gentleman and take her off my hands."

Wickham laughed at that. "Darcy wouldn't ... wouldn't marry a tart who tried to force his hand. Nor would he take advantage, the prude. Teased him ... called him a monk ... and he hated that. He wouldn't know what to do with a woman." He laughed again. "When he marries one of these society misses, I'll cuckold him since the only woman who'll marry him will do so 'cause he's rich."

Bingley laughed at this as well. "My sister claims he's got one on the hook. Quite a beautiful girl, though I can only assume that since my sister spoke so poorly of her appearance. Gossip in Town says she's an heiress, but Caroline says that can't be true since she swears he met the girl here in Meryton when we first arrived. Of course, she has gone to London now, and Caroline thinks she has deceived poor Darcy into marrying her while hiding the truth that she's the natural-born daughter of some nobody."

Wickham perked up slightly at this, sobering even more. "What's the chit's name?"

"Caroline swears she was called Elizabeth Bennet in Meryton but was introduced in Town as Elizabeth Tomlinson. She cannot understand why she has a different name now. Gossip says she and Darcy are courting, but then again, Caroline was pretty much cut from all polite society after Darcy threw her out of his theatre box for daring to approach him."

"Interesting," Wickham murmured to himself. "Say, I was hired by Longbourn's heir to learn all I could about the Bennets. What do you know about the family."

This led to an hour-long conversation when Bingley shared all he knew about the Bennets, their connexions in London, and Darcy.

"So, you intend to marry the eldest Bennet daughter then?" Wickham asked after they had talked at length.

"After Caroline's stunt in Town, she might be the best I can do. Bennet has hinted that he has convinced the heir to break the entail, or at least to surrender his interest in it, which means Jane Bennet would inherit. If I married her, I would eventually gain an estate, though I suppose it would require a significant infusion of cash to bring it up to snuff. I must see how badly Caroline has wrecked things for us in London before proceeding."

Wickham nodded at this and thanked the man for the information. While he had intended to return to Kent in a day or so, he decided his best bet was to make for London on the morrow, as he still had some of Mr. Collins' cash on him. If he were lucky, he would manage to sneak out of the inn without paying his bill, and then he laughed at himself. *No, I should just tell the innkeeper that Bingley agreed to pay my bill. He saw me with him tonight and probably wouldn't even question the matter,* he thought and laughed again. As soon as Bingley departed, he informed the innkeeper of the "agreement" and his intention to depart on the morrow.

* * *

Bennet was at a loss as to how to convince the trustees to release Elizabeth back to his care and sign the marriage contracts. He had spread the rumour of Elizabeth's engagement to Mr. Collins through Meryton, but he wondered if that was enough. If Elizabeth were not in Meryton, the scandal arising from her not honouring the engagement would not injure her, nor would it be enough to force the matter.

His thoughts of blackmailing Darcy fell flat when he realised that the scandal he suggested likely would matter little to Darcy. If his friend Bingley knew of his exploits, it was unlikely they were all that closely held a secret, and would the *ton* condemn a man such as he for refusing to marry the daughter of a tradesman, regardless of her dowry? Such a claim might injure him for a short time, but it would have little impact in the long run.

No, he needed Elizabeth at home, for if he could convince her to agree to marry Mr. Collins, then the trustees would surely not deny her. When the Gardiners came to Longbourn for Christmas, he would do all he could to ensure Mr. Collins compromised her in such a way that would guarantee the trustees would have to give their permission. He had not yet been notified about the change in trusteeship nor that Mr. Elliott was now officially Elizabeth's guardian.

* * *

Upon receiving the first letter from a friend detailing Darcy's alleged courtship of a wealthy heiress, Lady Catherine dismissed it, confident that her nephew would ultimately yield to her long-standing insistence on his marriage to her daughter. Her influence, however, had waned, unbeknownst to her, as her friends were well aware that the proposed arrangement existed only in her imagination. Lord and Lady Matlock had vehemently denied it for years, but Catherine, residing primarily in the countryside, remained oblivious to the diminishing impact of her assertions.

The second letter, unsigned and filled with accusations against the lady Darcy was supposedly courting, fuelled Lady Catherine's ire. The allegations, including scandalous gossip from Meryton about the girl's parentage, stirred her determination to rush to London immediately and confront her nephew for not adhering to his mother's wishes.

Her daughter, Anne, held a vastly different perspective on the matter. Uninterested in marrying her cousin or residing at Pemberley, Anne detested children, disliked travel, had no penchant for reading, and frankly, did not care much for her cousin. Fitzwilliam amused her to some extent, but Darcy did not, and Anne was resolved to go to great lengths to thwart her mother's attempts at arranging the match.

Aware of Darcy's intentions through letters smuggled by her companion from her cousin Jonathan Fitzwilliam, Anne was ready to thwart Lady Catherine's plans. Thus, when Lady Catherine declared her intent to drag Anne to London on a Friday afternoon to coerce Darcy into marriage, Anne employed her customary method of getting her way.

"Mother, I implore you to reconsider. I am too unwell to travel such a distance," Anne pleaded weakly, feigning a sudden bout of nausea.

Her companion, Mrs. Jenkinson, responded calmly, "Miss Anne, I believe a small dose of the tonic will alleviate your discomfort and ensure you are fit for the journey in due time." This was not the first time the two had planned such an act, and both women knew how to induce spontaneous bouts of vomiting.

With that, Anne reluctantly accepted the tonic, knowing the ensuing bout of illness would successfully disrupt her mother's plans.

As the effects of the tonic took hold, Lady Catherine's frustration became evident. "Anne, this is sheer obstinacy on your part! We will leave for London today, and you will marry your cousin as soon as might be arranged."

Anne managed a feeble protest, "Mother, please, I am not well. I cannot endure such a journey today."

Lady Catherine continued to insist, "Nonsense! You will accompany me, and we shall end the boy's delays. You will be Mistress of Pemberley."

Adding weight to Anne's objections, Mrs. Jenkinson intervened, "Lady Catherine, perhaps it would be best to allow Miss Anne some rest. A hasty journey in her condition may exacerbate her indisposition. You know she is often unwell."

After another bout of Anne being ill, accompanied by her nearly swooning, Lady Catherine was convinced to delay their departure for another day or two.

From the letter Anne received that very morning, she knew that were they to delay her mother from departing until Monday, Darcy would have departed London for Pemberley. Lord Matlock would still be in Town, and he should be able to dissuade Lady Catherine from pursuing the matter further.

Chapter 21

Together with Mary, Jane wrote a letter to tell her cousin what they had overheard their parents say about the marriage arranged between Elizabeth and the heir to Longbourn.

Dear Lizzy,

Mary and I have overheard our parents discussing a matter that has left us bewildered and uneasy. I'm uncertain how much of this you are already aware of, but it appears our father has orchestrated a marriage arrangement between you and his cousin, the heir of Longbourn. Somehow, and I cannot fathom the details, they have convinced Mr. Collins to relinquish his rights to Longbourn in favour of accepting your estate. The specifics of this are unclear to us, especially since we were unaware you possessed an estate. However, they plan to force the issue when you return at Christmas with our Uncle and Aunt Gardiner, when Mr. Collins is meant to compromise you. We strongly advise against your return, although we are unsure of where else you might find refuge. Perhaps our aunt and uncle could assist you in some way.

Since your departure, Longbourn has been changed. Mama and Papa frequently engage in discussions, particularly in Papa's study, revolving around various matters, many of which seem to concern you. Despite our attempts to eavesdrop whenever possible, much of what they say remains incomprehensible. While we believe it is in your best interest not to return to Longbourn if possible, I do hope that, someday, our paths may cross again. They are also spreading rumours about your engagement throughout the town, with Mr. Collins being praised for his willingness to accept you as a bride. However, contrary to what Mama and Papa have allowed to circulate, it appears they know you are not our uncle's natural child. Instead, they assert that you are the legitimate heir of an estate somewhere, the daughter of Papa's sister, though they do not plan to disclose this information until the matter with Mr. Collins is settled.

If you encounter Mr. Darcy while in London, please inform him that his friend — assuming their friendship remains intact, given what we have heard — is spreading stories about him in Meryton. Mr. Bingley is accusing Mr. Darcy of ruining his sister and others, then refusing to marry her. These tales portray him as a rake of the worst kind, although Mr. and Mrs. Hurst deny everything, asserting that Mr. Bingley is merely retaliating against his friend for not adhering to the Bingleys' plan for him. It is indeed a peculiar situation.

Papa has also mentioned Bingley's story, albeit without some of the embellishments circulating in town. I know Papa visited Netherfield not long after Mr. Darcy and another gentleman visited nearly a week ago, a time frame coinciding with the beginning of these stories.

Miss Bingley has returned to Netherfield, but she isolates herself and refuses to meet with anyone. I dare say the rumours her brother has spread about her have only intensified her reluctance. While Mama still harbours hope of my marrying Mr. Bingley, I have started to question the wisdom of such an alliance. If Mama attempts to coerce the matter, I believe I could find a way to journey to London, as Uncle Gardiner will not force me into a marriage against my will.

I earnestly hope the information our parents have shared about your inheritance is accurate. When you finally have the opportunity to visit your estate, would you consider extending an invitation for us to join *you? We would be devastated if you were to return only to be forced into a marriage with Mr. Collins. He visited for a fortnight, and his presence was insufferable. He rarely bathes and emits a foul odour; you would not find happiness in a union with him, Lizzy.*

Regrettably, I must advise against writing back to us unless you can disguise it in some way. Perhaps Charlotte could be persuaded to convey a letter or two if you include one in a letter to her. Writing directly to Mary or me would likely result in our parents intercepting the correspondence.

Be mindful, Lizzy, and may you find the strength to navigate these challenging circumstances.

We love you and hope you are well,

Your cousins,

Jane and Mary

This letter arrived at Gracechurch Street on Friday while Elizabeth and Mrs. Gardiner were having tea with Lady Matlock. Mrs. Gardiner noticed it when she returned home after visiting and sent it with a messenger to Matlock House.

Elizabeth received it just after Darcy arrived back at Matlock House. He had returned home for a short time after Mrs. Gardiner left to begin making the arrangements for his party to depart on Monday and to ensure that the guards Fitzwilliam had found knew to find Elizabeth at his uncle's home.

He returned an hour or so later, accompanied by three large men who were to act as footmen. However, their primary task was to protect Elizabeth from harm. These men accompanied Darcy into the sitting room where Elizabeth and Lady Matlock sat discussing the letter that had just arrived. After the introductions were made, one of the men went to sit outside the room while the other two retreated to the room assigned to them so they could rest and plan.

After the men departed, Darcy came to sit next to his fiancèe, accepting the letter she handed him. "What's this?"

"My cousins, Jane and Mary, have written to warn me of what they have overheard in Longbourn and Meryton. We already knew much of what my aunt and uncle have plotted, or at least suspected, but the third paragraph concerns you and your former friend." Elizabeth paused as she allowed him to read the letter.

"Blast it all! I am astonished that Bingley would speak of what occurred at Netherfield, nor can I understand his purpose in speaking ill of me." He stood and paced as he considered why his former friend might speak in such a way about him. "Your uncle likely visited him after he realised I had stayed at Netherfield for a time, and Bingley tried to make me out to be a rake and a cad to justify why I had left. Damn him! I never considered him such a fool before, but he is obviously much more of one than I ever dreamed."

"Calm yourself, William." Elizabeth stood and moved to where he paced, laying her hand on his arm to force him to stop.

"I apologise, Elizabeth. I am angry that my friend, my former friend, could spread such lies, especially when I have remained silent about his sister's efforts to compromise me. Even if they never reach London, I cannot understand his purpose in speaking so."

"Uncle likely encouraged him to speak ill of you as he sought ways to discredit you. Mr. Bingley, too, likely wanted to hurt you, though perhaps he was merely describing himself as he spoke of you. *You* once spoke of your former friend as something of a cad with women, though he never went so far as to ruin one."

Darcy took a deep breath as he continued to calm himself. "You are right. It is the kind of thing Bingley would do — blaming someone else for what he has done; it is likely he elaborated to make matters seem worse than they were.'"

"Miss Bingley's reputation in London is quite ruined after that night at the theatre, Darcy. I cannot imagine her brother's words would be believed, as your honourable reputation is well known. Everyone knows she has been after you for some time, so anything she or her brother say would be perceived as anger at your failure to comply with their ridiculous plans."

Lady Matlock moved to stand near her nephew and his intended. "There are too many other things to worry about right now. Does my husband or Mr. Elliott know when to expect Bennet to come to town?"

"Elliott was to write to Bennet today to ask him to come one day next week to meet. However, I have sent a note asking him to wait as I think it is better to delay bringing him to London until we are wed."

"Did Mr. Elliott agree to the delay?" Elizabeth asked.

"I am waiting for his reply. My butler knows to forward any response here since I did not want to be parted from you while we waited. I brought the settlement to review with you, as promised, along with the books from Briarwood."

Darcy then asked permission to speak privately with Elizabeth, and Lady Matlock directed them to the library, where they could use tables to spread out the papers. The discussion that followed was lively as they debated several points within, though Elizabeth could find little fault with it. She was impressed when she learned the extent of her dowry, which had begun at twenty thousand pounds but had grown to nearly fifty thousand pounds invested in the funds. The income earned from Briarwood had also been invested over the years, and that account had nearly seventy thousand pounds in it.

"Gracious!" Elizabeth exclaimed. "I cannot even fathom such amounts. Had Mr. and Mrs. Bennet treated me differently, I would have easily shared my wealth with them and even ensured Mrs. Bennet had a home if her husband passed away before her. I hope I can invite Jane and Mary, at least, to visit us, though I wonder if their parents will allow them once they learn we have defied them."

"It is possible, but we will do what we can for them. Will you write them in reply?"

"Mrs. Bennet will likely read any letter from me, so I must be careful not to reveal our plans. I will send a brief note thanking them for writing and letting them know I am well, but without providing any details. Hopefully, they will understand my message. I have not written to Charlotte because I do not want her to be put in a position to have to lie should someone ask her what she knows about me. I must arrange for Aunt Gardiner to forward her letters if she writes to me. Though, I suppose I will not have to maintain my secrecy for much longer."

"That is true," he said, smiling at her as he brought her hand to his lips for a kiss. "Soon, you will be Mrs. Darcy, and we will let the whole world know it."

* * *

Wickham arrived in London and visited his paramour, Mrs. Edith Younge. After their failed attempt to abscond with Georgiana Darcy, they had not seen each other since their departure from Ramsgate that summer.

"This new chit, Elizabeth Tomlinson, is worth substantially more, at least a twenty-thousand-pound dowry plus an estate in the north. Not to mention, my seducing her would enable me to get back at Darcy for this summer. He imagines himself in love with the trollop," Wickham told her as he attempted to persuade her of his plan.

"George, you cannot possibly seek to cross Darcy again. You should worry about what he will do if he finds you sniffing around someone he cares about." Mrs. Younge was not willing to encounter Mr. Darcy again. She knew he was a gentleman and he would not harm a woman, but she had never seen a man as angry as Mr. Darcy after he learned of the plot against his sister. She truly believed he would kill George if he laid a finger on the woman Mr. Darcy was courting.

"Darcy will never harm me, as I am his father's godson. In all the years I have known him, he has never once acted against me, regardless of the provocation. He will surely not do anything to me now, knowing I can harm his sister's reputation."

"You are a fool, George, if you think that."

"Fine, Edi, if you will not help me, I will simply not share what I gain with you. If you lend me twenty pounds, I can hire some boys to help me keep watch on Darcy's house. Also, let me stay with you for a few days …"

She sighed heavily. "I can spare ten pounds for you, George, but I expect to be repaid soon. And you can sleep in the mews."

"Surely, Edi, you cannot expect me to sleep outside. Let me into your bed, dearest. You know you want me to warm you at night."

Another twenty minutes won Mrs. Younge's agreement to all he asked. He had the coins in his pocket and recruited a few boys to watch Darcy to see if he would lead Wickham to his heiress. While the boys did their work, he took the remaining funds and went in search of a drink and a card game.

Chapter 22

Unfortunately for Wickham, for two days, the urchins he hired to watch Darcy's house had little to report. It appeared that Darcy left his home each morning to travel to his uncle's house, where he often stayed until dinner. On Sunday morning, Wickham caught a glimpse of Georgiana leaving with Darcy to go to church but missed seeing Elizabeth return with them to Matlock House after the service.

Later that day, however, he finally saw Darcy walk out with a woman toward Hyde Park, and she was definitely not his sister. Wickham had heard much from Mr. Collins on the beauty of his bride, though neither man had ever seen her. Mr. Collins assumed she was much like Jane Bennet in appearance and created an image of her in his mind, which he shared with his "solicitor".

Mr. Collins could not have been more wrong. Not about her beauty, as she was quite lovely, but not the statuesque blonde he expected. Instead, she had dark hair that clearly was struggling to remain pinned. She was shorter than Darcy, not even reaching his chin, though that was not surprising as Darcy was taller than most men. She was pretty but not classically beautiful, and, for a moment, he wondered what Darcy saw in her. Then she laughed. And then Darcy laughed … in public.

More than anything else, that told Wickham of the connexion between the two. It also would make them harder to separate, though that might work to Wickham's benefit. Perhaps he could persuade Darcy to pay a ransom for her, enabling Wickham to still live as he desired without saddling himself with a wife. The more he thought about it, the more the idea of an immediate ransom payment appealed to Wickham instead of having to deal with that fool Collins for years.

While he was contemplating this, he failed to notice the two rather large men who followed the couple, and he also failed to notice *them* notice *him* staring at Darcy and his intended.

Wickham departed the park and spoke to a few of the boys he had paid to keep an eye on Darcy. He pointed out Elizabeth to them and told them to report her comings and goings to him as well. He paid them a few more coins but not nearly as many as the man dressed in livery paid them a little later. With the promise of more coins, the boys easily informed the footman all they knew about the man: his current residence and the elements of his plan Wickham had inadvertently revealed. The footman was rather pleased with what the few coins had enabled him to learn.

Darcy, however, was decidedly not pleased. When they returned from their walk, he was dismayed to learn that Wickham had been there watching them. What the footman revealed displeased him even more: "It seems the gent was considering a few different options, including attempting to force the lass to marry him to ruining her outright. It seems he's settled on kidnapping her for a ransom. He saw for himself you care for her, and the fool didn't bother to tell the lads he hired to keep silent. The coins I gave them made them tell all they knew. He told the boys to keep an eye on the house another day or two, but as you'll be leaving in the morning, I think we'll be able to give him the slip."

Darcy frowned. "Wickham is not one to rise early, and his 'informants' will scarcely be able to follow us. We will need to ensure they do not see us arranging to leave — unless you can give the boys false information to report to throw him off."

The guard smiled at the thought. "I think it might work. We can have them report you are headed south or not even mention that you have left at all. Unless Wickham comes himself to check on things, we can have them report the same information they have been, so he will not know you even left London."

"Do you have enough coins? I will tell my butler to have plenty available for your use, although I suppose that means you will need to remain behind."

Once Darcy had matters settled to his satisfaction, he found Elizabeth and told her what he had learned. She was aghast at the thought that they had been watched while they were in the park but thought the deception a good plan.

"You said he has always been rather lazy; well, we will be able to use that to our advantage. He will keep wasting his coins, giving them to these boys who are only too ready to deceive him. His own sins will come back on him, and he will receive a little bit of repayment for the pain he has caused you in the past."

He smiled gently at her. "I love how you take my anger and turn it around into a much more pleasant emotion. I was furious when I came in here, but in only a few minutes, you have changed it into amusement. Will you always do that, my darling?"

She smiled back impishly. "I certainly hope so, William. Is it not the wife's responsibility to ease her husband's burdens? I suppose this is one way I will ease yours."

Looking around to ensure they were alone, Darcy leaned down and kissed his soon-to-be wife. "I look forward to having you with me always. Just your presence in the room makes me happy, and I feel far less burdened than I did before I met you. I cannot wait to have you to myself at Pemberley."

He watched her cheeks turn pink, and he laughed. "I love you, dearest Elizabeth … and I dearly love making you blush." He laughed again when the colour on her cheeks became even more pronounced.

* * *

The following morning, Darcy, Elizabeth, Georgiana, and Lady Matlock boarded one of Darcy's large travelling coaches to begin their journey to Pemberley. They took a different route out of London than usual, travelling further west from the start to avoid Hertfordshire and the route Bennet might take should he arrive in London sooner. A second carriage conveying their luggage and servants followed behind, but that was unobserved by any of those watching.

On Saturday, Mr. Elliott posted a letter to Mr. Bennet claiming a need to delay their meeting until mid-December. This gave them several weeks to get Elizabeth married to Darcy and allow the couple to take a short honeymoon before they had to return to London to deal with her uncle's deceit and attempts at manipulation. It was unlikely that Mr. Bennet had received or read the letter yet, though with all the possible threats to Darcy and Elizabeth's marriage, they were determined to take any precautions necessary to ensure they would not encounter anyone who might delay them.

This proved wise as Mr. Bennet received the letter early Monday morning and read it immediately instead of waiting to deal with it later, as was his usual practice. He was again angered at Elliott's dictating terms and called for his horse to be saddled immediately. Mr. Bennet rode to Netherfield to ask for Bingley's help, but when Bingley refused to do more than provide the address to Darcy's townhouse, he returned home, ordered his carriage and readied for the trip to London.

"Mr. Bennet! Mr. Bennet! Whatever is the matter?" Mrs. Bennet shrieked when her husband had come into the house bellowing orders for Mr. Hill, their butler, who also served as Mr. Bennet's man when needed, to pack a bag for a short stay in London.

"I am going to London to retrieve Elizabeth as I am tired of waiting for her trustees to act. I will send a letter to Collins telling him to meet me there, and we will take that girl to Scotland and make the two marry. If I must, I will lock them together in an inn if that is what it takes to get her married to the fool."

Then, ignoring his wife, he sat at his desk and quickly composed a letter ordering his heir to meet him in London as soon as possible, giving his brother's address. He ordered a boy from the kitchen to take the letter to Meryton and send it by express. Everyone in the house knew what the master intended, and while many were reluctant to do so, they also knew they could not refuse to carry out his orders. They were uncertain if Mr. Bennet would be able to carry out his plans, and prayed the Gardiners had known and were able to get Miss Lizzy to safety.

Mrs. Hill caught the boy's eye as he ran to the kitchen on his way to Meryton. There, the housekeeper pressed a small note addressed to the Gardiners and some coins into his hand. "Have the express rider go to London first and then on to Kent. It will delay Mr. Collins receiving it by at least a day, and perhaps the advance warning will allow the Gardiners to secret Miss Lizzy away," she whispered.

The boy nodded, then ran to the inn in Meryton, where he sent both letters with the same rider, giving him the order to hurry to London as quickly as he could, then to make his way to Kent far more slowly.

* * *

Darcy's carriage was well on the way toward Oxford, where they would turn north to head to Derbyshire. While it was not, perhaps, as fast a route to Pemberley as taking the Great North Road, they were well away from Hertfordshire and any places Mr. Bennet might stop. By nightfall, they were on the outskirts of Oxford and stopped at an inn for the night. The second carriage had travelled ahead at the last stop to arrange for rooms that night so they would be ready when the travellers arrived.

It was a merry party that ate a late meal and then retired to their bedchambers. Elizabeth and Georgiana were sharing one room, and one of their guards remained alert outside their room all night.

They continued that way for three more days and arrived at Pemberley late on Thursday. Elizabeth was astonished by her first view of the estate and immediately fell in love. When they arrived in the courtyard and began to disembark, a flash of memory suddenly passed through her mind.

"I remember being here once before, William. It is a faint memory, but I recall playing on the grounds, I believe. Maybe more about the estate will come back to me, although you mentioned our stay was brief; is that not correct?"

"You were here for, I think, a fortnight or so. It was just a few months after Georgiana was born, and we celebrated my birthday and yours with fireworks, the same as we had done the previous year at Briarwood. You were five, and I was twelve, and it was probably the last birthday I remember with fondness. Mother was ill, but she still did all she could to make it a happy time for us all. I am glad you remember, dearest."

"It already feels like home. I am so looking forward to exploring further. Thank you for bringing me here," she said, then forgot propriety for a moment and gave her intended an enormous hug. Darcy smiled broadly, much to the astonishment of his gathered staff.

Chapter 23

Lord Matlock arrived at Pemberley a little later that evening, having departed London early Tuesday morning. He had taken a more direct route and had travelled more quickly. A note was sent to the vicar at Kympton asking him to come to Pemberley the next morning.

"Are you content with this plan, dearest, a hasty wedding without any of your family around?" Darcy asked his bride before they retired that night.

"My darling Will, I do not want to delay. Too many seek to destroy our happiness, and by marrying immediately, we can thwart all their plans. I am no use to any of them once I am married."

"You are of infinite use to me, my love. You bring me a sense of contentment I did not know I could ever experience, and I relish your being by my side always after tomorrow. No one will be able to separate us then. And I will be able to protect you and speak on your behalf against those who sought to use you."

The two kissed deeply, and their cheeks burned brightly when Lady Matlock entered the room to admonish her nephew. "Fitzwilliam Darcy, you will marry her tomorrow. This type of behaviour will have to wait until then."

He stammered an apology, and the two quickly separated. Lady Matlock led Elizabeth toward the stairs, helped her find her room, and entered behind her.

169

"So much has happened over the last few days and weeks, and I wonder, my dear, are you prepared for what will happen tomorrow night?"

"What do you mean?" a nervous Elizabeth asked.

"Did Mrs. Gardiner have an opportunity to speak to you about what takes place after the wedding? I have no daughters, Elizabeth, and had hoped Darcy would marry well before Georgiana, so I would never have this conversation. However, you are here and are to marry tomorrow, and I am probably the only woman you can speak to about these things. Do you know what to expect tomorrow night — after the two of you are married? As much as I hate to say this to any woman, you should not wait to consummate your marriage. You would not want to give anyone grounds they might use to force an annulment."

"Oh," was all Elizabeth could manage for a few minutes. "I ... well, I know a little more than most girls, I suppose. I grew up on a farm and saw the animals ... and well, I, uh, asked a few questions. Mr. and Mrs. Bennet would not answer many of them, but the housekeeper, Mrs. Hill, explained a few things. My Aunt Gardiner did speak with me about, um, relations ... between a man and a woman after I turned eighteen, but said she would explain more when it was closer to my wedding. She told me a little more before I moved into Matlock House."

"That is a relief. So you are prepared, then? You do not have any questions?"

"I, um, I think I am prepared. As much as I can be. She said if I married for love, my husband would want to take care of me and treat me gently. She encouraged me to speak to Mr. Darcy and, um, to trust him."

Lady Matlock nodded. "Good. Then, I will allow the two of you to figure things out. I know your intended is probably just as anxious as you are. He was never one to seek out ... amusements ... like others have. My brother was exceptionally moral in his habits, and I believe he raised his son similarly."

"That is ... good to know," Elizabeth said hesitantly. As much as she liked the idea of her husband waiting for her, she wondered if it would not be better if one of them, at least, knew what they were doing. She attempted to control the tendency to flush as she realised where her thoughts had tended.

170

"Trust my husband," she thought and nearly said out loud. Though her marriage was to take place the next day, with all the problems surrounding them the last few weeks, she had not even considered what becoming a wife would entail.

Lady Matlock patted her hand and left the room, encouraging Elizabeth to sleep well. However, too many thoughts were swirling in Elizabeth's head, making sleep hard to find.

She was not the only one having trouble sleeping that night. Down the hall, Darcy was also tossing and turning in his bed as he contemplated the following night. As Lady Matlock suspected, George Darcy had raised his son to view the relationship between a husband and wife as sacred and encouraged him not to seek relief from other sources. Watching Wickham whore his way through school and cleaning up his messes made him even more cautious. While he knew the mechanics of the act and had heard plenty from other men — though many of those stories related to mistresses and courtesans and not wives — he had no practical experience. He knew the first time might cause pain for the woman but had heard his cousins mention how to lessen it somewhat. However, his cousin was not there, and he could not imagine asking his uncle any of these questions. While he might know something about deflowering a woman, it was not the kind of conversation he would have ever wanted to have with him.

Sleep remained elusive, prompting him to don his dressing gown and secure it around his waist. Opting for a glass of brandy and perhaps a book, he hoped the combination would usher in the much-needed repose.

* * *

While the Darcy carriages made their way to Derbyshire, several groups descended on London. A problem with the horses delayed Bennet's travel, forcing him to wait to leave until early Tuesday morning. Charles Bingley grew tired of his sister's whining and decided to beg Darcy for forgiveness, thinking he could re-establish the friendship away from his sister. Lady Catherine finally decided to leave her daughter at Rosings and would instead drag Darcy to Kent to marry her daughter. She would enlist her brother to force the issue with their nephew.

Wickham was watching Darcy House when the first person arrived outside. Mr. Bennet did not find his niece with her aunt and uncle in Cheapside, and the Gardiners could not or would not say where she was. He had Mr. Elliott's address and looked for her, only to be told by the butler that no one named Elizabeth Tomlinson or Elizabeth Bennet had ever been there. He decided to check for her at Darcy House, having obtained the address from Bingley.

That gentleman was fairly angry by the time he arrived and pounded on the door of the home. He was met by a stern-looking butler who was offended at someone having the audacity to pound on the door when the knocker was clearly off.

"The master is not home," the butler replied to Mr. Bennet's demand that he speak to Mr. Darcy.

"Where is he then?" His protest was interrupted as a large carriage arrived, bearing Lady Catherine de Bourgh's emblem on the side.

They both watched as the great lady descended from her carriage with the assistance of a nervous-looking footman. Wickham moved closer to hear what was being said. "I demand you take me to see my nephew," Lady Catherine exclaimed as she marched up the steps and faced the butler.

"Mr. Darcy has departed from London," the butler said stoically. "As I understand it, he intends to return to Town before Twelfth Night."

"Where did he go? Pemberley?" Lady Catherine demanded.

"I understand he headed west, madam. He did not inform me of his destination, but he was accompanied by Lady Matlock and his sister. Lady Matlock mentioned Bath, though it may have been Bristol. I cannot recall which."

"Was my niece with him?" Bennet interjected.

The butler stared at him in distaste. "I do not know who your niece is, sir. I suggest you search for her elsewhere."

"Then where is my niece?" Bennet demanded again.

"Sir, it is not my responsibility to know where your niece is. Now, as Mr.

Darcy is not in town, neither of you can have any further business with me or this house, and I ask you to leave."

"I will not," Lady Catherine replied tartly. "I will stay here."

"You will not, madam. My orders are clear; no one is to be admitted to Darcy House when the master is not in residence."

"Do you know who I am?" she asked, her voice rising angrily.

"I am aware, Lady Catherine, but my master specifically has said that you are not to be granted entry when he is not here. If you have a problem with that, I suggest you take it up with him."

She gasped at his audacity and stepped back, which gave the butler enough room to shut the door and engage the lock. He went into his office, wrote a note, and then sent a boy from the kitchen to track down Colonel Fitzwilliam.

Wickham had heard enough to know that Darcy had left town. *"How did this happen?"* he wondered. *"How did Darcy leave town without me knowing of it?"*

Despite what the butler said, Wickham was almost positive Darcy would have made for Pemberley, not to Bristol or Bath as had been implied. He knew his old friend would have wanted to go to Pemberley, and he was almost as certain that Miss Tomlinson or Bennet or whoever she was was with him.

Lady Catherine was still sputtering at having the door shut in her face, and she turned to Mr. Bennet to inquire about his purpose for seeking his nephew. "Who exactly are you, and who is this niece you are searching for? She is not the one spreading rumours that she is courting my nephew, is she? It will not be, as Mr. Darcy is engaged to *my* daughter. He will marry my Anne and combine our two great estates."

"I am Thomas Bennet, master of Longbourn in Hertfordshire, madam, and I believe the butler called you Lady Catherine. Would you be Lady Catherine de Bourgh from Rosings Park?"

She sniffed. "I am."

"The niece I am looking for is promised to the heir of my estate and happens to be your rector, Mr. Collins. It seems your nephew is assisting her in running from her intended. I do not know anything about this reported courtship with your nephew, but I assure you, I intend for her to marry Mr. Collins."

"You are her guardian then?"

"My niece has lived with me since she was five. I am the only 'parent' she has ever known. I am uncertain what caused her to act this way, but it is not her typical behaviour. I am afraid she has had a small taste of freedom and believes she can avoid the marriage arranged for her. For some reason, your nephew has taken it upon himself to aid her with this."

"My nephew is unlikely to act as you suggest. He is committed to fulfilling his duties, so if he has strayed, it is likely due to your niece's influence. I am willing to assist you in ensuring that my rector marries your niece. I left him at the residence of your relations on Gracechurch Street earlier. We will retrieve him from there, find your niece and transport them to Scotland, where they will be married. This will enable my nephew to complete his intended match with my daughter. You will accompany me to Bath, where we will search for my nephew and your niece and send them both to do their duties to their families."

"Yes, madam, I will happily go with you. I would appreciate your assistance in this matter."

Lady Catherine appeared to think about this for a moment. "Your niece, she is the natural child of your brother, correct? Where did this estate come from, the one you are offering my rector in trade for giving up his claim to Longbourn?"

"It is a long story, madam."

"Well, we will have time as we travel for you to tell it all. Wait until we have retrieved Mr. Collins, and then you can tell me about your niece and her inheritance."

Bennet was unsure exactly what story to concoct for this woman but considered the matter as they travelled to Gracechurch Street. He could not remember what he had told Mr. Collins, so perhaps he could goad Mr. Collins into telling the story.

Chapter 24

When Bingley's carriage arrived, Wickham was still standing outside Darcy House, trying to decide what to do next. He was lost in thought and did not notice the new arrival, but Bingley immediately recognised him. Unbeknownst to the two of them, the remaining "footman" hired by Darcy for Elizabeth's protection had witnessed all the day's arrivals.

Bingley angrily approached Wickham. "You owe me fifty pounds! I do not know how you convinced the innkeeper that I would pay your bill and gaming losses, but I do not appreciate being taken advantage of."

Alarmed, Wickham turned and saw Bingley. "Oh, Mr. Bingley, well, I am afraid that was an unfortunate misunderstanding. I do not have the funds on me right now, but I will ensure you are paid back as soon as possible."

"I sincerely doubt that," a voice that Wickham had never wanted to hear again claimed. "George Wickham, what the devil are you doing outside Darcy House? Darcy would be incensed to discover you here, and, well, you know me. I would just as soon run you through."

"I … I was hired to investigate a, uh, a missing woman. My, uh, my investigation led me here."

"To Darcy's house?" Colonel Fitzwilliam asked sceptically.

"Uh, yes. She absconded from her family's home on Gracechurch Street, and several people have reported seeing her in Darcy's company."

"He is telling the truth, Colonel. I met him in Hertfordshire a few days ago, and he told me that a rector in Kent had hired him to learn what he could about a lady named Elizabeth Bennet and her inheritance in the north."

"You are wasting your time. No one by that name has lived in Hertford-shire for more than twenty years. "

"Whatever do you mean, Colonel?" Bingley asked. Wickham attempted to sneak away, thinking the Colonel was distracted by Bingley's question. He was not, and his large hand dropped forcefully on Wickham's shoulder, holding him firmly in place.

"You should remain to hear this, Wickham; you will find it fascinating. To my knowledge, the only Elizabeth Bennet christened by that name in Hertfordshire died nearly twenty years ago, though she had married by then and was Elizabeth Tomlinson. She and her husband had one child, a daughter, also named Elizabeth Tomlinson. Unfortunately for the girl, both her parents were dead before her first birthday. Her grandparents raised her at Briarwood, their estate, but after they died the autumn following her fifth birthday, her guardian sent her to live with her relations at Longbourn, where she has been abused and ill-treated by her aunt and uncle."

"So, the rumours that she is the penniless, natural child of her deceased uncle circulating in Meryton are untrue?" Bingley asked.

"She cannot be penniless! It was reported she has twenty thousand pounds," Wickham cried in surprise. "My, um, client has a marriage contract signed by her uncle, Mr. Bennet."

"That contract is worthless as Mr. Bennet had no authority to act on her behalf. And she has far more than twenty thousand pounds. In addition to inheriting Briarwood, Miss Tomlinson has an additional inheritance held in trust. Your client, or better yet, the man you duped into believing you are a solicitor, will be very disappointed when he travels to Bath along with my aunt, as they will not find Darcy or Miss Tomlinson there. They are making their way to Pemberley and will be married long before those who would seek to abuse or manipulate them arrive."

"Darcy will marry that chit? What need has he for more wealth?" Wickham protested, growing angry and attempting to throw off the Colonel's hand to escape.

Fitzwilliam merely tightened his grip and caressed the hilt of his sabre. The combination of these actions caused Wickham to pause. "Did you have something else to say?"

There was nothing Wickham could say or do in this situation, so he merely shrugged.

"Now, Bingley, as I understand it, you and Darcy are no longer friends, not after your sister attempted to compromise him, and you chose to betray his friendship. You cannot imagine my cousin will ever forgive you, now or ever, can you? Why are you outside his house?"

"I had hoped to throw myself on his mercy, but I suppose there is nothing I can do to repair the relationship, is there?"

"It is possible that in two or three years, he might soften enough to speak to you on occasion, but Darcy publicly cut your sister after she brazenly approached him at the theatre a sennight ago and attempted to malign his soon-to-be-wife. I doubt he will ever acknowledge her again."

"She did what? My god! I had better settle Caroline into a permanent situation with a companion far from London before she ruins me." Bingley sighed as he did not want to deal with his sister.

"Perhaps, if you take her where she is not known, you will find someone willing to take her for her dowry," the Colonel replied. Bingley nodded and began to stride away.

"Oh, Colonel, if you do manage to get any money from that … scoundrel, know he owes me fifty pounds. He convinced the innkeeper in Meryton that I agreed to pay his bill at the inn, including debts of honour to several members of the militia. I have discharged his debts, as I had little choice, but Mr. Wickham owes me now. I may be attempting to become a gentleman now, but I know several men who would assist me in claiming that money from Mr. Wickham, should it become necessary." Colonel Fitzwilliam had never heard Bingley sound so menacing, nor would he have thought him capable of it, and he watched Wickham seem to wilt before his eyes.

"I will ensure you are repaid, Bingley. I doubt you are the only person Wickham owes money to," the Colonel replied, a dangerous glint in his eye as he considered an idea that might help him rid London of Wickham.

If matters could be arranged the way Fitzwilliam had begun to consider, perhaps they could banish the wastrel from England's shores altogether.

* * *

Friday morning dawned bright and clear in Derbyshire. Darcy and Lord Matlock met with the vicar in Darcy's study at nine in the morning. After examining the documents and ensuring all was in order, the vicar agreed that all was in order, and the ceremony could proceed. The wedding was to be held in Pemberley's library after Elizabeth viewed it and threatened to move into the room.

Lord Matlock escorted Elizabeth to Darcy before the couple took their vows.

The ceremony passed in a blur for the pair. They managed to say the necessary words, but the rest of the room seemed to fade when they locked eyes. In a matter of minutes, or so it seemed, the vicar pronounced them husband and wife. Darcy led his wife to the dining room, and the wedding party enjoyed a lovely meal specially prepared by the staff to celebrate the master's wedding.

Lord and Lady Matlock departed for their own estate at noon, accompanied by Georgiana. They would meet the Darcys in London in approximately a fortnight, though with the way the couple were staring at each other, they wondered if they should travel to Pemberley first to drag the couple to London with them.

Finally alone, Darcy took Elizabeth to the family wing to show her the mistress's chambers. During the first week of their marriage, the couple rarely left their apartment as their meals were brought to their shared sitting room. On two occasions, they sneaked from their rooms to a secret exit from the house near the family wing, created by some ancestor who wanted easy access to the gardens.

"A secret passage? How exciting!" Elizabeth exclaimed when her new husband explained.

Darcy grinned, amused by her enthusiasm, and opened the door that would take them outside. "Indeed, my dearest Ellie. This is a well-guarded family secret; in fact, I am not sure even Georgiana knows of it. My father only told me a few weeks before he died and said it is a privilege bestowed solely upon the master of Pemberley. Of course, I have chosen to share it with you, my love, just as my father shared it with my mother."

Elizabeth's eyes widened with anticipation as they stepped into the dimly lit corridor. The scent of aged stone and earth surrounded them, making the expedition feel even more clandestine.

"Oh, how marvellous!" Elizabeth said as they emerged into the evening air. "What other secrets does Pemberley hold, William? Despite it being winter, this garden is lovely. It must be bursting with colour in the spring and summer."

Darcy chuckled, relishing her excitement. "It is, my darling. I have little doubt you will spend much time here in those months. Now, there are a few other secret passages, but none as well-used as this one. It was designed by an ancestor who, like us, cherished the tranquillity of these gardens and sought a private escape."

The moon cast a soft glow on their surroundings as they silently stood there, watching the sunset to the west. Despite the cooler weather of late November, they found ways to express their love outside in the nature they both adored. Soon, however, they grew cold and hastily made their way back to their sitting room, startling the servants who had brought the evening meal. Each time they used the passages, they laughed when they startled a servant either inside or outside with their sudden appearance.

In the second week of their marriage, they spent more time in other rooms of the house. Since Elizabeth had only seen a few rooms before their wedding, Darcy took her on an extensive tour of the house, which took far longer than expected due to the many kisses exchanged behind closed doors. The servants quickly realised not to enter any room the couple were in together. Both were reluctant to do so when it came time to return to London but knew it was important to do their duty and allow Lady Matlock to introduce them as a married couple in London.

Both Darcys dreaded what was waiting for them in London, having little doubt their pursuers would be furious. Fitzwilliam had written to Darcy to give an account of Lady Catherine's, Mr. Collins', and Mr. Bennet's wild goose chase to Bath, then Scotland. They were expected to arrive at Pemberley in a few days, according to the reports they had received from the men who were following, which was the only reason the Darcys did not delay their journey. The Darcys would return to London before they arrived and were prepared for an angry confrontation.

Fitzwilliam also reported that Wickham had been dealt with but that he would only share the full story with them when they arrived back in London. This intrigued them, and as they made their way toward Town, they debated what their cousin had managed to do to the man.

Chapter 25

The carriage bearing Lady Catherine, Mr. Bennet, and Mr. Collins arrived at Pemberley late in the afternoon, three days after the newly married Darcys departed it. Similar to the way the butler at Darcy House had dismissed Lady Catherine, Mr. Reynolds, Pemberley's butler, refused the travellers' entry to the mansion, directing them to the inn in Lambton if they wanted to remain in the area.

"The Darcys left for London a few days ago," Mr. Reynolds stated matter-of-factly. He raised an eyebrow, adding, "If you had notified the master of your intention to visit, you could have saved yourself the trip."

"What of my niece? Where is she?" Mr. Bennet demanded.

"Who is your niece, sir? No strangers were at Pemberley with the Darcys while they were here. Lord and Lady Matlock did stay a night or two but departed for Matlock shortly after arriving," the butler responded before closing the door to the unwelcome guests, ignoring their protestations. If those in the carriage interpreted his words to mean Mr. and Miss Darcy instead of Mr. and Mrs, he felt that was their own fault for not seeking clarification. The ordinarily stoic man grinned when he reported the interaction to his wife, the long-time housekeeper of Pemberley. The couple had been employed at Pemberley since the master was a child, and they were more than delighted to send Lady Catherine packing.

Following this exchange, the three travellers were even more miserable.

Lady Catherine was particularly irritable, snapping at both of the men who accompanied her, laying blame on them for every difficulty that arose on their way. It had been a wasted trip; every step of the way had been just one more pointless chase.

Mr. Collins attempted to defend himself, but Lady Catherine was not in the mood for excuses. "You two have been nothing but disappointments on this journey. I should have undertaken this quest alone."

Mr. Bennet, usually one to maintain a detached air, grew annoyed. "Lady Catherine, cease your accusations. Blaming us will not change the fact that we still have no idea where your nephew or my niece is."

They had left London for Bath and spent two days searching for any sign of the Darcys, the Matlocks, Mr. Elliott, or Miss Tomlinson. They were not there, but they met a friend of Lady Matlock's who thought she heard the family might have intended to go to Bristol, not Bath, so the frustrated searchers made their way there.

They were not in Bristol either, but they found a former classmate of Darcy's who claimed to have received a letter from his old friend a few days prior stating his intention to take an underage heiress to Scotland to marry her there. He reported that the couple had grown tired of waiting for her guardian to agree, so they had used this trip with Lady Matlock as a decoy to circumvent the man and marry over the anvil.

Now tired, frustrated, and annoyed, Lady Catherine continued to snap at her companions for not travelling straight to Scotland as she had intended from the start. It took nearly a week to journey from Bristol to Gretna Green, but when they finally arrived, there was no record of Fitzwilliam Darcy marrying anyone, nor was there any evidence that Darcy had even been there.

"A wild goose chase, that is what this has been!" Lady Catherine exclaimed, frustration evident in her voice. "Bristol, Bath, and Gretna Green! I should have known better than to rely on anyone's judgment but my own." Determined, she demanded her coachman to convey them to Pemberley as fast as he could manage it, but the weather slowed them down, and a wheel broke, which caused them to lose an entire day.

Once again thwarted, the frustration in the carriage reached a fever pitch as their journey continued, leaving them questioning the reliability of the information they had received and the purpose of their relentless pursuit. They found rooms at an inn in Lambton and would hasten to London on the morrow.

* * *

Darcy read the express from his butler with a small, ironic smile on his face. "It seems, my love, that my aunt, your uncle, and his cousin have paid a visit to Pemberley. They arrived there, demanding entry the same day we arrived in London. From what Reynolds overheard, they have travelled all around the country in pursuit of us — Bath, Bristol, then all the way to Gretna, and finally to Pemberley — and have made each other quite miserable in the process. My aunt will be very displeased when they finally arrive in Town, but as we are married, there is nothing she will be able to do."

Elizabeth laughed as she read the letter over his shoulder. "Reynolds shut the door in their face just as Jacobs did here. Your aunt will not have appreciated being denied entrance at two of your homes as she sought to prevent you from making an 'improper' match with a 'penniless nobody'. From what you have said of the lady, her ire will be something to see."

The image her words evoked caused Darcy to grimace. "I have little doubt of that. I will send a note to my uncle informing him of their imminent arrival in Town. I am afraid we will need all the support we can muster."

His new wife laughed at the face he made. "She cannot be that bad, can she? Is she worse than Mrs. Bennet?"

"In some ways, they are similar, but, yes, she is worse. She is used to deference due to her rank as the daughter of an earl. Truly, she is referred to as 'Lady' because of her birth; her husband was merely a baronet. She runs Rosings as something of a despot; everyone is expected to do as she commands. She wastes the money she earns from the estate on ostentatious decorations and furniture to display her wealth and status. Lady Catherine believes her status as the daughter of an earl entitles her to issue commands to anyone and everyone within her reach. Your cousin Collins is likely a toadying fool who believes in her supremacy, that is, if he is like the others she had hired in the past."

"And my uncle believed he could force me to accept such a man?" Elizabeth shook her head in dismay. "I am still amazed at learning of his plans for me and how he would have traded my future because he was too unwilling to change his lifestyle of indolence for one of economy and diligence. I would have never agreed to his plans; surely, he must have realised that at some point."

"It is done, Elizabeth, and you never have to see your uncle again, especially after we confront him about his theft of your funds."

"Will he keep my cousins from me if we do this? How will we prevent his actions from harming them? Mrs. Bennet will allow the younger girls to ruin themselves if they are not careful, especially with the militia arriving in Hertfordshire."

"Elizabeth, we will do what we can; in fact, your Uncle Gardiner and I discussed the possibility of forcing Mr. Bennet to surrender guardianship of the four girls to him as a part of his punishment. I have not had a chance to discuss his suggestion with you yet, but we spoke of that as an option last night. We will still make him pay the three thousand pounds but promise not to go after the full amount if he surrenders the girls to Gardiner."

"Truly? Do you think he will agree?"

"Mrs. Bennet might prove more difficult to convince, but, yes, he intends to propose this to him as a way to prevent us from making a further claim. We have barely scraped the surface of what he likely owes, having spent so much time investigating other matters and, of course, getting ourselves married." He waggled his eyebrows at her, causing her to laugh.

"Yes, this conversation has become far too serious. We are alone, and you are much too far away ..." her voice trailed off as Darcy jumped up from where he sat and moved to snatch his wife out of her chair.

"Well, then, my impertinent wife, let us remedy that situation immediately," he said huskily before capturing her lips for a kiss that left them both breathless when it ended some minutes later.

*** *** ***

The note eventually was sent to the Matlocks informing them of the expected arrival of the objectors in the next day or two. This was not surprising to any of them, as the Matlocks had also received regular reports through Colonel Fitzwilliam from those who were following Lady Catherine's carriage around England. A return note suggested they all meet the following day to form a battle plan.

Quite a few people gathered in the drawing room at Matlock House the following morning. Mr. Elliott, Lord and Lady Matlock, the Gardiners, Colonel Fitzwilliam, and the bodyguards were all waiting when the Darcys arrived a little later than the agreed-upon time. The colonel teased his typically prompt cousin, who had developed a bad habit of arriving late to nearly everything since marrying his comely wife.

"Darcy, whatever has delayed my typically fastidious cousin this morning? Since you have arrived back in London, you have been late to every gathering we have had. What could be the cause?" the colonel asked, his eyes sparkling as he noted the tips of his cousin's ears turning red. Fortunately, he did not ask where Georgiana could hear him, but Elizabeth's eyes widened, and she coloured before walking away to join her aunt.

"None of your business, Jonathan. It is simply that there are two of us getting ready for most events, which takes a bit longer. You are neither married nor likely ever to be since you speak better of your horses than I have ever heard you speak of a woman. Women take longer to dress."

"I have noticed that with my mother, but that is why she typically begins getting ready before my father. Perhaps you should encourage your wife to do the same?" he jibed.

Darcy gave his cousin a dark look. "Stop, Fitz." he countered, knowing that his cousin hated the diminutive of his surname.

"Boys, that is enough from the both of you," Lord Matlock stated authoritatively. "Jonathan, you will not get the response you are hoping for from your cousin, so I suggest you drop it. And Darcy, well, I am glad you are happily married, but do attempt to be on time occasionally. This is an important conference, and we need everyone's input. We do not have time for this nonsense."

They all settled down, and Fitzwilliam recounted what they knew, including the latest update that informed them the de Bourgh carriage had stopped for the night not far from Hertfordshire. "I believe the skirmish may take place this afternoon."

"Skirmish?" Elizabeth questioned. "Are you expecting us to meet on the field of honour with swords and muskets?"

Fitzwilliam laughed. "Not quite, but I expect it to be fairly minor in the end. Lady Catherine will bluster, but ultimately, she will be forced to leave without achieving her goal. The marriage is already done; none of the parties who will arrive today will be able to put an end to it. Oh, and the problem with Wickham has been fully resolved now."

Darcy looked at him. "I have been anticipating your explanation as to how you managed it."

"I will enjoy telling you the story," the colonel replied with a cheeky grin.

Chapter 26

Lord Matlock looked between his nephew and son. "What on earth are you two speaking of?"

"Do you recall how Wickham was hanging about outside Darcy House before you all left London a fortnight ago?" Fitzwilliam asked his father. Receiving a nod, he continued. "Well, we hired the boys he used to report on your activities. They were quite willing to switch their loyalty for a slight remuneration, and we used them to feed Wickham bad information. When Lady Catherine and her … her retinue showed up, he was there, outside Darcy House, watching. He was still standing there a few minutes later when Darcy's former friend, Charles Bingley, appeared."

Darcy looked at him in astonishment. "You did not mention that part before."

"Yes, well, he said he came to London to apologise and beg your forgiveness. Anyway, Wickham had been to Hertfordshire and learned from Bingley that you were courting Miss Tomlinson in London. When Bingley left the tavern after the two had a long chat, the innkeeper demanded payment from Bingley for Wickham's bill. Apparently, he had run up quite a large tab – 50 pounds – and had intended to run out on it, but, after meeting Bingley, decided to stick him with the bill. Knowing Bingley, you cannot doubt that he paid it, but he was not amused and actually threatened Wickham when he ran into him here. Truly, I would never have guessed he had it in him. In fact, I would have expected him to take the loss without a word, but he had steel in his tone when he demanded that Wickham pay him back post haste."

Darcy agreed that "steel" was not a word he would have expected to use to describe Bingley.

"How long was he in Hertfordshire that he accumulated fifty pounds of debt?" Mr. Gardiner asked in shock.

"A sennight. More than half of that was in debts of honour to men in the militia there. A significant portion was for libations in the tavern; the smallest amount covered his food and bed for eight nights. He intended to skip town without paying but felt it would be easy to have Bingley pay for him."

"Who cares about Bingley?" Lord Matlock demanded. "What have you done with Wickham?"

"He has signed up for a stint in His Majesty's Navy. I doubt he will see the shores of England for many more years, as my friend who helped arrange for his entry into the service said it is not unlikely they will be gone for up to five or six years. And that does not even take into account how many landsmen and other sailors die during each voyage."

The assembled group began to discuss strategy for when the carriage conveying its miserable occupants would arrive. They briefly considered dismissing Mr. Bennet and Mr. Collins entirely but felt that would only add fuel to the fire. Instead, they decided to confront the entire party head-on with the news of the marriage between Elizabeth and Darcy, ending the delusions regarding other matches between Darcy and his cousin or Elizabeth and her uncle's cousin and heir.

* * *

Not long after the group sat down for an enjoyable luncheon, their peace was disturbed by the loud tones of Lady Catherine demanding entrance to her brother's house. They all rose from the table *en masse* before the butler or any other servants could arrive to inform them of their "guests" and moved to the drawing room where they would receive them. Elizabeth and Darcy sat beside each other on a settee, their hands gripped together and hidden in Elizabeth's skirts. They were surrounded by their family until all the best chairs in the room were taken, except for three uncomfortable-looking ones set in a row.

Once again, Lady Catherine's voice heralded her entry. "I demand you take me to my brother at once. He will tell me where to find my nephew, and between us, we will force Darcy to cast that strumpet aside and marry my daughter, just as his mother intended. We will unite the great estates of Pemberley and Rosings, and I will aid my nephew in taking his place in the world. With my help, he will become an Earl at least, if not a Duke, and head of one of England's richest families."

The guests remained seated when Lady Catherine all but shoved the butler out of the way when she stepped into the drawing room. She halted abruptly, taking note of the assembled guests, who remained seated and did not acknowledge her presence. Her eyes narrowed at seeing Darcy sitting beside a lovely young woman, and she noted the position of their hands covertly entangled within the lady's skirts. "What is the meaning of this?" she demanded.

Bennet entered on her heels. "Elizabeth Rose Bennet, what the devil are you doing in this house and with that man? You were to stay at the Gardiners, yet I have had to travel all over England in search of you. I demand you explain yourself." The longer he spoke, the louder his voice grew until he nearly shouted at the end.

Darcy stood. "You have no right to ever speak to her in such a way, and certainly not in my uncle's house. I can see time spent with my aunt has not made you any more reasonable than you were before your journey. As you well know, Elizabeth has never been a Bennet. What you do not know, however, is that she no longer bears the name Tomlinson. We married, above a fortnight ago, and she is now Elizabeth Rose Tomlinson *Darcy*."

All three of the uninvited guests demonstrated their shock at this announcement. Lady Catherine was the first to give hers a voice. Stamping her cane on the ground, she roared: "It cannot be. I demand you have this marriage annulled immediately. You were engaged to my Anne. It was the dearest wish of your mother —"

Lord Matlock cut her off. "Enough of your nonsense, Catherine. Our sister Anne never wished her son to marry your daughter. She might have agreed with you that it was a pleasant thought when they were both children, but you know as well as I do that Anne would have never demanded her son marry anyone he did not wish to, which also goes for your daughter. In fact, both George and Anne Darcy told me on several occasions they wished for their son to make a love match. I recall them both speaking of the possibility of little Ellie Tomlinson marrying Fitzwilliam one day after they saw them together at Pemberley. They were too young at the time, and neither George nor Mr. Tomlinson would enter into an agreement to force the issue, but I recall it being discussed even as early as that."

Elizabeth looked at Lord Matlock with incredulity. "Truly? My grandfather discussed the notion of our marrying one day with William's father? I am so pleased that our wedding would have made my grandparents and your parents happy, William."

The earl smiled at his new niece. "They did. I believe they both looked forward to watching you lead young Darcy on what they called 'a merry chase'. If I am not mistaken, you fulfilled their wish in this regard, as you had the lad quite tied up in knots."

She grinned unrepentantly at her husband. "Well, Dearest Will, was it a merry chase?"

"It was, indeed, my love. And I enjoyed every moment, little Ellie. I believe I have told you this before."

"Stop this nonsense," Mr. Bennet bellowed into the middle of these happy imaginings. "Whoever told you this was dissembling. While there may be someone named Elizabeth Tomlinson who was that little girl, you are not she. You are my niece, the daughter of my brother, Edward. His natural child, I would like to add."

Mr. Elliott stepped forward at this. "Unless there is another young lady named Elizabeth in your household, you are the one who is dissembling, Mr. Bennet. I have in my possession fifteen years of correspondence in which you reported on the activities of your niece, Miss Elizabeth Tomlinson. Moreover, after meeting Miss Tomlinson, I know that virtually everything you told me is false. Indeed, it appears that you diverted the very generous payments from Miss Tomlinson's trust intended for her education, clothing and allowance, among other things, for your own use, ensuring she was the poor relation you and your wife represented her to be. That, sir, is a crime; you could hang for it. We will meet soon to discuss how you will reimburse Mrs. Darcy for the funds you stole from her."

Mr. Bennet's eyes widened at this, and he spluttered through several attempts to speak.

Lady Catherine stamped her cane on the floor again, garnering everyone's attention. "I do not care about Miss Tomlinson or any matters related to her. We must return to the matter at hand. Darcy, all of society knows that you are engaged to my daughter. I will not allow you to jilt her."

"If that is so, madam, it is your own fault for spreading your lies about the fictional engagement. You are solely responsible for any harm your daughter suffers from this falsehood. However, I cannot imagine that many believed your tales as it has been many years since Anne has been of an age for marriage, and one has not yet occurred. Certainly, most people would have realised by now that you were merely stating your wishes on the matter, especially as no engagement has ever been announced. Whenever it was mentioned to me by anyone, I have denied it, as has my uncle. I know my father did the same while he was still living, though you were much less likely to mention the purported engagement then."

As Mr. Bennet had done, Lady Catherine could do little but gape at her nephew's frank denial of her wishes.

Lord Matlock entered the fray, his tone commanding. "Catherine, you will desist in your delusion that Darcy will marry your daughter. It will never happen. He is quite happily married to a lovely woman, and you can do nothing about it.

"Knowing you would eventually end your journey here, your daughter sent me a request. Upon her twenty-fifth birthday, Anne inherited Rosings in accordance with the will of your late husband. However, you have refused to relinquish your position, claiming her too ill to be Rosings' mistress. Anne has informed me that she is quite well, and while you were on your little 'holiday' and unable to interfere, she finally had the opportunity to take control of Rosings. She has asked for my support and assistance in finding a place for you to reside while she learns what she needs to do for her estate. My son, Jonathan, will resign his commission and assist her. Since Anne does not desire to marry, she has made him her heir."

At this, Lady Catherine clasped her chest and collapsed on the floor before them all.

Chapter 27

For several moments, pandemonium gripped the room. Mr. Collins swiftly reached his patroness, obstructing everyone's efforts to assist the lady. Darcy, Elizabeth, and the Gardiners observed from a distance as Lady Matlock and Jonathan sprang into action, urgently summoning servants for aid and dispatching a message for a physician. After a brief pause, Darcy stepped forward to physically remove Mr. Collins, recognising that his presence was impeding the necessary assistance others were attempting to provide.

"But ... my patroness ... Lady Catherine. She needs me," he protested.

"Right now, she needs you out of the way. You are impeding her gaining assistance, sir!" Darcy commanded as he, again, physically prevented Mr. Collins from moving around him to go to her. Mr. Collins continued to wring his hands as he stared at Lady Catherine lying prone on the floor.

Lord Matlock watched his sister collapse to the floor and, for a moment, felt a twinge of sorrow for her. Then he noticed her eyes twitching. He looked around him and observed Mr. Bennet moving toward his niece, a look of determination on his face.

"Enough!" the earl proclaimed, ending all the chaos. After ordering everyone back to their seats, he began in a somewhat calmer fashion, though no less angry. "Catherine, get up from the floor immediately, or I will have the servants drag you from there. There is not a thing wrong with you. And, Bennet, remain where you are. You are not to approach Mrs. Darcy

193

under any circumstances. We know about your plans for your niece, and you would not have been permitted to carry them out. Your agreement with Mr. Collins was invalid, as you were never her guardian. It was George Darcy, but when he died, it became Mr. Elliott here, who you have met and have been writing letters to for all these years. Even had you managed to marry her to Mr. Collins, Mrs. Darcy's estate would have remained in trust for her; it would never have transferred to her husband."

Lady Catherine sat up. "I am most displeased, brother," she croaked. "I am in shock that you could treat me as you have, ignoring my illness and demanding that I do more than I am capable of. It was always this way; even as a child, you would make demands of me that I could not possibly manage."

The earl was shaking his head. "It is ironic, is it not, that you cannot recognise your own behaviour in your child. Do you know that Anne faked the illness that delayed your journey from Kent? She used those same measures to prevent her from joining you on your fruitless journey. Her weakness started because you sought to keep her ill, but as soon as Anne realised it, she began to use it against you, just as you did to our parents all those years ago. You feigned illnesses to get your way as a child, and it will not be tolerated now."

"But Lord Matlock, my patroness is truly ill. Can you not see her? She fainted, sir; you cannot ignore that. A doctor must be fetched," Mr. Collins insisted.

"I do not know who you are or why you are here, sir. Get out of the way and do not attempt to tell me what I must do. In fact ..." he paused, then called for a footman. "Take this person out of my house. He has no business here and does not even have the sense to get out of the way."

"But sir, I am here because my intended is here. I am to marry Miss Elizabeth Bennet, and when we are wed, I will claim her estate as my own." The foolish little man was puffed up in his pride. "I have surrendered any interest in Longbourn because Mr. Bennet promised I would marry his niece. Once I had her estate, I would not need Longbourn as well. It was truly gracious of me to suggest such a transfer as it allows my cousin's family to have a place to stay when my cousin departs this mortal soil."

Lord Matlock stared at the rector in disbelief. "You will have to find someone else to wed because the woman you expected to marry is already married to Mr. Darcy."

Protesting the entire way and still believing himself engaged, Mr. Collins was removed from the house. Lady Catherine also objected to his treatment; judging from the volume she used to do so, it became clear to all in the room that there was nothing wrong with the lady.

"You have only proven my point with your complaints, Catherine. If not for Anne's request, I would throw you from my house, but I promised to keep you away from Rosings until she has things as she wishes."

"Rosings is mine, Malcolm; you cannot take it away from me. Anne is not strong enough —"

Lord Matlock interrupted his sister's tirade once again. "Did you not hear me, Catherine? Not only does the estate legally belong to Anne, but she is perfectly well and capable of managing it. Jonathan will help her as she learns, and, of course, Darcy and I will provide whatever assistance she needs. She will do well enough."

"Why does she not want me there to assist?" Lady Catherine's tone sounded almost petulant.

"Because you do not know how to assist without completely taking over," Darcy pointed out. "And, forgive me for this: you are incapable of successfully managing Rosings. You have nearly run it into the ground with your nonsensical decisions and frivolous spending. Since her twenty-fifth birthday, Anne has waited for you to leave long enough for her to exert her control over the estate. Had she attempted to insist upon doing what was her right, she feared you would drug her into complying with your continuation as mistress of Rosings. So, when an opportunity presented itself, she put her plan into action."

Lady Catherine was aghast. "I do not ... I do not understand. How could my daughter treat me in this way? It is infamous!"

"You have not listened to anyone besides yourself in years. Had Anne told you she wanted to learn to manage the estate, as was her right, what would you have said?" Lord Matlock paused for several moments, but when no answer came, he responded to his own question. "You would have told her she was incapable of it and was too ill to do what was required. You never bothered to listen to her. You have not listened to Darcy when he attempted to advise you on estate matters. He met with your steward behind your back to do what was necessary since, without his efforts, you would have bankrupted Rosings ages ago. As it is, he has advised the steward to ignore most of your proclamations. You advise your tenants, your vicar, the shopkeepers in town, the parishioners at the church you attend, and everyone you come into contact with, and most of them have learned to ignore your comments as the advice you give is often wrong if not outright foolish. No one has been able to tell you anything; now, no one wants to listen to you. Including your daughter."

" But ... where am I to go?"

"You can stay at the de Bourgh townhouse in town for a time, or you can retire to the dower house at Matlock if you prefer. Perhaps, once Anne is ready, she will allow you to live at the dower house at Rosings, but Anne wanted the opportunity to learn estate management without you there."

Lady Catherine's face had been growing more and more red the longer her brother spoke. This time, when she collapsed, everyone was far more concerned, as her face was nearly purple.

Lord Matlock struggled not to roll his eyes, but his son confirmed that she had truly swooned this time. The housekeeper who had been present for this entire exchange brought forth the smelling salts in her hand. Lady Matlock took them and waved them under her sister's nose. She twitched but did not wake, and everyone in the room grew more concerned.

"Father, we should carry her into a guest room. The doctor has been sent for and will hopefully arrive soon enough. She might have finally had enough, though I doubt it will keep her down for long. She will be up and protesting all the changes quickly enough. I hope she decides to remove to Matlock instead of remaining in London," Fitzwilliam said.

His father nodded, and soon, Fitzwilliam and Darcy had Lady Catherine secure on a makeshift litter, and the two carried her upstairs. The physician met them in the hallway outside the room, accompanied by the housekeeper and several maids.

"Darcy, take your wife home. The Gardiners have taken Bennet to Gracechurch Street. Apparently, he had not bothered to inform any of his family at Longbourn of his travels; Mrs. Bennet has written several nearly hysterical letters to the Gardiners requesting information," Lady Matlock said when he returned downstairs.

Darcy nodded at his aunt and then did as she insisted. Lady Catherine was far from his favourite aunt, but she was his mother's sister, and he cared for her as he cared for all his family. She had had a great shock this day after enduring weeks of rushed travel on a wild goose chase for which he had been at least partially responsible. Of course, had she not been so insistent on her own way, she would never have engaged in such extensive travel, but he could not help but feel a little responsible.

His wife put a stop to those reflections once they arrived home. "William, she had no right to demand you marry her daughter, as neither you nor Anne desired such a connexion. No rational person would have ever travelled hundreds of miles to force two unwilling people to marry. It is simply nonsensical."

He drew a deep breath and leaned his head back against the chair. "I know that Ellie, yet I cannot help but feel responsible."

"Did you inform your aunt you would never marry your cousin?"

"Several times. Anne and I both did."

"Did you give her any reason to doubt your word?"

"No."

"Did you ever propose to Anne?"

"No!"

"Then how are you responsible for your aunt's delusion? Call it what it is, William; she was deluded into thinking she could force you to do her will and would not desist no matter how many times she was refused. It is clear that her collapse was brought about by hearing that no one complies with her demands. She has been living with the mistaken belief that all revere her, though it seems that only Mr. Collins actually does. It was likely a shocking realisation for her."

Darcy nodded. "The previous rector acted similarly, but he only lasted a few years before he took another position and resigned from the Hunsford living. A few of her servants hold her in such reverence, but most merely placate her. In some ways, Anne has been far more active in the running of the estate than her mother realised for the last several years, especially outside the house."

"Now, you must stop thinking of your aunt for some time. What shall I do to distract you?" Elizabeth asked him.

He had a suggestion, and she followed it exactly. Once again, they retired very early that night.

Chapter 28

Mr. Collins was still standing outside the house when Mr. Bennet and the Gardiners exited, nervously waiting to hear news about what had occurred inside after he had been dismissed.

"Cousin Bennet, Cousin Bennet. How is my patroness, Lady Catherine de Bourgh? I have not seen the physician arrive yet. Tell me, is she recovered?"

A man brushed past them and gained entry into the house as they stood on the kerb.

"It appears the physician is here now. He will tend to the lady. Come, we should depart," Mr. Gardiner said to the anxious man. Bennet had ignored his cousin and already stepped into the waiting carriage.

"I must wait here so I might be of assistance to Lady Catherine," he insisted.

"You will do more by staying out of the way. Do you have a place to stay? We will give you a ride to your hotel."

Mr. Collins looked around him. "I am afraid my luggage is in the carriage of my benevolent patroness. I do not know where it may be at the moment. She has borne the cost of our travel so far; I do not have the coins for a night at an inn."

Disguising his frustration, Gardiner looked cautiously at his wife, who nodded slightly. "You may stay with us tonight, and in the morning, I will ensure my brother assists you in finding transportation to take you back to Hunsford. When we arrive at my home, I will send a note to Lord Matlock to request he send any luggage belonging to you or my brother."

"I must speak to my cousin tonight. I cannot understand what was said in there about my intended. Did I correctly grasp that the woman I was supposed to marry is now married to the nephew of my patroness? Did they marry in Scotland?"

Sighing loudly, Gardiner attempted again to direct the man to the carriage. "Yes, you and my brother do have much to speak of tonight," he replied in a tone that discouraged further questions. When that did not work, he simply did not respond further to the ridiculous man.

When they arrived at the Gardiner home, neither Mr. nor Mrs. Gardiner would allow Bennet to avoid speaking to his cousin to clarify matters. Mr. Gardiner sat in the study with the two men and attempted to help the vicar understand what had transpired.

"Elizabeth has been living with us since she was five; when her grandparents and my brother died, I was her next of kin," Mr. Bennet finally stated bluntly in an attempt to halt the man's onslaught of words. "She is my niece, but the rumour that she is my brother's natural daughter is untrue. My wife and I did not correct that story when it surfaced." Bennet continued to explain his niece's story — the death of her father, followed not long after by her mother and, finally, her grandparents. "She is, or was, Elizabeth Tomlinson, the daughter of my sister. Now, it appears she is Elizabeth Darcy."

"So you have been lying to me all this time?" Mr. Collins finally asked, shocked to learn that he had been deceived. "You made me surrender my claim to Longbourn while knowing I could not inherit this other estate?"

"No. You are still the heir to Longbourn; that has not changed." He cleared his throat. "Truthfully, I did not intend to cheat you out of your inheritance. Briarwood is a much more valuable estate. Had our contract been approved by Elizabeth's trustees, you would have been far wealthier than if you inherited Longbourn." Mr. Bennet attempted to clarify. "Since I was the one who raised Elizabeth, I mistakenly believed I was her guardian and could make arrangements for her marriage and negotiate her marriage settlement. As they appeared disinterested in Elizabeth for fifteen years, I fully expected her trustees to sign the contract and that you would marry her as planned. Believe me, I am as shocked as you are over what has occurred. You will still inherit Longbourn, but this will destroy me. The trustees intend to claim I have stolen from my niece. And it will ruin me if I do not continue to receive the stipend from Elizabeth's estate each month."

Bennet trailed off, and for several minutes, Mr. Collins could only stare at him as he worried about what might happen to Longbourn before he inherited it.

"What can I do to help you?" Mr. Collins finally asked.

"Return to Hunsford and remain there for now. Perhaps in a few months, you can return to Longbourn and marry my daughter Mary; she will make a good wife for you. In a few years, you could engage a curate to take over for you at Rosings and come to live in the dower cottage so you can learn estate management from me."

"But what of the marriage contracts that were signed? What of my receiving an estate now? I was to become the master of an estate in just a few months. Why would I marry your plainest daughter when I was to have your lovely niece?" Mr. Collins demanded. "No, this Mr. Darcy has taken my rightful wife, and I will have nothing more to do with your family from this day forward. I pray that your wife and daughters will have another place to live after you pass from this world, for I will have them cast out of Longbourn the moment I inherit."

Having finally understood that his cousin was attempting to manipulate him, Mr. Collins was determined to be done with this family. He would return to Kent, awaiting news of his patroness while hoping for her complete recovery. Vaguely recalling something about Miss de Bourgh being the true mistress of Rosings, he wondered for a moment what he would find when he arrived there.

* * *

Lady Matlock made plans to introduce her new niece to the *ton* during this time. As Christmastide was fast approaching, she had informed Darcy that they would remain in Town through Twelfth Night. There was not enough time to organise a ball specifically in honour of the new couple, and even if there had been, Darcy would not wish to attend an event where he was the centre of attention.

"You and Elizabeth can be introduced to society at my annual Twelfth Night ball, but you must be seen around town even before that. I know you attended a few events together before you were wed, but now that you are married, you must be seen out and happy. There are several dinners and musical evenings you have been invited to; not all of the events must be dances."

"I would be far more agreeable if I were permitted to dance with my wife. The strictures that say I might only dance with Elizabeth once per evening are ridiculous. As a newly married man, surely I would be permitted two, even three dances with my love," Darcy protested.

"It is not done, Fitzwilliam, as well you know. However, I will allow you to slip out after supper and not force you to remain the entire evening."

"I will agree, but only if I may dance the first and the supper set with Elizabeth."

Elizabeth laughed at his demand and the pout on his face as he spoke. "Darling, you are acting much like a recalcitrant child demanding your way. However, I would be pleased to dance the first and supper set with you at any event we attend that includes dancing. The harpies who would criticise a newly married couple for dancing together are not worth our notice. I would adore dancing with you, but I would enjoy a night out at the theatre even more. At the theatre, we can hold hands the entire night." She gave him a saucy grin, and her new aunt laughed.

"You are good for my nephew," Lady Matlock said, smiling at the light blush on her nephew's cheeks. "I have never seen him so happy."

Elizabeth turned her smile toward her aunt. "He makes me happy, too, Aunt. Now, we have three weeks until Christmastide and another two weeks before Twelfth Night, all filled with events your aunt will insist we attend. Unfortunately, I believe I will require a trip to the modiste to ensure I have fashionable gowns to meet the ton's expectations for Mrs. Darcy. William, do you think our estates can manage to fund the clothing I am certain your aunt will insist on my purchasing?"

He laughed, leaning down to kiss his wife, ignoring his aunt's presence. "Yes, my darling girl, I think that between the two of us, we can afford what you will require as my wife."

* * *

The next day, Mr. Bennet received a summons from Mr. Elliott, notifying him of a meeting scheduled for a sennight from then at the solicitor's office. He was charged with bringing any documentation about how the stipend for Miss Tomlinson's care had been spent over the last five years. Since Elizabeth had been in charge of keeping the books for much of this time, they doubted if Mr. Bennet could find anything to prove his claims of how the funds were spent for these years. As Elizabeth had brought several of these ledgers with her to London, Mr. Elliott and Lord Matlock wondered if he would attempt to create documents to support his claims or if his indolence would prevent him from doing so.

Bennet travelled to Longbourn to see what he could find to support his claims regarding what he had provided for Elizabeth over the years. He noticed that some of the estate's ledgers appeared missing, and he was concerned about how he would prove what he had spent on his niece without them. Briefly, he wondered if he could postpone the meeting but doubted it would be allowed.

Mrs. Bennet burst into his study upon receiving word that the master had arrived at home. "What I have suffered in your absence!" she fussed. "You leave for London, telling me you will only be gone a day or two, but then you do not return for over a fortnight. And not a word from you to inform me of your plans! I sent several messages to my brother in Gracechurch Street, and he informed me that you had gone off to chase down our worthless niece. Tell me, did you get her married? Will Mr. Collins still relinquish his claim on Longbourn now that he has Lizzy's estate? Why that child should have been left an estate, I will never understand. Will they continue to provide funds for us and our girls?"

"Madam, I demand you cease your fretting immediately. Matters are not yet settled; I must return to town in a sennight to meet again with the trustees."

"Again? What is yet unsettled? Are they still insisting upon that worthless child having a Season? I suppose she might attract a gentleman's attention with her estate, but what will happen to us if she does not marry Mr. Collins? What will happen when we no longer receive the stipend for her care? We will continue to receive it until she comes of age, will we not? What will we do if we do not?"

"Enough!" he bellowed. "I suggest you learn to live with less. Elizabeth will not marry Mr. Collins as she already married Mr. Darcy. It seems her trustees decided she needed protection from her family, though I am still unsure exactly how that came to be. Mr. Collins will inherit Longbourn, but I will encourage him to marry Mary instead. He is unhappy now, but I will ensure he does right by my widow. Now, leave me be. I need to meet with my brother Phillips. He will likely need to accompany me to London next time."

He also needed to arrange a place to stay, as he was told in no uncertain terms that the Gardiners would not be hosting Mr. and Mrs. Bennet any time soon. His brother was furious with them for not telling the truth about Elizabeth's heritage for all those years and for allowing the residents of Meryton to believe a lie that harmed her reputation. Likewise, they thought he had been remiss in not informing Elizabeth of her inheritance, not providing for Elizabeth appropriately all those years, and lying in his annual reports to Mr. Elliott. While the Gardiners would not refuse to see his nieces, they intended to completely cut off all contact with Mr. and Mrs. Bennet unless absolutely necessary. They assured Mr. Bennet they would do nothing to aid Mrs. Bennet should he pass away before her.

Bennet pondered that if the Gardiners knew he had lied, did it follow that Elliott and Darcy did as well? Was this demand for another meeting with the solicitors to hold him accountable? He began to be very concerned about this meeting and reflected on what had been said the previous day in Lord

Matlock's house for several moments. He wondered what they intended to do to him and what would happen if he failed to appear.

Chapter 29

Colonel Jonathan Fitzwilliam accompanied his cousin Darcy each year at Easter to pay a duty visit to his aunt and cousin. While Darcy was busy with estate matters, Fitzwilliam provided company for his cousin.

At one time, all three cousins had been great friends; however, that changed as Lady Catherine began to insist that Anne and Darcy wed. Darcy was focused on avoiding being entrapped by her demands, and the colonel ran interference between them. He and Anne had remained great friends while Darcy grew more distant.

Anne understood the retreat and was just as powerless to stop her mother's intrigues. She did not resent Darcy for his withdrawal, as she had known that Lady Catherine would have viewed any attention or kindness paid toward Anne as his agreement with her decree that the two would marry.

However, during those visits, she learned about estate matters from Darcy and did what she could to exert her independence without her mother knowing. Colonel Fitzwilliam was her loyal assistant, finding ways for them to meet with the steward without her mother's knowledge. Each year, they discussed the plans for the estate, with Darcy providing guidance while allowing Anne to ultimately make the decisions. With the help of her companion, Anne could exchange letters with her cousins without Lady Catherine's interference; through these letters, she became confident in her ability to run the estate.

As Anne's understanding grew, so did Fitzwilliam's. After listening to Darcy for years, he had a pretty good idea of estate matters and was excited at the prospect of helping Anne manage Rosings.

* * *

Fitzwilliam arrived at Rosings accompanied by his father and his late uncle's solicitor.

"Uncle Malcolm, Jonathan, I am so pleased to welcome you to Rosings." Anne greeted her guests in the drawing room. "Has my mother been dealt with?"

Her uncle nodded. "In a way. Anne, I, well, I hate to be the one to tell you this, but your mother collapsed when we confronted her. She is presently at Matlock House under the care of a physician. The attack weakened her, but she should eventually recover."

Anne was taken aback. "Am I responsible for her condition? Was it caused by my refusing to allow her to return to Rosings?"

"No, Anne, her attack had nothing to do with you. She was exhausted from travelling across the country, searching for Darcy and learning of his marriage in the way she did. But what caused the episode was her sudden realisation that no one truly listened to her."

"Oh my. That must have been a terrible shock for her."

"It certainly was. Do not be alarmed. This does not change our plans. Your mother will not return to Rosings; she will remain in our home for some time to try to recover. For the present, your companion will be an adequate chaperone for you while Jonathan is in residence, and the two of you will take control of the estate. You could marry, as it would make things easier for you."

"No, Uncle. I have finally gained my freedom. As much as I adore Jonathan's company, I do not intend to wrest control from my mother, only to willingly give it to another immediately. And Jonathan deserves more since I am not certain I will ever be able to truly be a wife to him."

"Nor would I ask it of you, Annie. I know you have desired your independence above all. Father, I wish you had not even suggested such an idea. Now, there are documents we need to sign before you and Thompson return to London on the morrow. Let us get what needs to be done completed so the estate will be legally Anne's."

The four moved into the study to do as the colonel suggested, and soon, the estate was fully in Anne's control. Anne gathered Rosings' servants and announced the transition.

* * *

A sennight later, Bennet arrived at the solicitor's office alone. His brother had refused to assist him further, claiming that he had already gone as far as he felt he could. Phillips felt slightly ashamed for his part in helping to manipulate Elizabeth's situation to aid the Bennets. Finally, he admitted to himself that his motivation had been selfish — he did not want Fanny Bennet to live with him and his wife when Bennet eventually passed.

Though he doubted he ever would, should he encounter Elizabeth, he intended to apologise for attempting to wrest control of her estate from her. Upon hearing the complete narrative from Bennet, particularly the revelation that the Bennets had received a quarterly stipend for her care, a sense of pity for the girl overcame him. He was grateful to know she had found happiness, especially after enduring years of mistreatment from Bennet and Fanny. Given the hardships she had faced, he believed Elizabeth deserved a measure of joy in her life, and he was genuinely pleased she had found it.

In the London solicitor's office, Bennet was facing a tough time. A dozen men sat around the table, and eleven were irritated with Bennet's recalcitrance. He stubbornly refused to admit that he was in the wrong.

"Frankly, you are getting off far too easily. The Darcys are well within their rights to demand far more recompense than they are requesting. Given the time and the inclination, the solicitors would likely find thousands more pounds you owe them. Were Longbourn not entailed, I would have little doubt they could claim the estate itself or demand you sell it and use the proceeds to pay back all of what you took from her. You should be grateful they are asking you for such a trifling amount as three thousand pounds," Mr. Elliott said when they were sitting in the solicitor's office.

"But you are demanding more than two years' income from my estate. How is such an amount ever to be repaid?" Bennet protested.

"When your brother died, Longbourn brought in a clear three thousand pounds per annum. You have allowed the income to decrease due to your lackadaisical attitude toward its management. Perhaps if you began to put more effort into managing your estate, you could make up some of the profits you have lost. Not to mention if you were to restrain your wife's spending ..."

"I am not sure she can do that," Bennet interjected.

"Controlling your wife's spending falls to you as her husband and the master of the estate. Tell her what she has to spend and make her stick to a budget," Gardiner retorted.

"Easier said than done," Bennet groused.

"You have a small fortune of books in your bookroom," Gardiner replied. "Since much of the money you skimmed from the stipend meant for Elizabeth went to purchase those books, you could sell them and repay her far more quickly."

"I could never sell the books. They are my companions, more than my wife or daughters. Only Elizabeth came close to providing the same intellectual stimulus."

"But you had no compunction in attempting to sell your niece to your heir," Darcy nearly growled at the man.

"How was what I did any different than what *you* did in marrying her? You married her so that you could retain control of her fortune."

"Mr. Bennet, I thought you were more intelligent than this. Surely, you know by now that notwithstanding our marriage, Elizabeth retains control of her estate and inheritance." Darcy had to keep himself from shouting at the obtuse man. "I am nothing like you. I married Elizabeth because I love her and want her to be my partner in life. She is witty, intelligent, and beautiful, and I am fortunate she accepted me. You, on the other hand, stole from her trust funds and plotted to steal her estate — you could be hung or transported for much less. You also mistreated her, neglected her, and forced her to do what you were too indolent to do yourself."

"It is quite easy to care about others when you have all that wealth at your feet," Bennet insisted.

"You have not been exactly poor. Fifteen hundred pounds per annum is more than most people see in their lifetime," Elliott put in. "To claim that a lack of funds prevented you from caring for your niece is absolute bunkum. You could have worked your estate to increase your income, but instead, you chose the path of sloth. Instead of working to keep your estate producing at the same level it was, you allowed the income to decline, relying on the money intended to provide for *a child* under your care."

Mr. Bennet scowled again, but none of the men cared that such statements made him unhappy.

"Now, here are the terms. The trustees, Mr. Elliott and Lord Matlock, together with Mr. and Mrs. Darcy, have agreed not to file criminal charges against you and your wife if you agree to the following." The attorney, Mr. Livesey, began to read off the stipulations. Mr. Bennet would be required to repay the couple three thousand pounds over the next six years and surrender guardianship of the remaining four girls to Mr. Gardiner. Mr. Gardiner is to be given one hundred pounds per annum for each girls' care, leaving Mr. Bennet with enough funds to keep Longbourn running, but not much more.

"As you are well aware, with a competent steward and modern farming practices, the estate could bring in nearly double what it presently does. It is up to you to increase the estate's funds. Failure to comply with these demands will have the Darcys suing you for the full amount you owe. That amount is presently undetermined, but we identified a deficit of three thousand in just a few days. Please note that this is with only the barest of efforts, so I do not doubt we could identify significantly more."

"My wife will never agree to this," Bennet complained.

"I am sorry, sir, but are you not the husband and the master of your estate? Your wife was complicit in your actions, was she not? Should she not suffer along with you in this?" Lord Matlock reprimanded him.

"She will be displeased, and I will have to hear about it."

"Then spend more time on the estate, taking care of what you should have been taking care of all along. Visit the tenants and encourage your wife to do the same. Perhaps you would not be in this situation if you had forced her to learn her place as the mistress of the estate instead of giving in to her every demand. After living on an estate for fifteen years, surely you cannot be entirely ignorant of what is required?" Elliott asked.

Mr. Bennet was seriously displeased; however, there was little he could do but agree. Before too much more time had passed, and with a minimum of prodding required, all the documents were signed.

"Now, Lydia and Kitty will be going to school as they require instruction. Mary will have masters hired to assist her, and a companion will be hired for her and Jane. The Darcys may occasionally host them, but neither you nor your wife are to have contact with any of your daughters directly. You may send letters to their guardians or their school's headmistress; if the letters are deemed appropriate, your daughters will be permitted to read them. Neither of you may criticise the Gardiners, Darcys, or anyone else in this room. You may not arrange marriages for any of your daughters; you have surrendered control to Mr. Gardiner.

"Finally, neither of you are permitted to write to the Darcys at all or to make any demands of them. There will be a financial penalty if any of these strictures are ignored, and I warn you, it is a substantial penalty. You have agreed to this in the documents you signed."

Defeated, Bennet left the solicitors' office, dreading what was to come.

Chapter 30

Mr. Bennet spent one final night in an inn just outside London before returning home. After leaving the solicitor's office, Gardiner pulled Bennet aside to inform him that he and Mrs. Gardiner would arrive at Longbourn in three days to collect the girls. That did not bother him nearly as much as when Gardiner told him that every book he had purchased in the last 15 years now belonged to Elizabeth and would need to be packed away as well.

As Bennet lay in the bed at the inn, he realised he dreaded telling his wife what had happened in London. She would moan and complain, especially about her precious Lydia being taken away. He was unsure how the older girls would react, though he knew informing Lydia that she would need to attend school would be a trial. Perhaps he would allow Gardiner to inform her. After all, he was now her guardian.

He wondered idly what would happen if one of the girls refused to go with the Gardiners. Would they allow her to stay if she demanded it? That would allow him to keep the hundred pounds he would otherwise have to send for her care, but half of that would end up as Lydia's allowance if she stayed. Mrs. Bennet would have fewer funds now to purchase new dresses and other fripperies. He briefly wondered if either Mrs. Bennet or Lydia would know how to live within a budget. Or willingly follow one if they did?

Naturally, Bennet had not read the contract he signed well and did not realise that Lydia or any girls could indeed refuse the Gardiners' offer. Nor did he realise steps had already been taken toward this and that nearly as soon as he left London the first time, those steps had already begun to be implemented.

Mrs. Gardiner would speak to each girl privately, explaining matters clearly. Each girl would choose, on their own, what to do. If they accepted the assistance of their uncle, they would be required to behave as gentlewomen with all the expected behaviour of one. The two youngest would no longer be out, they would attend school, learn accomplishments, and how to manage a household.

In return, they would be treated as daughters of the house, receiving all their needs and many of their wants, an allowance equal to what they received at Longbourn. It would also provide them with far greater opportunities and benefits from the association with the Darcys and Lord and Lady Matlock, though they would not be allowed to take advantage of it until they learned how to behave in society.

When Mr. Bennet arrived home, he discovered his books already boxed, preventing him from secreting away even a few for himself. In a fit of pique, Bennet chose not speak with his wife, letting her discover what was happening when his brother arrived. He did inform Jane and Mary by themselves to warn them and had asked the Hills to begin to pack his daughters' belongings.

Unbeknownst to the master of the house, the Hills already knew what was to occur and had begun assisting Jane and Mary. Neither expected Lydia to willingly leave her mother to attend school, though what Kitty would ultimately decide was a little less certain.

Seizing the opportunity, Jane engaged in several heartfelt conversations with Kitty, discussing the merits of living in London and attending school. Recognizing the potential negative influence of Lydia, Jane earnestly encouraged Kitty to distance herself from her younger sister before her behaviour adversely affected the family. A letter from Mrs. Gardiner detailing incidents involving a friend in Lambton had starkly illuminated the consequences of unchecked influence for Jane. In the past few weeks, especially after gaining insight into her cousin's experiences and her own parents' treatment of the girl who had come to live with their family, Jane had been compelled to confront a more realistic view of the world. These revelations, coupled with other unsettling occurrences during her father's absence, had awakened Jane to the darker aspects of life.

Mrs. Phillips heard enough of the conversation between her own husband and Mr. Bennet and began to spread the story of how the Bennets had treated their niece infamously. As the truth of the girl's parentage became known, many began to criticise the Bennets. Some older residents recalled the former Beth Bennet as a happy, joyful child and recalled bits of her in her daughter. They would have been pleased to know that Elizabeth would have enjoyed sharing stories of the girl's mother with her, as they had known and adored her.

"Will Lizzy be returning to Meryton? Will she remain with the Gardiners in Town? I have so many stories about her mother as a child that I would love to share with her," one of these older residents asked Mrs. Phillips.

"Mr. Bennet has been rather closed mouth about things, at least around me. Mr. Phillips had written a contract for Lizzy to marry Mr. Bennet's heir, but Mr. Phillips was not aware of the full extent of her grandfather's will or her full inheritance. He truly believed she was Edward Bennet's natural child, and the estate came from her maternal grandfather. He regrets ever assisting my brother with anything related to Lizzy's possible marriage," Mrs. Phillips answered.

"What does Mrs. Bennet say? She always treated Lizzy as a poor relation, but I heard from someone that Lizzy's estate paid the Bennets a hefty stipend for her care each quarter," another lady asked.

"That is one area where my sister has remained silent. She has always disliked Lizzy; she disliked taking her niece in and frequently complained about the cost of clothing and educating her. That does not make sense if they received funds for her support, but I cannot imagine my brother withholding that information from her." Mrs. Phillips was enjoying being the centre of attention and had little trouble with making up information she did not know. "I heard something said about her having a Season in

Town. Mayhap her guardian knows someone who might sponsor her. With her inheritance now, she will be able to marry extremely well."

"That should please Mrs. Bennet," Lady Lucas added. "It would have had she not ensured her niece would want little to do with her in the future. My Charlotte has had a letter from Eliza, or should I say, Mrs. Darcy. She has married; it seems Mr. Darcy met her often enough in Meryton that he fell in love with her. They apparently knew each other when they were children, and the estate Eliza will inherit upon her birthday is not too far distant from Mr. Darcy's estate. They encountered each other in Town. Actually, it was Mr. Darcy who escorted her to Town after learning of Elizabeth's true identity and assisted in removing her away from the Bennets' control."

This announcement made all the women begin to speak excitedly. They remembered the gossip when Mr. Darcy first entered their society of his having ten thousand a year and speculated about the size of Elizabeth's dowry now and the potential income of her estate.

"Truly, Mrs. Phillips," Lady Lucas said after the subject had been canvassed for some minutes, "Mrs. Bennet was foolish not to embrace Eliza into the family and treat her better. She constantly complained about the possibility of being thrown into the hedgerows when Mr. Bennet died, all the while having a girl living in her home who would have gladly cared for her all her life. However, she threw that away with her poor treatment of her."

"She resented that Mr. Bennet took an interest in the girl when they arrived at Longbourn. Lizzy was already quite intelligent, even as a small child, and Mr. Bennet spent time teaching her. That and Lizzy had things she would not, so she grew jealous of the child and could not get over that, not even in the interest of self-preservation. I do not doubt that she will attempt to do so now, especially when the facts of her marriage and inheritance become more publicly known, but Lizzy will not overlook how Mrs. Bennet has treated her before. My husband spoke of Mr. Bennet having to speak to some solicitors in London about the money he took for Lizzy's care and how it was used."

Both women looked at each other. They knew Mrs. Bennet frequently withheld items from Elizabeth that she willingly purchased for her daughters. On more than one occasion, they had questioned the matron's insistence on purchasing lower-quality items for Elizabeth or berating her for daring to use something that belonged to one of her daughters. "My husband refused to support Mr. Bennet when he went to London. I did not hear what all was said, but I heard raised voices the last time Mr. Bennet visited his office."

The ladies exchanged yet another glance. Just then, Mrs. Bennet approached with her daughters and did not seem to recognise the slightly chilly quality of the greetings. Charlotte, who had arrived in the group with her mother, spoke to Jane privately and told her some of the conversations.

Jane nodded at this news. "I am not surprised to learn that Mama will be censured. Lizzy's last letter told me a few of these facts, and the Hills have received a letter telling them to pack up most of Papa's bookroom when he left Town tomorrow. Those books now belong to Lizzy since they were purchased with her money. We will be going to live with the Gardiners, at least those of us who desire to. I am uncertain what Kitty will choose to do, but I feel Lydia will want to remain with Mama. Neither understands that things at Longbourn will soon change drastically."

At Charlotte's questioning look, Jane continued to explain more of what she knew from a letter from her cousin. Elizabeth had only given the briefest outline of what was expected to occur, but, combined with the letter to Mrs. Hill, was enough to let both women understand that Mr. and Mrs. Bennet were about to be held accountable for their actions against their niece.

Charlotte shook her head. "Mr. and Mrs. Bennet are not receiving all they deserve. Perhaps being compelled to live with less, without most of their daughters, and facing the disapproval of their neighbours will serve as adequate punishment. Has your mother not yet recognized the difference in treatment she is receiving?"

Jane looked over at where she was seated, next to her sister and Charlotte's mother. She could see the distaste in the other lady's faces, but Mrs. Bennet was crowing over something Lydia had said or done and how her dearest daughter was capturing the attention of so many soldiers in the militia. Then she turned to look at Lydia, who was acting similarly, bragging about

216

some of the more outrageous flirtations she had been engaging in. "If she remains at Longbourn, she will ruin herself within a year. Perhaps it is best that we are to depart."

"What of Kitty?" Charlotte asked, and both older girls turned to look at her.

Kitty appeared thoughtful, listening to Lydia but also observing the others around her. Most of the young girls were shocked at what Lydia was describing, and then Kitty turned toward Jane, who smiled gently at her. Kitty stood and went to sit next to her oldest sister. "I am afraid you are right about Lydia, Jane. I think … I think if I am allowed to leave Longbourn for London, I will go to London. Lydia will try to convince me otherwise, but I … well, perhaps it is best that I go to school to learn to behave."

Both women smiled at the girl. "I am proud of you for realising this, Kitty, but please do not speak to Lydia of it until the Gardiners arrive. We cannot be certain she will not speak to Mama, and since we think it unlikely Papa will, we do not want to run the risk of upsetting Mama too soon. I prefer to wait as long as possible for her to learn what will come."

"She speaks of Mary marrying Mr. Collins now instead of Lizzy."

"Mary will not marry Papa's heir. We will have the opportunity to meet men in London, well, not you, not yet, but Mary and I will be introduced to good and eligible men who would make good matches for us. Lizzy has agreed to give those of us who go to the Gardiners a dowry, and that will assist us in finding matches who are worthy of us."

"You will not marry Mr. Bingley?" Kitty asked, having heard much about that match from their mother as well.

"Mr. Bingley is not all he seems. I believe he thought he could settle for me after his sister nearly ruined his family, but I will not allow myself to be used in such a manner. I would not accept a man because he believes he can do no better than me." Jane spoke unnaturally firmly, and Mrs. Bennet heard.

"Has Mr. Bingley offered for you? He left for London some days ago without holding the ball he promised. Have you heard when he is to return?" Mrs. Bennet asked excitedly.

"The Hursts remain at Netherfield, as I understand it, but Mr. Bingley is taking his sister north to settle her somewhere with another family member. Mrs. Hurst said she doubts he will return any time soon. And Mama, I told you, there is nothing between Mr. Bingley and me. He paid me a little attention but no more than anyone else in Town. I have no expectations of him. Not to mention, Mrs. Gardiner has said he has a poor reputation in Town. A connexion with him would not aid me or my sisters." Jane said this last, hoping it would stop her mother's constant references to him.

"Yes, I have heard vague rumours about him from Town. Mr. and Mrs. Hurst are very pleasant, and I hope they will remain for some time. However, I heard the other sister, who believed she was superior to everyone, ruined herself in polite society. Both the Bingleys have been cut from most invitations, and no one in Town will receive them," Mrs. Phillips inserted.

Mrs. Bennet gasped at that, and then the conversation returned to the matrons speaking of gossip from London. There was a mention of a ruined girl in Meryton now that the militia was quartered there, and warnings were issued to all the ladies to keep an eye on their daughters since many of the men in the regiment were unknown to the local society.

As usual, Mrs. Bennet believed the warnings were meant for others, not for her or her girls. She spoke of Lydia being a great favourite with many of the officers and how she was sure to attract the most handsome among them. Lydia heard this comment and bragged that she would be the first of her sisters to marry and that she was looking forward to being the wife of a dashing soldier. Some of the ladies heard this and merely shook their heads, knowing that the life Lydia spoke of was unlikely to happen. The conversation shifted once again, and soon, all the ladies returned to their own homes, speaking of the Bennet family and how they hoped the eldest three would not be ruined by the youngest.

Chapter 31

Never particularly astute, Mrs. Bennet did not realise that the residents of her town had begun treating her differently or notice that her daughters were acting strangely. Unbeknownst to Mrs. Bennet, Jane, Mary, and Kitty had begun to spend time above stairs helping each other pack those things they wanted to take with them.

Therefore, she was quite surprised when her brother and sister arrived in a large carriage followed by a wagon two days after her husband returned from London

"Brother, Sister, what are you doing at Longbourn?" the matron said when she greeted her unexpected guests.

The Gardiners turned to look at each other, and Mrs. Gardiner rolled her eyes. Her husband had to hold back the laugh that threatened, though he seriously considered throttling his brother-in-law as he stood there looking at the two, his gaze defiant.

"I told Bennet of our plans before he left London. We are here to take Jane and Mary to London with us. Kitty and Lydia may come too, but they will be enrolled in school if they choose to come."

"Choose?" Bennet bit out while Mrs. Bennet cried out in dismay.

"You mean to take all my daughters? Why?"

"Bennet agreed to all of this on Friday. Since your family will be required to pay restitution for taking what did not rightfully belong to you, we agreed to assist by taking the girls to London with us. Granted, none of them will be forced to come, but they will live with our rules. My wife will speak to each of them individually and will explain what we expect from them under our roof and allow them to make the choice," Gardiner explained.

"None of my girls will want to go with you. You have wasted your time in coming here, Brother," Mrs. Bennet said with a measure of certainty.

It surprised everyone there when Mary was the one who contradicted her mother. "Actually, Mama, Jane and I have already decided we will go to London. Kitty believes she would like to join us, though she wanted to speak to my aunt first, to be certain. She is already looking forward to going to school. Our things are packed and ready."

Mrs. Bennet stood there gaping. Lydia looked at her sisters hatefully. "Well, I will not go. No one will tell me what to do, nor will they make me go to some school. I will remain here with Mama."

"Thank you, my dear girl. You and I will be pleased here together, and I will give you what I would have spent on these ungrateful girls."

"You will find your funds cut substantially. You and your husband are to repay Elizabeth the three thousand pounds you stole from her, and you will send one hundred pounds for each girl to me in London for their upkeep. Yes, you will have fewer people in your home, but you will have significantly less income. The three of you will have about nine hundred pounds remaining, although that amount could increase if Mr. Bennet is more diligent about the estate. The funds from Elizabeth's trust will no longer be paid, so you will only have what Longbourn earns to live on. There will not be enough for extravagant purchases."

"Nine hundred pounds," she screeched. "How can you expect us to live on that?"

"You will need to learn to live within your means," Gardiner said adamantly. "Kitty, go and have your chat with my wife while the bags are loaded. Are you already packed as well?" At Kitty's nod, he began directing the men with him to load the boxes and trunks waiting to be loaded. He ignored his sister's complaints, Lydia's foolishness, and Bennet's attempt to placate his wife.

Jane and Mary spoke to the Hills and were waiting just inside the foyer of the house, not wanting to go outside where their parents and Lydia were still arguing. Mrs. Gardiner approached them from behind, startling them both.

"I should not be, but I am astounded he did not say a word to your mother before our arrival."

"He has said little to anyone since returning from this last trip to London," Jane informed her aunt. "He has spent most of his time in his bookroom, although few books remain there now."

Mrs. Gardiner nodded at this information. "He did not want to deal with your mother and her complaints. Now, it will be just the three of them, and without his books to keep him company, perhaps he will be forced to interact with them more."

A loud voice from outside interrupted their conversation. Mrs. Gardiner continued, "I need to speak to Lydia and at least offer her the chance to come to London. She will not accept it, but she must be offered the opportunity." Reluctantly, she went off to do as she said and followed the sound of yelling. "Lydia!" she shouted, getting the attention of the combatants. "Come, child, we must speak."

"There is no point in the two of us speaking; I will not go to London to live with you, and I do not want or need to go to school. I will stay right where I am."

"Lydia, your parents will not be able to provide you with the dresses and other things you are used to. Their income will be cut quite significantly. School would allow you to learn how to act in society, and eventually, you might even be able to be presented at court."

"I do not care for any of those things. I will marry an officer and attend dances and parties every night." She crossed her arms across her chest as she spoke, giving Mrs. Gardiner quite the eyeful.

Mrs. Gardiner sighed heavily. "Lydia, the life you would live as an officer's wife is not merely dances and parties. It will be far more difficult than you are imagining at present. Come, let us sit down together and speak directly. Then, you can make an informed decision."

"No!" cried the spoiled child. "I will remain right where I am, until I marry my officer."

"Has someone proposed to you already? Are you in a courtship?"

Lydia laughed. "Heavens, no. I will marry soon enough, but I have yet to choose my husband. I will not allow myself to become an old maid like Jane. Imagine being three and twenty and still unwed. No, I will be the first of my sisters to marry, and I am the youngest." She laughed again and walked away from her aunt.

Shaking her head, Mrs. Gardiner approached the girl's mother. "You must speak to her. Marrying a militia officer is not the life she imagines it is. She would have to follow her husband to whatever camp he is presently posted to and would have little to live on. You will all have to begin to economise, but as an officer's wife, she would have far less than she is presently used to. No new dresses and likely no maids to do the work. She is unprepared for such a life; you must speak to her."

"Oh, la, Maddie. Lydia will do very well as an officer's wife and will be much admired. Now, I cannot understand why you are here and are taking all my daughters away from me."

"Your husband agreed to it, in part to prevent the Darcys from demanding you repay even more of what you stole from Lizzy. She cares enough about her cousins to want them to have a better life than what they are likely to have here. Jane and Mary will live with us in London while Kitty will attend school for a year to learn additional accomplishments. What accomplishments can your youngest daughters claim other than being pretty and lively? They will need more than that to attract a suitor eventually, and they will be exposed to far more at our London home than they have been in Meryton."

"You said Lizzy married that rich Mr. Darcy; they met in Meryton. Perhaps Jane will encounter Mr. Bingley in London, and he will finally be convinced by his friend to propose. Surely, Lizzy would like to see her favourite cousin settled well. When that happens, I will not have to worry about my other girls, as Mr. Bingley will surely help see Jane's sisters well settled."

"Mr. Bingley is not in London, nor is he an eligible suitor for Jane."

Mr. Gardiner stepped up to the pair just then, indicating to his wife that all was ready to depart. "Fanny, as Mr. Bennet will likely not bother to inform you, I will tell you what else he agreed to. You are not allowed to write letters directly to any of your daughters who reside under my roof. You may send letters to me and my wife for us to read, and if they are appropriate, we will pass them on to your daughters. For Kitty, the headmistress will read them before passing the letters on. That includes letters from Lydia since she will remain here with you. Likewise, you are forbidden from writing to Elizabeth Darcy or her husband at all. Do not even attempt it, as those letters will be sent back or dropped into the fire unopened. Neither Elizabeth nor her husband ever want to hear from you or Mr. Bennet again. In the contract that Mr. Bennet signed, any violation of this will result in a penalty of ten pounds per incident. You are not to request anything from your daughters, including introductions or funds, and that continues when they are married. If any of the girls wish to write to you, they will not be prevented from doing so, but know that any letter that comes into my house from you or your daughter will be read first by me."

Mrs. Bennet's mouth dropped open. "I cannot imagine writing to Lizzy anyway."

"Can you not, madam? You sent Lizzy several letters when you believed she was residing with us before you learned of her marriage. First, you demanded she return so she could marry Mr. Collins, and when you learned that would not happen, you wrote to remind her that you had raised her and treated her as a daughter. You also asked her if she would not mind sending you fifty pounds each month now that she had so much money and an estate to boot. You asked her to agree to house you and any unmarried daughters when Mr. Bennet died, claiming to have done such a great service by taking her in when no one knew she had anything. You have always known about the stipend you received for her care and have used it for your benefit while treating Elizabeth as though she were an inconvenience."

Mrs. Bennet stammered but had no way to defend what she had done. She complained of her ill-treatment, but Gardiner and his wife had already boarded the carriage behind the girls, and, ignoring the caterwauling, he tapped the roof with his walking stick. The carriage jolted into motion, while Mrs. Bennet watched it leave, finally dumbstricken.

That silence lasted all of five minutes. Mr. Bennet had long ago retreated to his bookroom, where his wife found him several minutes later. She opened her mouth to speak but looked around, finally noticing the empty shelves.

"What happened here?" she asked, distracted from the topic she had come to speak of.

"Since most of the books I had purchased in the last fifteen years were purchased with money from the stipend, it was determined they belonged to Lizzy, not me. They were boxed up and sent to her. I was left with only the estate books and whatever books were here before we came."

"My brother said you agreed to all of this. You never said a word to me. How did the girls know to be packed ahead of their coming? And why did you not tell me any of this? What are we to do now? My sister said we would have to live on something like nine hundred pounds per annum. That is less even than the income of Longbourn." Mrs. Bennet would have continued asking questions, but her husband silenced her with a glare.

Mr. Bennet sighed heavily and explained to his wife, finally, what had transpired in London. She listened in stunned silence as he explained all that had happened, or at least most of what had happened. He was unwilling to tell her of Mr. Collins's threat to leave them homeless in retaliation for lying to him about Elizabeth.

Chapter 32

Mrs. Bennet sat staring at her husband in disbelief. "How could you have agreed to all of this?" she demanded, growing angry with her husband for being his usual taciturn self. "You have known this for days and had opportunities to tell me since returning but did not say a word to me."

"If I had told you, I would have only had to listen to you complaining about the situation for days. Now, it is done; there is nothing you can do about it, and you still have Lydia with you. It is not as though you cared much about the other girls anyway. Perhaps Jane a little more than the others, but you ignored Mary and Kitty." Mr. Bennet was already tired of speaking and only wanted his room to himself. There were still a few books left to distract him, and if he were careful, perhaps he could purchase a few more at a second-hand store.

She huffed. "How will we manage to live on so little? Do you have a plan to increase the income of the estate? You have let it decrease in recent years, as you have become reliant on having the money from Elizabeth. What happened to the plan to have Mr. Collins marry Mary? She is no longer here to make her marry him; will the Gardiners enforce the contract?"

"There is no contract, nor would your brother have required Mary to marry where she did not wish. We will simply need to learn to get by on less. I suppose I can continue some of the improvements Lizzy started, but I do not know how much they will help. Perhaps they will not miss them if we do not send the funds to London to either the Darcys or the Gardiners. That will allow us to keep more for ourselves. You only have yourself and Lydia to dress now, and since Lydia is desirous of getting married, that will mean one less person to be responsible for. There are other places within the household where you can save on expenses; sit down with Mrs. Hill and see what can be done."

For the second time that day, Mrs. Bennet was stunned into silence. She did not know what to think about everything she had been told. Silently, she left her husband's bookroom and went to her sitting room to consider matters over.

* * *

Mrs. Bennet was not a woman used to introspection. She was much more likely to find a way to blame others around her, and that is what she did. She was in her sitting room for less than fifteen minutes when she began to believe herself ill-used. Feeling faint, she began calling for Mrs. Hill to bring her her salts. As she waited, she shrieked for Lydia to join her, and the two began to form a plan.

"Lydia, we must go to London to meet with Lizzy. She will surely recognise you, her cousin, and will want to take you in and help you make a good match. Since her other cousins have forsaken us, and she sees you have stayed with your parents, she will want to assist you. We will convince her to provide you with all the best clothes and introduce you to the *ton*."

"La, why would I want any of that? I want to marry an officer who wears a red coat. Several handsome men in the militia will do quite well. And now that all my sisters have left us I will have all their dowries, will I not? Surely I will be a far greater prize with five thousand pounds all to myself?"

"Perhaps you can still marry an officer, but one in the regulars. Now that you have so many more opportunities, you will not want to settle for second best."

Mrs. Bennet's words made Lydia pause for only a moment. "No, I believe that Denny or Carter will do quite well. Captain Carter is likely the better choice, though Denny is more handsome. I am certain I can make them both fall in love with me."

"Still, if we go to London and get Lizzy to purchase you fine dresses, they will fall in love much more quickly. Not to mention all the ribbons and lace Lizzy can purchase for you."

Lydia seemed to consider this. "I suppose I can spare a few days. Perhaps a few days out of their company would help the officers realise how much they would miss me." She thought for another moment. "But we cannot be gone too long. I would not want Mary King or Maria Lucas to take my place."

Mrs. Bennet agreed and told her they would remain no longer than a sennight in London, believing that her niece would pay for her daughter's gowns to be expedited. She asked Mrs. Hill to begin making the arrangements, including informing the driver of their intention to depart in the morning. "And you must have him discover Lizzy's new address in London. Mr. Bennet must have it somewhere in his office."

"I am sorry, madam, but I am afraid that is impossible," the housekeeper replied.

"What do you mean?" Mrs. Bennet asked.

"Mr. Bennet has forbidden you from using the carriage to travel to London."

"Why?" she demanded.

"My understanding is that you are not welcome there. The Gardiners will no longer recognise you, so you cannot stay with them, and Miss Lizzy, or rather Mrs. Darcy, wants nothing to do with you. She would not welcome you in her home."

"But I am the closest thing she has to a mother. I have raised her since she was five or six years old. How can she not want me to visit?"

"You will have to speak to your husband, madam. And in case Mr. Bennet has not yet informed you, Mr. Hill and I will leave here in a fortnight. We have been offered another position and have decided to take it."

"What!" the matron nearly shouted. "You cannot leave me. Who will I hire as a housekeeper if you depart?"

"Madam, your husband informed us that he can no longer afford to keep us at the same salary as we have been receiving. When another position was offered, we could not turn it down. We have a month before arriving at our new posts; we informed your husband this morning of our desire to depart."

"But I need you here. I cannot possibly run Longbourn without you. Surely, you would not mind the pay decrease since you are so desperately needed here."

"No, madam, my husband and I know what we are worth. The new position not only pays us more, but we have been promised a cottage in a few years when we decide we are ready to retire. We would not have that at Longbourn," Mrs. Hill persisted.

"Fine, then leave now. Do not bother to remain. Do not take anything that does not belong to you, and I will have someone check to ensure that all my jewellery is where it belongs."

"Miss Jane and Miss Mary packed up much of your jewellery. Some pieces were purchased with money that rightfully belonged to Miss Lizzy, I mean, Mrs. Darcy. It will be given to her, and she will decide what to do with those pieces."

Mrs. Bennet spluttered in her rage. Without waiting to be dismissed, the housekeeper left the mistress's room and headed to her room. Her trunks, as were her husband's, were already packed, and she informed him of what the mistress said. "We are departing immediately. Mrs. Bennet was none too pleased to learn that we had accepted a position elsewhere, and I dared not tell her where we were to go. The wagon is still waiting?"

Her husband smiled. "It is. We will make our way north to Briarwood. The housekeeper and butler will remain to teach us our duties for a month or two, but then we will be left in charge. I truly do not know what will happen at Longbourn now, as neither Mrs. Bennet nor Miss Lydia has any idea how to run this household or any other."

Mrs. Hill chuckled. "The mistress truly believed she'd be able to convince Miss Lizzy to purchase them new clothes after how she had treated the girl. Should we inform Mr. Bennet we are departing?"

"No. I doubt he will miss us, and the mistress told you to leave, right?"

"She did. Is anyone else accompanying us?"

"No, but I gave references to several who thought they would be seeking a new position soon. I do not trust Mr. or Mrs. Bennet to do the same, and I doubt the estate will have enough to pay any servants soon. I ensured everyone was paid a quarter ahead."

"You are a good man, Mr. Hill. At least we can be certain they'll be taken care of. How long do you think they'll last?"

He merely shrugged, and the two departed to board the carriage that would carry them and their belongings north.

* * *

When Mrs. Bennet stopped blustering, she nearly called for her housekeeper again before recalling that she had most likely departed by now. She scowled at this fact and instead called for Lydia.

"What?" she demanded petulantly when she showed up at her mother's door. "I was about to walk into Meryton."

"Not by yourself," Mrs. Bennet said in a rare show of protectiveness. "I will walk to town with you. We will visit my sister and see what can be done about finding a new housekeeper."

"Why do we need a new housekeeper?" Lydia inquired.

"The Hills have been offered a position elsewhere and left to take it. It was most inconsiderate of them. Your father has been most vexing about the situation with the girls and Lizzy. Do you know he knew they were to depart and did not say a word? I am so glad you chose to remain with me, Lydia!"

"I stayed so I could marry an officer. I will be the first of my sisters married, and they will all come home to see me wed. They will be quite envious of me, especially Kitty," she crowed. "We will invite all the officers to the wedding, and they will form a guard of honour as we depart the church. It will be so wonderful."

"But then you will have to go away from me, Lyddie. You should not be in such a rush to leave me, my dear girl. Imagine all the ribbons and dresses I can purchase for you now. With your sisters gone, I can spend all my money buying pretty things for you."

"But Mama, you have always said how important it is for us all to find husbands and marry as soon as may be. Why should you tell me differently now?"

"Oh, Lydia, I would hate to lose you so soon after all the rest of my daughters. I always knew you and Jane would marry and leave me someday, but I thought I would have Mary or Kitty still at home to keep me company. If you marry and leave, it will only be your father and I at home. I am not certain how I will stand that."

"La, Mama, but someday I will have to leave. You would not want me to be an old maid, would you?"

Mrs. Bennet was not confident about this but knew it would not be the same to have a married daughter visit her as it would be to have an unmarried one living with her. Still, Lydia was determined, and she wanted her baby girl to have the very best she could.

Soon, they arrived in Meryton and went straight to the dressmakers to have new clothing made for Lydia. Since there would be no trip to town, at least not for now, Mrs. Bennet was determined to purchase a few things to make Lydia stand out from the other girls in their small village.

Hearing, "I am sorry, Mrs. Bennet, but you will need to pay for all items in cash before you order," shocked the matron when the dressmaker refused even to consider making a new dress for Lydia. After hearing several similar comments in each of the shops they entered, both ladies were somewhat confused, so they decided to pay a call on Mrs. Phillips to find out what they could from her.

Chapter 33

Mrs. Phillips felt a distinct lack of enthusiasm about her sister's impending visit, especially given the recent surge of gossip swirling around the town regarding her. It was evident that Mrs. Bennet remained oblivious to the rumours that had originated from Mrs. Phillips herself and had since escalated. Much of the community's ire was directed at the Bennet parents for their perceived mistreatment of their niece over time. While the younger Bennet sisters had occasionally been guilty of unkind behaviour toward her, neither Jane nor Mary had been implicated in such actions.

"Sister, I am very disappointed in you. Clearly, you have not heard the news in Meryton. If you had, you would know that the whole town is most upset that you and Mr. Bennet have lied to us for years. You allowed everyone to believe Lizzy was the natural child of Edward Bennet when you knew she was actually the daughter of Elizabeth Bennet Tomlinson. All these years, you have treated her like a poor relation and been given sympathy and praise for taking in a child with nothing. All the while, you were receiving a stipend for her care, which was nearly equal to Longbourn's annual income. How could you?"

Mrs. Bennet stammered, but before she could form a coherent thought at the unexpected accusations, Lydia burst in.

"What do you mean? Do you mean that Lizzy is not my uncle's bastard child?"

"Lydia!" Mrs. Phillips reprimanded. "You should not even speak like that, nor is it true. Lizzy is your cousin, but she is your father's sister's child. And she was respectably married to a landed gentleman when the child was conceived, though he had died by the time she was born. The child came to live at Longbourn after both her parents and her grandparents died."

"Mama and Papa always said she was Uncle Edward's natural child. She is poor, and my parents were generous to allow her to live with us," Lydia insisted while Mrs. Bennet continued staring open-mouthed at her sister.

"Your parents were paid a generous quarterly stipend for allowing her to live with you. That money was intended to be used to ensure Lizzy and all of you girls, really, were well educated and had accomplishments. Instead, it was diverted to provide your parents with many unnecessary indulgences. If not for the money received from Lizzy's estate, you would not have had all the nice dresses and things you do. Since the money was not spent on Lizzy as intended, and your father lied to her guardian, your parents have to repay Lizzy. Her trustees have already seized your father's books and your mother's jewellery purchased with her funds."

"What difference does that make? Lizzy is married to that boring Mr. Darcy and will have loads of nice things."

"Lydia, they ruined Lizzy's reputation by allowing everyone to believe she was illegitimate. They never told Lizzy who her real parents were. They allowed the citizens of this town to believe she was your uncle's natural child. She is the legitimate daughter of your father's sister, Elizabeth Bennet, who grew up at Longbourn and was admired by many people here. Lizzy has been an heiress her whole life. Instead of knowing that, she thought she was a penniless relation, indebted to your family for her care. She was denied knowing about her parents, knowing her heritage, and many of the advantages she was born to. How would you feel if your entire life had been a lie? She deserved better."

"La, Aunt Phillips, I do not understand why it even matters. All has turned out well enough. As I said, she captured a wealthy husband despite all of that."

"You are a fool, Lydia Bennet, just like your mother. You should both leave my home and not return. You will not find a warm welcome in Meryton any time soon. Everyone knows you will be required to retrench and that your three most intelligent daughters have chosen to forgo the name Bennet for Gardiner. Sister, you should know that no one will have anything to do with you after this, and do not think that such an offence will be forgiven soon. Not by your daughters, not by your niece, and not by your neighbours."

"What do you mean, Agnes? How does everyone know all of this? Why should they think of this as some sort of offence? What have we done wrong?" Mrs. Bennet asked, having heard all her sister said, though not taking it in and clearly not understanding why *she* should be censured over it.

"You have lied for years to everyone in this town. They are upset at you for your deception and feel offended that you have not told the truth. Why, when arriving at Longbourn and discovering your niece there, would you allow it to be told that she was the illegitimate daughter of your brother? You and your husband knew the truth and did nothing to correct the misunderstanding. Instead, you encouraged the lie and spread it about for years. No one would have thought poorly of you had they known the truth."

Mrs. Bennet stared at her sister. "Lizzy will forgive us, and then you will all regret not being more accepting of us. She will invite us to London, and there will be grand parties that we will be invited to while you remain here in Meryton."

"You are delusional if you believe that, Fanny. Lizzy might, one day, forgive you, but she will never invite you to London. Had Lydia gone with the Gardiners, she might have included her in an invitation once she is old enough to attend such things, but since she chose to remain at Longbourn, that will never happen now."

"Who cares about London? I will not have to go to some stuffy school like Kitty and learn to be boring. I will have fun here."

"Your family will not receive any further invitations to any events in Meryton. I dare say Kitty will have far more fun than you will." Mrs. Phillips had begun to look at her youngest niece in something like contempt, finally realising just how foolish she and her mother had become. Not long ago, she would have been of a similar mind to her sister, but realising the depth of her sister's deception had forced Agnes Phillips to look at things differently. That and the sound talking to her husband had given her for bandying the Bennets' business about town.

Lydia continued to insist that she would do as she liked, but it was cut off by her uncle entering the room. "No one in town, including the officers, will have anything to do with the Bennets. You, Lydia Bennet, are a fool for turning down the opportunity to better your life by going to your aunt and uncle's home. Unless Thomas turns things around and begins paying attention to the estate, you will have very little to live on, as he scarcely has enough to pay what you owe in town. Not only that, but as I understand it, your housekeeper has left, and the two of you will be far too busy to visit anyone. I suggest you return home and remain there for some time. You will have much to learn, especially you, Lydia. No officer will marry a woman who does not know how to do anything to care for the home, as most of them live hand-to-mouth. The officers cannot afford servants and will not want to marry a woman who does not know how to cook, clean, or keep her mouth shut."

Lydia and Mrs. Bennet were offended by Mr. Phillips' statements and left the house in a pique. "We will show them how wrong they are, Lydia. I will speak to Mr. Bennet about hiring a new housekeeper as soon as we return."

They were disappointed upon arriving home and finding Mr. Bennet on the estate. They could not speak to him about hiring a new housekeeper; instead, Mrs. Bennet had to speak to the cook and maids about the evening meal. Mrs. Bennet could not answer several questions, and Lydia was too bored to pay attention to any of them. But she remained with her mother as Kitty was not there to entertain her.

"This is boring," she complained.

"If you want to be married, you must learn to deal with problems such as these. Perhaps my sister was correct when she said that you need to consider such things if you want to be an officer's wife. Most of them live in barracks designed for single men — in fact, I am not certain any of the officers, other than Colonel Forster, has even mentioned the idea of taking a wife. I wonder why none of them are married."

"What does it matter? Please, Mama, can we do something more fun?"

"No, Lydia, you need to learn how to care for a household. If you were married, you would need to know how to do all these things."

Over the next several weeks, all of Mrs. Phillips' predictions came true. No one from the neighbourhood visited Longbourn, and all attempts to visit others were denied. Lydia was most upset that none of the officers paid a call, and her mother would not allow her to walk to Meryton by herself. She was so disappointed she attempted to sneak out one night to pay a call, but her uncle Phillips found her and promptly returned her home. Her mother was so upset that she locked Lydia in her room each night to ensure she could not escape again.

All three Bennets were rather miserable. Mr. Bennet could not retreat into the silence of his bookroom as he now had to ride out on the estate regularly. Nor could he escape into another world of his books since he only had a handful remaining and no ready funds to purchase any more. What money they did have was required to purchase the necessities, and at the end of the quarter, they barely had enough to pay the remaining servants.

The two letters Mrs. Bennet sent to the Gardiners were both returned with notations that the requests for funds were inappropriate and that complaints about the situation they found themselves in were not welcome. A more official notice arrived from the solicitor informing them that the payment to the Darcys and the funds for the care of the three girls needed to be sent immediately lest Mr. Bennet be thrown into debtors' prison and additional funds be demanded based upon the terms of the agreement.

It was all very depressing for Mr. Bennet, who had intended to keep those funds for himself. He wondered what would happen if he disappeared, but then he realised how much trouble that would be. While part of him did not care much about what happened to Mrs. Bennet and Lydia if he should disappear, he realised how selfish that thought was. It did not stop him from contemplating it, though he did not attempt it. Instead, he put more effort into making the estate profitable and found he could make a couple of minor improvements, though he regularly wondered if it was all worth it.

Chapter 34

In London, the newly married Darcys had put their foot down with their aunt regarding the number of entertainments they would attend. While that lady would have liked them to participate in multiple events per day, sometimes multiple events in one evening, neither Darcy nor Elizabeth desired that. Instead, they stated they would be willing to attend only a few events a week, but certainly not every night.

Of course, they also decided to leave a few evenings open to host a dinner party or two for some of their friends. A few nights after the Bennet girls had settled into London, the Gardiners were invited for dinner.

"Jane, Mary, and Kitty, it is so good to see you," Elizabeth said as she greeted her cousins before introducing them to her new sister. "How are you adjusting to living in London? And Kitty, are you excited about attending school?"

The three cousins, particularly Kitty, had felt uncertain about their reception and were immediately put at ease by Elizabeth's cheerful greeting. The four ladies exchanged hugs as they sat near each other and then began to speak together about what had been happening while they were parted. While Jane and Mary had spoken to the Gardiners about Elizabeth's true heritage, Kitty still had several questions. The next hour was spent informing the entire party about things that had occurred in the last months, both in London and at Longbourn.

"Lydia did not want to go to school and opted to stay with Mama. However, I wonder how long she will remain at home, as she is determined to find a husband and be the first of us to marry," Kitty said. "Mama has always told her that she is pretty and lively and will surely attract a husband. Our Aunt Gardiner has been explaining to me how wrong that attitude is and how poor a match it would be."

"I think the Bennets will find their reception rather poor in Meryton now," Mr. Gardiner said. "My brother Phillips writes to inform me that the news of your heritage has come as a surprise to most of the townspeople, and they are censoring Mr. and Mrs. Bennet for allowing the lie of your birth to be believed for so long. Lizzy, your mother was a great favourite in Meryton. Many there would like to tell you stories about her now that they know the connexion. She was also known for her kindness to others and her liveliness of mind."

Mr. Darcy laughed. "I believe my wife would call that impertinence. I have also noticed that she tends to shy away from praise, ducking and blushing at any commendation directed towards her kindness. Despite our relatively short time in matrimony, I have observed that she prefers to operate quietly in her benevolence. Our stay at Pemberley lasted just a fortnight, yet it was evident she had earned the favour of many among our staff. I believe that some already prefer her over me."

As expected, Elizabeth's cheeks turned a bright shade of pink, and she attempted to redirect the conversation toward someone else. Her family saw this and allowed the conversation to shift, though they grinned at his antics.

"The Hursts are still in residence at Netherfield, although Mr. and Miss Bingley have left for the north. They should remain there for some time as neither will be welcome in London for the present. Should we ever wish to visit Meryton to allow you to speak to those who knew your mother, they would welcome us, Elizabeth," Darcy told his wife.

Jane Bennet gasped at this. "What has happened to Mr. and Miss Bingley, Mr. Darcy?"

"I have cut the connexion with them after Miss Bingley attempted to compromise me with her brother's full knowledge. He did nothing to prevent her, nor did he attempt to warn me. I did not make the attempt public, though I did inform my aunt in case any gossip reached the *ton*. I was content to let matters be, but then Miss Bingley attempted to approach me again and disparage my wife, though she was only my intended at the time. The cut became public knowledge then, though still not the reason for it. As I understand it, Miss Bingley returned to Netherfield with her tail between her legs. Mr. Bingley attempted to seek me out to apologise when he finally realised what she had cost him, but I had already left town to marry my Ellie by then. However, he and my cousin Jonathan had a conversation that finally persuaded him to leave town with his sister for good."

Elizabeth looked startled at this. "I did not know Jon played a role in his decision to depart. You did not tell me the entire story?"

Darcy coloured slightly then. "Yes, my dear, well, there was part of the story I have not told you as I have only recently learned the entire matter. It is…" he cleared his throat awkwardly. "… it is not the kind of story one speaks to young ladies about."

The unmarried ladies coloured, feeling all the awkwardness of his words, while the two married ladies smirked at their husbands. "Yes, we will speak later, husband. This sounds as though it may prove interesting."

Mr. and Mrs. Gardiner chuckled, knowing their 'niece' would force her husband to tell her all later. The Lizzy they had known as a child was impertinent and tenacious, which some might call stubborn and little had changed about her as she grew.

Once again, the conversation shifted as Mr. Gardiner asked Darcy about the Fitzwilliams and the de Bourghs. "The doctors believe Lady Catherine suffered from a fit of apoplexy and that it is unlikely she will ever return to what she was. Her brain appears to have been affected as she can only make muffled noises and can only move slightly. She remains unable to speak.

"Anne is doing well and, with Jonathan's help, has successfully replaced her mother as mistress of Rosings."

"Your cousin has inherited the estate now?" Jane asked. "Is Jonathan her husband?"

"No, Jonathan is our cousin, Lord Matlock's second son and a colonel in the regulars," Darcy explained. "Or he was a colonel, as he intends to resign his commission. As my cousin Anne does not intend to marry, she will leave the estate to him."

Gardiner explained matters more to his nieces, including the chase across England that had given Anne de Bourgh time to displace her mother as mistress of the estate and, ultimately, Lady Catherine's collapse when she finally learned that her edicts were widely ignored.

"What of Mr. Collins?" Mary asked. "He was a fervent admirer of Lady Catherine, and Mama had wanted Lizzy to marry him, though once it became certain she would not, she had fixed on me as his partner."

"Mr. Collins will not marry any of you unless you wish it. You three have a home for a lifetime with us, and your cousin has graciously given each of you five thousand pounds as a dowry. That money will support you to live independently should you choose never to marry, though you will never be asked to do that," Gardiner explained.

"Lizzy, you must not do that," Mary cried. "Our mother and father have taken so much from you; you should keep what is yours for yourself. We will be well without it."

Elizabeth smiled at her cousin. "Truly, Mary, it is no burden to give these funds to you. William and I will have plenty to settle on any future children, and you are welcome to reside at any of our homes whenever you wish. You are my cousins, and what your parents did — the lies they told and the money they spent — does not reflect on you. It would not be right for me to take out my anger at them on you three. Lydia has chosen to remain with her parents rather than take the opportunity to better herself, and the three of them will have to live with the results. I will forgive them, as is my responsibility as a Christian, but that does not mean I will ever speak to them again or recognise them as a member of my family."

The others nodded in recognition of her words. Jane might have wanted to persuade her cousin to forgive the Bennets and someday receive them but recognised that, at the moment, such an effort would be fruitless. Her thoughts regarding her parents were too unsettled to do such a thing, as she was uncertain if she would ever want to see them again.

Just the night before, the Gardiners had spoken to their nieces about legally adopting the name Gardiner in place of Bennet. Jane was of age and could decide whenever she wished, but Mary and Kitty were legally wards of the Gardiners. The paperwork Bennet had been forced to sign gave Mr. Gardiner complete control to make any decisions regarding the girls and ensured they would have their share of their mother's dowry when she passed. Despite Lydia's thoughts otherwise, each of the girls still had their dowry of one thousand two hundred fifty pounds and were entitled to one hundred pounds per annum from Longbourn for their father's lifetime.

Mary returned the conversation to a previous one. "How has Mr. Collins adapted to the change in his patroness? I cannot imagine he would respond well to the change in circumstances."

Darcy laughed. "I had a letter from Fitzwilliam yesterday. He is not impressed with the clergyman and has threatened to contact his bishop to have him removed because, legally, Anne should have appointed him, not Lady Catherine. It is astounding that such a foolish man could even pass the ordination examination."

"But he will still inherit Longbourn someday, will he not?" Kitty asked again. "What will happen to us when that occurs?"

"Nothing will change, Kitty. You are no longer dependent on the Bennets and will have a home with us for as long as you wish," Mrs. Gardiner reassured the girl. Something in how she said it told Elizabeth that this conversation had been repeated many times over the last few days.

The butler arrived to announce that dinner was served, ending this conversation. The discussion over dinner was far less fraught as they discussed the various events the Darcys would attend. Elizabeth invited her family to attend the theatre in a sennight, hoping the three girls would have appropriate clothing by then.

Kitty hesitated, asking to remain behind with Georgiana on the outing. As the evening progressed, Kitty and Georgiana gravitated toward each other since they were of a similar age. Soon, the two were conversing happily, and Georgiana shared her experiences regarding school with a much relieved

Kitty.

When the evening ended, all felt a little more comfortable than they had earlier. Jane, Mary, and Kitty felt that nothing had changed between them and their cousin, which they had feared, given how their parents had mistreated her. However, they were relieved that Elizabeth did not hold a grudge against them for their parents' actions.

* * *

When their guests left, Elizabeth and Darcy retired. Nearly as soon as the couple were in bed, Elizabeth began to ask Darcy more about what had happened with Mr. Bingley.

"Bingley was caught with a gentlewoman, well, a married gentlewoman, and Jonathan used this as leverage to encourage him to depart London. Between the matter with Wickham and now this, it truly was best that my former friend not be anywhere near London for a time," Darcy explained.

"When you say 'caught', you mean he was caught *in flagrante*, do you not? With a married woman? That is terrible. And did I know of Bingley's connexion to Wickham?"

"I believe I told you that Wickham had crossed Bingley in Hertfordshire, leaving my former friend responsible for fifty pounds of debt at the inn. Bingley threatened him when they encountered each other in London before Wickham fled. In fact, two of Bingley's men caught up with Wickham a day before he boarded the ship and beat him quite severely. It was one of the reasons Wickham was so willing to leave and join the navy, not to return to England for some time. As I understand it, Wickham was rather battered. While I should not be pleased with such a result, I cannot be disappointed. I confess that I am a little sorry I could not participate in the beating, and I know Jonathan feels the same."

Elizabeth laughed a little at this. Like her husband, she felt that Wickham got what he deserved, as she had heard many tales of his treatment of women, especially of Georgiana. While she would not want to see anyone deliberately harmed, she could not help but feel this was just retribution.

Not wanting to dwell on this news, Elizabeth quickly used what she had learned in her weeks of marriage to thoroughly distract her husband from all thoughts of his former friends.

Chapter 35

The Darcys lived up to their agreement with Lady Matlock, attending various balls, parties, and other entertainments over the next several weeks. Elizabeth Tomlinson Darcy made quite a splash in society, leaving few with no opinion of her whatsoever, whether positive or negative. Most admitted that she was the perfect wife to the solemn and taciturn Darcy, as she could prod him into something approaching agreeableness. The first time the pernicious peeresses of London society noted a smile on the gentleman's face while speaking to his wife, many realised that the rare sight indicated the mutual love between the couple.

Some women remained jealous that someone else had won the prize they sought. In truth, they could find little to dislike about Elizabeth. Those who thought to embarrass her soon realised that she had a biting wit and was unafraid to use it to put these women in their place. Once it became apparent the new Mrs. Darcy was rather formidable, such attempts ceased.

Lady Matlock's Twelfth Night ball was Elizabeth's official introduction to the *ton*. Most had encountered her in some form by then, and her reputation was well known. Attempts to discredit her had ceased, and many were determined to befriend her. With the two estates joined, the Darcys would be a powerful family in England, with significant wealth in their control.

Elizabeth's gown for the evening was a sight to behold, making her appear a vision of elegance and grace. The dress was light rose-coloured silk, draping beautifully on Elizabeth's figure, enhancing her natural beauty. The bodice was cut in a daring style that hinted at the delights that lay beneath and tempted Darcy to refuse to allow Elizabeth to attend. While it revealed nothing, Darcy did not want others to admire his wife's assets, insisting they were all for him.

"Ellie, must we attend tonight? I would much rather remain at home. My aunt's balls are always a crush, and we have already spent more than a month in Town. Everyone has already met you, meaning there is no good reason for us to attend tonight."

She laughed at him. "William, I have noticed you only call me Ellie when you are trying to convince me of something. I will have to keep that in mind for the future. And yes, we must attend as your aunt intends to announce our marriage officially. It is not a secret, but she intends to honour us tonight. We cannot miss it, as I feel certain she would send someone after us if we failed to appear. No, dearest, we will need to attend this final event, and then in two days, we will depart to Pemberley."

Darcy scowled. "But I will not be able to dance with you as often as I wish. We will only be permitted to dance the first, and the supper sets."

Elizabeth moved to stand close to her husband and stood on her tiptoes to whisper in his ear. "But, my darling, I believe I am feeling a little ill, and we will make our excuses after the supper set so we can return home sooner. Your aunt promised to allow it if we wished, so she cannot complain when we leave before the meal."

"My brilliant wife," he whispered huskily before tilting his head down to kiss her.

* * *

As Darcy predicted, the event was well-attended, though not technically a crush. Lady Matlock frowned when the two stood across from each other for the supper dance, and her expression was nearly a scowl when she saw them sneak out before the meal was served. However, most of the rumours about the couple were positive, speaking of their evident love for each other as they flaunted propriety at the event to dance with each other three times, leaving Lady Matlock with little to be displeased about.

She did have a few words for the couple when they departed. "I am seriously displeased with you, nephew, but as it has not seemed to have had a negative effect, I suppose you will be forgiven. It is good that you are to depart from Town soon, as I believe the two of you are too newly married to be in public."

"Aunt, you are the one who has insisted we remain. I would have left for Pemberley weeks ago had you not demanded we attend tonight," Darcy protested with a knowing smirk at her.

"Yes, well, you have been seen, and now it is best if you depart. Travel safely and enjoy your time in the country. I will see you in the spring. Georgiana will remain with us at Matlock House until you return in a few months." Lady Matlock gave them both an imperious look and sent them on their way.

The day after the ball, the Darcys slept late and visited the Gardiners one final time before leaving. Jane, Mary, and Kitty had decided to take the Gardiner name, which would be made official later that month, and Kitty was looking forward to attending school. A companion had been hired for Jane and Mary, who was also helping to instruct them in some of the accomplishments they lacked.

In the last weeks, Jane had already gained a suitor, a Mr. Ayres, an investor in Gardiner's business. Like Mr. Bingley, his fortune had been made in trade, and he sought to eventually purchase an estate, although he did not expect to do so for another decade. Jane liked the man, and he appeared to be interested in her for more than just her beauty. However, her experiences made her a little more willing to question the motivations of such a man. Without Mrs. Bennet pushing her toward any man, she felt she could take her time and get to know him well. For the moment, and on such a slight acquaintance, she had little to say to her cousin about the man.

Gardiner and Darcy spoke for a time in the study. Gardiner had received a letter from his brother Phillips regarding the Bennets, including Lydia's attempt to escape, which he had thwarted. Mrs. Bennet kept Lydia very close to home, as she did not want to lose her companion any time soon, especially as none of the women near Longbourn wanted anything to do with Mrs. Bennet after her infamous treatment of her niece. The anger of that had still not faded, and Mrs. Bennet and Lydia's actions, when they went into Meryton, had done little to cool it.

"They remain as foolish as always and seem incapable of learning their lesson. My sister still speaks of coming to London and having Lizzy purchase her and Lydia's clothing, but Bennet has thus far been able to prevent her from coming. He has managed that by keeping the carriage unusable, and Mrs. Bennet needs more funds to carry them to London in a coach. Since the Hills left, Mrs. Bennet has had to take far more of an interest in the running of the house, including directing the servants, as they truly cannot afford to pay a housekeeper what she would deserve. My sister says they are getting along well enough, though they expect Lydia to attempt to escape again soon. So far, she has been prevented from ruining herself, but I fear it is only because she has lacked the opportunity."

"Is there someone who could be persuaded to marry her so she does not? She is young and foolish but a product of her environment. What she wants most is to be married, and were she to marry someone who could teach her to behave, perhaps she could be saved." Darcy and Elizabeth had discussed the girl, and while Elizabeth was disinclined to do too much for her as she had been rather cruel to Elizabeth at times, she knew that the influence of her parents had made her so.

"Lydia is insistent she will only marry an officer. I suppose one might be persuaded, but neither Phillips nor I are inclined to invest the funds that would be required," Gardiner replied. "No, the officers in Meryton have been warned and will not touch Lydia, not even for a roll in the hay."

Darcy frowned. "Then perhaps she is safe enough for now. Her family are social pariahs, and she is, presumably, learning how to run a house and maybe a few other useful skills. If she matures through all of this, she may be fit to marry someone in a few years."

Gardiner merely shrugged, and the two discussed some investment opportunities for the rest of the visit.

* * *

The journey to Pemberley took longer in early January than it had in November due to the condition of the roads as they travelled. Darcy and Elizabeth enjoyed being in each other's sole company for several days and not having to interact with others as they had in Town.

When they arrived home, they were again greeted by their staff, who welcomed them home with alacrity. The winter months passed peaceably as the couple learned more about each other and came to love each other more deeply. During this time, they visited Briarwood twice, and Elizabeth had been delighted the first time they travelled to her estate.

With Elizabeth's marriage, she was now officially in charge of the estate, and they had gone there the first time to help get the Hills settled into their new roles as the housekeeper and butler. Briarwood was larger than Longbourn, which meant Mrs. Hill had different responsibilities. Elizabeth wanted to acquaint the couple with what was expected of them and find out what assistance was needed.

Briarwood was newer than Pemberley, having been built less than a century ago rather than the nearly two centuries Pemberley had stood. Still, it was an excellent example of the early Georgian style built on only a slightly smaller scale than Pemberley. It boasted over 100 rooms, including ten apartments in the family wing and another fifteen or so in a separate guest wing. There were several drawing rooms and sitting rooms, and though its library was smaller than the one at Pemberley, it was no less full.

After settling into the master suite upon their first visit to Briarwood, they visited the nursery. Elizabeth expected that she would have spent quite a bit of time in that room and looked around, hoping that something would inspire a memory of her childhood. The room was vaguely familiar to her, in that hazy way common to one's earliest memories.

She and Darcy recreated some of his memories from that room, lying on the floor and reading together, playing with some blocks they found in a corner. Still, nothing shook loose any concrete memories, though speaking of the time they spent together was enjoyable. Darcy recalled far more than she did, having been seven years older, and Elizabeth appreciated his effort, no matter how silly they felt at times. When they decided to stop reminiscing, they spent several minutes speaking of the children they hoped would someday inhabit these same rooms. That led to a rather childish dash toward their own rooms again, and a supper served in their private sitting room.

Before breaking their fast the next morning, Darcy took Elizabeth to the great hall where the family portraits were displayed and showed Elizabeth her grandparents.

"Allow me to introduce you to your esteemed ancestors, my darling Elizabeth," Darcy announced with a charming smile, his hand sweeping towards the portraits adorning the walls of the great hall.

Elizabeth's eyes sparkled with curiosity as she observed the paintings. "How fascinating," she murmured, studying each portrait with interest.

Her attention lingered on the images of her grandparents, a sense of melancholy washing over her. "It is sad, I think, to see these portraits of them," she remarked softly, a hint of nostalgia colouring her tone. "They looked very happy together. I wish I remembered them better."

Darcy nodded in agreement, his gaze lingering on the portraits as well. "Indeed, they were remarkable individuals, and they left behind a wonderful legacy in you," he added, his voice filled with respect. "I remember your grandparents a little; your grandfather was a very good man. My father admired and respected him. I happened across one of his journals, and he wrote about speaking to your grandfather about pairing the two of us one day."

Hand-in-hand, they moved a few steps further down. "Here is your father, Elizabeth," Darcy said gently, embracing her.

"I wish I had known him or my mother. Since the Bennets never mentioned my mother existed, I wonder if any of the portraits in Longbourn were of her. I will have to ask Mrs. Hill if she knows of one, though, even if there is, it is unlikely I would ever see it." Hearing the sadness in her voice, Darcy leaned down to kiss her forehead but did not speak, hoping his presence was enough.

Elizabeth was able to ask her housekeeper later that day, but neither Mr. nor Mrs. Hill was aware of there being one. There were a few portraits in the estate, but not many, as that was not something the current or past masters of Longbourn had ever considered worthwhile.

Before they left the estate, after having visited for a little over a fortnight on this trip, they discussed what to do with it moving forward. The admiral, who had been in residence for six months, had departed shortly after Christmas, so the estate was once again uninhabited. Elizabeth and Darcy had discussed possibly leasing it again or keeping it available for their visits. Still, by the time they were to depart, they had yet to determine the best course of action.

"If we lease it, then we will be unable to visit. I would like to see the estate in the summer to see if it spurs any memories from the time I spent here as a child. Bits of the house seem slightly familiar, but since I seem to recall pieces of the summer I spent with you more vividly than others, I wonder if we could spend a few weeks here in the summer — near our birthdays — if you would not mind." Elizabeth whispered these thoughts to her husband on the last night of their stay at Briarwood as they lay in bed.

"I would be delighted to spend the month of our birthdays here at Briarwood, especially if it sparks memories that have been long hidden. I remember more than you do of that time, and perhaps my memories will help to inspire yours." He moved his head down to kiss her, and soon, that kiss deepened until any discussion about the estate was forgotten.

The following day, they sat next to each other in the carriage that would take them back to Pemberley. "I think the Hills are doing well with their new duties, and I hope you are pleased with how the estate is faring," Darcy observed to his wife.

She nodded, an action he felt more than saw, as her head was tucked beneath his chin as they sat snuggled together — for warmth, he had claimed. "Everything about the house seemed to be in good repair, and the tenants were just as content as those at Pemberley. You have done well in managing the estate over the years."

Elizabeth felt her husband shake his head. "My father put it all into place, and I merely continued what he did," he returned.

That caused his wife to laugh, and he smiled despite knowing she was laughing at him. "You have often said I take compliments poorly, sir, but you are the same. You cannot accept praise any better than I."

Once again, he used the most effective method he had for silencing his wife when she teased him, so he kissed her, keeping her silent for some time after that, hoping she would forget what they had been talking about.

Chapter 36

On their return to London, Elizabeth and Darcy accepted the Hursts' invitation to break their journey at Netherfield. After her brother had left, Mrs. Hurst discovered she was with child. Since the thought of an extended journey had not been welcomed by either Mr. and Mrs. Hurst with her in that condition, they had opted to remain.

Mrs. Hurst was nearing her confinement and, without the presence of Miss Bingley, had managed to become friendly with some of the matrons in town. As the residents of the grandest house in town, the Hursts had held several small entertainments, which made the denizens of the area appreciate them further.

Despite her advanced condition, with Elizabeth visiting, Mrs. Hurst decided to host several of the other local matrons, including some of the older townspeople who wanted to tell Elizabeth stories of her mother as a child.

"I hope you do not mind, as I know your stay is short, but so many wanted to apologise for what they believed — the lies the Bennets allowed to spread and even encouraged — and to tell you about your mother. Many here held Beth Bennet in great respect and would like to tell you stories about your mother's childhood. In fact, that is one reason we asked you to remain for a Sunday, as some were unwilling to visit Netherfield but hoped to see you at the church in Meryton," Mrs. Hurst explained.

"I would be pleased to hear stories of my mother," Elizabeth replied. "I would like to visit the tenants at Longbourn but am uncertain what kind of reception I would receive from the Bennets were I to encounter any of them. Mrs. Bennet was rather unkind to me before, and now, well, I cannot imagine she would be happy to see me."

"She is very bitter, and her bitterness has only deepened by her rejection from the society here in Meryton," Mrs. Hurst replied, having heard much of this news from Mrs. Nicholls in preparation for the Darcys' visit. Both ladies felt it best that the Darcys know what might happen, so Mrs. Nicholls and Mrs. Hill had broken their rules regarding gossip to better acquaint Miss Lizzy with the situation at Longbourn.

"Mrs. Bennet's isolation has taken its toll, and being in the company of her remaining family has done little to alleviate her discontent with her situation. Lydia remains spoiled and demanding but is now without access to any society, as none of the local girls will speak to her, nor will the members of the militia. Those who once flirted with her now ignore her since they have been told in no uncertain terms that a connexion to that family will only cause problems for them. Without her other daughters to keep her company, Mrs. Bennet has largely confined Lydia at home to attend her, making Lydia even more petulant. That, combined with her one attempt to 'escape,' has led to her mother keeping a close rein on her, but they only make each other miserable with their incessant complaints about their poor treatment.

"Meanwhile, Mr. Bennet has become somewhat more diligent in tending to his estate and is managing to augment his income, but instead of channelling those additional funds to his wife, he has chosen to indulge in his own pursuits, acquiring a few books for personal pleasure. Many in town speculate how long his diligence will continue once he obtains more books. According to the servants' gossip, when he does speak to his wife, it is even more sarcastic and biting than before, and the three consistently contribute to each other's unhappiness."

"Then it would be best to avoid encountering them while we are here. Our trip would have been short regardless, but I do not desire Elizabeth to be accosted in any way," Darcy interjected, feeling rather protective of his wife. Ever since meeting her — first as a small child and later as an orphan who had been mistreated — he had always felt protective of her. However, on their journey from Pemberley to Netherfield, it had become apparent to both Darcys that Elizabeth was likely with child.

His off-handed remark on the absence of her courses, combined with the vague nausea that she had begun to feel, only made worse by the motion of the carriage, had made them speculate about her condition. They would speak to a physician in London to confirm this as well as to Mrs. Gardiner, who was the closest thing to a mother Elizabeth could remember. However, they were reasonably certain of the prognosis, and Darcy felt very "mother-hennish" with his wife.

For the moment, Elizabeth was inclined to be amused by his cosseting of her, though once they reached their London home, she intended to speak to him seriously about it. She was content to cease riding and other things he had suggested, but she was not inclined to have him follow her around for the next several months.

In this case, Elizabeth merely gave her husband a speaking look before allowing the conversation to drift to other matters. The next afternoon, the ladies of Meryton had been invited for tea and would drop in as they could to visit with Elizabeth. Since the following day was Sunday, the Darcys hoped to speak to others after church, and then on Monday, the couple would depart for London. They appreciated the Hursts' invitation, especially considering Louisa Hurst's condition, and thanked them for allowing them to visit during this time and arranging for the visitors.

Soon, however, both women expressed a need to rest before dinner. They all retired to their rooms, though Darcy left after his wife slept to seek out Hurst.

"What else can you tell me about the Bennets?" Darcy asked once both men had a glass of port in hand and were playing a game of billiards together. Darcy noticed that Hurst was far more sober than he had been on other visits and had started to lose some of his excess weight.

"Little more than my wife has heard through the gossip. Mrs. Bennet's sister is the one who told all; her husband is the solicitor Bennet used in his attempt to take your wife's estate from her. Most do not think Phillips knew the full truth when he wrote the documents, but they feel he should have asked more questions. However, his wife informing the neighbourhood of Elizabeth's true status, which must have come from Mr. Phillips himself, has granted them clemency from the matrons."

Darcy nodded at this and took his turn in the game. Several minutes later, he spoke again. "What do they say about the youngest Bennet daughter?'

"If she had a chance, she would ruin herself and is likely unhappy that she has been prevented from doing so. However, the men of the militia have been warned against her, and frankly, they are unwilling to engage the girl after her family was censured," Hurst shook his head and grinned slightly at his friend.

"How are Mr. and Miss Bingley doing?" Darcy asked, wanting to redirect the conversation.

Hurst sighed heavily. "At least as unhappily as the Bennets. Miss Bingley is even more of a shrew than before and is unwilling to consider any of the men who might have been willing to marry her for her dowry. Unfortunately, they are unwilling to tie themselves to her once they meet her, so ... my brother finds himself at an impasse. He is unwilling to force his sister to marry; truly, he cannot force her, but he wishes to get her out of his house any way he can. Obviously, neither can return to London ..."

Here, Hurst trailed off as he knew Darcy knew all the particulars. "They are far from here, and as Bingley is content for us to remain until his lease ends at Michaelmas, we will remain. We will likely go to my parents' estate once Louisa has the baby and has recovered from the birth. It is time I learned to manage it, and now that we do not have Caroline tagging along with us, we can go there again. My parents never did care for her taking on airs as she did and forbade her from visiting the estate."

Darcy did not reply to Hurst's comment. Nor did he want to mention what they suspected about Elizabeth's condition. Hurst, a quiet man, did not add anything else, and the two played until their wives joined them for dinner.

As expected, the next day was busy at Netherfield as many women dropped by to speak to Elizabeth. Much to Elizabeth's surprise, Mrs. Phillips had managed to sneak into Longbourn and retrieve a miniature of Elizabeth's mother. Mrs. Phillips felt no shame for what she had done since she believed the picture rightfully belonged to the child who had never had the chance to know her.

"Thank you, Mrs. Phillips," Elizabeth said after staring at the portrait for a long moment. Unlike Mrs. Gardiner, Elizabeth did not feel comfortable referring to this lady as aunt now that she knew the truth. Nevertheless, she valued her effort in retrieving the painting, regardless of its means. Elizabeth was delighted to have an image of her mother as a young woman painted a few years before her marriage to Frederick Tomlinson. It was undeniable that the two shared many similar characteristics, and beholding this picture brought Elizabeth a sense of closeness to her mother.

Other ladies crowded in to tell Elizabeth stories of her mother, who had been of a similar temperament to Elizabeth herself. Beth Bennet had also preferred the outdoors and had loved reading, both of which were the traits that drew Elizabeth's father to seek her out when they met. The two met in town, having quite literally run into each other in a bookshop. Frederick Tomlinson found out just enough about her to seek her out and eventually came to Meryton briefly to court her. It had taken six months, but he had loved her enough to pursue her, even on such a short acquaintance and despite her lack of traditional "accomplishments."

Elizabeth loved sharing this story with her husband since he had often expressed that most of the "accomplishments" so heralded in society were a perfect waste of time. He believed gentlewomen should learn valuable skills like helping tenants, assisting their husbands or fathers with estate matters, reading, and other skills such as climbing trees and skipping rocks — both were lessons he had taught her as a small child. He had also taught Georgiana these things and encouraged her to learn more than just the usual accomplishments for women.

Darcy was delighted to listen to what Elizabeth had learned that day about her mother. He and Hurst had elected to stay out of the way of the myriad

256

of ladies who visited. However, Darcy listened to her excited stories readily enough and was pleased that she now had stories of her mother as a child to reflect on.

On Sunday, the four attended the church in Meryton. Those attending church who had not visited Netherfield the previous day were pleased to see Elizabeth and speak to her about her mother. They were also interested in seeing her married to Darcy, as they had heard about the marriage, though they had yet to see her or her husband since they had departed from Hertfordshire in the autumn.

After being greeted by the whole of Meryton, or so it seemed to Darcy, the Netherfield party could finally depart the churchyard, only to come face to face with Mrs. Bennet.

"How dare you show your face here, you grasping, conniving, baseborn child? I cannot believe you are treated as royalty here when I am reviled for taking you in and caring for you as a child," she snarled into Elizabeth's face.

"Madam, had you treated me with respect and care, you would not be facing any difficulties from your neighbours. You have deprived me of much, and while I am perhaps sorry for you, you have brought this all upon yourself. It was your choice to treat me as you did and conspire with your husband to steal from me," Elizabeth replied quietly.

Her voice rose only slightly as she continued. "The fact that you continue to lie to your neighbours, to me, and to yourself just proves how foolish you are. Three of your daughters have elected to no longer live with you because of your actions, and the last one will ruin herself the moment you allow her the slightest bit of freedom. You are too blind to see anything outside the reality you have created for yourself. If you choose to blame me for the misfortune which has fallen to you, so be it, as your bitterness has no effect on me. I am happy, I am loved, and despite your best efforts, I am married to a wonderful man. I have discovered my true heritage, not the false one you attempted to create for me. I know who I am and can look forward to a future where I will be loved and cared for all my days. What do you have other than anger and bitterness? Your family and friends have rejected you because of your own actions; it has nothing to do with me. The sooner you learn that lesson, the better off you will be."

With her husband's hand securely on her back, Elizabeth glared at the woman before turning on her heel and walking away. And while Mrs. Bennet looked angry enough to attack, she glanced around and saw the disdain on the faces of all who were still standing there, having witnessed the confrontation. Her shoulders slumped in recognition of the futility of it all, and she slowly slunk away.

Chapter 37

Elizabeth and Darcy relished the time spent with the Hursts on their final evening before departing for London early Monday morning. They had enjoyed spending time with the couple; Darcy had known them for years, but in the past, when Bingley had been his friend, he had spent very little time conversing with Hurst. Mrs. Hurst was almost entirely unknown, but Elizabeth and Darcy believed she had likely changed somewhat by being out of her sister's presence. She seemed softer than before, which could also be due to her impending motherhood.

The Darcys made a brief stop in London on their way to Rosings. While there, Elizabeth visited her aunt and confirmed her suspicion that she was likely with child. All that remained was to await the quickening, expected to occur soon. Darcy was content with this, as Elizabeth had chosen not to consult a doctor for confirmation, being already sure of her condition. Summoning a doctor would undoubtedly have caused a commotion in the household, something Elizabeth wished to avoid to preserve their secret a little longer.

They collected Georgiana from the Matlocks so they could travel together to Rosings. Georgiana and Elizabeth had only spent a few days in company, though they had corresponded frequently. Georgiana would remain with them when they left Rosings for Pemberley. It was unlikely they would return to London for some time after that due to Elizabeth's pregnancy.

Adjusting to being in company with others was difficult for Darcy and Elizabeth. For much of the last months, they had been alone. Granted, there were always servants about, and they had their individual responsibilities to attend to. Still, they had not had to balance their desire to be alone with the need to entertain others. The few days they spent at Darcy House before going to Kent had been awkward as Elizabeth was used to being with Darcy in his study as he worked. In London, others needed her attention, particularly Georgiana, who regularly sought the couple out. Instead of evenings spent cuddling in their sitting room, they were forced to eat in the dining room with Georgiana before moving into the music room or the drawing room for music and conversation.

When they boarded the carriage to begin their trip to Rosings, Darcy helped his wife first, then Georgiana, into the carriage and paused when he entered, not knowing where to sit. Every time they travelled, he and Elizabeth sat together on the forward-facing seat, but this time, Georgiana was in his spot. Ruefully, he glanced at his wife and saw her own apologetic look. He took the seat across from his wife and angled his legs so they touched hers, and in this way, they maintained a connexion as they travelled. Before long, Elizabeth claimed she was tired and wanted to rest against her husband, so she switched seats to sit next to Darcy. Soon, she was leaning against his shoulder with his arm around her, and both had drifted off into a contented sleep.

The carriage stopped after travelling for about three hours to rest the horses and to give the family a chance to stretch their legs. After Elizabeth and Georgiana refreshed themselves, they joined Darcy for a small meal in a private room that he had arranged. It did not take long for the three to resume their journey. When Georgiana entered the carriage first, she sat on the backwards-facing seat, allowing her brother and sister to sit next to each other on the opposite bench, as she had overheard her sister whisper to her brother that she preferred that seat as she did feel slightly nauseated travelling backwards. Not knowing the reason for the change, Elizabeth smiled gratefully at the younger girl.

"Thank you, dear. I will confess that I prefer to sit this way but have become used to sitting beside my husband when we travel. I appreciate the sacrifice," Elizabeth said as she patted her sister's knee.

Georgiana felt herself grow embarrassed at the affectionate gesture, something she was still learning to accustom herself to now that she had a sister. "I noticed you were a bit uncomfortable, and since I am comfortable either way, I do not mind giving up this seat for the two of you," she replied quietly. Darcy just smiled at her in appreciation.

When they arrived at Rosings, they found the estate doing very well, much better than it had under the control of Lady Catherine. Anne and Fitzwilliam worked well together and had already begun making several changes to increase the estate's profitability. They sought Darcy's advice on how to distribute the income fairly — Anne wanted Fitzwilliam to receive at least half the profits, enabling him to marry as he wished once he found and convinced a woman to accept him.

Fitzwilliam was quite content to remain as the heir and rely on the income from his father's allowance and his savings from his salary during his years in the army. This was the only area where the two significantly disagreed, and they sought Darcy's opinion on making things equitable between them. They were a few days into the visit before Fitzwilliam and Darcy hid themselves away to discuss the matter.

"Truly, Fitzwilliam, what Anne proposes is completely reasonable. If she splits the income from the estate with you, then you can both be independent, and you will feel you are able to marry. I know Anne never intends to marry. You need an heir to pass Rosings to," Darcy argued with his cousin.

"I have agreed to help Anne manage the estate. I have surrendered my commission in the army, so I have the funds I have saved over the years in addition to what I received for my commission. In essence, I am acting as a steward for Anne. I do not believe I ought to receive any more than that and certainly not half or more of the proceeds from the estate. That is rightfully Anne's," Fitzwilliam protested.

"Do not be an idiot. Anne wishes to share the proceeds with you, recognizing that your role surpasses that of a mere steward. Essentially, you are the master of the estate, and Anne heavily depends on you. She intends this for your benefit, acknowledging that she would never exhaust the estate's income. She desires to witness you marry and have children, aspiring to play the role of their 'aunt' and indulge them. She seeks to live vicariously through your happiness. Therefore, accept her offer and bring her joy by providing 'nieces' and 'nephews' for her to spoil."

Fitzwilliam grimaced. "Is that what this is really about?"

"In part. She also wants to ensure you stay here and believes that giving you a stake in the profits will do that. I know you would have remained even without it, but she wants some kind of guarantee."

"I would have stayed regardless," Fitzwilliam sighed heavily.

"I know that, Fitzwilliam, and Anne knows that. However, she wants some measure of happiness. Anne wants some family nearby and hopes you will provide the family she has never had. Elizabeth and I will have a family and visit occasionally, and Georgiana will do the same, but neither of us is here. She wants you to live the life she cannot."

Again, Fitzwilliam sighed, dropping awkwardly into a chair as he considered the matter. "Fine, I will sign whatever agreement she wants, but how does she intend for me to find a woman to marry? I believe I have met everyone here of marriageable age, and none struck my fancy. If I go to London, and it is known that I will inherit Rosings, I will suffer what you did — all manner of women will want to throw themselves at me. I have seen the connexion you and little Ellie have, which is what I want. You knew it the moment you saw her again, did you not? It was immediate. I have never felt that with anyone, and there is no guarantee I ever will."

"I do not believe I immediately fell in love with Elizabeth when I saw her again, but I was struck by her kindness. That and the sense of familiarity I felt when I looked at her. We met every morning for a fortnight before I asked her for a courtship, and then matters did progress quickly. I knew I was in love with her when I finally asked to court her, but I wanted to give her time to come to the same conclusion. Our prior connexion helped us resolve matters faster, and of course, Elizabeth's situation with the Bennet family was there, pushing things along. Otherwise, we might be marrying now or have only been married a short time."

"So you do not recommend marrying in such haste?" Fitzwilliam teased, having recovered some of his composure as his cousin spoke.

"I am not certain that haste is not warranted in some situations, and I do not regret for a moment the speed in which Elizabeth and I were able to come together. However, it was a unique situation that brought us together, and I would recommend that whoever you consider, you consider fully what marriage to them will mean. I had to earn Elizabeth's trust, especially after it was shattered by learning of the deception of the Bennets. We still occasionally have to counter issues that are offshoots of what those people did. I told you that Mrs. Bennet approached her, and even knowing the entire town now knows the truth, she still referred to Elizabeth as baseborn. It took all I had to maintain my equanimity in the face of her lies, but my Elizabeth was brilliant. She was poised and imperturbable as she confronted that harpy. I do not doubt she still believes her lies, but that is because she is a bitter woman who relishes blaming her problems on all but herself. From what Elizabeth has said, she lives in a state of agitation, never accepting her own role in her problems."

"She is an idiot, and you said one of her daughters remained with her?" At Darcy's nod, the former colonel continued. "I wonder if we could find a way to introduce her youngest daughter to a good man who would take her in hand and teach her to be responsible. I believe Elizabeth said her youngest cousin was enamoured with the military?"

"Yes, she is, but no, she is not the wife for you, Jon." Darcy was adamant about not introducing his cousin to the girl.

"Oh, I was not thinking of myself. But I do know a man who might be willing to marry a pretty girl who needs a lot of training. He has enough money that he would not need a significant dowry, but a little would help," Fitzwilliam suggested.

"I will have no part in it, and neither will Elizabeth. You have met the Gardiners and can speak to Mr. Gardiner on Miss Lydia's behalf. But I do not want to know about it. Elizabeth agreed to fund dowries for the three who left Longbourn but will give nothing to Lydia. Let Bennet himself come up with something for her."

Fitzwilliam stood and smiled at his cousin before knocking him on the shoulder. "I will not say a word unless I am successful. Come, let us speak to Anne about my surrender to her plan, and then I will spend a month or two in London to see if I cannot find a woman who will agree to become my wife. With luck, I will be as happy as you by year's end."

Darcy laughed at his cousin's antics. They sought out the women, and Darcy immediately went to sit beside his wife, kissing her hand, much to the amusement of the others.

Chapter 38

The Darcys remained at Rosings for another fortnight before returning to London with Fitzwilliam in tow. Despite their intention of a short stay, they were in town for a sennight before finally turning their carriage north toward Pemberley.

While in London, they visited with the Gardiners again. Darcy was annoyed with his cousin for having already mentioned his idea of marrying off Lydia to a former soldier and reiterated his intention to remain out of the matter.

The Darcys hosted a family dinner in town, sharing the news of their expected addition. The Matlocks, Mr. Elliott, and the Gardiners attended, offering well wishes upon hearing the announcement.

Jane's suitor, Mr. Ayres, had recently requested a formal courtship and attended the dinner with the family. It appeared the two would marry soon. Fitzwilliam finally met the Bennet girls that night — now officially Gardiners — and while he had noticed Jane's beauty, Mary had intrigued him. The two spoke for some time that night, and Darcy wondered if Fitzwilliam would decide to pursue her or if he would attempt to find another.

Mary had grown quite a bit in her time with the Gardiners and was a far more interesting conversationalist than she had been while in Hertfordshire. The influence of the Gardiners was evident in several areas; Mary was dressed in a more flattering way, and her hairstyle was softer, but more than that, she exuded a confidence she had not had before.

"So, Miss Mary, how do you enjoy living in town?" Fitzwilliam began, attempting to learn more about the girl.

"I greatly appreciate the opportunity to learn from masters. My aunt and uncle have hired a music master who has helped with my playing, and I have enjoyed learning French with my cousins. I am perhaps old for such things, but nonetheless, I am pleased to be granted the chance."

Fitzwilliam nodded and spoke a sentence or two in French, and she responded. He corrected her pronunciation of a phrase, but soon, the two turned the conversation to other topics.

Elizabeth caught her husband's eye as he spoke to Lord Matlock and Mr. Elliott and nodded toward the pair. He winked at her in reply as the two had discussed the possibility. They would not have pushed them together but thought they might benefit from the connexion, even if they only became friends.

Before too much longer, the guests began to depart, though Fitzwilliam remained behind the rest. He and Darcy disappeared into the study while Elizabeth and Georgiana retreated to their rooms. When Darcy joined Elizabeth in the bedroom a short time later, he smelled of whisky, Fitzwilliam's preferred beverage. Elizabeth waited impatiently while he disrobed and finally joined her in bed.

"He wanted to ask about Mary and her general situation. He is interested in knowing more about her. He attended many of the same society events I did, and I believe he became just as jaded as I was before I met you. He attracted some attention but was pursued less since he was a second son and would not inherit an estate. But that does not mean he did not see the same inanity I did. I believe Mary interests him in part because she is so different from most women he has encountered."

"What did you tell him?"

"To take his time and come to know her well. He will be in town for a month or two before he returns to Rosings, and it might be possible for him to invite the Gardiners to visit Rosings for part of the summer. It is an easy distance, and the children could accompany the family if they wanted to."

"What did he say about his conversation with my uncle about Lydia?" Elizabeth asked after a minute or two had passed.

"Not much. I asked him why he even bothered pursuing it, and his answer amused me." When he did not immediately continue, his wife poked him in the side, and he laughed.

"He believed that removing Lydia from the house would be yet another way of exacting revenge against the Bennets. Mrs. Bennet currently has Lydia as a buffer, and he interpreted what we told him as holding on to her daughter tightly because she wanted company. He thought having the two stuck alone in that house would be a proper punishment. No one else in Meryton will visit them, and Mrs. Bennet has never bothered with visiting the tenants, so that will leave her with nothing to do but torment her husband, and he will plague her in return."

Elizabeth chuckled. "That does seem a fitting punishment. Perhaps it was unfair to Lydia to give her the choice to stay or remain, but had the Gardiners forced her to leave, she would have made life difficult for everyone. Nor do I think she would have remained at whatever school they enrolled her. Jon may have the right of it."

"Bennet did cede guardianship of all four of his daughters, so Gardiner would be within his rights to demand Lydia come to town. He also has the right to sign the marriage contract. However, I am adamant that we will not fund Lydia's dowry."

Sighing, Elizabeth agreed. "We have discussed it, and I agree. I was willing to fund her dowry had she left the Bennets willingly, but if she has to be coerced into leaving, she does not deserve to be rewarded. She will receive her hundred pounds per annum from her father and her share of her mother's five thousand upon her death, but I will not give her anything else."

"Thank you, Ellie. I did not want to push the issue, but I wanted to ensure we agreed. Luckily, we will have left town long before this comes to be. Fitzwilliam will need to speak to his friend, and then the Gardiners, before someone will have to convince Lydia to agree." He sighed deeply. "It is out of our hands, is it not? And we have more important things to concern ourselves with. My aunt and uncle were surprised by our news tonight, but I do not think they were displeased." His hand moved down to caress the slight bump that had recently appeared on her abdomen.

"Your aunt was less pleased with the idea of our not attending the Season next year. The baby will likely be born in the autumn, but still, I do not relish the idea of travelling with an infant. I would prefer to wait one more year. And I do not think Georgiana minded delaying her presentation. She will be eighteen rather than seventeen when she debuts."

"I have no objection to delaying her presentation indefinitely, but I know I must let her go at some point. I hope we can find a good man who will love her as much as I adore you. Now, come here," he said as he kissed her. "I want to have a conversation with this little person, and then we must sleep. Are you ready to return to Pemberley, my love?"

Elizabeth laughed at him but nodded her agreement and laughed some more when he moved down her body to proceed to have an entire conversation with their unborn child. It was quite late when they found their rest that night; their excitement over the coming child was demonstrated several times over.

* * *

A few days later, they began their journey to Pemberley. It was early April, and while they could have remained for the last part of the Season, neither Elizabeth nor Darcy desired to do so. Georgiana was also ready to return to the country, as she had been in London for some time.

Spring soon faded into summer, and as August approached, despite Elizabeth's advanced condition, they journeyed to Briarwood to celebrate their birthdays as they had planned on their first visit. Among the surprises Darcy prepared for his wife, the one he looked forward to most was the fireworks he had purchased for her birthday. On the first of August, the Darcy party arrived at the estate, followed in the coming days by the Gardiners, including Jane and her new husband, the Matlocks, and Anne de Bourgh. Anne had not travelled that far in many years, but since she and

Jonathan had begun to run Rosings, she had grown healthier.

It was not entirely appropriate for her to travel so far, as she was in mourning for her mother, who had finally succumbed to her illness in June. Lady Catherine was not truly mourned by any who knew her — perhaps Mr. Collins had been sorry for her demise, but she had been such a termagant that few missed her. It was sad to realise that no one really missed her, but she had not been the kind of person who inspired devotion.

With all their guests having finally arrived, everyone enjoyed the various entertainments that were planned. Elizabeth and Darcy explored a few places they had visited as children, and Darcy recreated a few of the scenes he remembered. Fitzwilliam assisted with this several times but was frequently distracted by courting Mary.

On the evening of his wife's twenty-first birthday, the party at Briarwood had a grand celebration with a dinner that included all of Elizabeth's favourite dishes. Afterwards, they moved into the ballroom where Darcy had hired a few musicians to play for dancing. The couples danced for a while before it was fully dark outside and they moved onto the terrace to view the fireworks.

Darcy stood behind his wife when the lamps were extinguished, ensuring the family would be able to see the fireworks well. Elizabeth jumped slightly when the first firework exploded and moved into her husband's embrace. Without thought, she turned slightly, kissed his cheek, and whispered an endearment, calling him her "Dearest Will."

That moment sparked a memory, and suddenly, she was four years old and in a younger Fitzwilliam Darcy's arms. She saw him flushing as she kissed his cheek and heard the fireworks around her.

She smiled and turned around fully to face him. "I remember, Will. It is just the tiniest scrap of a memory, but I suddenly saw myself in your arms, kissing your cheek and making you blush. I saw my grandparents and your parents standing around us, watching us, and they were smiling back at us. Thank you, my love, for recreating this moment for me."

Ignoring the fireworks and the family gathered around them, he leaned down to kiss her passionately. He felt the baby move against him as he crushed his wife to him and knew that the best thing he had ever done in his life was to find himself worthy of Elizabeth's trust.

Chapter 39

While the rest of the party remained only a little over a week after Elizabeth's birthday celebration, Mrs. Gardiner and Mary stayed behind to see Elizabeth through her confinement. Darcy had wanted Elizabeth to give birth to their child at Pemberley. Still, Elizabeth's desire to celebrate her birth at Briarwood and recreate one of her few memories of her grandparents had convinced him to make the journey. However, he had only agreed if they remained at that estate through the child's birth and for the following month or however long it would take for both Elizabeth and the child to be ready to travel.

Since Mary was to remain at Briarwood, Fitzwilliam begged his cousin for an invitation to stay, claiming he needed advice on managing the harvest. The two had been courting for several months, and the gentleman found every opportunity to spend time with his preferred lady. Her guardian had graciously allowed the two to exchange letters that summer since Fitzwilliam had been needed at Rosings, especially after Lady Catherine passed, and he was technically in mourning for part of that time. Due to their distance from Rosings and the difficult relationship between Darcy and his aunt, the Darcys had elected to mourn for a shorter time.

Darcy was unwilling to let the occasion pass without teasing his cousin a little, so he agreed but added a caveat. "I would appreciate your assistance since I will have to travel back and forth between here and Pemberley several times. You can assist me by acting as my go-between. If you travel to Pemberley, you can stay several nights at a time, allowing me to remain close to my wife."

Fitzwilliam's face fell, making Darcy smirk. "Surely you realise you are the best person to travel back and forth during this time. You are always welcome at Pemberley."

"But Mary will be here," Fitzwilliam said, as close to whining as Darcy had ever heard him.

"Yes, she and Mrs. Gardiner will be here to assist my wife as she prepares to give birth. Miss Gardiner —" he emphasised her proper name — "will be far too busy to court during this time."

Again, Fitzwilliam looked disappointed. "I suppose I can be of aid in this way. But you do know that is not why I asked to remain."

"I thought you wanted to stay to get experience with the harvest. There will be much to oversee both here and at Pemberley. You can gain valuable experience speaking with both me and my steward."

Finally, Fitzwilliam saw the slight smirk on his cousin's face. "Damn it, Darcy. When did you learn to tease like that? You know I want to remain to court Mary. And your wife will not need that much assistance, at least not until she actually enters her confinement. And then Mary will not be necessary."

Darcy frowned then. "Yes, she and Georgiana will likely need to distract each other. I will be very grateful for your presence while she labours, as I believe I will also need someone to distract me. I ... I wish to be with my wife when she gives birth, but I was told that it was not appropriate for me to be in the room. Ellie would like me with her, but Mrs. Gardiner and the midwife have declared I am unnecessary and would be a distraction. Mrs. Hill will be there for her as well."

"You are worried." It was not a question.

Darcy blew out a long breath. "How can I not? Mother was so ill after giving birth to Georgiana and never fully recovered. I know Ellie is far healthier than she was, but I still worry for her. She lost both her parents before she reached her first birthday. We speak about so many things but never about this."

Fitzwilliam eyed him thoughtfully. "Then perhaps it is time for you to trust her with your fears. You spent much of your courtship worried about earning her trust after it had been abused by her family, but have you trusted her with your biggest fears?"

Darcy considered this for several minutes. "I think she knows a little, but I have never said it explicitly. I suppose this is something we should speak about. I am not certain that I will not still worry, but it will allow Elizabeth to share her concerns as well."

Not being able to add significantly to the topic, Fitzwilliam just nodded. After a moment, he seemed to have considered something. "I know it is not the same, but Anne always feels better when she can speak to me about a situation she is dealing with. She does not always want me to do anything, merely to listen."

Nodding, Darcy acknowledged the truth of that statement, as it was something he had also noticed about his wife. After a terse farewell to his cousin, he sought out his wife. "Dearest," he began, "I know we have discussed my remaining with you when you give birth ..." he trailed off, uncertain how to continue.

"Yes, I would like you to be with me, but my aunt and Mrs. Hill both feel it is better if you were not. I ... I will not demand it of you, but I would like you to be with me. I know it is not the custom."

"I would like to be with you, Ellie, but I confess, I am afraid."

"Afraid? Of my giving birth? Or are you afraid I might die as a result?"

"My mother died as a result of giving birth. She was not very healthy even before she became with child, but the act of giving birth was traumatic. She never recovered." Darcy's head was bowed slightly, but he held tightly to his wife's hand as they spoke. Elizabeth used her other hand to lovingly caress the dark curls on his head.

"I am healthy, my love, and not weak. I vaguely recall your mother, sitting with her after she gave birth. We spoke of it — in the nursery at Pemberley, do you recall?" He nodded, and she continued. "I know you were a child, but you have told me often your mother was never particularly healthy.

Your aunt confirmed that Lady Anne lost several children between you and Georgiana, and each time, she was weaker afterwards. She was bound to her bed almost entirely through her confinement with your sister, was she not?"

Again, Darcy only nodded, moving his head to lean it against the back of the settee. Elizabeth continued to caress his hair, giving comfort as they spoke. "I am well, dearest. I feel certain I will be with you for many years yet."

"I know, Ellie, but it does not mean I do not worry about you. So many die in childbirth or just after due to fevers and other various ailments."

"Will being with me while I labour help or worsen it?"

"I do not know," Darcy admitted. "But I would prefer to be with you than without you, wondering how you are faring."

"Then it is decided. You will remain with me until my aunt feels you need to leave. We will speak with her of our determination together."

In the end, the conversation with Mrs. Gardiner was irrelevant. Elizabeth gave birth just a week after this conversation, and Darcy was gone most of the day. He arrived at the last moment and was the first to hold the new baby.

"Should we also name her Elizabeth, after her mother and grandmother?" Darcy asked.

"Perhaps as a second name," Elizabeth replied tiredly. "What of Hope?"

"Hope Elizabeth?" Darcy asked. "Why Hope?"

"I have undergone many changes since we met, but all my life, I hoped for more. Once I learned the truth of what my aunt and uncle had done, I wondered if there was anyone I could trust, and you have been a constant. I learned to trust you, and you have given me all I hoped for and more. This, our daughter, is the living embodiment of the hope and trust I have found in you."

Darcy leaned down to kiss her. "I love you and am so glad you have given me Hope. It is the perfect name for this little angel."

She laughed. "Angel might be a stretch. After all, she is my child. Recall what I was like when demanding you and Jon entertain me."

He merely shook his head, but he did smile broadly. "I do remember. You trusted me then to care for you, and you can always trust me. I will take care of our daughter just as well as I do you."

Epilogue

Not long after Elizabeth gave birth, Fitzwilliam finally worked up the nerve to propose to Mary. He had sat with Georgiana and Mary in the final moments after he and Darcy returned from the fields and had seen the two girls worry about their sister and cousin. The three spoke of trivial things to distract themselves, but Fitzwilliam realised how much he wished to be in a similar position to his cousin, waiting for the woman he loved to give birth to their child. He wanted the happiness Darcy had found.

And he believed that happiness was to be found with Mary. He had come to admire the lady very much over the last months. Right then, while everyone anxiously awaited the new arrival, it was not the time to ask, but soon it would be.

He found the time almost a sennight later.

The couple were walking in the maze near the house. They had been accompanied outside by Georgiana, though she had drifted away without either realising it. When they reached the centre, Richard seemed to recognise that they were alone and took the opportunity to propose.

"Mary, my dear, we have courted for months now, and through our time together and the letters we have exchanged, I have come to admire you greatly. I cannot imagine another person I would want to walk beside me as I manage Rosings with my cousin Anne. The two of you get along extremely well, so I think we would live together well enough. Would you ... do you think you would marry me and be my wife?"

"You admire me?" she asked quietly.

"I do, very much. But truthfully, Mary, I ..." he sighed heavily, not comfortable with shows of affection. "... the truth is that I love you very much. I do not want to be parted from you. I made the excuse of learning about the harvest to remain nearby. I wanted more time with you than just exchanging letters."

"I love you too, Jonathan. And, yes, I will marry you," Mary replied before Fitzwilliam pulled her up and into his arms. The two kissed for several minutes before a giggle alerted them that Georgiana had found them.

They shared their news first with her, then with the Darcys, who were in their private sitting room admiring Hope. Next, they sought Mrs. Gardiner to inform her, who passed along her husband's blessing for the pair to marry.

Soon, it was decided that the couple would marry in London after Easter. The Darcys anticipated being able to travel by then. However, they had no plans to partake in any part of the Season, choosing to visit the Hursts instead. After the birth of their son, the Hursts had officially assumed the lease of Netherfield, opting to remain in Meryton, where they had grown fond of the local society.

During the Darcys' stay at Netherfield, news of the Bingley siblings' destiny reached them. Faced with Caroline's persistent ability to deter potential suitors, the duo had resolved to embark on a new adventure — quite literally. In August, they had set sail for Nova Scotia with a firm determination to find prospective partners willing to marry them in that distant land where no rumours of their reputations could reach them.

The visit to the Hursts would also allow the Darcys to visit some of the others in Meryton who wanted to see little Hope and check on things at Longbourn.

Since Fitzwilliam first mentioned the idea of marrying Lydia off to a soldier, he had taken the necessary steps to put it all into action. He had found a retired soldier, the retired Major James Waverley, willing to marry Lydia Bennet, knowing that his task would be to turn a selfish, spoiled child into a suitable wife.

As the major had been successful at turning boys into soldiers, Waverley felt he would also be successful with a wife. Instead of the harsh discipline of the military, he used other methods to encourage good behaviour, including supplementing her pin money for good behaviour and taking it away for improper behaviour. He also rewarded her with dresses and ribbons when she acted appropriately, and, surprising them all, she learned reasonably quickly.

Mr. and Mrs. Bennet had differing opinions of their youngest child marrying — Mr. Bennet was pleased to have one less person to provide for, though he had been a little annoyed at being required to send one hundred pounds per year to her husband. Each quarter, the various solicitors had to send him warnings to forward the required funds, as each quarter, he hoped it would be forgotten so he could keep that money for himself. Each quarter, he was disappointed when no one forgot.

Mrs. Bennet had cried and fussed and pretended to be ill when Lydia informed her of her desire to be wed to the handsome soldier who had shown up with a marriage contract already signed. Lydia did have the choice of accepting him, but she was intelligent enough to realise that this was the only way she could leave Longbourn. No one in their village had anything to do with her family, and she was bored with always remaining at home. Marriage to a soldier, even if he was retired, seemed more exciting than remaining with her parents.

After days of her mother feigning illness, Lydia married the former major anyway, and Mrs. Bennet now only had her husband for company. She continued to refuse to visit the tenants, and Mr. Bennet only took a cursory interest in ensuring their health and well-being. There were moments when one or the other thought they would run mad if they were forced into the other's company any longer. However, neither ran mad; unfortunately, they remained well enough.

To his detriment, Mr. Bennet decided he had paid enough toward his debt to Elizabeth and had stubbornly refused to heed the warnings about what would happen if he did not do as required. Darcy arrived with a writ from the magistrate and had the gentleman sent to the gaol for a fortnight.

He spent most of the time demanding to be released and, if not released, insisted he be brought a few books.

Sir William did not give in to his former friend's demands, and while he did bring him books, they were not the kind of books he expected to receive. Mr. Bennet did receive his account books from Longbourn with explicit orders to write the necessary bank drafts to the London solicitors so he could be released.

It took another four days for him to comply. This scenario was repeated at least once a year for the next four years until the money he owed to the Darcys was repaid. The hundred pounds he was required to give annually to each of his daughters continued to be a struggle. He also tried it with his sons-in-law, but two of them were far less willing to play this game, and after a serious talk with the two former soldiers, he never attempted that particular stunt again in his life.

Kitty had been older than most of the other students when she first attended school. After a year and a half of instruction and having mastered a variety of accomplishments, she became known for her drawing and portraiture. She began creating portraits of the members of her family, particularly the youngest members. Her first portrait was of little Hope Darcy; the Darcys were delighted with the image and brought Kitty to Pemberley for a summer to make additional drawings and portraits of the little girl. A year later, when Jane and Mary had their first offspring, Kitty also captured the images of those children.

When Georgiana had her presentation and come out at the age of eighteen, twenty-year-old Kitty debuted with her. While both girls had several suitors, Georgiana Darcy was far more sought after than Kitty Gardiner, though neither girl found someone who cared about them enough to tempt them into marriage.

The following year, Georgiana met a viscount who was interested in more than just her dowry. When her Season was cut short by the impending birth of Elizabeth's second child, the viscount followed them to Derbyshire, begging a friend to allow him to stay at a neighbouring estate for several months while he courted the heiress.

They married a few months later, and just shy of ten months after the wedding, when Georgiana gave birth to a daughter, Kitty visited her estate and met her future husband.

Georgiana had invited her friend to visit as she recovered from the birth. It had become an expectation that Kitty would capture the first image of any children born into the extended family, so when the viscount's younger brother arrived with the same intention, it became something of a competition between the two to see who could create the better portrait.

One afternoon, Kitty entered a room quietly, not realising the viscount and his brother were already there. Before she could announce her presence, she heard the young man insult not only her drawings but her person as well. From then on, she avoided him and ceased any attempts at conversation with him.

At first, he was unaware that Kitty was avoiding him and deliberately attempted to provoke her into speaking with him. The two remained at the viscount's estate for another month, and each left with conflicting feelings. He desperately wanted to get to know the lady better while she hoped never to encounter him again.

They met several more times over the next year before they finally had an honest conversation, and he confessed his interest in her. The couple courted for a year after that before she accepted his proposal of marriage. After their marriage, they continued to visit their families to capture special events, and eventually, they even travelled to the continent. They never had children of their own but adored all the cousins, nieces, and nephews they travelled to visit.

As the years passed, the large extended family continued to grow. Fitzwilliam and Mary eventually had three children, two boys and a girl, and were very happy at Rosings. "Aunt" Anne de Bourgh was very involved with all her nieces and nephews, especially those who lived in her home. She never married but lived far longer than anyone anticipated and was very happy to remain a much-loved aunt.

Jane's husband eventually purchased an estate not far from Rosings in Kent. The two sisters were close and enjoyed raising their children near each other. Jane gave birth to five children, four girls and one boy, and the cousins spent every summer together. Her children also referred to Anne de Bourgh as their aunt; no one cared if they were unrelated.

Lydia occasionally joined the families when they got together in the summers. She and her husband only had one child, a daughter, and Mr. Waverley treated his daughter in a similar fashion to his wife to ensure she did not grow up as spoiled as her mother had.

Darcy and Elizabeth had five more children after Hope, four boys followed by one more girl. The oldest son, named George Frederick after both of his grandfathers, inherited Pemberley, while the second, William Alexander, inherited Briarwood. Their other sons, Jonathan Edward and Tomas James — the name Tomas was chosen as a nod to Elizabeth's maiden name, not her uncle, a point they made clear — inherited smaller estates which George Darcy had purchased many years ago in case he had a second son.

All of their children, girls and boys, were taught to care for their estates and their tenants and were provided with the best education their parents could manage. The libraries at Pemberley and at Briarwood were both well-used and well-loved by all of the Darcys, and the children were taught the importance of being trustworthy in everything. One by one, their parents watched them find love and marry. While life was not always easy, Elizabeth and Darcy did everything together, falling increasingly in love with each other as they did. Time and time again, they expressed how grateful they were to have found each other again as adults and thankful that the trust which had begun in childhood would continue for a lifetime.

About the Author

I first read Pride and Prejudice in high school and, in the last few years, have discovered the world of JAFF. After reading quite a few, I thought that perhaps I could do that, and these are my attempts. I write under the pen name Melissa Anne.

I began my career as a newspaper reporter before becoming a middle school English teacher and then moved to high school to teach Literature. I presently live and work in Georgia, although I grew up in East Tennessee and claim that as home. I've been married to a rather wonderful man (something of a cross between a Darcy and a Bingley) for nearly two decades, and we have three children.

Contact me at melissa.anne.author@gmail.com

You can connect with me on:

f https://www.facebook.com/profile.php?id=100092746207347

𝒫 https://www.instagram.com/melissa.anne.author

Subscribe to my newsletter:

✉ https://dl.bookfunnel.com/5row1akr7w

Also by Melissa Anne

Finding Love at Loch Ness

A modern tale based loosely on Pride and Prejudice. American grad student Elizabeth Bennet visits Scotland for a month to finish her master's thesis in history. She encounters William Darcy first at the airport and then again on a tour of Loch Ness. A quick friendship develops, and eventually discover love. Join our dear couple as they travel from Scotland to East Tennessee and back as they conquer fears and a few challenges in their quest for happily ever after.

This adaptation uses the names and characters from Pride and Prejudice but has few events of the original. Disclaimer: this story is sweet and low angst and only loosely based on P&P.

Includes a bonus short story: The Man Cold

Hearts Entwined

A slightly more immature Elizabeth Bennet meets Fitzwilliam Darcy London two years earlier than in canon. As a second son, Darcy has chosen the life of a barrister so there are fewer obstacles in their way, and they quickly fall in love. Using the fortune left to him upon his father's death, he invested with Gardiner to make his own fortune, making it easier for the two to wed, along with a legacy set aside for second sons by Darcy's grandfather, the late Earl of Matlock.

Despite this, our dear couple's path is not always easy, as challenges arise as they marry and come together. A vile Mrs. Bennet and Jane's resentment over Elizabeth's good fortune cast shadows over their happiness. The presence of George Wickham and the manoeuvrings of Caroline Bingley further complicate their path. However, despite these tribulations or perhaps because of them, they learn together to surmount them, ultimately weaving their hearts even more profoundly together.

Also available as an audiobook narrated by Stevie Zimmerman

Responsibility and Resentment
A conversation that changes everything ...

What if Elizabeth Bennet and Fitzwilliam Darcy spoke honestly to each other in Kent and clarified any misconceptions prior to his making his proposal? What would happen if Mr. Bennet made an ill-fated attempt to resolve the issue of the entail only to create a much bigger problem for his family and Mrs. Bennet were even more of a shrew than in canon? What if Mr. Bennet had a secret reason to encourage the couple to marry quickly and before returning home? Will they ever be able to overcome the resentment that results from Mr. Bennet's manipulations or from Mrs. Bennet's subsequent behaviours?

Join Our Dear Couple as they find happiness together sooner than in canon but still have to fight against outside influences that seek to destroy it before and after their wedding. A story where responsibility is accepted by some and shirked by others, leading to resentment that requires effort to overcome. Will it be enough?

Also available as an audiobook narrated by Stevie Zimmerman.

The Accidental Letter

A short, angst-free novella that occurs in the months after Hunsford. Darcy, realizing his mistakes, confesses his misdeeds to Bingley earlier, even before Elizabeth has the chance to visit Pemberley. As a result, Bingley returns to Hertfordshire in June, while Darcy retreats to Pemberley to reflect on his actions. Meanwhile, Elizabeth, who has discovered her love for Darcy, writes a heartfelt letter expressing her newfound feelings. However, she unintentionally loses the letter, which she had intended not to post, but just as a way to express what she felt.

Unexpectedly, Bingley stumbles upon the misplaced letter and, assuming it was Elizabeth's intention to have him deliver it, promptly sends it to Darcy. Although Bingley is aware that there has been a disagreement between Darcy and Elizabeth, he remains unaware of the details. Upon receiving the letter, Darcy is filled with a mix of emotions and promptly makes his way to Hertfordshire to seek clarification and resolve their misunderstandings.

This is a short novella of around 25,000 words and is written with minimal angst, ensuring that our dear couple, Mr. Darcy and Elizabeth Bennet, ultimately find their happily ever after.

Now available as an audiobook read by Emily Wylie.

A Different Impression

What if Darcy had been distracted by an act of kindness and never uttered his insult at the assembly? What if Mr. Bennet became aware of his youngest daughter's behaviour, and did something about it, and left his bookroom for a time? What if Caroline Bingley were revealed as a shrew much sooner? What if Darcy was less arrogant and came to realize his attraction to Elizabeth much, much sooner?

Join Elizabeth and Darcy as they pursue their happily ever after. There are still villains at work in this story who desire to see the couple separate, but they are much more easily defeated when our dear couple are working together, without so much pride or prejudice getting in their way.

What Happened After Lambton

Darcy and Elizabeth meet at Pemberley months after the disastrous proposal in Kent. A frank conversation and several apologies lead to the couple getting engaged much sooner than in canon.

After Kent, Darcy had confessed all to his cousin Colonel Fitzwilliam, including Wickham's presence in the militia in Meryton. Fitzwilliam keeps an eye on Wickham and prevents the elopement, meaning that Elizabeth's stay in Derbyshire is not interrupted. That does not keep Wickham from creating problems for the couple, even after Wickham is tried for desertion. Mr. Bennet is unhappy about the engagement, and Jane is … too easily led by those who do not have her best interests at heart. Mrs. Bennet and Lydia are foolish and remain so.

This story follows what might have happened had Darcy and Elizabeth gotten engaged upon meeting at Pemberley.

Made in the USA
Las Vegas, NV
02 March 2024

86601510R10173